THE LAST TO GO

THE LAST TO GO

A Family Chronicle

Rand
Richards
Cooper

HARCOURT
BRACE
JOVANOVICH

San Diego   New York   London

HBJ

Copyright © 1988, 1986, 1984 by Rand Richards Cooper

"Sparkling Celluloid" was first published in the October 1984 issue of
Ladies' Home Journal magazine, copyright © 1984 by Meredith Corporation.
"My Father's Hot Little Numbers" was first published in the October 1986
issue of *GQ*, copyright © 1986 by The Conde Nast Publications Inc.

Requests for permission to make copies of
any part of the work should be mailed to:
Permissions, Harcourt Brace Jovanovich, Publishers,
Orlando, Florida 32887.

Excerpt from *The Whitsun Weddings* by Philip Larkin
reprinted by permission of Faber and Faber Ltd.

Library of Congress Cataloging-in-Publication Data

Cooper, Rand Richards.
The last to go: a family chronicle/Rand Richards Cooper.—1st ed.
p. cm.
ISBN 0-15-148430-9
I. Title.
PS3553.0623L37 1988
813'.54—dc19   88-10908

Designed by Michael Farmer
Printed in the United States of America
First edition
A B C D E

To CBC and LHC

Contents

Acknowledgments

I wish to thank my editor, Daphne Merkin, for always demanding my best; my agent, Gloria Loomis, and her assistant, Beth Vesel, for their faith and support; Alice Weil for her intelligent reading of many of these stories; and the students, faculty, and staff of the Williams School in New London, Connecticut.

"Home is so sad. It stays as it was left,
Shaped to the comfort of the last to go.
As if to win them back. . . ."

——Philip Larkin, "Home Is So Sad"

THE LAST TO GO

I

Sparkling Celluloid

She rages against junk. She's alone in the house, upstairs again in the storage room off Toby's old bedroom. The Slatterys have always called this the Junk Room. Mary Ellen can peer down along the warping rafters and see the hood of her station wagon in the garage below. The room is uninsulated and drafty. In January the wind drives through the Junk Room, rattling the door; Toby used to push an old chest against it every night. Keeping out monsters. Finally his father attached a lock.

Recently Hendrick has been up here, too. "You telling me he never insulated this place?" he said. "Trying to heat the whole neighborhood?" The next week Hendrick brought a roll of fiberglass insulation, and here it still sits, a gauzy pink thing that looks like a tremendous strawberry dessert. "Think of the money," he said. Hendrick likes to think of the money. He slaps his forehead, giving her advice, scolding her. But she doesn't know about all these things, fiberglass, blown gaskets, the IRS.

She has finished sorting through the kids' old books: Nancy Drew and the Hardy Boys, Someone or Other and his Flying Dirigible, a pair of Living Bibles. *Little Women. Great Pass Receivers of the NFL. 100 Experiments to Do at Home.* Out of the last she remembers Toby and Lydia making telephones of tin foil, string, and orange juice cans. Now all these books are on their way to the Salvation Army.

Here I come, she thinks; the woman who gives things away.

For months Mary Ellen has been cleaning. She started with the rooms downstairs, purging them of the Oriental throw rugs, the Constable and Brueghel prints. Methodically she scraped from the wood floors a decade's worth of varnish laid down in good faith by their cleaning lady, Stella. The walls she painted white. The living room she filled with light furniture, simple chairs with earth-toned burlap sacking for seats, and lots of glass. A new look, cheerful and lean, Scandinavian.

She hasn't touched the basement yet; it's too depressing. If it weren't for the sad facts of plumbing and heating, she'd seal it off completely and throw away the key. Hendrick has helped her move loads of furniture down there, the stuff she couldn't or wouldn't sell. The mahogany buffet, the armoire resembling nothing so much as an ogre with rickets, the brocade love seat. In those days, she likes to think, we coveted heaviness and darkness to the last bureau. But she knows these were her parents' things. That's why she keeps them. Daniel had nothing when they met.

There is one window in the Junk Room, a miniature, nine panes facing north. The middle pane is a rainbow arching out of pink cumulus. The glass is set in lead. Before they were married, while Daniel was still in medical school, his roommate, Jerry, was an amateur glazier. Jerry eventually opted out of surgery, is a dermatologist out in Ohio. "What a life," Daniel would say, shaking his head. "No night calls."

Now the sun lights up that rainbow. There is a scuttling of leaves on the roof outside. She can hire Todd, the boy next door, to rake and bag them. Tonight is Halloween. Sharon, the only one of her children still at home, and her boyfriend, Fred, are going to take care of the trick-or-treaters while she and Hendrick go to the movies.

In the corner she finds her mother's old trunk, the one with the brass studs and deep-cut floral patterns. Inside are old Halloween costumes. Here is Lydia's skeleton suit and dancing señorita gown, her astronaut helmet dangling scraps of tin foil. Here is Toby's Frankenstein mask.

She piles it all on the floor. Here is a Mexican sombrero, part of the Pancho Villa outfit Daniel wore to one of their annual masquerade parties. She can't remember what she herself wore. Yes, he was a handsome Pancho, with the billowing sleeves and the cross-brace of bullets she'd fashioned out of old lipstick canisters. He hunched over a bit and swaggered, trying out some Spanish he'd picked up in the Southwest and making it sound just right; he never did anything unless it was convincing.

That hat was the real thing. They'd picked it up in Nogales. He was with the Public Health Service in Arizona; she was ostentatiously pregnant with Toby; Lydia was just two. But Nogales! That night, when they drove back to their reservation town, it was cold, too cold for Arizona. Snow was falling and collecting on the rail fences, snow light as talc. Lydia was quiet, asleep for once. Daniel drove with one hand on her belly. She could feel the foot of the unborn child pressing upward now and again, and she thought, *Here is my husband's hand and my child's body and only my skin between them.*

The bottom of the trunk yields loose bits of costumes. Gypsy beads, a wizard's wand, a grotesque nose. What to do with it all? Who will take it?

She twirls the wand like the majorette she never was and looks from the bright heap of costumes to the window. That rainbow was a promise between them. They were moving from apartment to apartment, and he said the pane would wait until they got their own place, their first. Then it would be the highest window.

Well here it is, baby, she thinks, and here I am!

3

The shoe Mary Ellen flings at the window is Sharon's from kindergarten, a party shoe. Throwing the shoe, she trips backward and sits down on Hendrick's roll of insulation. The window is broken. A car is turning in the driveway. No one ever told her about fiberglass: and her hands, when they go to her face, are stuck with tiny pink needles that won't come out.

Toby enjoys surprises, both giving and getting. Coming home today is a surprise. He finished his psych midterm in the morning; an hour later he was on the road, heading south.

The day is clear. It's a long stretch down through New Hampshire, but Toby keeps music rolling from the tape deck. He switches from Dvorak to the Stones to Ella Fitzgerald, and he's into Connecticut. He taps his foot to the music.

Maybe he'll do the old scarecrow trick tonight, just like Halloween in the old days: the raggedy jacket stuffed with leaves, a pair of ripped jeans, the old fireman's boots, the Frankenstein mask if he can dig it up. He'll sit half hidden by bushes at the front door, waiting to terrorize people. No one notices the doorstep dummy until it comes alive, groaning, reaching for your leg. The last time he pulled the stunt was five or six years ago; it worked like a dream until Nate Holover and Greg Aston, remembering the ruse from the year before, sneaked up through the bushes and blew him away with firecrackers.

Nate Holover. His parents both lawyers. The biggest, the loudest house in town. Everyone always screaming at each other. One whole summer Nate slept over at Toby's, escaping the arguments. Now Nate is an actor in New York. He appears in toothpaste ads, running up from the beach with a surfboard and a big smile. His parents are still together. It's the Slatterys who've come apart; in fact, it is Nate's father, Albert Holover, who is the lawyer for Toby's mother. Toby imagines Mr. Holover cross-examining his father. It is perilous to live in a small town. Passing the hospital, Toby thinks of his father in there somewhere, reading an x-ray, injecting an artery, breaking bad news. For twenty years, in waiting rooms and operating room

4

corridors, sometimes over the phone, he has been telling people, "I'm sorry. . . ."

Toby sits in his car in the driveway. He is looking up at October clouds the color of wet cement when a shoe bursts from the attic window. A dozen somersaults down the roof, and it lands on the drive. His sister's black Lab, John Henry, comes out from behind the bushes and sniffs the shoe.

There are shards of colored glass on the pavement. That'll be the rainbow, Toby thinks. He's surprised it's lasted this long. He exhales, thinking about his mother. Now a second projectile, this time a drinking mug—his father dabbled in pottery—takes out the remaining panes. Mom is up in the Junk Room again. He imagines her sobbing.

"Love for sale," Ella sings. "Love that's fresh and still unspoiled, love that's only slightly soiled. Whooooooo will buy?"

"Oh, shit," Toby says.

In the kitchen Toby and his mother sit talking. Toby swishes coffee in his mug. "So when's Hendrick coming?"

"Your guess is as good as mine, honey." Hendrick is as chronically late as Toby's father is punctual. "Last time he ran out of gas. On the bridge."

"Oh, jeez."

They laugh. His parents have grown so different since the split: his father so meticulous about details, his mother a walking tornado of lost checks, bills, car keys. Dr. Slattery, Toby realizes, is always taking out an emery board and filing his nails. In restaurants he calculates tips to the cent. It drives Toby crazy.

"I like Hendrick," Mary Ellen says. "He has red hair and rebuilds engines, and the first time I met him I thought he was a great big galumphing lumberjack of a man. His laugh comes from way deep down. Nothing at all like Daniel." One of Mary Ellen's cats leaps up onto the table, and she pets its long back.

"So you're going to the movies?" Toby says.

"Yup. I talked Hendrick into going over to that little theater in Westerly where they bring you peanuts and beer, and you get to throw the shells on the floor."

"I saw *Casablanca* there one time."

"Don't remind me."

"Sorry," Toby says. His father is a Bogart fan. Now Mary Ellen pushes aside her sandwich and lights a cigarette. She is so thin.

"You know, Toby," she says. "I've been on a real roller coaster. But the worst is behind me now."

"Good!"

"Everything's been up, up, up. I'm meeting all sorts of people. A man at Sharon's PTA asked me to go snowshoeing with him in the Catskills. He's a teacher."

"And you told him . . . ?"

"I told him to wait until everyone's divorces came through."

Toby smiles. "What's up with Hendrick's divorce?"

"Oh, the same. Still staying with his mother. He'll be glad to see you. He's such a funny bear of a man." Mary Ellen thinks about how Hendrick will come through the door, ducking a little, unnecessarily; he's tall, but not that tall. He'll clap her kids on the back. "Hiya, sister," he'll say, and "Hey, man."

"So it's been good with him?"

The question hangs. Hendrick is nice. He opens doors. And then there's always comedy—like the long-awaited trip out on his "boat," which turned out to be a tiny dinghy. He wrenched his shoulder trying to start the engine, and when they finally got out to the "island," it was no more than a smidgen of sand just offshore. Kissing him was less than a complete success; she minded, unfairly, the tobacco on his breath.

"He tells me war stories, Toby. He was in Vienna after the war. American zone, the occupation, all that. I'm praying nothing in the movie tonight reminds him of Vienna." She doesn't like most movies, but she goes anyway. The last one they went to was James Bond.

6

Hendrick pushed popcorn at her in the dark as the new James Bond escaped hand over hand down the cable from a stalled cable car, chased by a hulking moron with steel teeth. In the cinema lobby, and again later over coffee in the kitchen, Hendrick hunched his shoulders and opened his mouth wide. "Jaws!" he said, biting her on the shoulder.

Now she watches Toby take dishes to the sink.

"You shaved off your beard. It makes you look like your father."

"Mom . . ."

"Oh dammit, Tobias, I don't want to cry anymore." She stands, back to the wall. Her head turns from side to side, like a baby refusing the spoon.

"You know he took her up to Saint Auguste, Toby. Did you know that?"

Toby didn't.

"Oh yes. Can't you just see him showing her around? 'Now here's where we used to put on our skis, and here's where Sharon went to nursery school, and here's where Toby got hit on his little nose with a hockey puck.' I can see the tears welling in his poor, poor eyes. As if he had some right, as if something had been taken away from *him*."

"I know." Toby speaks softly. He remembers how they all used to ski together until his mother had a bad fall one year and never skied again. Nowadays his father skis more than ever before.

"Would you get me a Kleenex?" Mary Ellen says. "Hendrick doesn't need to see this. He's really a very kind man, Toby. He helps me. I do like him."

"So do I."

"Good. I know he tries too hard. He's like me; he just wants to be loved. Now Muriel's telling him she never really loved him. Maybe she and Daniel have been talking strategy." She jokes into the tissue, blowing a laugh through. "One of these days I'm going to wake up with enough courage to attack the basement. I'll just go

7

down there and do it," she says. "Everything will go. Hey, look—why don't you go pick Sharon up from practice? She'll be thrilled."

"Okay." Toby takes his car keys off the table.

"You know," says Mary Ellen, smiling grimly, "once your father made me touch a dead body. Did you know that? He and Jerry took me down one night to the lab. They made me close my eyes. I smelled that awful preservative. 'Open your eyes,' he said, so I did. There I was, my hand on the chest of this corpse. And Daniel was laughing. 'Meet Reuben,' he said."

"Jesus, Dad," Toby whispers.

"I was so furious with him, I called Mom and told her to get my room ready. But I was pregnant with Lydia."

"I can't believe Dad did that."

" 'Open your eyes,' he said. Well, my eyes are open now, baby!" She lights another cigarette. "You know, Toby, it took me a long time to open my eyes. When your father was running around with this girlfriend of his, I just didn't want to see it. He wouldn't admit it, and I wouldn't see it."

"What made you finally see it?"

She laughs, one soft *humph*. "You remember that hideous clock he gave me that summer, the one I hated?"

Toby nods.

"Well, I knew when I got that clock that he couldn't have been thinking about me when he bought it. But of course I let it pass. Finally one night he wanted to make love, and as he kissed me, I looked at the clock, and I just said to him, 'I don't know who you have on your mind, Daniel, but it isn't me.' " She pauses, and John Henry wanders over for his head to be stroked. "Now hurry up and get your sister," Mary Ellen says to Toby. "And keep your eyes open."

Toby kisses her on the cheek. There's a fine scar beneath his mother's eye, another running down her temple. She had a face-lift last Thanksgiving. "Damned if I'll let all this misery ruin my beautiful face," she had said. "It's not natural." And the best thing was this:

8

after the operation, when her head was wrapped in gauze and she looked like a war casualty, instead of hiding in the house, she went about business as usual. "What happened to *you?*" people would ask. She'd give a brave and impudent smile and say, simply, "I got my face lifted."

The first trick-or-treater wears a black cape and a black bucket over her head. Her parents hover behind.

"What are you?" Toby asks.

"Tell him, Dolly!" the father calls.

"Darth Vader," Dolly mumbles, taking an Oh Henry bar and turning to run.

Sharon and Fred sit on the steps, carving a pumpkin.

"Let's do something different. A Charlie Brown face with a big smile."

"Nah," says Fred. He's a junior at the high school, a wide receiver on the football team. "Pumpkin's gotta be scary."

"Oh Fred," Sharon says. "You're so conventional."

Toby stuffs his boots with newspaper, his jacket with leaves. Mary Ellen is inside, dressing for Hendrick. The sunset is spilling a dense pink, like cherry juice, on the horizon.

Fred works after school at a dry cleaner. "They're all nuts down there," he says. "There's this one chick comes in wicked hung over every morning, presses a few pants, then dumps a chair behind the coat bins and crashes out. Then this other guy, Harry, writes her name and number on all the shirt cardboards."

"You should get a raise," Sharon says. "You're the only reliable guy there."

"Try telling that to Mr. Carmady. He *likes* those guys. And guess what? They all think *I'm* weird."

They laugh. Sharon drips wax into the hollowed pumpkin. "How do you like it?"

"I don't know," says Toby. "Little too friendly, maybe."

9

"Same," says Fred.

"Typical males. No imagination. I'm going inside. Come on, Fred. And Toby, if Joey Brock comes by, please scare the crap out of him. He's such a jerk."

"I'll do my best."

"You'll know him. He's the one who drools."

Now Toby slouches down in the dead leaves, propped against the house. It's dark out, the moon is low and merry, playing in the maples like a child. He pulls on his Frankenstein mask, then the work gloves and, sweating lightly, half-hidden by the bushes, he waits.

A moped pulls over the curb onto the flagstone walk. It's Sharon's friend Duncan Hogarth. As usual, he wears a camera around his neck.

"That you, Toby?" Duncan calls. "Let me shake your paw."

"Hey, how'd you know?" Toby laughs, clapping his gloves.

"You got me once, remember? I was in sixth, you were in ninth. Sharon home?"

"Yeah. Fred's over. Go on in."

After Duncan come two more Darth Vaders, a coven of witches escorting a giraffe or a centaur, an Incredible Hulk, a Superwoman. Then another brother-sister team, the boy a walking telephone dial, the girl a receiver. The two of them are connected by a huge cord. Toby sits there watching.

"They better not have stupid apples," the boy says. "Or nuts."

"Slatterys always have Reese's," the girl says.

Sharon opens the door. "Don't call us," the boy recites, and his sister, "We'll call you." They get their Reese's.

"Told ya," the girl says.

No one notices Toby. Since the last time he did this, he's become more adept at lifelessness. He's happy, watching the parade of fantasies along the leaf-tickled avenues of their town, spying on the masqueraders in that unguarded moment before the door opens. He smiles beneath his monster mask.

Three big kids in navy sweatshirts come up the walk, carrying pillowcases. They have charcoal smeared under their eyes. "Sharon Slattery lives here," says one.

"Sharon Sluttery, you mean."

"Yeah, I'd like to hear you say that to Fred La Plante."

"Be realistic."

"Shhh."

The door opens. Toby hears Fred. "Well, well, well. If it isn't the Three Musketeers. You guys still trick-or-treating?"

"Yeah, yeah. Trickertreat."

"Well, here you go." Fred is giving out the candy. "One apiece. Now you boys be careful crossing the street, okay?"

"All right." "All right, already." "Hey, see ya, Shar."

The door closes. The loudmouthed one imitates Fred. " 'You guys still trick-or-treating?' Brilliant deduction."

"Shut up, Erik. Didn't see you doing jack shit about it." Toby listens to them grumbling as they slide away into darkness. "But how about that Sharon. I wouldn't kick her outta bed. . . ."

They are gone. Toby rubs his gloves together, tests his legs. Whoever comes next will feel the wrath of the monster. He practices groaning.

A car pulls to the curb. The trick-or-treater is huge, and he is talking to himself. "I'm gonna kiss me a bear. No, kiss me a *grizzly* bear . . ."

The voice belongs to Hendrick Hayden.

Inches from Toby's leg, Hendrick stops. He wears Levis, a heavily rhinestoned cowboy shirt, a gray Stetson. Holsters and six-shooters gird his gut. He draws a gun and jabs the air, twirls it, blows the smoke away, reholsters. He drawls, "I'm gonna kiss me a grizzly bear and rassle me a pretty girl. Oh, yeah. All right, folks. Here we go." He tugs the red bandana around his neck, the knot jutting to one side, reaches for the doorbell, and steps back, hands on his silver guns.

Now Toby groans, rolls his monster's head, reaches out for the cowboy's ankle.

"Chri—!" Back Hendrick leaps, off the step. "Jesus!" One of his cap guns goes off. If it were real, he would have shot himself in the leg.

"Hendrick, it's me," Toby says, unmasking. "It's me."

"Please sir, don't shoot," Sharon pleads from the doorway.

They are all laughing. Hendrick touches Toby's shoulder. "Man, you scared the whoop right outta me."

"I'm sorry," Toby says shakily. "I couldn't resist."

"Just when I've been practicing my John Wayne all day."

"Come on in. Do it for us now!" Sharon calls.

They stand in the foyer, the five of them, Toby with his mask bunched up in his hand. "Hendrick," Toby says, "this is Duncan Hogarth, the famous high school photographer."

They shake hands. "Saw your picture of Fred here catching that long bomb last Saturday." Hendrick turns to Fred. "Terrific catch, Frederick. Wish I could move like that." He pats his stomach above the gun belt.

"Hey," Fred says. "I wouldn't mess with you. No way."

Duncan wants a group photo.

"Where's your mother?" asks Hendrick Hayden.

"Upstairs. Getting ready. Let's go with the photo. When she comes down, we'll get one with her in it."

They cluster for the pose. Fred and Sharon, arms draped over shoulders, easy as old clothes. It always surprises Toby to see this; she's only fifteen. You know what I like about him? she says. His Fredness. Nobody else has it. Now she takes a stream of her long hair and makes Fred a moustache. Hendrick sucks in his gut, and it makes him look strong indeed, an idea whose time has not yet passed. He's taller than Toby, and that's another surprise. He's handsome, and a bit overinflated. Toby pulls on his mask.

Draw yer guns, marshall!

Moan, monster, moan!
He's gonna kiss him a grizzly and rassle a pretty girl. . . .
They draw closer; the light smacks; they laugh.
"Now, where's the old lady?"

She's in the basement, wearing her robe, facing the mess.

The place hasn't been swept in years. Huge scabs of plaster, peeled away from the wall, disintegrate into powder on the floor. Remnants of a practice flower arrangement she did with Lydia years ago, strips of bark suggesting Indian dugouts, remain fixed to the wall with putty, the vines that coursed among them long dead now. Here's an ancient school desk with inkwell and swivel chair and its saga of carved names. Daniel's mother was a schoolteacher. Why is it still here? Beside it, a whitewashed tin cabinet with the kids' heights marked and dated in pencil, and beneath that the old train set that was his and later Toby's, now a heap of battered Pullmans and twisted track. Years ago, they gave the kids permission to crayon the walls down here. *Sharon and Neal, TruLuv forever.* Now, who was Neal? And then those columns of numbers totaled in crayon: Toby 169— Dad 44. Ping-Pong matches. He and Toby stopped playing then. He hated losing.

"Quitter," Mary Ellen says.

She thinks about their divorce case. At hearings he actually smiles at her. He waits in the anteroom, hands in his pockets, jingling his keys. What for? What can they possibly say to each other? Twenty-five years of marriage have boiled away like vapor, leaving them with squabbles over money. In court no one cares about blame anymore. They just add up the figures, all business. So often she doesn't want to think about money; she just wants out. At the same time she is astonished, thinking about how she was never paid for all she did. She and everyone else.

"Dammit, Mary Ellen," she says. "What you did all those years was worth something!"

She turns in a circle, besieged by armies of the things they owned. Upstairs, she knows, her date is waiting for her. But now that she's here, she's got to make a start. There's so little she wants down here. So little she needs! She doesn't know whether to laugh or cry. A great faith in cleaning sends her striding through the junk.

There is noise on the stairs, but she's oblivious; she has found the box of Super 8 films they took in Saint Auguste, up in the Laurentians, over a decade ago. The reels sit in their canisters like giant coins, a chest of degraded treasure at her disposal.

She opens one, another, a third—takes the ends of film and twists them together. Holding this knot, she hurls the reels against the wall. Explosions of plaster. She opens the rest of the cases—there must be two dozen reels in all—and tears at them, abandoning herself, unraveling the opaque strands, the celluloid bubbling up at her, sparkling in the light like champagne.

II

The 5:42 out
of the City

All afternoon he's sure he's going to be late. As a favor to Mr. Foote, he is caddying for Mr. Kemper today, and Kemper has brought his thirteen-year-old nephew along, and the kid is hopeless.

"Better give him a driver, Danny," Kemper says to him as they stand under a wicked sun on the edge of the fairway, two hundred yards from the green. "Not much power in those arms."

Sighing inwardly, he selects the club and hands it over to the kid, who swats and misses, murdering the turf. Another group passes them, smiling and waving, and for the hundredth time he checks his watch.

"You in a hurry, Danny?" says Kemper.

"No, sir," he lies. "Not really." According to his calculations, he can still make it to the station in time for the arrival of the 5:42 out of the city; if he makes it, he may be able to catch a glimpse of Mary Ellen Matthews, his blind date for tomorrow night. He watches

15

as Kemper's nephew, with a wild flail, sends the ball squirting off into the bushes, and suddenly he knows: *This is the last time I will caddy, ever.* He is twenty-two years old, a college graduate, and in one month he will begin medical school in the city. It is time for life to start.

It has been a strange summer. After graduation in June, he packed his stuff up and drove the fifteen miles from his fraternity house to his parents' home. Getting out of the car and looking at the small brick structure, he felt like a stranger. Then his mother came barreling out the front door, calling his name.

They treat him like a hero. His mother boasts about him so much that whenever he sees her friends coming up the front walk, he slips out the back door. On his birthday she presented him with a cake with candles in a big *M.D.* It made him feel like a child. Afterward he stood out in the backyard watching trains careen past, coming from the city. He knew that moving back into his parents' house and commuting to med school would kill him. Deep in thought, he didn't hear his father come up behind him, didn't know the old man was there until he felt the hand on his shoulder.

"We're proud of you, Dan," his father said. "You've done everything we expected of you, and more. From here on, what you do is up to you."

He loves his folks, but they belong to his past, not his future. The narrowness, the grinding seriousness of their lives, the cycle of bridge games and church luncheons and Masonic picnics and visits from relatives—he will never belong to this. The man he most admires in the world is Mr. Tobias J. Foote, a lawyer and businessman for whom he is working as a chauffeur. From caddying for Mr. Foote three summers ago, he has worked his way up in the man's good graces. The day his acceptance letter from medical school came, he wrote Mr. Foote; a week later came a one-line response: "Instead of handing me drivers this summer, how would you like to *be* my driver?"

As it has turned out, there is more to the job than driving. In addition to chauffeuring Mr. Foote to meetings in his black Packard touring car, Danny runs errands for Mrs. Foote, drives their fourteen-year-old daughter to dance lessons and to the stables where she rides one of the family's four horses, and helps the gardener and house-keeper around the house. On occasion he returns to the golf course to caddy, either for Mr. Foote himself or—like today—for one of his friends or associates.

It is Mr. Foote who has set up the blind date for tomorrow night. "I want you to take out the daughter of a friend of mine, Danny," Foote said to him. "Ralph Matthews's daughter. She's a great girl. Been out of college a couple of years, works for a fashion magazine in the city." Pausing to let Danny think about it, Foote stuffed tobacco into his pipe and lit up. He talked between huge puffs, staring at the flame from his lighter going down into the bowl. "Ralph's sick. Bad heart. . . . Doesn't have much time left."

"Does she want to go out with me?" Danny was unsure.

"Don't you worry," Foote said, waving his smoking pipe at him. He took out his wallet and handed Danny a brand-new twenty-dollar bill. "Take her out and show her a good time Saturday night. You can take the Packard."

As the sun slips lower in the sky, the heat seems somehow to intensify, and he is sweating freely. They are on the seventeenth, the next to last hole he will ever caddy. It is a momentous feeling. He watches Kemper's troll-like nephew, whose name is Buddy, tee up and take a practice swing. "You're looking up early," he says, "and it's pulling your whole body up." He turns to Kemper and adds, "I hope you don't mind my butting in, sir."

"You kidding? You know this game better than I do." Kemper winks as the kid, who looks ludicrous in knickers and a Bobby Jones cap, plants himself over the ball, backswings calmly, and lofts a good drive out onto the fairway, well over 150 yards.

"Wow!" he says, his mouth wide open.

It's five o'clock sharp as they reach the clubhouse. Danny hurries to his car and is thankful when it starts. He imagines himself behind the wheel of the Packard, the radio murmuring, his passenger a beautiful girl whose long legs disappear into the shadows under the dashboard. He knows Mr. Matthews slightly, caddied once in a foursome of his three years ago—a silent, pear-shaped man, pale and worried-looking. Asking around, he has found out through a friend of a friend that Matthews's daughter usually takes a 5:15 train out of the city, arriving at 5:42 at a station in between her town and the town where his parents live. He plans to be there.

As usual, there's a gang of caddies at the hot dog stand across the road, and they wave and call out to him as he drives by. Sometimes he stops and has a smoke with these kids, but today he has no time for them and so just hits the horn, hard. The sound reverberates through his rickety Nash and he smiles, watching them all become miniature in the smudged glass of the rearview mirror.

It is the hottest day in the summer, she is in a hurry, sweat is pasting her blouse to her back, and there's nothing she can do but laugh. Here she is, working for a magazine whose pages are full of cool, graceful girls and women while she herself, dissolving in the heat, has all the grace of a melted pistachio ice cream. It's so damn silly.

At least it's Friday. She stands for a second on the sidewalk outside the office. Buses across Independence Square are lined up to pick up children visiting the Liberty Bell. She pities the drivers.

"Reconsidering my proposal?" says a voice behind her.

She turns smiling to its owner, an older man, fair-haired and handsome. "Which one, Mr. Cheevers?" she says, lifting her eyebrows coyly. "There have been so many."

"Touché," he says, walking off. Cheevers is the editor of the cosmetics department, where she works. She chuckles, thinking about the things he says to her. It's all a game, and they both know it—he is forty-something, and divorced. But it's a game she likes to play, teasing with him at the office, on one occasion even going out to lunch with him. It makes her boyfriends exquisitely jealous. Oh, what a *dream* our editor is, she says. Their foreheads furrow and their lips pout, and she knows she will never marry them.

She walks up Chestnut Street, the spikes of her spectator pumps tock-tocking on the sidewalk. She is thinking about the men who have wanted to marry her in the past three years: Troy, who went to Dartmouth and works with his father as an architect, and who promises to build her any house she wants, anywhere she wants; Roger, who tells her she looks just like Lauren Bacall in *To Have and Have Not*; Bill, who is older and has been in the service; Stuart, who brings her huge bouquets, which she turns over to her mother. Then there's her old college beau, Pete, who writes her long and desperate letters from California, and, most recently, Bob, the fantastically good-looking Bob. Blond, 6 feet, 3 inches, strong, he is the kind of man who makes her feel helpless just by looking at her. They met at the shore last summer; in the fall he started calling her for dates, and by Christmas she told her parents she thought he was the kind of man she could marry. When they told her it was all wrong, she argued with them. "You don't want me to marry anyone ever, do you?" she said at dinner one night. Her father leaned across the table, dabbed at his mouth with his napkin, and said to her calmly, "No, my dear— we just don't want you to marry *him*."

"Why not?" she pouted.

"Because," her father said, aiming his bulging eyes at her. "Because *you* don't really want to—do you?"

A week later, her father had his first heart attack, and Bob proposed to her. She told him she would have to think about it, and that's what she has been telling him ever since. When her younger brother, Bennett, asks her how things are going with "the big blond Viking god," she answers "Oh, he's a dream," but deep inside she knows it isn't going to happen; she doesn't want him enough. They are all sweet, her suitors, but she doesn't want to marry them. She puts them off with gentle "maybes" and "not yets," and they keep dating her, ardently repeating their promises until one day they disappear, and six months or a year later she hears that they are married. Then, in spite of herself, she feels betrayed. Sometimes she fears she will die a virgin, and it will be her own fault.

Hurrying past window displays at Lord and Taylor, she makes it to Broad Street station just in time to catch the 5:15 Paoli local. Businessmen at the two bars in the station are pouring drinks into themselves, checking their watches between gulps. Seeing them, she worries about her father, who has had two heart attacks, a small one and then a not so small one, in the last eight months. She is afraid for him, and as she makes her way to the concourse and boards the train, she remembers a dream she has had, a terrifying dream in which her father died, her brother married, and her mother went away, leaving her all alone in the house, calling out their names.

The train sits on the track for five minutes, an unexplained delay that doesn't bother her but that annoys some of her fellow riders, men in three-piece suits who sigh loudly and rustle their newspapers with extra emphasis. She says "Thank you very much!" to the conductor who punches her ticket, and then pulls off her white cotton gloves, soaked with sweat. Anyone who cares can now see that she isn't married or engaged. But everyone else is either reading or staring dully ahead. Sometimes she wonders if she is the only real, live person in the world.

Finally they begin to move, lurching through the darkness under Philadelphia; she looks at her reflection on the window, warped as if in the hollow of a spoon. I don't look that ugly, I don't look that ugly, she says to herself—but oh Christ, maybe I do. She wards off thoughts of her father by focusing on her weekend. Tonight there is the movies with her girlfriend Carolyn, and tomorrow something risky, a blind date with the chauffeur of a friend of her father's. Normally she stays away from blind dates, but this time she has said yes—mostly to keep Bob from taking her out and delivering the ultimatum she suspects he has been nerving himself up for, but also because her father's friend, Mr. Foote, has arranged this in order to cheer her up. If she refuses, he will think she is depressed beyond measure about her father, and will feel badly.

The train is crowded, and there are standees. The conductors swing through the aisle, making a song out of the names of the stops. She looks out at the tenements of Philadelphia, block after block of dreary row houses with laundry crowding the balconies. There is the sulphury smell of poverty, and a view of smokestacks billowing foulness from a chemical plant. Every morning, women who work at this factory board the train wearing curlers under their scarves; she likes to watch them put on their makeup and carefully remove the curlers.

Now she remembers something. If Carolyn's information is reliable, then this chauffeur of Mr. Foote's, this Danny Slattery, is going to be at the station when she gets off. She reaches into her sling shoulder bag for her mirror but then thinks better of it. If he is going to come sneaking around, she reasons, then he can take what he gets. She laughs to herself, imagining streaking her whole face with lipstick and prancing out on the platform like a banshee, scooping up one of these dour executives in her arms and soul-kissing him, right there in front of Mr. Pathetic Chauffeur. She loves to turn the strategies of men back on them.

The sharp scent of fresh-cut grass edges into her thoughts, and she looks out to see trees and lawns. The train hurtles past a golf course. She watches the tiny figures with their metal sticks winking in the sunlight, and thinks of her father, who loves golf, lying at home in bed. He claims he is fine. She wants to believe him and almost does, but then she remembers him that night at the dinner table just after Christmas—dropping his spoon onto his plate, reaching to grab his shoulder, a look of confusion and fear on his face. That look doesn't leave her mind, and even now, though it must be eighty-five degrees in the train, she shudders as she thinks of it, shudders all the way down to her fancy pumps.

He reaches the station at 5:35. There's no time for him to go home and clean himself up, but that's okay. He doesn't plan to be seen. The parking lot is half-full; there are taxis and empty cars and some cars with wives sitting behind the wheels reading magazines and kids hanging out the windows. He parks the Nash at the far end and crosses the lot, scouting for the best vantage point. Technically, checking out a blind date in advance is cheating. But he has been burned in this situation before, and some features of this setup strike him as dubious. He hopes Foote has not set him up with a monster.

It has been a strange summer for girls. The college girls have gone home, and all he sees are the girls from his old high school. He has gone out with some of them, even managing to get one of them, Sally Rathburn, to go with him to the Jersey shore for a weekend. But it meant nothing, and he knew it—knew it even as he was taking her clothes off over her perfunctory protests in a small, rented beach cottage. "If you do anything stupid, Danny," his father has said to him, "you sure better be prepared to live by it."

His father has nothing to worry about. These town girls belong to his past, not to his future, and he will do nothing stupid with them. He wonders what kind of daughter Mr. Ralph Matthews has. He tries to recall the man, what car he drives, what kind of game he shoots, how his clothes look. A big car sticks in his mind—fancy, maybe a Bentley; this image brings with it a vision of a girl, and for a second he is sure he has seen the daughter. But the image blurs and dissolves, and all he is left with is Matthews himself, and his musty aroma of sternness, shrewdness, and wealth.

The train is late. He looks across the tracks at two-family houses on a ridge named after a Revolutionary War hero. Beyond this, houses spread out and get larger, small yards become big lawns, and the town where Mary Ellen Matthews lives gradually begins. As a child he sometimes pedaled his bicycle over there, admiring the cool greenness of the place, wondering where its center was and never finding it.

His own town is noisier and dirtier, crowded with kids playing baseball in the streets, mothers digging in gardens, fathers sliding themselves under cars up on blocks. People have always worked themselves ragged in his neighborhood, and they are proud of it. He remembers his father ten years ago, before the war, limping slowly up the front walk at twilight after a twelve-hour shift at the shipyard, one hand pushed against his groin to hold in the hernia he tried to ignore for five years. One night he came in red-faced and flustered: a workmate of his named Howard Trent had fallen on the tracks, fainting from sheer exhaustion as the two of them crossed the platform. "I hear a sound behind me, and when I turn around there's Howard, lying there bleeding." In the years since then, his father has told the story over and over—how he picked Howard Trent up and carried him to the drugstore, how he watched as the druggist stitched up Howard Trent's cut jaw. He tells the story as an adventure, but Danny hears it differently. To him it sums up the life his father and his buddies have had to live. Work like a dog until one day you drop. It's not where he wants to be when he is sixty, his father's age.

Now the track twangs, and people begin to gravitate to the edge of the platform. The train leans around the corner, its brakes shrieking—and suddenly he thinks he remembers the girl, standing in a broomstick skirt in the sunlight next to her father's big car. As the vision takes shape, he is afraid he has invented it, for what he sees is the girl of his dreams, his ideal: slender, smiling, hair lifted by the wind, one eyebrow slightly raised, mischief in her glance. As the train stops, he suddenly doesn't seem to know what to do with his hands. He puts them in his pockets and then takes them out, then puts them in again. He waits for the doors to open.

She almost doesn't make it off. As she rises to leave, the strap of her bag catches on the seat, jerking the bag off her shoulder and scattering her things in the aisle. Only the conductor watching from the door saves her, and she thanks him with a big smile.

The sun is low, just over the top of the station, and she raises a hand to block its blaze. People crowd the platform. Next to her one of the executives folds his newspaper twice and slaps his leg with it, and she can't tell whether he means frustration or satisfaction. Men whose faces reveal nothing bore her.

She sees the family Buick in the lot, and though she can't see who is driving, her mother or her brother, she throws up a hand and waves. She is showing off shamelessly for her blind date, and she knows it. As far as she can tell, there are four possible chauffeurs. The first is dark-haired and baby-faced, hanging back in the shadow of the station with his hands in his pockets; the second is short and stubby, carrying a briefcase and wearing an ill-fitting suit; the third, leaning against the corner of the building, smoking a cigarette, is dashing but dissolute-looking around the eyes; and the last, slim and intense-looking, wears a pencil-line moustache and glances about from side to side, almost frantically, through horn-rimmed glasses.

As she walks slowly toward the car, a blast of the horn tells her it is her brother behind the wheel. The dismal certainty hits her that the chauffeur will turn out to be the short and stubby one, and for a moment she considers calling Mr. Foote and begging off. She has dated short men before; they fill her with an irresistible urge to laugh.

There are fewer people on the train than he expected; if she is on it, he will see her. Most of the passengers are executives, some of them only a few years older than he is. They carry briefcases and newspapers, and coats folded over their arms. He hears cars starting in the lot behind him. A child's voice calls out, "Daddy!"

No one at all matches the vision of the beautiful girl in the sunlight, and he begins to suspect it was a figment of his imagination. The only girl who fits the general description is a wan creature in brown who crosses the platform, hunched over her purse like an old lady. The image of Mr. Ralph Matthews comes to mind, and he smiles despite his disappointment: how typical of such a man to have a daughter browbeaten into plainness.

He is already thinking of the cool shower awaiting him at home when, in the last second before the train begins to move, a girl jumps off the last car, and it is her.

Her hair is much shorter, but aside from that, she is just as he envisioned her, lighter somehow than everything else, as if a mutinous ray of sunshine followed her everywhere. For a moment she seems to catch his eye, and his hands tighten in his pockets, but her glance sweeps past, and he knows she hasn't seen him in particular. When she walks quickly toward the parking lot stairs, he doesn't follow. He doesn't need to. All he needed to see was the way she came down from the train, her skirt billowing, eyes already taking in the scene on the platform, her mouth smiling ironically.

It is a mouth made to be kissed. He jingles the keys in his pocket as he heads back to the Nash, picturing that mischievous smile and saying to himself, *This is the girl I will marry.*

It is Saturday evening, and he is in the Packard, driving to pick up the girl of his dreams. He is wearing his seersucker suit and white bucks, and a brand-new bow tie. Mr. Foote has given him his blessing, telling him, "Good luck, Danny boy," when he went to pick up the car. He feels lucky, and sings as he drives.

The car around him is vast as a continent. He thinks about the route they will take into the city after he picks her up. He wants no mistakes, no missed exits, no backing and turning. They are going to Old Bookbinder's, an expensive restaurant he has driven Mr. Foote to several times. As soon as he saw her at the station, he knew where he would take her; the reservation was made over the living room phone, which he took around the corner into the hall, out of the hearing range of his mother. He hopes that everything will go smoothly, that he will order the right wine and pronounce the dishes the way they are meant to be pronounced.

Very few of the streets in Mary Ellen Matthews's town are called "streets"; they are roads, ways, circles, avenues, boulevards, and places. Driving slowly, staying well below the posted limit, he feels the Packard as an extension of himself, something he has never felt before, though he has driven the car fifty times. The hum of tires on pavement rises to him through the leather of the seats; a pebble loudly pings the underside of the wheel fender, and he winces. He waves to a boy in a Phillies' cap riding a bicycle, and the look of admiration he gets in return fills him with a strange elation. He wishes his fraternity brothers could see him now. *There we were*, he will write to them, *just the two of us in a spotless '49 Packard . . .* His words won't be good enough, but he'll say them just the same. *She's a great girl. I'm crazy about her. . . .*

He arrives at her street and, following Mr. Foote's directions, which he has memorized, counts four houses from the corner. At the stone gate he turns right, into a circular cinder drive. There is a green Buick, and he parks next to it. After checking himself in the rearview mirror, he gets out and gently shuts the door behind him.

Dust settles in the wake of the Packard. He turns from it to look at the house, a stone fortress with ivy-covered gables, six in all. The front walk is made of flat shards of stone, which look like marble; someone has clipped the borders of grass in between these shards so that not one blade of grass lies on the stone. At the Footes', that might be his job.

Standing at the door, he straightens his bow tie, takes a deep breath and, seeing no doorbell, lays his hand on what appears to be a knocker. But when he goes to lift it, nothing moves. His hand slips off, and he experiences a moment of sheer horror, imagining laughter from every window. Then instead of lifting, he turns; the mechanism moves smoothly, and a gravelly ring echoes on the other side of the door.

When the doorbell rings, her first thought is to keep her father from waking up. So she runs down the stairs and is still trying to catch her breath when she sees him through the glass panel beside the door. She is surprised to see that her blind date is not Short and Stubby, not the Brain or the Rake—it is Baby Faced and Dark. He is standing there with his hands in the pocket of his seersucker suit, and she likes the look of him. He looks older now than he did on the platform, and better.

She opens the door. "Mary Ellen?" he says, throwing her a fairly good quizzical look, as if he has never seen her before.

"Yes?" she says, innocently, as if she is expecting no one.

"I'm Dan Slattery." He pauses. "Your blind date."

She lets him hang for half a second, then laughs. "Well, hel*lo* there," she says, opening the door wide and backing away to give him space to pass. She shoots him a look of coy bafflement and watches his face closely as she asks, "But haven't I seen you somewhere before?"

He knows she knows. She can tell. And he likes it. "I don't think so," he says, looking right at her. "But it's funny—I have the same feeling too."

She steps aside and lets him by—he is taller than she thought— and, smiling, follows his clean scent into the room.

III

The Butcher
of Hartford

After two years out west, Dan and Mary Ellen Slattery moved back east to find that Mary Ellen's mother was dying. Leaving Arizona, where Dan had worked as a doctor to the Navajos, they drove in their red '47 Chevy with their two small children, Lydia and Toby, and Dalmatian puppy, Waldo. Singing songs and laughing at passing cars, they talked about the life awaiting them in Connecticut, where Dan had landed a residency in neurosurgery.

"Your father's going to be a brain surgeon," Mary Ellen said to her year-old son. "And what do you think of that?"

Dan held up his hands and waved his fingers. "Yes, folks," he said. "The precious fingers of the brain surgeon."

When they got to Philadelphia, Mary Ellen's mother was in the hospital. The little bump behind her ear she had gone in to have taken off had turned out to be something very wrong. Dan spoke with the surgeon, then took Mary Ellen aside and told her, in a low, calm voice, that her mother had cancer and was dying.

"Oh God," Mary Ellen said, collapsing in his arms. "She always told us she would die if we put her in the hospital."

"Don't be silly," Dan told her. "This thing has been growing inside her for years."

After the funeral, Dan took them all up to Connecticut. Mary Ellen had imagined a small clapboard house with a lawn and garden; her heart sank as he drove them through dingy brick tenements right in the center of Hartford. "Here we are," he said, pulling into a lumpy paved lot.

It was an awful apartment. The water pressure in the shower was weak, the radiators clanked, there were cockroaches, and at night they could hear in detail the horrific arguments and reconciliations of the couple who lived above them. "Hey!" Dan shouted toward the ceiling one night. "I'm a doctor and I'm trying to get some sleep!"

There was silence, and then a voice called back, "I'm a plumber, and I don't give a fuck!"

Day followed dreary day. Mary Ellen felt drained by her children. They had little engines inside them, and she was their fuel, disappearing drop by drop. The messes she got herself into were pitiful. One day she was feeding Waldo, while watching Toby eat in his highchair and keeping an ear open for sounds of distress from Lydia, out playing in the tiny yard. The phone rang; it was the garage, calling to say that the Chevy had a blown head gasket. Hanging up, she went back to the sink, lost in worry about the $150 they now needed to fix the car; without thinking, she picked up a knife and licked it off. She gagged: it was the knife she had used to serve Waldo his dog food. She threw the knife into the sink as Toby, distracted momentarily from the business of smearing puréed sweet potatoes across his forehead, looked up at her with a bobbing, wide-eyed wonder. Then she couldn't remember whether the man at the garage had said $150 or $1500.

"I'm a failure," she said to Daniel that night. "Do you want to trade me in?"

29

"Well," he said, "I did run an ad. But no one seemed interested."

"In you or in me?" she said, hugging him.

They joked, but beneath it all she often felt that, unlike her husband, she just wasn't good enough or tough enough for the life that faced them. She missed her mother. After her father's death seven years earlier, she had grown even closer to her mother, and out in Arizona she had come to rely on the twice monthly letters from home, full of recipes, town gossip, and tips on handling sick or cranky kids. She and Dan had laughed at the letters, with their solemn pronouncements on the minister's gout or the closing of a favorite hamburger stand, but now that they had stopped, Mary Ellen saw how much she had cherished them. "I feel cut off," she said to Dan.

"I'm sure," he said, smiling. "How will we make it without the Gout Report?"

"I miss Mom."

"You have me. I'm here."

"I know," she said. "But sometimes I just need her. Why can't she be here?"

"Everyone has to go sometime," he said.

He had his own struggle to fight. As a first-year resident, he worked seventy hours a week, sometimes more. He would leave on Saturday morning, and she wouldn't see him until Monday night. It was like being married to a secret agent. When he did come home he was exhausted, dragging himself through the door, unshaven and rumpled, as the kids screamed to play with him. One night he actually fell asleep on the couch while Lydia rode him, bouncing up and down and yelling "Horsey! Horsey!"

"You poor man," Mary Ellen said, shaking her head.

He worked so hard. In Arizona he had done easier things, setting legs and stitching cuts, delivering babies; sometimes when the going was slow, he had taken out his electric clippers and set himself up as a barber. Now his life was packed with disasters. People from auto wrecks, people with tumors, paralyzed people—death filled his days and nights, twelve or sixteen or even twenty hours running. It made her feel guilty, burdening him with her own small problems. Sometimes she found herself getting angry. "Why do they do this to you?" she asked him one night.

"Everyone has to go through it," he said. "That's just the way it is."

They had no money. In addition to his minuscule salary, they lived off their savings and off money left to her by her parents. Every nickel mattered. This bothered Dan; she could see it when he read letters from college buddies who by now, six or seven years out of school, owned houses in the suburbs, bought new cars, and took trips with their families to Florida. He read these letters aloud to her, wincing. "Gee," he would say, "Old Jimbo is really raking it in."

"So what?" she said. "Who wants to be married to someone named 'Old Jimbo' anyway?"

Their friends were other residents and their wives. One night a week they got together with Jack and Marcie English and Peter and Jo Ann Schlosser. To save the cost of babysitters, kids were brought along and put to sleep in the back room while the grownups played cards and drank beer. The men talked about their boss, a tyrannical chief neurosurgeon named James Edgar Howells, renowned for browbeating young doctors and seducing young nurses. When the men told of Howells's escapades, they rocked back in their chairs, laughing hard; inevitably, someone's child would wake and wander into the room, blinking and confused.

The stories about Howells disturbed Mary Ellen. Known as a brilliant surgeon with no tolerance for indecision, he humiliated residents in front of patients and berated nurses in the operating room. His favorite target was his own OR nurse, a hunched-over old woman named Buben, who had worked for him for years. "Buben, goddammit!" he would shout, if the slightest thing went wrong. "Are you trying to ruin my operation?" And finally, the men hinted, Howells was "quick with the knife"—when the choice was waiting or cutting, he invariably cut.

"Why do they let him get away with it?" Mary Ellen asked.

"Well, he's never actually *hurt* anyone," Peter Schlosser said, smiling. "Or at least he hasn't killed anyone."

"And besides, who are 'they?' " Dan said. "*He* is 'they.' "

"Well, I don't care how important he is," she told him. "He must be a terrible human being."

Then there was Howells's womanizing. Twice divorced, he was said to be a prime despoiler of young nurses. He had cleared the way for his philandering, the men said, by doing disk surgery on his most recent wife and then—when she continued to complain of pain—dispatching her to a mental institution, where she languished while he divorced her. "So if I ever operate on you," Dan said to her, laughing, "you'd better heal quickly!"

According to Marcie English, the residents were terrified of Howells. He was a famous surgeon who presented papers at conferences all over the country, and at the hospital he controlled the whole game—operating time, referrals, letters of recommendation. "Watch them when they talk about him," Marcie told Mary Ellen. "They're like little boys, and he's the Boogey Man. One night Jack told me quite seriously that Howells keeps a jar with a brain in it in his kitchen."

Mary Ellen saw something else. "I think you all *like* that madman," she said to Dan the night he told her the story of Howells's ex-wife.

"It was just a joke," he said.

"But it's not funny, what he did to her. The man's a butcher."

"I know it's not funny," he said.

"Then why don't you do something about him?"

"What can I do?" he said. "I'm nobody here." He looked at her and frowned. "What's wrong with you tonight?"

"I just liked it better when you were somebody, that's all." She was thinking of Arizona. "Remember the girl on the reservation who died? Little Angelica?"

"Sure," he said. Little Angelica had been the daughter of a Navajo and a Mexican migrant laborer; she had come into the clinic with appendicitis, and Dan had sent her on to the hospital in Tucson, where she died the next day, during surgery.

"Remember how you called the hospital in Tucson to send her flowers, and they told you what had happened, and you came home and cried and cried—?"

"Of course I remember," he said, a sharp edge in his voice. "It's only two years ago."

"Is that all?" she said. It seemed like eons. The memory of him sitting on the edge of the bed weeping was too much for Mary Ellen, and she began to cry herself.

"Hey," he said softly. "What is it?"

"I don't know," she said. "Everything."

"Hey," he said. "Baby, baby . . ." He patted his knees, and she went and sat on his lap. "All this—" his gesture included the apartment, Howells, all of Hartford—"it's just temporary. Before you know it we'll be free. We'll be on our own somewhere with our kids and a big white house, free and easy."

"I know," she said. She buried her face in the warmth of his neck. He stood, still holding her, and carried her into the bedroom. Soon they were naked, clinging to each other in the darkness as the sound of traffic leaked in through the window. She remembered him asking "What's wrong with you?" in that same annoyed way five months earlier, after a visit from his parents when she had been grouchy both to him and to them. What was wrong, she realized now, was that his parents, to whom he seemed indifferent, lived on, while hers, whom she had adored, were dead. Sometimes, wickedly, she wished his parents were dead, too.

"What is it, sweetness?" he asked. "Thinking about your mother?"

"I'm so bad," she said.

"Sweetheart?"

"Just tell me you love me."

"Of course I do. Of course I do."

On a warm morning in June, nine months after their arrival in New England, Mary Ellen saw her mother.

She had taken the kids down with her to do laundry in the basement. The light at the foot of the staircase was not working. With Toby in his stroller and Lydia hanging onto her hand, Mary Ellen headed into the blackness of the hallway, aiming for the far end, where a weird light, foggy and blindingly bright, poured in from the washroom windows. There was a sweet smell of decayed leaves and rat poison; Mary Ellen felt lightheaded. She blinked; her mother was standing in the light at the end of the hall.

It was only a flash. But with a certainty that flooded outward from her stomach, Mary Ellen recognized the Sunday church clothes, the maroon dress and matching pillbox hat, the black snakeskin clutch bag that her mother held in front of her with both hands. She smiled at Mary Ellen, then vanished into the laundry room.

"Mom?" Pushing Toby's stroller and dragging Lydia, who began to whine, Mary Ellen hurried to the end of the hall. The laundry room was empty. A washing machine churned loudly with someone's load of clothes.

"Liddie?" She turned to her daughter. "Did you see someone?"

Her daughter's eyes went wide.

Mary Ellen took the girl by the shoulders. "Did you see Grandma Matthews?"

Lydia shook her head, then turned and ran out of the room.

Upstairs she called the hospital and had Dan paged. "Can you please come home?" she said weakly. "Something happened."

"Are the kids okay?" He sounded very young and far away.

"Yes. It's me. Something happened to me."

"I'll be right there," he said. "You hold on."

She fumbled through the kitchen drawers until she found a cigarette, her first in months. Then she sat down and pictured the look on her mother's face. Her mother's full lips were smiling, her eyes slightly unfocused. It was an expression of serenity.

Soon she heard Dan pounding up the stairs. "What is it?" he said, lurching wildly through the door. His gaze landed heavily on her cigarette.

"I just saw my mother," she said.

"What?"

"I just saw my mother, down in the laundry room."

He glanced around the room, past Toby sitting placidly in his stroller, to Lydia playing in the living room. Annoyance pinched his face; she could see him fighting it back. "Are you drunk?" he said.

"No."

"Then would you mind starting over?"

She took a drag of the cigarette and watched her own trembling hand carry it away from her. In a low voice she told him what she had seen. He listened, eyebrows knitted, his hand creeping over his mouth and hiding his expression. "Why are you looking at me like that?" she said.

He took his hand away from his mouth. "Listen," he said, glancing at his watch, "we'll talk about this tonight."

All afternoon in the apartment, she kept peering into doors and mirrors, expecting to see her mother again. Dan called twice from the hospital. "I'm thinking about that rat poison down there," he said gravely. "Those fumes could be hallucinogenic. I'm going to check into that."

"Dan," she said to him that night. "Do you believe I saw my mother?"

"I believe you saw something," he said.

"Well, it wasn't rat poison fumes," she said. "It was my mother. Can't we just leave it at that?"

"Sure we can." He put his arm around her and guided her toward their room. "Why don't you leave everything to me tonight and get yourself some sleep."

In bed she lay with her eyes open, awake in every cell of her body, waiting for her mother to come to her. She thought about the house in Philadelphia, now sold to strangers; she went through it room by room, from the pantry, where canned beans and fruits towered to the ceiling, to the washroom where Lillian the housekeeper ironed with an old-fashioned iron heated in a brazier of coals, to her father's study with his portraits of presidents and his leather ledgers stacked high on the desk. Her mother's death had cut her loose from all of that, and now she drifted perilously across her own life, freighted with precious children, steered only by her husband. Sometimes, looking at him, she felt a rush of panic; it was as if with her mother's death she had married him a second time, in a ceremony whose vows, though frighteningly solemn, were muffled and unclear.

She thought about her first date with Dan Slattery—a blind date not long after her father's second heart attack. She had answered the doorbell in stockings; the house, when her father rested upstairs, was hushed, like a church. She remembered standing at the door and hoping that the person on the other side would be a man she could swoon over, a man smart and handsome and funny, a man who could make everything smooth for her. After their second date she brought him back into the house, and as they stood talking in the hall, her father called her upstairs. He wanted to meet this young man, he said.

"Now, Dad?" she said. "It's midnight."

"Does he turn into a frog?" Her father waved her toward the door. "Bring him up."

So she brought him up. They went in, and there followed an awkward moment as her father, propped up against the headboard of the bed, inspected her date as if sizing up a sack of potatoes. "I'll bet you're a Democrat," he said finally.

"Yes, sir," Dan said, shooting her an urgent, questioning look. "That's all right, that's all right," her father said. "It won't last."

Then he laughed, and Dan relaxed. Her father asked about medical school and explained something technical about his heart condition, which Mary Ellen didn't try to understand. They were beginning to talk about golf, when Mary Ellen coughed politely into her hand. "Dad," she said. "Don't you think you should get some sleep?"

"All right, all right." They said good night. When her father reached up to shake her date's hand, his eyes shone with a strange, aggressive light; looking down, Mary Ellen saw how hard he was gripping, saw both men's hands going white and red around the fingers. She turned away. "You take care of yourself," her father said to Dan.

"Good night, sir," she heard Dan say a second time.

Out in the hall afterward, she felt inexpressibly sad, and he took her in his arms and held onto her. "I know," he said into her ear. "I know." A month later her father was dead, and she and Dan were engaged.

Now she lay awake, listening to her husband and daughter playing with the dog in the next room. The lights of cars skated across the wall, and every now and then a siren erupted. She was still wide awake hours later when Dan got into bed, kissed her once on the back of the neck, and fell instantly into a deep, snoring sleep.

Each June, the residents' party was held at the home of the chief of neurosurgery. When Mary Ellen found she was expected to socialize with the infamous Howells, she refused. "I won't be a guest at that butcher's house," she said.

"Don't do this to me," Dan said, holding his hand over his heart and groaning in mock agony. "Everyone has to show up. It's crucial."

Grudgingly, she went along.

The day of the party, Dan shaved in the morning and again in

37

the afternoon. He stood in front of the closet for ten minutes, unsure what to wear. They left the babysitter with a page of instructions and the phone number of Howells's house; in the car on the way over, she watched Dan fingering his bow tie and sneaking glimpses of himself in the rearview mirror. The city eased itself into the shaded quiet of West Hartford, where houses were large and gardens flourished. Dan peered out the window and asked her how much she thought each house cost. She had no idea, and accepted his estimates. The neighborhood reminded her of where she had grown up.

"I miss having trees," she said.

Howells's house was an ivy-covered, gabled Tudor. A sign on the driveway read Back Achers. "It's hard to picture such a horrible man having such a beautiful home," Mary Ellen said as they parked.

He turned to her. "Remember what you promised? Forget the stories, forget the rumors. No accusations, no controversy, none of this butcher business—"

"I know, silly," she said. "I'll be a model of pleasant hypocrisy."

"Now you're talking," he said.

The party was in the backyard, a yard like those of Mary Ellen's childhood, isolated from neighbors through artful placing of trees and bushes. They found Peter and Jo Ann Schlosser, standing by a meticulously tended rose garden with a couple Mary Ellen knew she was supposed to know. Peter was in Bermuda shorts and tennis shirt; Dan in his seersucker suit was overdressed, and knew it. "Why didn't anyone tell me it was a beach party?" He looked around, frowning. "I may have to pull a quick change," he said, tugging at his bow tie.

They all stared at him. "I brought some other clothes, just in case," he added.

"Marvelous," said the woman Mary Ellen was supposed to know. Dan headed off. Mary Ellen knew he was annoyed; he liked every little thing just right.

Jo Ann Schlosser was telling a story Mary Ellen had heard at least three times, about a burglar who broke into their apartment as she and Peter lay in bed. Not wanting to hear yet again the part where the burglar shines his flashlight up and down Jo Ann's naked body, Mary Ellen excused herself. "I'm just going to take a peek around," she said.

She headed vaguely toward the bar, a long table with a punch fountain at the end. Beyond this, a grove of small Japanese maples led to a cluster of hedges, which Mary Ellen recognized as a topiary garden. People stood talking in the yard, and she was surprised by how many she didn't know. Several of the residents' wives were pregnant. Their husbands touched them lightly on the waist or elbow as they sipped drinks and talked to each other. Mary Ellen imagined all of them spread out across the country, buying houses, meeting neighbors, helping their kids with homework. She wondered where everyone would end up.

"Lost?" a voice behind her said.

She turned to face a tall, handsome man in his forties, holding a glass of punch in each hand. "Lost?" she said.

"You were staring at these maples as if you didn't know what country you were in." He talked as if resuming a conversation broken off moments earlier. "Put these trees in native soil, they'd be twice the size," he said. "Do you garden?"

"A little," she said.

"Well, what do you make of this hedge arrangement?" He raised one of the punch glasses to point at the topiary.

"I like it," she said, looking at the miniature shapes of giraffes, elephants, bears. "I've never really seen one before."

"Very European," he said, a touch of contempt in his voice. "A Renaissance ornament developed by murderous Italian princes. To reassure their wives that the world was a beautiful place." He sipped one of the drinks. "Of course, the whole thing should be bigger. It really loses the point if it isn't done to scale."

"Oh, I don't know about that," she said.

He shrugged. His smile was a burst that quickly faded, like

fireworks. He had graying hair hanging almost shaggily over a face of prominent, bony features. They were the kind of good looks that she supposed were what people called "craggy." She raised an eyebrow at the punch glasses. "Are you drinking both of those yourself?"

"Oh, I'm sorry," he said, handing her one. "What an idiot I am. Actually, I got this one for my wife." He paused. "Then I remembered I'm not married anymore."

Before she could say anything, he was off and running again on the subject of gardening, frowning now at the hedge garden. "Pretentious, isn't it?"

"No," she said. "I like it."

"You don't think it's a little bit—effeminate? For a man living alone?"

She sipped her punch. The thing about punch was, you never knew exactly what was in it. "Well," she said, "I think he's a pretty horrible man, but I don't think he's a fairy."

She was about to elaborate when she saw Daniel rounding the bar in his checked Bermuda shorts. As soon as he saw her, he changed directions and came quickly her way.

"Honey?" she said when he pulled up. "Is everything all right?"

The craggy man laughed. "Slattery," he said. "This is your wife? We*elllll* . . ." He drew the word out. "She was just giving me the bottom line on topiary gardens—and the people who own them." He winked and raised his glass to her, then moved off toward the garden.

"Oh, no," she said to Dan. "You're kidding me."

"What did you say to him?"

"I told him I thought Howells was horrible."

"You didn't." He slumped standing up. "Why?"

She felt tricked. "He disguised himself," she said. "I thought he would be older. And uglier. And meaner." She started to take a sip from the punch, but annoyance flooded through her, and she handed the drink to her husband, who drank it off in two hard gulps.

"I'm sorry," she said to him.

"Oh well." He wiped his lips. "Just promise me one thing: you won't talk to him unless I'm there." She agreed, and he took her hand and led her back to the rose garden, where Peter Schlosser was doing his Nixon-Khrushchev routine.

When Howells approached her a second time, during the volleyball game, she tried to ignore him. She was standing on the sideline, watching, when he appeared next to her. Once again he launched breezily into conversation. "What do you make," he said, "of the whole controversy about competitive sports?"

"Of *what*?" she said, turning to him.

"Sports." He waved a hand loosely at the volleyball game, a gesture that reminded her of a brilliant and ironic professor she had had in college. "We tell our children to run around competing with each other. Win, win, win, we tell them. Be the best. Some people call this training for teamwork, others call it combat practice. The old playing fields of Eton dilemma. What do you think?"

"I think . . ." Mary Ellen decided to disagree with Howells whenever possible. "I think this is just an innocent game of volleyball."

"No doubt," Howells said, pursing his lips and brooding. On the volleyball court, Dan leaped high and made a hard, winning shot over the net, his teammates cheering. "Hmmm," said Howells. "Did he play ball in college?"

"As a matter of fact, he did," she said. "Basketball."

"I see," said Howells enigmatically. They watched Dan playing. "Competitive, isn't he," said Howells. "Good reflexes, too. Comes in handy for a brain surgeon."

"You know," Mary Ellen said, changing the subject, "it was pretty rude of you not to introduce yourself before."

"You're right." Howells nodded. "It was damn rude. But there's so much malicious gossip floating around, sometimes I go incognito. You know what I mean?" He scratched his forehead and looked at her. There was something playful and yet wounded in his expression that made her like him in spite of herself. She wanted to ask him about some of that malicious gossip—his face seemed to say *Go ahead, fire away*—but just then Dan made another heroic, leaping shot and turned, smiling, to where she stood. His face clouded when he saw her there with Howells.

"Adios," said Howells, as Dan began moving her way.

In a remote corner of the game, where she could dodge or duck whenever the ball threatened to come near her, Dan grilled her about her conversation with Howells. "I thought we had an agreement," he said first.

"But he just came up to me," she said. "I couldn't get away."

"Well, so what did you talk about? Did he say anything about the incision I did on his subdural last week?"

"No," she said.

"Did he mention arteriograms?"

"You know," she sighed, "I do on occasion talk about something other than my husband's surgical procedures."

He made a stricken face. "You didn't say anything I'll regret, did you?"

"No," she said, pouting a little. "We talked about sports."

"What?"

"Yes," she said nonchalantly. "And I was surprised. He seems to hate competitive sports. I think he thinks they're harmful."

"Hah!" Dan turned away and barged back into the game, played a couple of shots, and then floated back to her.

"What was that 'hah' for?" she asked.

He smiled widely at her and wiped sweat off his forehead. "Howells," he said. "He was a big football star at Harvard in the Twenties. Lineman. Ferocious. 'Horrible Howells of Harvard,' they called him."

"You're kidding me," she said. Her gaze shot to the side where they had been standing, but the butcher was gone.

42

"Why do you never tell the truth?"

Only under cover of darkness and semidrunkenness could she speak to James Edgar Howells this way. She glanced over toward where Dan, searching for the bathroom, had gone into the house. All evening she had felt mounting indignation at the thought of Howells roaming his backyard like a prince, telling lies with his ironic, haunted smile and then disappearing. No one, it seemed, had the courage to tell him off. Now here she was. "Is lying a policy with you," she said, "or do you just enjoy it?"

"What do you mean?" he said.

"First you come on like some stranger," she said, "and trick me into insulting you. Second, you tell me you hate football, and then it turns out you're the Horrible Hulk of Harvard or something."

He smiled. "Don't you think perhaps alcohol is affecting your judgment?"

"Yes. It's improving it."

"I see. Well. He paused, pursing his lips. "Any other questions?"

Mary Ellen felt like a runaway train, unable to stop herself. And Howells seemed willing to let her say anything. "Yes," she ventured. "Did you really operate on your wife and then get her committed?"

"Anything else?"

"Do you really keep a brain in a jar in your kitchen?"

Howells looked both thoughtful and amused. "Come with me for a minute," he said, taking her arm.

She let herself be led off. They went around the bar and garage, through a cloister covered with wisteria. "Where exactly are we going?" she said.

She wasn't sure she liked Howells's silences; she was used to men who kept up a running banter. Howells unlocked a door in the side of the house; she followed him down a half-flight of stairs into a room full of mahogany and fluorescent lights. There were books everywhere.

"Your study," she said. "What are we doing here?"

"Dispelling myths." He moved to the nearest bookshelf and took down a fat book titled *Clinical Psychosis*. "First, I've already explained to you why I don't introduce myself. Second, yes, it's true that I did play football in college. In fact, if I hadn't had the pleasure of personally fracturing someone's fibia and then seeing the bone extrude through the skin, I might still be a big fan. And here—" he handed her the textbook—"here is the answer to question number three. If you read the stuff on paranoid schizophrenia, you'll know as much about my ex-wife as I can tell you." As Mary Ellen flipped aimlessly through the book, Howells took down a glass jar containing a small, pickled-looking something in yellow fluid. "Here is question number four," he said.

She started to shake her head, then remembered. The brain.

"That's right," Howells said, reading her face. He put the jar on a teak coffee table in the middle of the room and stepped back from it. "Now this is no ordinary ten ounces of cerebral tissue," he said. "This brain belonged to a friend of mine, a physicist and poet. The most brilliant man I ever met." He named someone Mary Ellen had never heard of. "Before he died, he authorized me to study his brain."

Howells paused to give Mary Ellen the chance to question him. When she didn't, he went on. "That was two years ago. I did some research and got in touch with leading neurogeneticists here and in Europe. It came down to two of them, one in Geneva, one in Michigan. Both of them wanted the brain."

"But you didn't give it to them?"

"I decided they just didn't know enough to do justice to it. I wrote to them and told them so."

"You mean you decided to do the research yourself?"

He looked startled. "No, no, no," he said, chuckling. "No, I don't have the faintest idea how to unlock the secrets of this magnificent organ." He tapped the jar. "I stand before it as a Neanderthal."

Mary Ellen stared at the soft, vaguely repulsive folds of the brain. The thought that she carried one of these inside her, that her children and husband and friends did, too—this stole her breath away. It was like a secret that should never be told.

"Mesmerizing, isn't it?" Howells said. "And we neurosurgeons—we have only the most primitive notions of how it works." His face was lit by a strange elation. "We are like commercial artists," he said, "hired at inflated wages to do touch-up work on the ceiling of the Sistine Chapel. We don't know how the thing was painted in the first place. We only hope we don't screw it up too much when we do what we have to do."

They stood in silence, staring at the brain. Mary Ellen felt the way she had felt in the basement of the apartment three days earlier, when she had looked up and seen her mother. Anything was possible; there was nothing she could rule out. "Do you think it's possible . . ." she said. ". . . Do you think people can make contact with the dead?"

He didn't laugh at her but frowned in a way that Mary Ellen took to indicate deep thought. "I have two sons," he said. "One of them is a corporate lawyer in New York. The other was a paranoid schizophrenic, like his mother. Ten years ago he ran away, and I never heard from him again. Sometimes I wake up in the middle of the night, a car goes by, the lights sweep across the wall, and then I hear Jimmy, calling my name. Sometimes he sings."

The story made her shiver. She looked at Howells, watched him lost in thought, his face all angles and furrows. The way he acted, the way he had explained himself to her—it cast into doubt everything she had heard about him. "Any other questions?" he said.

"One more," she said. "Why me? Why take me off and tell me these things?"

"You really want to know?"

She nodded.

"Two reasons. First, you reminded me of someone I was in love

45

with once. Someone I would have married if I had been less of a horse's ass."

"And second?"

"Second, neurosurgeons bore the hell out of me, if you want to know the truth."

They stood close. She smelled his presence, heavy and slightly sweet, like molasses, and felt herself leaning closer into it. "I should get back," she said.

A handful of people remained in the yard. The bar was gone; a man was folding chairs and stacking them on the back patio.

By the time she saw Dan, he had already spotted her. He was plowing across the yard like a missile, aimed straight at her. She watched his white socks glow in the darkness as they pumped up and down, up and down.

"*Where* have you been?" he said when he was ten feet away from her. When he saw Howells standing in shadow behind her, he stiffened. "Oh—Doctor," he said.

"I've just been showing your wife a few things in the house," Howells said. He slapped Dan on the shoulder. "You're a damned lucky man, Slattery."

"Don't I know it, Doctor."

They left. Darkness and silence surrounded them as he took her arm and dragged her across the front yard toward the car. "Ouch," she said. "You're hurting me."

He stopped. "Do you think this is some *game?*" he hissed.

"What do you mean?"

"I mean you—disappearing with Howells like that."

She opened her mouth but couldn't find words, and he barged on. "Do you have any idea how important that man is to us? Do you have any idea what it means if he doesn't like someone?" He snapped his fingers. "One false step, and the only job I can get is in Nebraska. Do you want to go to Nebraska? It's cold and very flat."

They came to the car. She opened the door for herself, and they sat there. She watched his fingers flexing on the steering wheel. "But he did like me," she said meekly.

He started the car, and they drove in silence. He took the corners fast, and the Chevy squealed and strained. She watched his face appear and disappear in the light-dark-light-dark of streetlights flashing overhead. Each time, she expected him to emerge smiling. But he didn't.

"Maybe there's more to him than you know," she said finally.

"What does *that* mean?"

"Well, maybe he's actually a very nice man."

"*What?* The butcher, the horrible human being?" He brought her own words back to her. " 'Oh Dan, why don't you *do* something about him?' "

"Well," she said, "that was before I met him."

"I *see*. And how exactly did he win you over? Did he take you down into his office?"

"As a matter of fact, he did."

"Oh, Jesus," he said, shaking his head. The light flashed, and she saw his upper lip, curled into a smile. "I guess it's a relief to know that my wife hasn't insulted the world's foremost neurosurgeon—she's just been seduced by him. This'll play well at the hospital." He assumed a lewd voice, dripping with insinuation. " 'Say Dan, I hear Howells was showing your little lady a thing or two the other night.' Jesus!"

"Oh, Dan, come on . . ."

"Then again, you're certainly not the first woman in Hartford privileged enough to see the inner sanctum."

"Are you jealous?" She didn't know what to make of his reaction. "It was all perfectly innocent. In fact, I don't even believe all those stories anymore."

"Oh really? Why not?"

"Well . . ." She wanted to be able to explain herself to him.

"He just didn't act that way. Not at all. I mean, he's intelligent and deep, and kind of . . ." She groped for the right word. "Kind of wistful."

"Wistful."

"Yes. I think he knows how people see him but doesn't know what to do about it. You know what he showed me down there?" Briefly she told him the story of the physicist's brain, painting for him a picture of Howells's deep concentration, of the haunted look on his face. "Granted he's arrogant," she said. "But maybe he has reason to be. I think he may be a genius. Maybe all of you can't see that because you have to take orders from him or something."

"Are you done?" he said when she stopped.

"Done? I've told you everything that happened, if that's what you mean."

"Good," he said. "Because now I can tell you something." He turned to her, and she saw his teeth as he smiled in the dark. "I've heard that whole story before."

"What whole story?"

"The brain business. Almost word for word. From one of the ER girls, an LPN named Eileen. Pretty girl, about twenty. Nice kid." He glanced sideways at her, as if that was supposed to mean something. "I guess Eileen had a similar little visit with Howells, and got pretty much the same show. Except that I think with her it was a chemist's brain."

"A chemist's brain? No, it was a physicist's brain."

"Yeah, and tomorrow it'll be a philosopher's brain, and the next day Einstein's brain." He sighed. "The point is that it will be whoever's brain he wants it to be. The whole thing is just some hype he cooks up to entice gullible females."

"I don't believe you."

He shrugged. "Well, you might want to talk to Eileen. I guess her show ended a little differently than yours did, though. Seems there were a few other organs Howells was interested in displaying. . . ."

48

"Stop it, please." She needed to get her thoughts straight. Was it possible she had been duped somehow? She flashed back through the events of the evening, seeking some edge to hold onto. "He also told me about his ex-wife," she said.

"And what exactly did he tell you?"

"Well, I never knew she was schizophrenic. I thought he just committed her to get rid of her."

They came to a stop light, and he laid his head on the steering wheel. "I can't believe you let him con you with this hype," he said. "Did he get around to the line about his son?"

"What line?" she said.

"Oh, how his son was a brilliant kid, was stricken with devastating psychosis, and ran away, never to be heard of again. How he misses the kid, etc., etc., the whole dogfaced soulful business?"

"What are you saying?" she said.

"I'm saying it's all a crock. I happen to know from a patient whose son went to school with Howells's kid that the kid was just a spoiled brat who got kicked out of three schools and then got his girlfriend pregnant. Howells finally threw him out of the house and told him he never wanted to see his face again."

He was waiting for her to come back at him. But she had nothing left. "Is there anything else he said that I can translate for you?" he said.

She leaned her head against the window. The neighborhoods outside had gradually deteriorated, and now they had reached the part of the city where they lived. She saw garbage blowing around in the gutter and quietly began to cry.

"Hey," he said. "It was just a joke, that last thing I said. I didn't mean anything." She cried into her hands, and he went on in a soft voice. "Everything's okay. No harm done tonight. Really."

She tried to gather herself together. It was like collecting pieces of a puzzle scattered across a huge floor. "I feel so alone," she said.

"I'm here."

"Do you still love me, even if I am a gullible female?"

49

They reached the parking lot. He turned off the engine and faced her, wiping a tear off her cheek. "I'm crazy about you," he said, his voice confident and round. "Come on. Let's get some sleep and forget all about this."

They walked across the lot to the back steps. Above them, light shone where the sitter kept watch over their children. He caressed her face, and she saw his wedding band gleam; taking his hand, she closed her eyes and kissed his fingers, pressing her lips into the tiny hairs on the backs of his knuckles.

"Better be careful," he joked, laughing. "Those are the precious fingers of the brain surgeon you've got there."

She pictured him in the hospital in Philadelphia, describing the cancer growing inside her mother; in the kitchen, staring at her cigarette; in the car, his upper lip smiling. Closing her teeth around his index finger, she bit down, hard. *It was just a joke*, she said to herself, as he jerked his hand away.

IV

Straight Down the
Fall Line

All week long Dan Slattery was nagged by a feeling that something was wrong. He felt it in his office as he saw his last patient and dictated a surgery report into the dictaphone; in the driveway as he hoisted his suitcase and the kids' duffel bags into the car; at the airport, kissing his wife, Mary Ellen, and six-year-old, Sharon, goodbye as the skis in their canvas sacks sank down the baggage chute; and he felt it again minutes later as the jet pounded down the runway and careened improbably upward, bearing him and Toby and Lydia west toward the Rockies and skiing heaven. Dan looked out the small, rounded window and searched the pattern below him in vain for his wife's station wagon. The feeling of something being wrong didn't speak its name but tugged mutely at his sleeve. He chalked it up to missing his wife in advance. "Hey Dad." Toby, his eleven-year-old, leaned across his lap. "It's gonna be powder three feet deep out there, right?"

"Right, Champ." Together he and his son looked out at Connecticut, its brown barrenness speckled with the remnants of snows demolished by a January thaw. "Hey Liddie," he said to his daughter. "Take a look at your home state?"

But Liddie just shook her head, and Dan realized, looking at her tight lips and her face frozen white beneath its freckles, that his daughter was terrified.

"You okay, honey?" he said.

"Fine. I just—don't—want—to talk."

"Well, that's a new one." Dan laughed to ease her mind; failing, he turned with his son to watch America drifting by in ribbons and checks below.

"Dad, is Mom nuts or something? I mean, I can't believe she didn't come."

"Who's going to take care of Sharon?" Dan said. "And besides—" he glanced at Liddie—"your mother and planes don't mix too well, if you know what I mean."

With this explanation, Dan picked up a spy novel he'd been reading and sank into it. He thought he saw Lydia shoot him a glance of terror, wonder, and blame, as if reading at thirty thousand feet were a reckless insult to whatever god kept the plane aloft. And indeed there soon followed a spell of turbulence. The craft heaved, the seat belt light went on, and Lydia jammed her eyes closed. "I hate it when it does this," she whispered.

Dan's heart went out to her. It didn't seem fair for an eighth grader to be preyed on by fear. And meanwhile his son went on merrily talking. "Dad, is Mr. Tackler meeting us at the airport?"

"I don't think so, Champ. He's probably skiing right now."

"Cool."

"You like Mr. Tackler, don't you."

"Yeah. He's cool."

"*SSShhh!*" hissed Lydia, her eyes still closed. As she shushed them, the plane rocked sideways, and she clutched Dan's arm with a strength that astonished him.

52

The previous spring—the last time Dan and his wife had skied together—Mary Ellen had had a bad fall at Stowe. They were coming down near the top and had just negotiated one of the sharp curves of the upper Nose Dive when Dan looked ahead and saw Mary Ellen fall on the top of a sharp mogul. She landed almost gently on her back but then slid over the top of the bump, out of view. When Dan raced to the spot, he saw her sliding down the pitch, out of control. "Get your feet downhill!" he shouted. He skied hard to catch up, swooping down past his wife's discarded ski poles, nearly falling himself, finally catching up to her lying in a heap, sobbing but unhurt, by the side of the slope.

Dan helped her collect herself and walked her down to the bottom, snowplowing along beside her with her skis on his shoulder. On the way down, Mary Ellen seemed calm, but in the base lodge something broke inside her; she shuddered and wept and refused to go back out.

Throughout the off-season this aversion grew. At several parties during the summer, Dan heard his wife tell the story of her fall, and each time it seemed to acquire a new danger: a looming pine, a windmilling ski, a patch of blue ice. The length of the slide grew as well: twenty yards, forty, fifty. Once Dan teased her about it ("Are you sure there wasn't a lift tower somewhere in there too, hon?"), and she shot him a brutal look; he pulled back, apologizing. He blamed himself, he told Mary Ellen, for having taken her on a tough slope late in the day.

By September Dan had begun to feel that the only way he'd ever get his wife to ski again would be to kidnap her and lead her blindfolded to the nearest chair lift. Then Marc Tackler called from Denver. He and Faith and the kids were planning a week in Aspen in early February; they'd rented a big condo and wanted the Slatterys to join them. Marc Tackler was the one who, almost ten years earlier, had introduced the Slatterys to skiing, taking them to a beautiful ski resort above a frozen lake up in Quebec, in a town called Saint

Auguste. More than they had imagined possible, Dan and Mary Ellen had fallen in love with the place. You could stand at the top of the slope and look down across the frozen lake to where smoke rose from chimneys straight up into an utterly blue and windless sky, like ropes to heaven. They all slept late and stayed up late, drinking with the young Canadian instructors, until two or three in the morning, when Mary Ellen would drag Dan off to bed, up to their room over the curling club. Somehow the idea of making love over a rink where people bowled strange discs and whisked dwarf brooms was exciting. Every year thereafter Dan and Mary Ellen returned to the resort above the frozen lake, returning even after Marc Tackler had been transferred out West. They started bringing their kids with them to Canada, and as the years passed, they concentrated more on skiing and less on carousing. The memories of stumbling out to the slope at noon, hung over, seemed quaintly reckless. They became experts.

It was impossible, Dan knew, for Mary Ellen to refuse the Tacklers' invitation. When he announced it at the dinner table, the explosion of delight from Toby and Lydia was so strong that he barely heard Mary Ellen, in a wan and worried voice, agree to go. The next week he brought home new ski clothes for everyone—corduroy jackets, denim warm-ups, all no-slide surfaces. Mary Ellen smiled. She seemed to have put the nastiness of her spill behind her.

Then, in December, Marc Tackler called Dan at the office with bad news. Faith and the kids weren't going to make it. Faith, he explained, was taking a psychology class which she refused to skip, and Ricky—Marc's son, a year older than Toby—had just had his appendix out. The upshot of it was that Marc would be the only Tackler there, the condo was no go, everyone would have to find a different place to stay. He recommended a hotel near the slopes.

Dan went home to relay this message with a feeling of doom. And sure enough, the expression on his wife's face when he told her the news was unmistakably one of relief. "So Faith isn't going," she said. "Hmmm . . ."

All December they tossed it back and forth, but Mary Ellen prevailed, claiming she'd have fun with Sharon while the rest of them were gone. So they headed west, a fragment of a family, wearing their no-slide jackets. Dan couldn't help feeling that if he'd handled things differently, more sensitively or perhaps cleverly, with some kind of brilliant strategy, they would all be going together.

Not only was Marc Tackler not at the airport in Denver, but no one by that name was registered at the hotel in Aspen that Dan and the kids checked into. It was late in the afternoon, and the three of them walked through the town and up toward the slopes, Toby and Lydia pointing at fat Texans wearing Stetsons, Dan half expecting his old friend to pop out and surprise them from behind one of the odd pastel-painted Victorian homes. At the bottom of the mountain, they watched skiers taking last runs. The kids' eyes traveled up and up and up. "This is the big leagues, gang," Dan said.

The next morning they were the first people up the lift. The whiteness below them was unblemished by even a single rock or patch of ice. Toby pounded the chair lift, trying to hurry it up. "Let's *move* this sucker!" he said. There were no safety bars on the chairs, and Dan told his kids to sit well back. "I don't want to spoil my week," he joked, "by having to scrape either of you off the slope with a spatula."

And then, finally, they were skiing. They threw themselves down the broad slopes, shouting as they went. Looking at the endless snowfields, Dan kept expecting someone to appear and take it all back. There was none of that famous Colorado powder, but plenty of moguls to keep them busy. The kids loved the bumps, Liddie absorbing them with her powerful legs, Toby using them as launching pads. What Dan loved most was that fleeting, almost nauseating sense of imperilment that came when you pitched yourself from the top of one bump straight down into the trough of the next. It was an intoxicating feeling Dan had also known while white-water rafting, while making love with his wife early in their marriage, and while deep at work at the operating table. He suspected that if he flew planes, he would feel it there, too, in the cockpit.

At other times, though, he was appalled by the recklessness of skiing. Having filled out his kids' school physicals year after year, he knew their weights—Lydia a solid 120, tall for her age, Toby hovering just under 100—and he winced at the picture of those precious masses turned, with his approval, even his urging, into human missiles. On the second afternoon Dan watched as his daughter, descending gracefully toward him, was nearly struck by an idiot veering at her wildly from behind. As Dan stood helplessly watching, he was aware of an impossible, physical urge to stretch his arm out forty yards and pluck his daughter off the slope.

He didn't mention that moment to Mary Ellen in his nightly call. Instead, he tried to convey to her the kids' excitement at having discovered the Old West. They were ranging the town like bandits, he said, and soaking him for cash.

All week long Dan was surprised to see how well the kids did without their mother. He himself felt incomplete without his wife, as if he had awakened to find all his teeth painlessly pulled, and was scouring his blank gums with his tongue to find them. On the second afternoon, his son solemnly told him, as they rode the chair high over the steep drops of Ajax Mountain, that it was "probably better" Mary Ellen hadn't come. " 'Cause now," he said, "we don't have to stop every five seconds and talk."

"That's not a very nice thing to say, is it, Champ?" Dan batted his son lightly on the back of the head. "Your mother gives it her best."

"I know, I know," his son said. "But—well, she'd never ski *that*." And he pointed below them to the twisting plunge of an expert trail.

Mary Ellen asked about Marc Tackler, and Dan had to report the mysterious truth, that their old friend simply hadn't shown up.

Worried, Mary Ellen thought they should call Faith in Denver, but Dan assured her that if anything terrible had happened, they'd know it. He was convinced that Marc would show up soon. And in fact the next morning Dan found him, against all odds, on the slopes. Dan never forgot the way a person skied, and when he saw, way over at the edge of the trail, a dark figure flash by with the supreme effortlessness of a river in a ravine, he knew it was Marc Tackler. He lit out after him but couldn't catch up, had to guess blindly at two forks in the trail, and then luckily found him in one of the lift lines. He skied up beside him and said "Single?!" right into his ear.

"Daniel, old man!"

"Marcus!"

They shook hands awkwardly through their ski gloves, like astronauts, and Marc Tackler moved over to let Dan into the line. In fact Marc had not been single—he had been positioned next to a young woman—but as soon as Dan cut in, she found someone else. Within a minute they were aloft, Marc hugging Dan's shoulder with his right arm while reaching with his left under his coat to produce a flask, ludicrously disguised in a jacket of tricolor sponge as a ham and cheese sandwich.

"Same old Marc," Dan said to Mary Ellen, phoning home that night.

That assessment turned out to be both true and untrue. In Connecticut years earlier, Marc Tackler had been known, fondly, as the Great Flirt. But what before had been a big game was now in Aspen, Dan immediately sensed, for real. Marc took Dan to a loud club, where he kept one eye turned to the huge bar mirror on which were reflected women passing in jeans, in tight stretch pants and coveralls. "Some pretty crazy flora and fauna in the Rockies, Daniel," he said. Dan also looked at himself and Tackler together in the mirror. While both of them were approaching their forties in reasonable shape, they were doing it differently: Dan with his graying hair looking almost dignified, a gravity he knew he could crack wide open with a quick smile; Marc youthful with his round face like a jack o'lantern, devious and merry, under a college kid's head of sandy hair which curled over his collar in the back. Only on a second, closer glance could you see the lines around Marc Tackler's eyes, the fleshiness of the round face, the slight paunch that had accumulated over his belt.

The two men sat drinking Scotch. Though Dan would have preferred a table, they sat on stools at the bar. Dan remembered how comfortable Marc Tackler had always seemed in bars, where Dan himself had for much of his adult life felt vaguely, ludicrously ill at ease. He mentioned he'd expected to find his old buddy checked in at the hotel, and Marc glanced at the mirror, laughed his pumpkin laugh, and said no, he'd thought the place would be good for Dan and the kids, but that for him it was, well, "a little too family."

Dan felt he had to speak. "Marcus, tell me," he said. "Are you and Faith in any trouble?"

Marc tossed back his Scotch and thudded the glass hard on the bar. "Hell no," he said, grinning. "Just up to my old degenerate tricks, that's all."

As they went on talking, Dan tried to remember what exactly those old tricks had been. There had always been wild stories about Faith and Marc—of skinny-dipping parties, mattresses hauled into the middle of the park, partners traded for an evening. But the Slatterys had largely dismissed the stories; Faith Tackler, they were sure, just wouldn't do such things. Dan, who often secretly pictured people as animals, thought of Faith as a camel—awkward and yet graceful, though wholly without any trace of the camel's sulk. Among the relatively few people he knew who never told a joke or funny story, Faith was the friendliest. At the Slatterys' annual costume party, the joke was that Faith always wore a mask so that no one could see her embarrassment when Marc inevitably began shedding his costume in a 2:00 A.M. striptease. Dan had believed, without ever putting it in words, that Faith's overt goodness and Marc's overt badness had made for a happy balance. And so he wasn't quite sure what to make of it when Marc mentioned to him that two young women were going to meet them for drinks in that same bar the night after next. Amazing skiers, Marc said. Knock your socks off.

"Will we get to use a table instead of bar stools?" Dan joked.

"Maybe even a booth," Marc Tackler said, smiling and waving for more Scotch.

The next morning the kids were up at dawn, gloating and stamping their feet at the prospect of a foot of new powder, the first three inches of which had already fallen when Dan had lurched out of the bar with Marc Tackler a mere four hours earlier. "Dad, come *on*, let's *go!*" They raced back and forth between their room and his adjoining one, pulling on their clothing layer by layer and appearing finally at his bedside fully clad, staring at him through their goggles like Martians. Dan groaned and rolled over. "Dad," Toby said, "this is *pow*der!"

And so it was, powder lighter than they'd ever dreamed. Dan's grit-your-teeth, forward-lunging style didn't work in the deep stuff, and again and again he fell into the luscious depths of it. "Stay back on your skis a bit," Marc Tackler, who had met them at the base lodge, called to him. "And relax! Go with the flow!" Dan thought this advice dubious, but he followed it; he loosened his grip on himself the slightest bit and suddenly was home free, rocking his turns effortlessly through the snow. "Sweet and easy, isn't it?" Marc said at the bottom of the run. Indeed it seemed almost too easy, almost like cheating.

Marc's inclusion made the group a foursome, convenient for riding the lifts. Toby got a chance to ride with Marc and hear stories of the U.S. Ski Team tryouts twenty years earlier, where Marc had brushed shoulders with some of the world's greatest skiers. Meanwhile Dan rode with Lydia who, to his great pleasure, had turned out to be the most enthusiastic powder hound of them all. Dan had never seen her so happy. Often he felt unable to reach his daughter in her world of horse posters, folk songs, and hushed phone calls. But on this day he was literally right in her tracks, following her down through the immense snowfields, watching the plumes of snow she sent up and the long dark hair flying out of the back of her cap. He crossed her tracks with his own to produce elegant figure eights, which together they admired, Liddie looking up behind them with astonishment. "We did *that?*" she said. When Toby skied over, he looked up at the tracks, followed them down to where they ended at Dan and Liddie's feet, then said to his older sister, "Wow, that's cool!" He went on to add that she'd better do as much of that as fast as she could, because when she woke up one day and found herself turned into a *woman*, she'd have to start wearing some stupid pink coat, slow down to three miles per hour, and stop on every mogul to *talk*.

"You make talking sound like a Communist conspiracy, Tobe," Dan said.

"But women don't know how to ski." He looked up at Dan, then turned to Marc Tackler. "Do they, Mr. Tackler?"

Smiling at Dan, Marc said to Toby, "I wouldn't quite say that, superstar. I know some women who could ski circles around your father and me all day."

"Mrs. Tackler, for one," Dan said to his son.

Marc laughed out loud, as if to say touché, and skied off, accelerating straight down the hill. "Wow!" said Toby.

On the lift minutes later, Marc pointed to a woman skiing beautifully beneath them, on the steepest pitches near the top. "Suzy!" he called out to her. But she was gone, leaving only a swizzle trail in the powder. "That was one of 'em," Marc said.

Dan turned to his friend. "Are you serious about tomorrow night, Marcus?"

"That depends what you mean by serious."

"I mean, is this just another parlor game, or are you really planning on sleeping with one of those girls?"

Marc Tackler laughed. "I might have to sleep with both of them," he said, "if you don't do your part, Daniel."

Dan pounded the joke flat with a look of stony seriousness. The chair lift whisked them toward the unloading station at the summit. Marc looked at him and then shook his head. "You remember the lists Faith and I made, Daniel?"

"Lists?"

"Sure you do." Marc's brow furrowed a little. "Faith and I had these backup lists. In case we ever got tired of each other. We wrote down our fantasies—people we secretly desired, places we'd like to go to have affairs. Everyone thought we were kidding." His voice trailed off.

"So now you're going to the backup list?"

Marc Tackler ignored the question, smiling at Dan as the two men raised their ski tips for the unloading platform. "I gotta tell ya, Daniel," he said. "For a while there you were Numero Uno on Faith's list."

Dan almost blurted out, *Really?* and couldn't keep from smiling as they skied down the ramp onto the crown of the mountain.

That night he was going to tell Mary Ellen about this, but at the sound of her voice answering the phone, he pulled back. In his mind he saw the girl called Suzy, plunging rhythmically through the deep powder.

"Is that you, Dan?" his wife's voice floated to him over the ocean of static. "Hello? Hello?!"

He waited another second before speaking into the void. "Must be a bad connection," he shouted. "I lost you there for a minute." And then, speaking quickly, he began telling his wife about the beautiful figure eights he and Lydia had made in the snow.

Before meeting Marc Tackler the next night, Dan took the kids to dinner and an early movie. The film was a western, and as Dan watched good guys and bad guys stomp and bluster about town, he began to feel curiously cheerful about the evening to come. He was going, he told himself, in the spirit of scientific inquiry. He would know when to excuse himself.

Leaving the kids back at the hotel with permission to stay up another hour, he traipsed back out onto the streets. Snow glittered in the moonlight. Dan breathed in deeply, a giddy feeling, and imagined himself a gunslinger heading to bust up the saloon. He thought of his name perched atop Faith Tackler's list of secret fantasies and laughed out loud. When he and Mary Ellen had first moved to town, the Tacklers had seemed to him the kind of couple who had it all—going skiing and sailing, zipping around in Marc's little sports cars. They were the life of the party; when they moved away, the rest of the group knew that things would never be the same. Now, arriving at the bar with the big mirrors, Dan stood in the street, took a deep breath, and wondered how things had changed.

He found Marc in a corner booth, looking distracted and glum. "I thought maybe you'd done the sane thing and stayed home," he said.

Dan smiled. "As a former zoology student, I maintain an interest in the flora and fauna of all places. Have the plans changed?"

"No," Marc said. "They're still coming."

Dan settled into the booth and tried, in vain, to joke his friend out of whatever was troubling him. "What's wrong, Marcus?" he finally asked.

Tackler sighed deeply. "Daniel, I owe you an apology. I'm sorry about this whole thing."

"What whole thing, old buddy?"

Marc Tackler wouldn't look up. "Tell me something," he said. "You ever wake up in the morning, glance over there at the other side of the bed, and find yourself taking a good, long look? I mean really *looking* at her face, close up? And you see the folds, how loose the lips are, how the whole face sort of drips off itself?"

Dan stared, his hand over his mouth. He could feel his fingers squeezing his own chin. In fact he had never looked at Mary Ellen that way. Or if he had started to, he certainly hadn't allowed it to go on. He knew his wife was beautiful.

"And then," Marc said, "and then she wakes up and you see she's looking at you the same goddamn way. Oh, boy."

Not knowing what to say, Dan said nothing.

"Look, Daniel. I'm not saying it's right, all this business. . . ." He gestured across the bar toward the door through which, presumably, the two women would at any moment appear. "I'm just saying that at this point, it's the only way I can seem to keep things going. I mean, we just got so *tired*, Faith and I. Didn't you?"

Dan shook his head slowly and looked into Marc Tackler's eyes, sunk beneath their heavy lids.

"You never just wanted to say, 'Hey, fuck it all, there's gotta be more than this'?"

"No," Dan said. He had had his chances, he knew—some nurses at the hospital were more than willing to break up a marriage—but he had never bitten. "Nothing like that."

"I mean, you never get the feeling that something—you don't know what—something is just missing?" There was a pleading look on Marc Tackler's face. His hands with their pudgy fingers spread themselves out over the table. "You never get a feeling like that?"

Dan shook his head slowly. "No," he said. "Nothing that doesn't go away."

There was a silence, and then Tackler collected his hands like a deck of cards, clapped them together, and vigorously nodded. "You know we always said you two had the perfect marriage. We'd throw a party, you two couldn't wait to get home. It was all over your faces. Sometimes I'd drink a toast when you left—'The Slatterys are gone, let the real madness begin!'" Marc frowned, one half of the frown twisting up into a smile. "Actually, I was jealous. Faith, too. It was really pretty appalling, how little we wanted those nights to end."

Dan thought about this until Marc tapped him out of it, nodding toward the door. "Here they are," he said. Two young women stood surveying the crowd. Marc stood up, and his hand pushed on Dan's shoulder, keeping Dan down in the booth. "Don't worry, old buddy," Marc said with a tired and humble smile—a look Dan had never seen on his face before—"I'll keep you out of this. Watch me head 'em off at the pass." And Dan did watch as Marc Tackler swiftly crossed the room and greeted the girls with a big smile. Throwing an arm around each and talking a mile a minute, he hustled them out of the bar.

Back at the hotel two Scotches later, Dan found he did not feel as cleansed and relieved by this turn of events as he knew he should. He kept imagining Marc Tackler's toast after his and Mary Ellen's early departure—"Let the madness begin!" It occurred to him that on many, if not all, of those early nights he had wanted to stay but instead had dutifully followed his wife out. It seemed to him now that she had urged him to leave. Or had she? One way to settle this question would be to call Connecticut—the nightly call he hadn't yet made tonight—but by the time Dan arrived back in his room, it was 11:30, 1:30 in the morning back East, and the last thing he could imagine doing was waking his wife to ask her who had led whom out of a party six years earlier. He knew how touchy his wife could be when roused from deep sleep. Years of late calls from the hospital had trained Dan to wake at the first hint of the telephone's jangle, before his wife stirred; he would have it off the hook by the second ring, and, taking a second to tug himself up out of sleep, he would talk in a hushed voice, huddling with the phone at the very edge of the bed while his wife slept on behind him. Some weeks it seemed he couldn't make it through a single night without being awakened, and even now as he stared at the phone in his room, he could feel resentment welling up in him, a sudden resentment at the years of stolen sleep. He glared at the phone, a squat black presence hogging the corner of the room, its big white dial like an eye. And suddenly Dan felt rage stealing his breath, driving him to do nothing other than take up his ski pole and ram it home, straight into the eye.

Only a vision of the kids appearing at the door kept him from doing this. What would he say to them in their pajamas?

Knocked back a step toward sanity, he put down the ski pole he had actually picked up, sat down on his bed, and took three deep breaths. Slowly, item by item, he took off all his clothes, uncharacteristically allowing them to remain scattered on the floor around his bed. He knew he was confused, knew also that the best remedy for it—as he had often told his wife—was sleep, and knew finally that however beautiful the vacation, it would be good to get home again, where things made sense. For a half-moment he began to ask himself, had he really wanted a woman? Was that what this was all about? But reflexively he banished these thoughts, still half-formed, from his mind and sank back under the covers. Flicking on the bedside lamp, he picked up his spy novel, wherein fake people were busy poisoning and garroting each other across several continents, and read himself to sleep.

The last two days at Aspen were smooth and happy ones. They did not see Marc Tackler again; Dan told the kids he'd had business back in Denver. They all skied hard the last afternoon, trying to squeeze every last thrill out of the mountain. But Dan's mind was already back in Connecticut; as a result, he had his only bad fall of the week, roaring wildly out of control over a sharp ridge, into a spectacular somersault. "You okay, Dad?" the kids, poling over toward him, breathlessly called.

"I'm okay. But I'm afraid your old man is just about all skied out."

"You look like the abominable snowman," Lydia said, giggling.

"Yeah, Dad, that was awesome!" Toby said gleefully. He looked back up the hill above them. "I bet Mom's fall wasn't half that bad, huh!"

"Worse. Sixty yards straight down the fall line. On blue ice."

Dan watched as his son tried to take this in, and something

briefly nagged at him when his son's face, like a cash register totaling a long list of purchases, showed a sum of admiration for his mother. Dan pushed this nagging feeling away from him and skied off, down toward the hotel and their packed bags and rented car. Whatever craziness had seized him in the room two nights ago, it had passed, it was over, and it was time now to forget it.

The hustle and bustle of checking out, the kids' loud laments, then the spectacular, jagged beauty of sunset in the Rockies as they drove toward Denver—all of this kept Dan occupied. But something was out there still, some nagging thought like a window left open somewhere in the house, letting in cold air. Dan finally found it just as the jet was lifting them into the blackness above Stapleton Airport. Toby was at the window, face pressed to the glass, Dan in the middle, and Liddie on the aisle, sitting rigid, eyes closed. As the plane rose, its engines and air ducts whooshing tremendously as if they were being inhaled into the heavens, Dan looked across the aisle. A woman about his age or a little younger was gripping the armrests on both sides. Knuckles and tendons bulged under the pale skin of the back of her hand, and as Dan stared at the hand, he heard within himself a voice calling out, maliciously, for air pockets, for wind shears, for wild roller coaster turbulence. Shocked and ashamed, he covered his face with his hand. But the voice wouldn't stop—and now, queasily, he recognized it, a recognition so ugly and wrong, he knew he would never tell anyone about it and would do his best to forget it. For he'd heard that voice up on the Nose Dive at Stowe: the voice that wished him not to stretch out and pluck his wife off the slope but rather to push her along a little, the secret voice that chuckled as his wife went sliding down on her back, arms and legs waving in the air helplessly like a bug's; the bewildering voice that, even as his real husband's voice yelled "Get your feet downhill!," chanted perversely within him: "Faster! Faster! Faster!"

V

Boy Bringing Wreaths

When people ask Dan Slattery what he does for a living, and he tells them, and their eyes light up with amazement, he wishes he could make them know the truth—that it's a job, brain surgery, much like any other job. "It's really just glorified plumbing," he'll say. "I could teach you to do it."

No one believes him.

There was a time when he wouldn't have wanted them to, when he saw their disbelief as a return on his investment of years of training and sacrifice. Still, out of modesty or politeness, he kept saying it— "You could do this"—until one day he realized that he believed it. His days were ordinary: the patients whose physical problems he could describe but whose lives he knew next to nothing about; the dictaphone he spoke into each afternoon, effortlessly summing up his cases; the x-rays, which like any picture told you some things but never as much as you'd like to know; the scalpels and drills and cotton pads that seemed to him as self-explanatory as spoons and napkins. Anyone could do it.

He's not sure how or why things changed. But when he overhears his wife telling the kids how their father once cried and cried all night after losing a patient, he feels as if this happened in some other person's life, a third person he was invisibly watching. The person he is now could not have done that. Confronting a difficult surgical procedure, like the carotid endarterectomy he has to do next week, he thinks exclusively of the technical challenges; he calculates probabilities and speaks calmly and clinically of them to the patient. *We want to go in and open up the artery, clean it out, and close it up. The procedure has approximately a three percent morbidity. If we don't do it, there's a twenty to twenty-five percent chance of an incapacitating or fatal stroke within the next five years. . . .* Watching his patients make the awful calculations he asks them to make, he is unmoved. He has no doubts. He has seen it so many times before, he knows when there is no choice but the one that invokes his knife, and he knows the patient will arrive at it. Fear of doing nothing will smother fear of doing something.

Only one thing gets to him. Sometimes a patient will say to him, as the carotid case did today, "Hey Doc, I'm not worried about myself, but I got four kids, ya know?" and then his heart flip-flops, and he thinks about his own children.

"I know," he says, meaning it. "I hear you."

"Can you press it now?" The kid added more weights to the bar.

"How much?" said Toby.

"This here's twenty pounds, them on the end's ten, the bar's ten again. You figure it."

Ninety pounds. Toby looked past the street to the school, where Bernie the janitor was dumping trash. He watched the old man unhook the garbage sack from its frame and chuck it upside down into a green bin.

"Can ya press it? Huh?" The kid was hassling him again.

"No sweat." Toby bent over. Taking deep breaths, he squatted over the bar, keeping his back straight. He knew about backs and lifting from his father. Toby groaned. The ninety pounds was over his head.

"Damn close," the kid said. "You couldn't press no more. Now lemme try." The kid bent over the bar. His arms were covered with scars and bites, and there was a little white curlicue on his crew cut where no hair would grow. Toby watched him bring the barbell to chest height and stagger around under it. "Give it up, Roy," said Toby. "You'll kill yourself."

"No . . . fucking . . . way," he said, but the weights crashed down. He stayed bent over them, breathing hard. Toby thought of the kids who hyperventilated at school. Ten deep breaths and hold the last one, arms around the chest, squeeze, squeeze, SQUEEZE.

"You all right?" He looked down the hill to the river, where old men in squashed hats sold paper bags full of sandworms.

"Guess I aint but ten pounds weaker than you, huh Toby? Damn."

"Guess so." In the house behind them, someone turned on a TV, blasting it up loud. The building was dirty pink, with white trim gone filthy around the door and locks stacked like a totem pole. In the movies, doors like this were always getting kicked in by the cops. Toby knew that if his parents saw the place, they would change their minds about him sleeping over there, and fast.

"But that aint nothin, ninety. I seen my brother Ronald press one-forty." Ronald Carswell was the kid's half-brother. He and Toby had been in Little League together. Roy didn't look much like Ronald, but there was one thing, Toby thought, that both brothers had— terrible breath, like rotten carrots.

Slattery leaves the office at 6:15, a half-hour later than he likes. He waits for, and then in the rearview mirror watches, the plume of blue smoke twirling up from the exhaust pipe of his Corvette. Rubbing his neck with his hand, he looks among his casettes for Beethoven's *Eroica*. The afternoon, he notices for the first time, is beautiful. To Slattery, it is a problematic beauty, for each summer brings plagues of motorcycles which gnaw the town like locusts, leaving surgeons to cope with their devastations. Already, though it's only early June, they've begun their cruel work: just this morning Slattery spent four hours working with the plastic surgeons on a motorcyclist scraped off the road down near the Point. The kid had left half his face and all his intelligence on the fender of a Good Humor truck. Slattery hears himself telling his children about it. They'll ask about his day, and he'll loosen his tie and swirl the Scotch in his glass. Sometimes he mumbles, and they think he's tired. He is tired.

Then there was the Mead kid in the office again, with new backaches and headaches. Slattery had spent the afternoon glumly reading EEGs, and just as he was closing the file for the day, Donna buzzed: "Roy Mead to see you, Doctor."

"Does he have an appointment?" Slattery joked, then went out to usher the kid into his office. A ragged child with a pinched, weaselly face, Roy Mead jumped up on the examining table and, glancing furtively around, began unbuttoning his shirt. "Doc," he said, "them pills you gave me. They didn't stop the pain."

"Well, Roy, sometimes these things take time." Slattery tried a gentle firmness. "Have you fallen down recently? Strained your back?"

"I been doin some liftin. But this pain aint in my muscles. It's like it's right inside in my spine, ya know?"

Slattery nodded. Because the boy wanted it, he pushed and probed at the scrawny back and listened with a stethoscope to the strong heartbeat. He shuddered in sympathy for the doctors whose offices crowded Roy Mead's future and made a mental note to talk with Sharpe, the staff psychologist. Maybe Sharpe could spare an hour or two for the kid.

"Roy, go ahead and put your shirt on. I'm going to give you something for this pain." From his desk he produced a mild analgesic.

"Thanks a lot, Doc," Roy said, misbuttoning his shirt so that when he reached the top, he had a button and no hole. "And you tell Toby I got new weights, and he should come over and do some liftin. . . ."

Now Slattery powers the Corvette past beaches littered with last winter's seaweed, kids tossing Frisbees, the exclamations of a few umbrellas skewered into sand. He'll have to talk to Mary Ellen about Roy Mead. Last week when Toby asked to sleep over at the kid's house, she shrugged him off. But Slattery knows they can't keep having it both ways. Who was it, he wants to ask her, who answered the doorbell and invited this kid into their lives in the first place? All he wants is a little consistency.

The sun blares over the ocean to his left. He cranks up the music, hoping that the symphony rebounding within the small car will like a bellows blow from his mind all thoughts of the Mead kid, of the office, of the motorcycle disaster, of the carotid endarterectomy looming next week. He hits the volume again, and the symphony, a deaf composer's tribute to an emperor in exile, crescendoes. "Ah, Beethoven," he shouts. "Where would we be without you, old man?"

After two miles of pleasant beaches he turns the car inland, though it is the longer way home, instinctively circumnavigating Berryman's Point, where the biker crashed and burned. For a surgeon never wants to see, and scrupulously avoids, the places where his business is made.

Mary Ellen has never for one minute forgotten the first angelic image of the boy bringing wreaths. And on the whole, despite the failing grades, awkward picnics, devilish tricks with the dog, on the whole it hasn't gone too badly. She doesn't understand some people's pessimism.

"He's weird. He looks at me funny. And Lucille said his brother chopped off some guy's ear." Sharon, in second grade, sees him every day. She and Toby set the table as Dan and Mary Ellen sit with a drink. Lydia is in the TV room, strumming her guitar.

"No way," says Toby. "And besides, it's his half-brother."

He rang at the front door last December, the buzzer that always sends their Dalmatian, Waldo, raving and farting madly through the front hall. When she opened the door, he stepped back, scared of the dog. The wreaths were hung on his arms like donuts, shedding a sprinkle of needles on the packed snow at his feet. He wore sneakers with his scout uniform, and no jacket. Oh, you must be freezing to death, she said, and he answered, Just a little, ma'am.

"What's that brother's name again?" Her husband stares into his pipe as he stuffs it with Borkum Riff.

"Ronald. Ronald Carswell. Listen, Roy asked me to sleep over—"

"That Ronald isn't the nicest boy, is he, Toby?" Mary Ellen says.

"Whaddya mean?"

"Rides a motorcycle for starts," Dan says.

"It's a *mini*bike, Dad. And he never takes it out on the road."

"It's got two wheels, right?"

"Dad," Toby says. "Whadda you know anyway? You never even rode one."

"No, but I know lots of folks who have. I spend whole afternoons scooping their brains out of their nostrils—"

"Daniel!" She hates it when he talks this way. Some things kids just don't need to know about. That was Roy's problem. He had seen too much too soon. That first day when she asked the boy in for cocoa, she saw it all: the inner child calling out, *Save me, save me!* She could have wept. He needed to sell five wreaths for his scout badge, and she bought all of them.

"He was in again today," her husband is saying now. "He's got headaches, he's got back pain."

Sharon says, "He plays hooky."

"Only sometimes," says Toby. "What are you anyway, some kind of judge?"

"And he beats kids up. . . ."

On impulse she had invited him back to go Christmas caroling with them the next weekend. He came wearing only earmuffs on his crew-cut head. Soldiering along in Toby's old boots, he pulled out a fifty-cent tin harmonica, and before she could call out, "It's too cold!" he had it in his mouth and his lip was stuck to it. Later that night she watched him trying not to grimace as he drank hot cocoa. The next day she went to see the school social worker.

She puts a hand on her daughter's head. "Now, honey," she says, "let's not gang up and be mean. And I'm sure if Roy has backaches—" she glances at her husband—"it's for a reason."

"Amen to that," Dan says.

"So Mom," Toby says to her, "can I sleep over there tomorrow, or what?"

She feels suddenly ganged up on. "As I said, Tobe, why don't we hold off on that and have Roy over here for a picnic, so we can share him."

"What is he, a pie? I *never* get to sleep over there."

She looks at Daniel just sitting there. Legs crossed, smoking his pipe. She feels he's watching them, to see who will win. "Look, Toby, I just don't know how much I like that half-brother being around."

There is a frustrated silence, then Dan gestures with his pipe. "Tell me one thing, Champ. Is this Ronald Carswell really bad news?"

"He kicks little kittens," Sharon says.

"Gimme a break, Judge," Toby says. He turns to them. "Really, Ronald's an okay guy. It's just that people always get on his case. We were practically friends. But he always had this dirty uniform that kinda grossed me out."

"Thanks, Champ." The table finished, the kids dash off to join their sister in the TV room.

When they are alone, she speaks first. "He's sixteen years old, this half-brother. He drives—"

"Honey. Let's talk about Roy."

"Roy's fine; we'll have him here Saturday. It's this Ronald—"

"Honey, face it. You don't want Toby sleeping over at Roy's."

"That's not true!"

"It's Roy you're really afraid of."

"You have no idea what I'm really afraid of!" She sighs. "I'm not afraid of anything."

"Look. Let's be rational. Roy's a tough kid. He's dirty, he swears, he skips school, he has bad teeth, he's ungrammatical. He's a hypochondriac—"

"Dammit, Dan, you weren't there when he came with the wreaths. There he was, in the thick of winter, wearing old sneakers."

"All right, fine. It was beautiful. But let's be clear on this: either we take this kid on, or we don't. Okay?"

She looks at him, sitting there with his scrubbed teeth and his pipe going *fft fft fft* at her. He wants to be logical, he always says—drive everything to its logical conclusion. He sees things coldly, a murderous rationality, really. She wants to sting him. "It's people like you," she can't help saying, "who gave us the atom bomb."

"Now there's a helpful observation."

They are silent. The kitchen fills with smoke from her cigarette and his pipe. She watches him move to the Dutch doors, swing them open to look in at the three kids. Lydia is playing her guitar. "*Golden slumbers fill your eyes,*" she sings. "*Sleep pretty darling, do not cry, and I will sing a lullaby.*"

"Oh, that one again," he says to Lydia. "The hippies smoking grass in their marijuana den. Golden slumbers, all right. Psychedelic dope. Freaking out."

Their daughter groans. "He's sitting with his girlfriend and singing her to *sleep*. They *love* each other, that's all."

"They love each other's grass."

74

"Oh, Dad, you can't say anything. You're not qualified. You're half a century old."

"Thanks a bunch." When Dan turns back to Mary Ellen, he is wearing a smile, and she feels herself smiling back. Actually, she thinks, it isn't true: at present he is only four-tenths of a century old, and she is a little bit more.

If they only knew, he told himself again.

He spent the afternoon playing with gunpowder. Roy Mead had a Hellman's jar full of the slate-gray dust. The kid sat on a rotted tree stump in the Meads' backyard, lighting small snakes of gunpowder, looking over toward school and cursing his teachers. "That fatass Hauer, I hate his guts. Sits up there chewing them chopped liver sandwiches at lunch, you gotta listen to his fat mouth go clack clack clack. You can hear the fuckin celery."

"Yeah." Toby remembered those sandwiches.

"He don't let me come home lunchtime. Makes me sit there. Someday I'm gonna sprinkle some a this on his sandwich." He sifted through the dust in the jar. "Hey Toby, you aint gonna tell your mom about this, are ya?"

"Think I'm nuts?"

"Your mom," Roy said, "she's pretty cool. I mean she aint like most moms." Toby thought about his mother, about how she still came to tuck him in at night. *Sleep tight*, she always said, pulling the covers up around his neck. *Sweet dreams*. "Yeah," he said to the kid. "She's okay."

Roy's yard dumped into a gorge where the railroad tracks passed. There were rusting bikes stripped of wheels, a broken rake, empty tuna cans. Fifteen feet up the embankment, hanging over the track bed, they made a small, thorny wall of branches. From it they laid down a thin line of gunpowder reaching to the tracks. Roy put a nickel on the rail. "Hauer," he said.

In their bunker they waited for the train from New Haven.

"Most moms," Roy said, "I wouldn't care what they knew I done."

They felt the train in the soles of their sneakers. Toby knew its approach well, the way the train popped out of the gorge to a sparkly view of river and ocean on your right, and on your left the park with its hot dog stands, the worn-out softball fields, the restored colonial mill and its grinning water wheel. A white cross painted on an abandoned foundation. Jesus Lives! It jumped out at you—

"Light it! Now!" The kid screamed in his ear. Toby lit it. The powder fizzed and sparked; the train was gone.

At the track, Roy picked up the nickel, flattened like gum. "Crash diet," he said, elbowing Toby. On the face of the coin, Toby could still see a faint outline of Washington's face.

"Now what?" he said to the kid.

They went to the pier and fished off it. They ripped off two candy bars at a pharmacy. They played Vietnam. "You be the gook," Roy said. "Over here, Charlie! Hey! *Duh-duh-duh-duh-duh.* I just strafed you to death." At 6:30 they went in to eat. Pots and dishes were everywhere in the kitchen. The frying pan on the stove had yellow fat sprinkled with bits of old meals. Toby held his breath.

Roy's mom was watching the news. She wore jeans and a shirt that billowed way out, like she was pregnant. She sat with her feet up underneath her, and her hand picked at stuffing bulging out of the arm of the couch. Toby could see the strap of a bra along her shoulder and turned away from it. The news was about the war. A lot of Americans were getting killed.

"We're hungry," Roy said.

Mrs. Mead shook her head at the screen.

"*Duh-duh-duh-duh-duh-pkoo!*" Roy strafed the room. His mother turned and yelled at him.

"Would you please *stop* that?"

"Then get us something to eat."

Silence. Then Mrs. Mead looked at Toby, smiling suddenly at

him with pointy teeth, and pulled a strand of hair back over her ear. She was young for a mother. "Hot dogs in the fridge," she said. "Boil em."

With their hot dogs they walked up toward the laundromat at the top of the street. From here Toby could see the hospital and his father's office. A dark red Corvette passed; Toby ducked inside the laundry.

"Don't worry," the kid said. "It aint your pop. But I bet he cruises in that sucker, don't he?"

"Yeah," said Toby. Actually, his father didn't drive very fast at all in his shiny new car. The only fast driver Toby knew was Mr. Haft, their weird old neighbor who drove an old smashed-up Oldsmobile but burned rubber every time he pulled out of his driveway.

The laundromat was deserted. There was a smell like the town pool, where little kids pissed. The light in the long room was harsh, and at the end was a Coke machine. Toby wandered toward it as if toward an old friend.

"Don't put no money in," the kid said. He knelt in front of the machine, ear cocked like a safecracker. "You want Coke?" He reached far up into the slot and came down with a Coke. "You want Sprite?" He pulled one down. "We got Sprite."

"How're you doing that?" Toby sat down next to him.

"This old machine, I'm like his doc. Like your pop." He shook a Coke can and sprayed it on the wall. "You know, your old man— he's all right."

Toby nodded. Roy took more sodas. Soon they were surrounded.

"Yeah, your old man's all right. He don't come down too hard on you guys."

"Are you kidding?" Toby said. "He's always on my case."

"And what about your sister's case?"

"Whaddya mean?"

"The other day I seen your sister with this freak. Some faggot with a pony tail."

"Oh yeah. Jeremy."

"That guy blows dope like there's no end. I seen him down the Bridge with them other freaks. Your pop lets her do that shit?"

Toby looked at a huge ball of dust on the floor between two washers. "What can he do?" he said. "She's fifteen."

The kid shrugged. He was doing bow and arrow motions at the soda cans. "He could tell them freaks to crawl back under their rock."

Toby thought for a second. "Where's your father, Roy?"

"California. He sells cars. Got himself a big fuckin house on a lake. Bigger even than your house."

Toby's mother had told him something very different. He didn't say anything about it.

"Yeah. Sells them little sports cars from France." Roy Mead sprayed another soda on the wall. "You still going to boarding school next year?"

"No. They don't want me to."

The kid nodded, still doing the bow and arrow thing. "I had me this slingshot once. Rubber tubing for the sling. You could hit the fucking water from here. Kill squirrels at fifty feet, no sweat. Then Ronald, he swiped it."

A woman came in with a huge basket of laundry. She started their way but, seeing them, turned and went to the far end of the aisle. "The thing about freaks," Roy went on, "is they got no respect. Who knows what they're doing to your sister. But maybe they don't have no freaks at boarding school."

"Maybe."

"Shit, I'd go. You gotta be crazy to stay here." For the first time Roy looked up from his imaginary slingshot and saw the woman. He laughed through his nose. The woman threw all her laundry in two washers, then walked quickly out, taking her basket and detergent with her. Through the window Toby watched her get in her car, close the door, and sit there. After a minute she locked the door.

"Yeah, I'd bust my butt outta here if I was you," the kid was saying. He started firing the slingshot again, harder and faster. "The problem with this town, it's too full a freaks. Freaks, drunks, and bums."

In the kitchen Slattery watches as Toby shows him and Mary Ellen the hyperventilating stunt everyone's doing at school. "You hold the tenth breath really hard," Toby is saying. "Then someone squeezes you from behind. Like this." He hugs himself.

"It looks like the Heimlich maneuver," says Mary Ellen.

"But it's just for fun."

"It has no therapeutic indication," Slattery says. He thinks about the emergency tracheotomy he did one night, years ago, in a steak house. The man had swallowed a piece of sirloin the wrong way and was soundlessly asphyxiating. People pounded on his back and loosened his tie, uselessly. A woman screamed when he, Slattery, took hold of the steak knife and held it up to the light. It was sharp enough; he entered the trachea below the obstruction, and breath resumed through the hole, gratefully, spraying blood. Ten years later, Heimlich showed that a simple bear hug from behind would send the piece of meat flying out. Deep inside, Slattery has never really believed this.

"It's like dreaming," Toby says. "Watch, I can even do myself a little." He breathes with exaggerated heaviness, spreading his feet to anchor himself.

"Toby. Please don't." Mary Ellen watches as her son sucks in harder, smiling, lifting his chin with each inhalation like a sinking man. She turns away. Toby reaches ten and holds it, hugs himself.

"Here Tobe," Slattery says. "Show ya something." He crosses and puts his hand lightly to his son's neck, thumb on one side, index finger on the other. In his fingertips Slattery can feel the strong pulse of two carotid arteries, the vascular drumbeat of his son's life. He presses on them expertly.

"Daniel—!" Mary Ellen shouts.

He lets go. Released, his son drops easily to the floor and lies there in an oxygen-thin ecstasy, mouth eerily grinning.

"Dan! What do you think you are doing?"

He's not sure what he's doing, or why. "I'm sorry," he says flatly. He thinks of the neck he'll rummage through next week, the arteries he'll try to scrape clear. He knows no work more delicate or more dangerous. When he did the arteriogram, the guy screamed as the needles went in. He feels like Dracula, the way necks are offered up to him.

"I'm sorry," he says again, shaking.

"Well, you should be," his wife says. She is helping Toby to his feet. "Oh *wow*, Dad!" his son says, smiling. "Amazing! Just like Mr. Spock."

"What do you mean?" Slattery says. Waves of helplessness and remorse wash over him as Toby, rubbing his face back to life, elaborates:

"The Vulcan Death Grip, Dad."

They spread their sleeping bags over foam mats on the screened-in porch. Roy's radio picked up stations from Indiana and Illinois. Car horns blasted by on Yantic Avenue. But it wasn't enough to cover the noises from the next room.

Roy had said nothing when the car pulled up. Footsteps, a low voice in the hall, a door closing. Roy turned the transistor up. Above his head Toby began to hear a rhythmic *taptaptap* in the wall.

"How far's it to Indiana?" Roy said.

Toby closed his eyes to picture a map. "Must be a thousand miles. More."

"You gotta cross Canada to get there?"

"No. Hey Roy, what's that noise?"

"Shit. I thought maybe you hadda cross Canada." The kid talked about cousins he had in Canada, cousins who said he could visit whenever he wanted and with whomever he wanted. He went on and on, but finally there was a pause, and Toby heard a man's cottony voice groaning, *Ohh baby, ohh yes . . .*

"Ohh, oh my God, oh God," yelled Roy's mother through the wall.

Jesus, Toby thought. She's getting laid.

The bed rattled and was quiet.

"Roy. Hey, Roy." The kid was rolled over on his side. "You asleep?"

"I get these headaches. Like I kinda black out. It's a bitch."

"Yeah." A mosquito whined at Toby's ear. He slapped at it, and the noise stopped completely, as if he had killed the last mosquito on earth. Toby thought of reaching out and patting the kid on the shoulder. But he closed his eyes and pictured the ratty squint, the sarcastic mouth, the fake sideburns that the barber made. He lay there holding his breath. He felt sorry for the kid, but he knew that within hours he would be telling the story to his friends, to Nate Holover and Chip Butler and maybe even Midget Weinberg; he would tell it complete with all the noises and sounds he had heard, and maybe a few extra ones.

Roy sat up. "Let's cruise, huh Toby? I can't stand this fuckin hole. Bugs're killing me."

"Sure," Toby said.

No lights were on in the houses they passed. The clock at the laundromat said twenty after two. Across the railroad tracks was the hospital, lit up like Manhattan. Roy Mead was keeping his mouth shut for once. It made Toby want to talk.

"I went to see my dad operate last week," he said. "This guy had a ruptured disk. They had to hack a big hole in his back."

"Yeah." Roy nodded. "Me, I get these *fuck*ing headaches." His voice exploded on the words, then was quiet again. "It's like my brain's falling off or something. That's why I go see your pop." They stood in the light of the laundromat sign, which showed a woman shoving laundry in a machine and smiling. "My mother, she keeps giving me orange juice. Like that'll do shit." Roy took a shot with his invisible slingshot, hard. He picked up a rock.

"Vitamin C," Toby said.

The kid turned in a circle. He put his hand on his forehead and stomped the ground once with his foot. "It gets so bad, I just aint able to think. I aint able to fuckin *think!*" And he heaved the rock up.

The Plexiglas came down in sheets, big black letters falling on Toby's head and shoulders. The housewife's nose was as big as his hand.

"Jesus fucking Christ, Roy!"

The kid turned around, squinting. "You cut?" he said. Toby wasn't. Inside the laundry the wall of dryers stared them down. They ran.

They didn't get far. A car pulled up in front of them as they crossed the basketball courts behind school—a car with a flashing red light on top. Roy hid behind the trash bins, and for a horrible sliding moment, Toby was alone in the shock of headlights. He blinked. Doors winged open, a police radio spat static, and a voice yelled, "All right, Ronald, get your ass out here."

Roy came out kicking a can. "I aint Ronald," he said.

Oh fuck, oh shit, Toby screamed silently to himself as two policemen walked toward them. One took out a notebook and a stub of pencil. The other cop had a moustache, and a cigarette between his fingers.

Toby never knew cops smoked. It scared him. Asked who he was, he showed his library card. He tried not to look at Roy Mead. The cop with the pencil took notes. "You're in trouble, you know that, Toby?" he said.

The kid broke in, "We didn't do nothin. You can't prove nothin."

The cop spoke to Toby. "What're you doing out here in the middle of the night?"

"It's a free country, aint it?" Roy Mead said.

"I'm just sleeping over, sir."

"Go ask his pop. His pop's office aint but two blocks—"

"Shut up, Carswell. Now, Toby. Why would someone run if they didn't do anything?" He jerked his head toward the laundromat sign. It looked awful.

"I . . . I . . ." Toby tried not to cry. "I didn't break it."

More static from the radio. The two cops huddled together for a second, then the first cop put his pad in his pocket. "We gotta go check something out. Let's say we meet you gentlemen back here in half an hour." He put his hand on Toby's shoulder, hard. "Now don't let anyone talk you into taking off. We know who you are," he said, tapping his breast pocket.

When they were gone, Toby sat down on the ground. He wondered how many laws they'd broken. It made him feel sick to his stomach. Not even the thought of boasting about this to Nate Holover could make the terrible sickening feeling go away. "Jesus, Roy," he said. "We're dead meat."

"They can't prove nothin. But anyway, that school up Cheshire aint so bad. Ronald, he rebuilt two engines up there."

"Jesus, Roy, you think I can go to reform school? I can't believe this."

"Hey. You come outta Cheshire, sometimes they get you a job."

"Roy. They're going to arrest us, asshole."

The kid looked up the street. "Not if we blow this place, they aint."

"Where're we gonna go? They got our names, addresses, everything."

"Canada."

"Great, wonderful." Toby couldn't believe it. The kid was pointing over his shoulder, as if Canada was just down the block. "I mean, really constructive, really brilliant, Einstein. Christ. You couldn't think your way out of a wet paper bag." Toby didn't care what he said now. He could just see his father groping for the ringing phone.

We have your son down here, Doc. Toby leaned back and looked up at the school, jamming itself into a sky made creamy-coffee by the lights of the city. He tried to calculate the hours he had spent in that building, learning to read and write and multiply. And now it all came down to this.

He would have to tell them everything. It was the only way. Then he'd have to fight the kid. That's what it had been pointing to all along.

"They say there's big mountains up there in Canada. And they got bears."

Toby nodded.

"We'll hop a train. They got mountains and bears, they gotta have trains. That's what I'm thinking."

Officer, he recited silently. *He broke it. Him. And his mom's at home getting laid.*

Cigarette embers blew from the cruiser window. There was a second car and a new cop. He looked hard at Toby, and the first thing he said was, "Hey. Aren't you Doc Slattery's kid? Doc Slattery who lives up the corner of Frog Hollow and Bay?"

Toby nodded.

The new cop smiled. The note-taker closed his notebook and put away his pencil. The cop with the moustache scuffed out his cigarette under a black shoe.

As the cars pulled away, shadows moved like huge cats on the playground. Toby followed the kid out of the schoolyard. He looked at his watch; it said 3:00.

Roy kicked a can, splitting the silence on School Street.

"Your pop, he's all right," he said. "He knows people, don't he?"

Toby said nothing.

Outside the dingy house was a dingy Cadillac. It was pink and smudged, like the house, but in the light it looked purple. A train thundered by, screeching out of the gorge sharply lighted, a few heads outlined like puppets in the little boxes. Then it was gone.

They stood staring at the car and the house.

"One a these days," the kid said, "we're gonna take care a that sucker. Me and Ronald. Just pull the brake and let her fly. Right into the fuckin river."

In the operating theater he holds up scrubbed hands to receive the gloves: thousands of times he has done this, and still it seems to him an awkward, helpless posture. He turns to the table, where a profusion of canopy and shroud separates him from his patient.

The incision is routine. He's got Barry Baylor assisting, with three neuro OR nurses, the Green Berets of the RNs. They're going for the left carotid artery; the right, less severely occluded, can wait. Cutting and clamping, swabbing and cauterizing, they ferret their way in.

"So you've been working on that backhand of yours," Barry says to him.

"Didn't know you were so concerned."

"Let me warn you, old partner. Any advance on your part will be met with an appropriate response." They laugh the surgeon's laugh, all mouth and no body. Barry has just come through a messy divorce, and he's high on survival, pouring his energy into tennis and boat building and Martha, his new—his new what? Slattery can't come up with the word. "Clamp, please," he says.

It is slow going. Reaching the targeted artery, they'll have to clamp it on both sides of the incision spot. If a clamp should slip with the artery laid open, a riot of bleeding will follow.

"How're the kids?" Barry says.

"Chugging right along. Lydia's all taken up with the guitar-campout-folksinging scene. She's hanging around with some pretty far-out looking creatures, but so far they seem harmless. Hey—you

85

by any chance remember a guy named Howes, Al Howes? Disk I did about five years ago?"

"Can't say I do."

"Neither did I. He's a patrolman in town. Seems Toby was out fooling around with some kids the other night, and one of them threw a rock through the sign at that laundromat over on Yantic."

"*Through* the sign? Beautiful."

"Right. Well, next morning I get a call, and it's this guy Howes. He was one of the cops on the scene. Recognized Toby from Little League. He's got kids on one of the teams, I guess. Anyway, the guy was so pleased with the disk job, he felt he owed me one. He let me square things with the laundromat guy." He laughs. "Toby's gonna be cutting grass and washing windows till he graduates from college."

"So your son is in with some big-time criminals," Barry says.

"Small time, small time," Slattery says. "Suction, please."

Slattery can joke about it now, but the fact was that Mary Ellen hadn't taken it well at all. Waking to answer a call after midnight, he found her smoking in the john like a schoolgirl, nervously, and she confided to him a vision of Roy she'd dreamed. She saw him larger but still crew-cut and smudged and not smelling quite right in their kitchen, short of cash, head averted, talking tonelessly of impractical schemes. How could you tell what boys would grow into? What could you really do? So many things were determined long, long before you could do anything about them.

"Here we go." Slattery's own voice calls him back. Thick as a man's little finger, the artery sits denuded of tissue, fat, and muscle. Violence and a measure of art have prepared it thus. There is no small talk in the room now as Slattery hunches to cut. He observes a slight, permissible tremor in his own hand; this never flattens out, no matter how often one does the job.

He makes a small slit. Suction. There—they've nailed it: a marble of hardened cholesterol clings to the arterial wall, dangling there as if held by a mysterious, static charge, like a balloon at a birthday party. "You little bastard," murmurs Barry. It is their enemy, this residue of easy American life. Tenderly, they scrape.

As thoughts return, Slattery finds himself unbuoyed by the success of the operation. It is routine. He has saved so many people, he doesn't even remember them. They come up to him on the street, smiling mistily, shaking his hand, and he hasn't the faintest idea who they are. He hopes their hands are clean.

Ten thousand hours in sterilized vaults have made him fussy about dirt and disorder in the outside world. He files his nails daily, appalled, even as he scrapes and flecks the cuticle, at his own primness. His wife's failures with a road map or a balanced checkbook loom before him not as annoying details, but as assaults on principle. But what principle?

I'm sure a career in surgery will suture liking, a high school lab partner punned in their yearbook. Well, he has done it. What he always wanted to do.

"Close her up for me, will you, Barry?"

"Sure thing." Slattery reads mild surprise in his partner's eyes. He normally does his own closures—in fact, he is considered something of a fanatic about it. But today he is tired. This morning Mary Ellen woke up and said, cheerful once again, "Maybe we shouldn't try to push so hard with this Roy thing after all."

By the OR door there's a mirror. Slattery stares at himself. Blood, spritzing through the arterial sutures, has touched his shoulders, mask, and bonnet with scarlet. Sadly, his eyes return to him knowledge of the campaign of attrition Mary Ellen will run to rid them of the boy. The unanswered phone call. The forgotten birthday card. The lengthening gaps between invitations.

It won't take much. And he will concur in it. The only lives he knows how to save are the lives of complete strangers.

He feels limp, a Raggedy Andy man. A bloodstained specter,

masked and hooded, glares back at him from the other side of the mirror.

"Hey, old partner." He turns, laughing and waving two gory claws, Bela Lugosi-like, to Baylor, still hunched over their success. "Now do I go out and talk to the wife?"

VI

The Yardman

The Slatterys always had mixed luck with yardmen. A lot happened on their acre and a half of earth, and finding the right man to cope with it was never easy. The grass was patchy under the huge maples out front. Fallen mulberries dissolved into rot, dandelions puffed and popped, garbage floated off the street and throttled the pachysandra, a drunken woman drove her Pontiac through the hedge right into the magnolia tree. When Dan and Mary Ellen first moved in, they had done the yard themselves. It was more picnic than work: they'd bring out trowels, clippers, a transistor radio, a bottle of wine. But the yard grew more and more ragged, until finally they caved in and hired someone.

No one seemed to last. There was an old Spaniard who spoke no English, then a young paroled felon named David, who came to them through a church outreach program and wandered off after two months. There were a couple of college kids named Sam and Ricky who did atrocious work. Jakus Swoboda was next, a weathered, gentle man whom Mary Ellen met when he stopped to help her change a flat tire. He tended their yard lovingly for two summers before dying suddenly of a heart attack. Then there was Bob Treat, and trouble began.

Treat made Mary Ellen nervous right from the first day, when he pulled up in his old Ford Fairlane with its ludicrous, menacing fins. He shut the door with great care, as if he intended to keep the car forever. He had a swirl of tattoos half-hidden by his T-shirt sleeve. That first day Dan and Mary Ellen gave Treat the tour of the yard, then drank iced tea with him out on the patio. The man's eyes were light blue and watery, his black hair sharply parted and Brylcreemed, and a shade long. One of his front teeth was chipped or unevenly spaced, and he tongued it noticeably, his mouth slightly open as he gazed out over the yard, nodding once or twice as Dan explained the place.

"I think he's an alcoholic," Mary Ellen said to Dan that night.

"Whatever gives you that idea?" he said.

"I'm not quite sure." She pictured the yardman's thin, pale face. "Maybe the way he guzzled that glass of iced tea."

Dan laughed. "He was thirsty. It was eighty degrees out there."

"I know, I know it's ridiculous. I just like to be able to trust someone who's always going to be around." As she spoke, she saw Dan smiling with a smile he reserved for certain favorite issues. "You're thinking about Stella, aren't you," she said.

Stella was their cleaning lady, an older black woman who came on Thursdays. Because she was old and slow, Dan felt she did nothing, and every few months he would hint that they should let her go. But Stella did everything that Mary Ellen needed her to do, and besides, Mary Ellen enjoyed their lunches together. Dan and their fourteen-year-old son, Toby, liked to tease her about Stella; they would pick up filthy rags and hobble around the living room, swiping randomly at the furniture and calling out to each other, "Is it lunch time yet,

Miz Slattery?" It drove her crazy. She got tired of justifying Stella to Daniel. "At least I can trust Stella," she said to him now. "That guy today, he gave me a strange feeling."

Dan smiled at her. "He may not be the most charming person. But let's face it—charm doesn't cut lawns."

"I know, but—"

He cut her off with a wave of his hand. "I'm a neurosurgeon. I may be the Marquis de Sade in my private life, but if I can take out a ruptured disk and make someone feel better, I'm an angel to them. I trust Treat as a yardman. The rest is frosting on the cake."

So they hired him. And the yard prospered. It was Treat who revived the magnolia tree struck by the woman in the Pontiac. He made sod grow in the dead areas of the yard and removed the blighted hedge with his blue car, tying ropes to the root clumps and driving away into the street. In the wound he planted azaleas.

"Treat's a wizard," Dan said in the middle of the first summer.

But something about him continued to bother Mary Ellen. He was too polite. His habit of appearing out of nowhere at the back door, with a simple request, unnerved her. He might ask for a can of oil and stand there smiling, humming softly and tonguing that tooth. He was sneaky, his sea-blue car appearing in the drive soundlessly, as if he cut the engine in the street and coasted up to the house. During his cigarette breaks he liked to just stand there in the yard, leaning on a spade and looking up at the house with his wide, watery eyes.

He was insolent as well—a fact her husband seemed blind to. One Saturday morning she went outside to find Treat in the garage, huddled with Toby under the hood of her station wagon. "Toby," she said sharply. "What do you think you're doing?"

Her son gave her a half-bold, half-fearful look. "Mr. Treat said we could," he said.

She rushed in and alerted Dan, who followed her out, sighing.

"What're you up to there, Bob?" he said to the yardman when they got there.

Treat hauled himself out of the engine and wiped his hands on a rag. "Just showing the kid here what a cylinder is," he said.

"But that's *my* car!" Mary Ellen said.

"Didn't figure he'd be working too much on mine." Treat tongued his tooth and smiled. "And when's the last time you changed them plugs? They're pretty shot." He stared at Mary Ellen. "She firing all right for you, Mrs.?"

Back in the kitchen, she asked Dan how he could let the yardman get away with it.

"With what? With teaching Toby about engines? With fixing your car?"

She snorted. "Fixing it! He's probably booby-trapping it."

Dan stared at her. "What is it about this guy that bugs you so much? He's a good man."

But that's where Dan was wrong, she was sure of it. She thought about the people who had worked for her parents when she was a child. There was Ilsa, the Hungarian cook who smelled like sausages and dust, and Lillian, the limping housekeeper. Out in the yard was Crow, an old man who had lost a finger in an accident and who used to play baseball with her brother, Bennett. Thirty years later, it was hard for her to know how good these people had been as gardeners and cooks, but she was sure they had been hired less for outstanding skills than for an air, intuited by her mother, of trustworthiness and warmth. Her father, she recalled, had done much of the actual gardening, working side by side with the jovial Crow. Though a serious, even somber businessman, Mary Ellen's father had loved flowers. She could remember his excitement when he came home for the first time with color film for their home movie camera; he and Crow had headed out into the yard and shot a whole reel of zinnias, roses, and nasturtiums.

The only yardman she had found like Crow was Jakus, the

92

chapped and weary old man. Jakus would stare long and hard at what he was about to trim, as if each bush represented a precious life in his charge. "Jakus—now there was a good yardman," she said to her husband one evening as they sat on the screened-in porch and watched Treat loitering in the yard.

"Jakus was a terrible yardman," he answered. "A nice old guy but a terrible yardman. Now *Treat*, on the other hand, is a good yardman."

But Treat was up to something. Mary Ellen felt watched. The yardman always seemed to be working the part of the yard closest to where she was in the house; she could hear him rooting in the bushes, humming tuneless songs. No sooner would she undress to take a shower than the bell would ring, and when she came down, wrapped in a robe, there he would be at the back door, licking his lips and asking politely for water.

"Give me evidence," Dan said to her as Treat's first summer drew toward a close. "Give me something that would stand up in court."

The only thing really troubling Dan that summer was his sixteen-year-old daughter, Lydia. The trouble was Lydia's new boyfriend, a seventeen-year-old boy named Jeremy who drove a van, listened to rock music, and wore his lank hair halfway down his back. When the boy had started coming around, Dan and Mary Ellen had teased Lydia about him. "The only people who had hair like that when we were your age," Dan told her, "were mental defectives." Lydia bristled; were they trying to say Jeremy was a crazy person?

"No," Dan said, smiling. "Just that he looks like one."

They tried to be reasonable. They said nothing about the long and secretive phone calls, about the strange clothes their daughter began to wear, the tie-dyed shirts with no bra, the necklaces made of leather. They said nothing when they saw the two of them passionately soul-kissing on the porch. But there were some things they couldn't ignore. Their main source of information about Jeremy was their son, Toby, and it was through him they learned that the boy had been kicked out of boarding school the year before, presumably for smoking marijuana. Worse, their son told them, Jeremy often hung out at the Bridge, a notorious embankment by the river where kids often got into trouble.

"This kid is bad news," said Dan, "and it really eats me up to see Lydia wasting her time on him."

When confronted, Lydia shrugged. "I've never been to the Bridge personally," she said. "But I bet some of the people down there are good people."

Dan ignored her. "And is that what Jeremy was kicked out of prep school for, smoking pot?"

Lydia shot a vile look at Toby, lingering by the fridge. She gathered her long hair, pulled it back off her neck, and fanned herself with it. "Sometimes it's like you guys convict people without even hearing their side."

"So," said Dan, crossing his arms. "What's his side?"

Lydia began to talk, but then looked up at her father and stopped. Her eyes filled with tears. "Oh, you wouldn't understand," she wailed, getting up from the table and flinging herself out of the room.

"I guess we wouldn't," Dan called after her. "We probably wouldn't understand someone burning his draft card, either. . . ."

What bothered Mary Ellen more than the boy himself was the distance he was causing between her and her daughter. It was clear to her that Lydia believed there existed a world of passions and allegiances that she, Mary Ellen, knew nothing about. She wished she could convince the girl that she, too, had been young and in love and desperate, that she had been chased by boys and had wanted to give her soul up to them. But when she tried to explain it, she could see her daughter's eyes glazing over with a look that said, *I love you, Mom, but what you're saying has nothing to do with me.* Still, Mary

Ellen spoke out. "Don't let a boy feel too sure of himself," she told her daughter. "Make yourself rare on occasion."

"But why should I play games?" her daughter said. "What if I just want to be with him?"

"Of course you do. But it can't hurt to hold back a little. Make him do the work."

Her daughter laughed. "Mom. This isn't a contract negotiation. It's a re*la*tionship."

Mary Ellen tried to look at Jeremy fairly. The hair was a big problem for her, and she tried to imagine him without it, sometimes raising her thumb when he wasn't looking to blot out the hair and assess his real looks. One time he came in wearing a fedora with his hair up under it, and she was shocked by how good-looking he was—a square jaw and a fine, laughing mouth. He reminded her a bit of Pete Joachim, her old college beau.

Gradually, through conversations with her daughter and Jeremy around the kitchen table, she realized that she liked the boy. He was happy and sincere, and had a big heart. Every June he spent three weeks working at a camp for retarded children. His convictions were real, and when he talked about older friends who had burned their draft cards, she sympathized, thinking of Toby, who in four years would be old enough to go to Vietnam. "This is a ridiculous war, Mrs. Slattery," Jeremy said to her. "I think it's patriotic *not* to participate in it."

Eventually, Mary Ellen let her daughter know how she felt. "I can see what you see in him," she said. "Though I still hate that hair."

Lydia smiled. "Can you maybe convince Dad he's a nice person and smart and all that?"

She couldn't do that, but what she could do was protect some of Lydia's secrets—not rushing to Daniel, for instance, when she found the butt of a sweet-smelling, home-rolled cigarette in the pocket of Lydia's jeans. She felt guilty not telling him about it, but in his eyes she could see him just waiting for a reason to banish the boy, and she didn't want to be the one to supply it.

Dan continued to seethe at the presence of Jeremy. "That kid's up to no good," he said one evening, as the two of them watched Lydia, with daisies tied into her long hair, walk bouncily down the back drive to the boy waiting at the street.

"What makes you think so?" Mary Ellen said.

"Just look at him sometime. You can see he's a congenital liar."

"Hmmmm," said Mary Ellen, raising her eyebrows. "Think that would stand up in court?"

He didn't seem to get the joke; he just sat there, stroking the hair on his arm and frowning.

Every August they had a big garden party, and this year, the tenth anniversary of their moving to town, Mary Ellen wanted to do something truly spectacular. She envisioned an outdoor buffet and dance floor under a big tent. Treat, who worked an extra day to help set things up, seemed to take pleasure in sneering at her plans. It was frustrating. When Dan was around, Treat was meek; alone with her, he grew bumptious and suggestive. When she asked him to take special care with the hedges and bushes, he rubbed his chin and asked, Did she have anything particular in mind, or would just cutting them be okay?

"That will be fine," she said tightly.

They disagreed about all the logistics of the party, particularly about the dance floor; Treat insisted it was too close to the garden. People would step in the flowers, he said. All afternoon he kept coming back to the topic, until she finally stood up to him, putting her hands on her hips and saying right into his face, "It looks nice that way, and it's going to stay that way!"

He shrugged. "Okay. You want people tangoing in them pansies, it's up to you." They weren't pansies, but marigolds, and he knew it.

When she came back two hours later from picking Sharon up from her Brownie meeting, Treat was nowhere in sight. She went into the house. Passing through the living room, she glanced outside and saw, with horror, that something had gotten into her garden, trampling a whole swath of marigolds.

She found Treat in the front yard, standing with electric clippers over the andromeda. She was sure he had seen her coming out of the corner of his eye and had turned the clippers on so that she had to yell and then tap him on the shoulder, whereupon he put his finger to his ear and insolently smiled. She yanked the cord out of the socket on the side of the house, and his clippers ground to a stop.

"What happened?" she said.

He feigned innocence. "Where?"

"In the garden—what happened in the garden?"

"Oh, that." His blue eyes quivered ever so slightly. "Well, I was doing them hedges just like you said, when all of a sudden a big dog comes hauling through the yard—"

"A dog?"

"Yeah, a big brown dog. He comes running through the yard—"

"You did this, didn't you?" Her voice was a whisper.

"Now, whoaaa, hold on a minute, Mrs." He shook his head and showed her a fresh pink scratch on his forearm. "See this? That's where I tried to tackle that big dog. I was trying to *save* them pansies, not hurt 'em."

"*Marigolds!*" She stomped her foot on the grass. "They are marigolds!"

Treat smiled. "Look, Mrs., I aint no flower man. I'm just a yardman."

That night she complained to Dan. The yardman, she told him, was fighting a war of nerves with her.

"Sounds frightening," he said.

"I'm serious," she said. "Did you see those marigolds?"

"I did," he said, "and I must say I find it hard to envision Bob

97

Treat tap dancing through the flower bed. Maybe there really was a big brown dog."

The next day was Treat's regular day. She tried to stay away from him, but around noon he showed up at the back door with his inevitable request, this time for a plastic garbage bag. When she gave him one, he thanked her and then, before she could close the door, cleared his throat and added, "By the way. I guess the doc believed me, huh? About them pansies."

She felt suddenly calm. "He didn't believe me at first, Mr. Treat. But when I told him that the big brown dog outsmarted you, then he believed me."

Smiling, she shut the door in his face.

All afternoon she felt elated. Having handled Treat, she found that she could forget about him. She couldn't hear him coming through the walls. He couldn't get to her.

She floated on this feeling until slightly after three, when she heard her younger daughter scream in the yard. Running out, she saw Sharon standing rock still on the front lawn, staring down at her bare feet.

"Honey?" Mary Ellen called.

Sharon turned toward her a look of outrage and sadness. After a second of bewilderment, Mary Ellen realized something was missing from the picture. Her daughter was standing over a ragged hole in the ground where their mulberry tree was supposed to be.

The tree, along with various dogwoods and magnolias, had been planted by the previous owner of the property. Of all these decorative plantings, it was the mulberry tree that the kids had loved the most, eating its berries, smearing their faces with them, making jam. Now Mary Ellen bent over to hug her sobbing daughter; she saw a trail of leaves and flattened grass where the tree had been dragged away. *Treat*, she thought.

She found him coming around the side yard, whistling and brushing his hands off. Holding Sharon close to her side, she walked right up to him.

"Who in God's name told you to take down that mulberry tree?"

The yardman read the hysteria in her voice. For once he could not meet her gaze. "Look, Mrs., that tree was ready to go. That tree was dead."

"Let me see it." She spoke with mathematical precision. He stepped aside. The tree was in a small trailer hitched to the yardman's Ford. Flossy roots dangled over the side, and the branches still had green leaves. Sharon began to cry.

"Leave," Mary Ellen said to Treat.

"Look, Mrs.—"

"Leave right now, please. Leave and don't come back."

"It's dead, I'm telling you."

"Leave or I'll call the police."

When he saw she meant business, he stopped talking. He pursed his lips, shrugged, then without another word lowered himself with exaggerated care into his hideous blue car. When the throb of his engine had melted entirely away, Mary Ellen went to the garage, fetched a broom, and swept from the driveway the dirt and twigs the yardman had left in his wake.

The evening of the party was warm, the air polished by an afternoon thundershower. At sunset Mary Ellen stood on the patio and watched friends socializing in small groups in the yard. The pastel cottons glowed in the soft, rich light. Toby and Sharon moved around the yard, carrying trays of Mary Ellen's stuffed mushrooms and tiny sausages. "Where's that Lydia?" someone asked. "Getting too old for us?"

Lydia was up in her room, sulking because Dan and Mary Ellen had refused to let her go for an overnight trip on Jeremy's boat. For two weeks she had hinted at the boat party without ever asking directly; when she finally raised the question and they said no, she acted as if they had gone back on their word.

"I thought you trusted me," she had said.

"It's the situation we don't trust," Mary Ellen said. "Maybe there aren't enough life jackets on the boat. Maybe there'll be a storm."

Lydia laughed. "We're not going to New Zealand. We're just going out in the Sound and anchoring there."

Dan put his head in his hands. "A cruise to nowhere with you and three pot-smoking seventeen-year-old males. All night long. Remarkable."

"Dad. He can't make a special trip in just to drop me off at midnight."

"If you're special enough to him," Mary Ellen reasoned, "he'll make a special trip. Don't you think?"

No, she didn't think so. She went up to her room and stayed there all afternoon; while they prepared for the party, they could hear her quietly playing her guitar and singing sad songs.

"Sometimes I feel I'm losing her," Mary Ellen said to Dan.

"In the long run," he said, "she'll thank us." He kissed her forehead. "Let me be the heavy if you want to."

The party helped Mary Ellen forget about the Treat fiasco and about her concern for her daughter. She drank Scotch and danced with Dan; leaving the dance floor, she cut back into the living room and was surprised and pleased to see Lydia, standing by the piano, talking to Holt and Sherry Humphries. Lydia looked shockingly sexy in her short cut-off jeans and loose, wildly colored T-shirt; Mary Ellen smiled as she watched the husbands of her friends noticing Lydia's long and slender legs. They would pass by, heading for the patio, drinks in both hands, their first look triggering a second look, which, when they saw whom the legs belonged to, was either furtive or amused.

You will have a lot of men after you, she wanted to tell Lydia. *Take your time.* Instead, she simply touched her daughter's arm as she passed by, and continued on, through the room into the hall beyond, and then out the front door into the night.

The yard was breezy and dark. Wind heaved the maples to and

fro far above her. She remembered the midnight walks she used to wake Lydia for as a young child; the two of them would go out on the lawn and listen to the voices of trees. All her life she had treasured the feeling of being heralded and protected by trees swaying overhead. She almost invariably had little in common with people whose allegiance was to wide-open places; these made her feel tiny and lost. *Please, God*, she had prayed at night as a little girl, *don't ever let me be alone.*

She walked slowly across the front lawn, her shoes in her hand. The light curling around the edge of the house and the muffled hilarity of the party comforted her. Closing her eyes, she floated into the sound and landed in her imagination as a ten-year-old, playing with her brother, Bennett, in the upstairs hallway in their house in Philadelphia as her parents threw a party downstairs. Bennett was the Shadow, she his lovely friend and companion Margo Lane, both of them crouching in their pajamas at the top of the staircase. The grownups played the piano and sang songs late into the night. Her brother's pajamas were paisley, and he was very proud of them. Lillian, the housekeeper, who limped, came to check on them in their rooms, and they stuffed pillows under the blankets and hid under the bed, watching her feet hobble by.

It was still so real. Her mother had been dead for thirteen years, her father for twenty, and yet there they were before her, at the piano, singing, her mother turning the pages as her father played with his brown vest unbuttoned and his sleeves rolled to the elbow, singing German songs passed down from his grandparents: "*Ich habe mein Herz in Heidelberg verloren*" and "*In München steht ein Hofbräuhaus, eins, zwei, suffah!*" It was as real to her as anything she had lived since. And yet they were gone, both of them. Mary Ellen's sharpest memories of her father were of his dying. She had been living at home then, two years out of college, and working for a magazine in Philadelphia. Her father had one heart attack and then another and another, each one worse than the one before. They knew he was going. Coming home from work, she would see his car in the driveway, think of him resting in his bed, and feel a huge and terrifying chasm opening inside her.

It drove him crazy, the way they all walked on tiptoe around him. He wanted to face the facts, calmly and rationally. One afternoon he called Mary Ellen into his study. "I have a few things I want to get on paper for your mother," he said. "You're elected to type."

"Sure," she had said.

He motioned her to a chair and began reading to her from notes. "First," he read, "recognize that death is the normal method of final departure." She looked up, and he waved her on, frowning. "Billions have gone before me, and billions will come after. Therefore, your attitude should be rational and not emotionally hysterical."

She had typed as he went on to detail his burial, right down to the casket, which apparently he had already chosen. Mary Ellen looked up at him and saw how ill he was, his good suit hanging on him like a costume. She began to cry.

"Control yourself, Moo-Rye," he said. "I'm not dead yet."

But within three months he was. And now, twenty years later, the thought of his ceasing to exist could still fill her with a desperate loneliness, which her husband, whose parents still lived, could not understand. He thought it sentimental for a forty-plus-year-old woman to feel as she felt about her parents. Still, she cherished every little thing of theirs that she had managed to save, and hoped that wherever they were, they could see her now and take pleasure in the fullness of her life.

She opened her eyes and looked at the cars parked along the street. It was funny to think of each couple getting into their own car and heading, from several towns, to her and Dan's house. She went down the line, looking at the station wagons, the little sports cars, a couple of boring sedans—

Her eye stopped on one car, familiar and yet out of place, whose outline filled her with alarm. She saw its hammerhead top and rear fins, and sank back into herself like a stone.

He was here.

Turning, she walked around the house, as quickly as she could without running. The tent loomed golden in the backyard, and the people milling under it looked tiny. Her eye scanned the crowd wildly until she found Dan, standing at the side of the dance floor near the garden.

He was talking with Treat. The yardman was gesturing wildly; Dan shook his head, then nodded. Treat had something in his hand which he kept waving, and she could hear his voice over the music now, vehement and ugly. She hurried over.

"What is he doing here?" she said to Dan.

"Remember what I told you, Doc," Treat said, and Mary Ellen saw out of the corner of her eye that he was swaying back and forth.

"He's raving drunk," she said.

Dan snorted. "You're telling me."

"Doc . . ." Treat held up the object, a flat piece of wood like the cross-sections of trees that are varnished and made into tables or ash trays, only smaller.

Dan sighed and winced. "Mr. Treat would like us to believe that this is from the mulberry tree—"

"Right smack from the center," Treat said.

"And that the wood is bad."

Treat held the slice out to her like a piece of pizza. "The wood is *shit*," he said proudly. People on the dance floor were beginning to shy away from them; a moat of empty space had formed around the yardman. "Look," she said to Dan. "Can we at least get off the dance floor?"

They walked out toward the lawn in single file, Treat tiptoeing along the strip of grass between the dance floor and the garden like a man on a tightrope. "Get him out of here," Mary Ellen whispered to Dan ahead of her.

Out on the lawn the yardman resumed his drunken show, poking with a finger at the heart of the wood, which began to crumble and fall out in pieces. "Look at that," he said. In spite of herself, Mary

Ellen looked into the pattern of swirls and concentricities. Then she pushed it away.

"Listen, Bob," Dan said. "This really isn't the time or the place—"

"That tree was alive," Mary Ellen said. "It had leaves."

The yardman's voice was slurred but strong. "You get any berries from that tree this year?"

"Some," she said.

"But none too many, right?"

She said nothing.

"And less than last year, right?"

She looked at Dan. *Do something*, she thought. But he was just standing there. So she turned to Treat. "You're drunk," she said.

"Hallelujah," he said.

Finally Dan moved. "Bob," he said, "we can talk about this when you're in better shape." He put his arm on Treat's shoulder and levered him around in the direction of the street. "But I really don't see any way of going on with this arrangement."

Suddenly weary, Treat allowed himself to be led off. As he went, Mary Ellen couldn't resist a last shot. "He shouldn't even be around children," she called.

It was a mistake. The yardman's slumping shoulders jerked up, and he turned on her. He looked at the chunk of wood, now hollowed like a doughnut, and for an awful second Mary Ellen felt sure he was going to hit her with it; instead, he turned and lofted it high into the air. They listened to it crashing through branches in the Kreuzmanns' yard.

The sound seemed to revive Treat. "Hey," he said, waving his arm wildly. "You wanna see somethin fascinating, Doc? Come on, I'll show ya." He tongued his tooth with pleasure and started off, passing the hole where the mulberry tree had been, and tramped into the pachysandra on the side of the house.

"Hey," Mary Ellen said. "Watch it."

But Treat paid no attention. He was bending down in the darkness. "Come on in here, Doc. I want you to see a real mystery here."

"Look, Bob," Dan said, "I'm hardly going to walk right through the garden. Just tell me what it is."

"Better than that," Treat said cheerfully, "I'll bring it to you. I'm sure even the Mrs. here won't mind me tearing up this particular tree here." He came back through the pachysandra and held out to Dan a small green plant.

"What is it?" Dan said.

Treat chuckled. "I'll give you a clue. You smoke it, and it aint tobacco."

They were silent. "Where did this come from?" Dan said in a tight voice.

"You know," said Treat in a conspiratorial whisper. "This makes little girls' minds go blooey." He made a wet, exploding sound in his mouth and craned his neck to look up toward the light in Lydia's room.

"You—" Mary Ellen took a step toward Treat. "You are—I won't say what you are!" She turned and walked into the house.

Inside she splashed her face with cold water in the bathroom, then walked to the far part of the house, away from the party. In the TV room she turned out the lights and went to the window. Overhead she heard again the faint sound of Lydia's guitar, while outside she could see her husband and Treat standing together on the sidewalk. The yardman looked shabby and small in the gray light from the streetlight. Dan appeared to hand something over to Treat, who shrugged and then folded himself into his car. She watched her husband wait until the yardman had driven off, then walk across the front yard. The gray in his hair shone bright in a shaft of moonlight as he walked back to the edge of the pachysandra. He was angry; she could read it in the way he stopped to collect himself, jutting his chin up and stretching his neck, touching the knot of his necktie. She wondered what he and Treat had said to each other.

When she met him at the door, he was holding the marijuana plant in his right hand, his left hand cupped under it to catch the dirt. He held it awkwardly and gently, like a wounded bird.

"Is she upstairs?" he said.

"I think so."

"You know," he said, moving to the stairs, "I had a feeling this was going on behind my back. I'll tell you one thing: this is curtains for our friend Jeremy."

She started to say something but was cut off by the appearance of friends spilling into the hallway from the living room. "Hey, kids," said Jack Cousins. "Where have you been?" Behind him were his wife, Claire; Sam and Melissa Miller; and Charles Ludtke, wearing a paper hat and raising his glass. "The Prince of Wales requests the honor of your presence!" he said.

"We'll be right in," Dan said, smiling, and the gang piled back into the living room. No one seemed to notice that Dan held a marijuana plant in his hand. Mary Ellen wondered if any of their friends had ever smoked it. "You go on in," Dan said. "I'll handle this."

She nodded. Crossing to the living room, she passed herself in the mirror and was shocked by how drawn and fragile she looked. She hoped she could slip into the room unnoticed, and swung through the doorway close to the wall. But as soon as someone saw her, there were loud cheers. A bottle of champagne popped open in Charles Ludtke's hands. She saw colorful banners on the wall, and Toby and Sharon sitting on the sofa wearing party hats and stuffing themselves with cake.

"Happy Tenth Housewarming!" someone called.

In her mind Mary Ellen saw Lydia sitting in her room, facing Daniel. It was so hard to be a girl. Whenever her own father had scolded her, she had wept for hours.

"I think I'm going to cry," she said, putting her hand to her face.

They never saw Bob Treat again. The morning after the party they scoured the bushes around the circumference of the house, looking for more marijuana plants. Dan was in a foul mood. He talked about the careful research he would do before hiring a new man. "I'll get ten references if I have to," he said. "No more of this haphazard business. No more personality conflicts."

Jeremy Trumpy they did see again—many times, as it turned out, over the course of many years. Though Lydia was forbidden to see him that summer and fall, in winter they relaxed a bit, and by spring, when Jeremy had been accepted at Cornell, the Slatterys reconciled themselves to his existence. Jeremy never did burn his draft card, but instead went on to distinguish himself at Cornell and then to enroll in Harvard Medical School. His long hair gave way to scissors below and, prematurely, to baldness above, so that as a balding twenty-four-year-old medical student, he was practically unrecognizable as the hippie the Slatterys had once feared and distrusted. Dan forgot his old feelings and was even sorry when Lydia, deeming Jeremy "too conservative," declined his offers of marriage in favor of a succession of shady and unkempt musicians who treated her badly.

Several afternoons after the party, Dan and Mary Ellen sat on the screened-in porch, drinking Scotch. They could feel the oppressive absence of Lydia, who had gone into exile in her room and who would stay there for most of two weeks before calling a truce out of sheer boredom. Mary Ellen felt sorry for her daughter, but at the moment what she wanted to talk with her husband about was Bob Treat. She wanted to know just what had transpired between the two men out on the sidewalk.

"What did you do out there?" she asked after raising the subject.

Dan shrugged. "I fired him. Formally."

"Did you give him something?"

"No," he said. "Well. I gave him ten bucks."

"Why did you have to give him anything at all?"

He stirred his drink with his little finger, then licked it off. She wished he wouldn't do that. "Well," he said. "I guess we really didn't give him a heckuva lot of notice."

"You mean *I* didn't," she said.

He said nothing, and after a moment she could see he thought the subject was done with. She felt cheated. "You think he was right, don't you? About the mulberry tree, I mean."

"What?" He laughed. "Of course not."

"Then why did you give him ten dollars and not tell me about it?"

"I don't know—it wasn't important." He rolled his eyes and sighed. "I mean, what's ten bucks when you consider what we dish out on a party like this?"

She had something to say to that, but before she could compose it in the right way, she was interrupted by three trucks, which wheeled around the corner of Frog Hollow and Bay and pulled up noisily onto the sidewalk. The trucks were shiny and red, the lead truck emblazoned with a golden hawk. A driver got out and glared inscrutably into the yard. He was big and sunburned, with an orange crew cut; his head and neck were of a uniform width and color, making him look like a stump that had been shoved in a fire and was still glowing. Now he lifted a finger and beckoned to men in the other trucks.

"These must be the new guys," Dan said, putting down his drink.

"What new guys?"

"The Wilcox Brothers," he said. "Barry Baylor swears by them."

He went outside. Mary Ellen watched as Dan and the sunburned, stumpy man talked to each other, switching to hand signals as first one lawnmower, and then another, rocketed into life. The man made a circling motion with his hand, then saluted Dan back toward the house, as the Wilcox Brothers, all five of them, began to fan out over the property.

"Yup, that's them!" Dan shouted at her as he came through the door. "No more fooling around for us. These people mean business!"

For five minutes they tried staying on the porch, but it was impossible. The Wilcox Brothers worked relentlessly. Mown grass and fallen branches were zapped, chewed, and swallowed out of existence. Noise swelled and subsided and swelled again, the engines reinforcing each other and reverberating above the yard like helicopters in a jungle war. Each time Dan or Mary Ellen tried to say something, one of the blond, crew-cut Wilcox Brothers would hump by on a mower, spewing cut grass.

Inside, the two of them found different things to do in different parts of the house. Up in their bedroom, Mary Ellen changed the sheets on their king-sized bed, glancing out the window as the Wilcox Brothers did the side hedge between the Slatterys' yard and the Kreuzmanns' next door. The teeth of their electric clippers mashed back and forth, bits of leaf spraying into the air. Mary Ellen remembered the years they had done the yard themselves, Dan's push mower whispering in the deep grass. That time seemed impossibly distant and quaint.

After twenty-five minutes, the Wilcox Brothers packed up their trucks and left. In the silence that followed, Mary Ellen felt numb and violated; she thought of small things the kids might have left in the yard—a baseball mitt, a doll—and wondered if any of it could have survived. Finishing the bed, she turned down the blanket and carefully fluffed up the pillows.

The subject of Treat did not come up again that summer. In the fall his name began to surface as a kind of running joke: whenever anything went wrong, they would blame it on the yardman. When a trowel was missing, it was Treat who had taken it; when Lydia's guitar string broke, Treat's invisible finger had plucked it; when a car failed to start, its engine had been "Treated." Gradually the joke faded; they moved on to other culprits, and Treat was forgotten.

It is easy to forget partially, and hard to forget wholly. Years later Treat would be revived, at a time when Dan and Mary Ellen would dredge up item after item from the bottom of their marriage, spotted relics they would claim as weapons in a battle against each other. Neither would recognize the other's Bob Treat; each would forget some crucial way in which the yardman had touched him or her. Dan would forget how sympathetic he had been to the yardman that night on the sidewalk, how he had commiserated with him, had given him not ten or even twenty dollars, but fifty. And Mary Ellen would forget just how much she had not only disliked the yardman but actually *feared* him, enough to ask Dan after the party to change the locks on the doors. Arguing about the significance of Treat, they would stumble upon this small discrepancy—had they actually changed the locks or not?—and, as if grateful for some simple disagreement, would launch into discussion, only to discover themselves spinning dizzily into an uncharted universe in which not only interpretations but facts themselves could be called into question, where one could fail to agree about anything, from the year of a trip, to the weather of a remembered afternoon, to the color of a yardman's eyes.

VII

Canoeing

On the first day of camp, the boy called Kevin helped Sharon Slattery unload her stuff. Sharon had taken an early Greyhound up into Vermont, getting off at a gas station where a green van with a white pine tree painted on the side was waiting for her. The van driver, a ghoulish bald man with a mole on his forehead, drove her over cracked roads to the lake where the camp was set. They pulled in. Busy checking the images of a tennis court and a muddy beach against her memory of the camp's glossy brochure, Sharon barely noticed the boy approaching the van and reaching in back for her duffel bags.

"I know where you're going," he said.

By the time Sharon registered these words, the boy was headed off with her stuff. "What did he say?" she asked.

"That's just Kevin," the driver said, as if that answered her question.

"Oh." Sharon looked out at two girls trying to play volleyball on a field of spiky grass. "Well, what am I supposed to do now?"

The driver gave her a flat look with squinty eyes and a trembling eyebag. "Start having fun," he said, getting out and opening the door for her.

But Sharon was in no mood for fun. She was depressed, a fact that itself added to her depression as she drifted through the trivial business of registration, health forms, mailbox and cabin assignments. She was the first arrival in her cabin; she peered in, took in the imitation log walls and the smell of cobwebs and rock, and quickly decided she hated it. Her stuff was stacked by a bottom bunk; she flung herself down, tore her tape recorder out of her knapsack, put on Lynyrd Skynyrd and lay back with her eyes closed.

All afternoon people wandered in and out. Sharon decided not to budge until her friend Gina Loveday showed up. She put on her mirror sunglasses, chewed gum, and went through her tapes one by one, nodding and tapping to the music. Girls coming in looked at her and moved the other way. Behind her glasses Sharon rated them on an interest scale of 1 to 10, then on a looks scale. Nobody got higher than 6. She wrestled with boredom. *Camp sucks*, she thought.

She hadn't wanted to go to camp in the first place. She had planned a summer at the beach, hanging out and working on her tan. When Gina, her old best friend from fifth grade, wrote from Houston about the camp in Vermont, Sharon half hoped her parents would veto the idea.

They didn't. "Think you can handle six weeks away from all your admirers?" was what her father said.

"I'll miss you," her mother said.

That was December. In January and February she tried the idea out on her two friends, Serena and Alex, using it as leverage to see how much commitment to her she could pry out of them. She wanted to know how much they would miss her if she left for a month. But Serena, it turned out, was already going to the Cape with her family for July. The prospect of a summer with Alex was a bleak one. Alex was good only when taken together with Serena. Left alone, she lost all nerve and tended to gravitate toward the mall, like everyone else.

So Sharon was stuck. "I'm not old enough to work," she complained to her brother, Toby, when he came home from college for a weekend. "I can't hang around with Alex all summer, I hate babysitting, I don't want to go to camp."

"It's a terrible dilemma," her brother said.

The decision came to her, like many of her decisions, in front of the mirror. She was staring at her face and closely assessing its features: the eyes, acceptable in greenness but insufficient in roundness, the tiny nose spotted with freckles, the long auburn hair, which in its waviness reminded her of lasagna noodles. She squinted her left eye to bring it into symmetry with her slightly smaller right eye, and pictured herself riding a horse. She saw herself heading in slow motion toward a colossal sunset, all of her—hair, shoulders, breasts— bouncing freely up and down in slow motion.

The camp, said the brochure, had access to a stable.

Later, changing her mind about horses and Alex and everything else, Sharon tried to get out of it, but it was too late; she was committed. And by this time another factor had come into play, a dark secret that Sharon had stumbled onto: her father was having an affair.

She had first suspected something strange going on between her parents one night at dinner. She was talking about school, and for once, instead of the typical interrogation, nobody was listening to her. Looking down the table, she saw her mother completely off in space somewhere, biting her lip and staring at nothing.

"Ground control to Mom," she said.

At the other end of the table, Dr. Slattery began waving his hand slowly back and forth, as if at a hypnotized person. Mrs. Slattery snapped out of it, got up, barged into the kitchen, and began banging pots in the sink, creating sounds Sharon recognized as the universal signal of mother pissed-offness.

"What's up with Mom?" she said.

Her father just shrugged.

That night she lay awake. She pictured the millisecond of pure hatred her mother had flashed at her father. Her thoughts did pretzels until she ruled out every possibility except the one that wouldn't go away. Her father was having an affair. It explained the way her parents sometimes looked at each other, like people standing in front of the refrigerator with no idea what they wanted to eat. It explained her mother cleaning the house like a maniac, then getting tired and going to bed early at night, and her father taking up photography and hanging out in his darkroom in the basement. It explained the tight smiles and bizarre outbursts and rapid-fire changes of subject.

Lying in bed, where a lot of her best thinking happened, Sharon flashed on the wall of her consciousness a picture of her father in his Jeep driving to a big house on the beach where a blond woman waited on a sundeck. She surrounded the woman with potted palms, tried without much success to give her a face resembling the face of Farrah Fawcett, and watched as her father disappeared with her into the house. They came out on the other side, hand in hand on the beach, both of them now wearing minuscule bathing suits. On her father's face was a look of wild pleasure, as if he had smoked a huge joint and liked it. He and the woman were disappearing into the foamy surf as Sharon dropped off to sleep.

All spring Sharon watched her parents. Both of them treated her with undue kindness and called her more and more by old nicknames. On her fourteenth birthday they gave her an unprecedented load of presents. Waking very late that night, she found her mother standing by the windows in the front hall, smoking a cigarette. "You okay, Mom?" she said.

Her mother's head jerked an inch, then turned slowly to face her. "Couldn't sleep, doodlebug," she said.

Sharon watched the cigarette smoke churn in the moonlight.

There were other signs. Her father was sick all the time—he

kept getting colds—and instead of feeling sorry for him, her mother was pissed off. "Just because you're a doctor doesn't mean you have to stop taking care of yourself," her mother said. And the biggest sign of all, Sharon saw, was that her parents wanted her gone for the summer.

She told no one. Her brother and sister were off in other worlds. Toby had college to brag about; Lydia had her band. When they came home for a few days to visit, they couldn't see what Sharon saw, and she knew that if she told them, they'd say she was crazy. But she knew what she knew. Her father had a secret. In May she went into the basement one Saturday to do laundry and heard her father talking on the phone in his office. She couldn't make out the words, but the hushed, warm sound of her father's voice turned her stomach into stone. She was standing there like a mannequin when he came out smiling, and his smile ran through her like a current: it was the face he wore in her dream.

Her father took a strand of her hair and twizzled it. "What are you doing down here, Judge?" he said. "Wanna pay some of my bills for me?"

"Who were you talking to?" she asked him.

"Oh, Allan Durfee," he said, the smile still on his face. The thought of her father lying to her made her heart pound. Mr. Durfee was the man her father played tennis with every morning before work, at the ridiculous hour of 6:00 A.M. Sharon had never met him.

That night her dream took on new dimensions. She watched her father pull out of the driveway in his Jeep, dressed for tennis. Accelerating, he drove right past the courts, which were deserted, and arrived at the beach house. Up on the deck, the blond woman was waiting for him. Her face was blank, like a white plastic bag. Sharon watched her father and the faceless blond woman disappear into the beach house. She tried to direct the camera to one of the windows to see what went on inside, but the scene was canceled, as usual, by the Great Censor squatting somewhere in her mind.

115

Like most of her friends, Sharon spent a lot of time thinking about sex, but she considered herself hampered by lack of knowledge. She knew what went where, but not what it *meant*. What was she supposed to think, for example, what was she supposed to feel, when boys put their hands on her, their fingers in her? The woman who ran the ninth-grade Human Sexuality class, Ms. Monahan, spoke as blandly about "arousal" and "penetration" as Sharon's mother did about vegetables in the Stop 'n' Shop. Sharon sat in class and imagined Ms. Monahan flat on her back, moaning, face distorted, spreading her legs for a man whose back muscles flexed and unflexed like sponges.

She worried about herself. When she was ten, she and Gina liked to hang around outside the house of a boy named Tommy Schotte, a thirteen-year-old who, through outrageous stupidity, was still in fifth grade. They mocked his dumbness, but something about him intrigued them, made them want to parade back and forth in front of his house. When he came to the door or window, they fled; Sharon remembered the tingling in her stomach and the sweatiness of her palms. It was like the feeling she got when, lying in bed, she put both pillows between her legs, crossed her ankles, and squeezed as tight as she could. She told no one about this, just as she told no one about the way Tommy Schotte made her feel. She was afraid of him, and he disgusted her, yet she wanted to touch him, to stroke his arm, and she dreamed of him putting his hands on her.

Three years later, when a boy actually did put his finger inside her, she felt nothing. In her mind, she saw a picture of her body as the textbooks showed it, a cross-section with one leg and all her internal organs. She imagined a finger extending upward into this. For Sharon, this detracted from the ideal quality she knew the moment was supposed to have.

She wondered also about orgasms. How would she ever have one if she wasn't sure what they were?

The girls in Sharon's class talked a lot about making love. Serena and Alex and Sharon called it "canoeing" because of a poem Serena had written about a canoe ride she had taken with her brother, Richard, which Serena's father—an English professor—said was actually an erotic poem. So Serena and Sharon and Alex joked about who canoed and who didn't. Sharon knew who was supposedly on the pill, who had gotten pregnant and had abortions, but that didn't bring her any closer to understanding the thing itself—a thing, whatever it was, that she identified with Tommy Schotte, with the curve of his upper arm and the strong, almost disgusting smell of his body. Other people knew more about the secret thing than she did. Once she had picked an assignment notebook off the floor in home room. It belonged to Ellen Okker, a lazy and rude girl teachers said was brilliant; Sharon was about to go over and hand it to her when, flipping through the pages, she read, *I want Jerry's dick in my mouth. I want him to come inside me, I don't care what my stupid parents say. I want to suck him until he comes.*

Sometimes when she imagined herself doing it, she would hear herself saying *I love you I love you I love you* over and over again while holding on tight to the thick neck of someone whose face she could never see. But how were you supposed to know what to say? Would the man climbing onto her say, "I want to fuck you," the way they did in a book she had found once in her brother's room? If so, what would she answer? *Yes, go ahead, fuck me?* One Saturday afternoon she came home early from dance class and heard her parents in their room doing it—no words, just sounds, rustling, her father grunting, and then from her mother a single word: "Push." She wondered what her father said to the woman in the beach house. She remembered the sound of his voice on the phone, and how she felt it in her stomach.

When Gina showed up at camp, it was clear that she wasn't dealing with the same questions. It made communication strained. They were both four years older now, but the only changes Sharon could see in Gina were a new, modified redneck accent, and a habit of using words in ways that defied explanation. Gina talked about "not having faith" in a group's music, or going swimming in a "mongo" pool; when she met up with Sharon after lunch or an activity, she said, "So what's your alibi?" Gina made plastic necklaces, and ashtrays in Ceramics, and wrote letters home in envelopes pre-stamped by her mother. She loved the hiking trips, singing children's songs through the woods while the counselors called out the names of different kinds of trees. It was frustrating; the two of them were dealing with different realities altogether. Once Sharon tried to raise the subject of Tommy Schotte, and all Gina could contribute to the discussion was, "Yeah, poor kid." So Sharon told her nothing of the titanic issues that were crashing around inside of her.

During the first week, Sharon noticed that the boy who had unloaded her stuff always seemed to be hanging around. When she went to mail a letter at the office, he was sitting on the porch, tossing a bright pink tennis ball up and down. When she came out of the cafeteria, he was there, tooling around by the garbage cans. Three times she caught him staring at her. Once she thought he winked.

She went to Susy, a girl in her cabin who had been going to the camp her whole life. "Who is this kid, anyway?" she asked.

"His real name's Kevin," Susy said, "but we call him Gumby. His dad owns that gas station up the road."

Sharon knew the place. Tall weeds grew around the side of the building. "Does he *do* something around here?"

Susy laughed. "They let him help out because his dad fixes all their vans and stuff. He's totally perverted. Stay away from him unless you want to get constantly whaled on."

The next time Sharon saw him, on the steps of the mail room, she took a good look. With his hair parted high on one side, and his high cheeks and tiny chin and mouth, he did look like Gumby. He was thin and pointy and greenish-looking. He was fifteen, maybe a lame sixteen; it was hard to tell.

"What're you lookin at?" The voice came out of the little mouth like a snail out of its shell.

"Nothing much," she said to him.

He jerked his head toward the envelope she held. "Got a letter there, or what?"

"No," she said. "I've got a Cadillac disguised as a letter." She skipped with exaggerated lightness down the stairs and out onto the lawn. Behind her she heard laughter—a truly insane laugh, full of gargling—and then the *thump thump* of the pink tennis ball on the wall of the frame house.

"What's that kid's *prob*lem?" she said to Gina, back at the cabin. "Is he a moron, or what?"

Gina smiled. "I think he's sweet," she said.

Sweet? It showed how little Gina understood about anything. Gumby was pathetic. The family who ran the camp, the Darnelles, treated him like a raccoon or stray dog. "Go on, get outta here!" Mr. Darnelle would say, coming out of the office. And Gumby would leap sideways, just like a small animal, then sullenly drift off into the woods behind the office, hunching his shoulders and jamming his hands into his pockets. Sometimes Sharon would see him in the woods, just standing there, lurking in the shadows. One time he waved to her as she walked by on the cinder path. "Psssst!" he called.

"Yeah?" she said.

He came out a little from the woods. "Got some more letters from Mommy there?" he said, smiling.

Sharon was surprised at the whiteness and straightness of his teeth. She looked him over. His jeans didn't fasten quite right at the top; the zipper tracks didn't meet.

"Your fly is down," she said.

He didn't blink. "I keep it that way for girls."

"Give me a break," she said. *What a Gumby*, she said to herself as she walked away. But she could still feel his eyes on her, and the feeling caused a slight tingling in her stomach. When she got to her cabin, she had to resist the urge to turn and look back at the woods.

Gumby was not the kind of boy Sharon had much experience with. At school the Gumby types stayed down in the shop, playing with saws and hammers. Most of them lived in town, and sometimes when they drove out to the beaches, they got into fights with the boys in Sharon's neighborhood. In summer they always wore long pants, even in August, cruising around in jeans and no shirts. Some of them wore their hair up in red bandanas, which made them look like maids. They all smoked cigarettes and a lot of dope, and drank rum out of thin bottles. Sharon didn't admit it to Serena or Alex, but she liked to imagine herself riding with these boys in their fast, trashed cars.

Once she had gone out with one of them. His name was Carl; she had met him when he and his friends crashed a party she was at. They got thrown out—someone's mother freaked and called the cops—but by that time he had already found out Sharon's name and home room. The next week he came by her house on his bike. He called her up a few times, they went to the movies, and afterward he came over. She had made sure her parents would be going out. Inside, Carl looked around the living room and hallway like a tourist. "Hey," he said, "what does your old man do?"

"He's a brain surgeon," she said.

"No shit," said Carl. "I guess he's got some bucks, don't he."

"I wouldn't know," Sharon said. She watched Carl smoke a cigarette and kill it by sticking it under running water in the kitchen sink. "We'd better not stay too long," she said. "I don't know when they're coming back."

A few days after that, in the mall with a group of her friends, she saw him—and quickly looked away. When she saw him by her locker in school, she walked past, pretending not to see him. He never called or came by again. About a month later, her mother asked her out of nowhere, "Who was that boy who was calling you a while back?"

Sharon turned red. "Who, Carl?" she said. "That was probably Carl."

Her mother didn't look up from the sewing machine. "Do we know him?"

"I don't know," Sharon said. "I don't think so."

"He didn't sound like someone I knew," was her mother's answer.

Now, months later, Sharon wondered, what the hell did that mean? "I don't know what makes my mother think she knows everything," she said to Gina.

"Hey, I like your mother," Gina said.

"So do I," she said. "Except when I hate her. Like when she makes me go to church. Or dance." These things were in fact annoying, but what she really hated was the thought of Carl out there somewhere, thinking terrible thoughts about her.

One way to make up for Carl, Sharon told herself, was to be nice to Gumby. So when he waved to Gina and her as they walked in their suits to Swimming, she didn't try to avoid him. He was standing by the road, holding a brown bag. "Going swimming?" he said.

"No," said Sharon. "We're dressed like this for church."

"Har, har," he said. "Hey, look what I got." He shoved the bag at them; it was full of cans of beer. He looked around. "Let's go party," he said.

Gina looked worried. "Won't you get in trouble for that?"

"Hey," said the kid, "I can pass for eighteen, no sweat."

Sharon almost laughed out loud. "So what're you hanging around fourteen-year-olds for, then?" she said.

"You aint fourteen." He looked right at Sharon. His eyes swept down from her face to her bathing suit, down to her legs and slowly back up again. "I know what fourteen looks like, and you aint it. Sorry."

When they came back an hour later, wet, he was still standing there. The beer was gone. He stared at her again, and she stopped. "Do you just hang around?" she said. "You're like a human barnacle. Don't you ever *do* anything?"

"Got somethin in mind?"

A delicious thought came to her. "Yes," she said, smiling. "Tennis."

And so an hour later, not really believing it herself, she was waiting for him by the court. He showed up in jeans—long jeans— and boots that tore up the clay. His racquet was an ancient, warped Dunlap, which he swung wildly, running around every backhand to smash the ball with his forehand. Rallies were impossible. He was quickly out of breath; after half an hour he called to her, "Tired yet?"

"Only from chasing the balls you keep hitting out," she said. She went up to the net to get a ball; he came up on his side, leaned over, grabbed her shoulders, and kissed her. His tongue had rammed its way into her mouth before she could pull back.

He was smiling like an idiot. "Is that your idea of finesse?" she said. "If so, you're crazy."

"I know I am," he said. "You make me that way." He threw his racquet onto the grass and sat down. As she left, she could see the top of the brown paper bag sticking out of tall grass by the fence. "Any time you wanna party," he called after her, "I'm ready. I'll be the one making frog calls outside yer window."

Back at the cabin, Gina wanted the details. "Is he any good?" she said.

"He's horrible," said Sharon. She sat down on her bunk and thought about the taste of beer and cigarettes on Gumby's tongue. "He's the worst."

"I guess you were right about that guy," Gina said. "What a loser. If he ever showed up around our house, my dad would go through the roof."

Sharon nodded slowly, even though Gina, in the upper bunk, couldn't see her. She lay back on the flimsy mattress and tried to resurrect in her nostrils the sharp smell that wafted out from Gumby's armpits. It was like a street in a hot foreign country. As she went to sleep, she lay there listening to the roar of crickets and frogs, trying to pick out individual voices. She imagined showing up at home with Gumby, and she saw her father go through the roof—literally, shooting up out of his chair in the TV room, straight through the ceiling and roof, waving his pipe as he went, flying high above the neighborhood and city right into outer space, like a rocket.

After two weeks, homesickness blew through camp like a tornado. Walking by one of the little girls' cabins at night, Sharon heard a voice wailing, "*Maaaa! Maaaa!*" like a sheep. Standing in the mail line, she caught Gina opening the heart-shaped locket she wore around her neck, to peek at the tiny pictures of her parents she kept inside. Sharon's father wrote to remind her of her mother's birthday and to ask her what she thought about going to Florida over Christmas. She envisioned the three of them in the kitchen, about to leave, all of their suitcases standing by the back door. It was a good image, and she let it sit in her mind for a while before rereading her father's letter word by word for clues to developments in his secret life. There were none.

On the same day she got letters from Alex, who was predictably sitting on her butt at home, and from Serena, who had a foxy new boyfriend up on the Cape. *I'm not canoeing,* Serena wrote, *but I'm doing a lot of sailing.* In her mind Sharon imagined Serena's boyfriend, saw him as blond and thin; the image got more and more Scandinavian-looking until it fused with the image of Bjorn Borg. She tried to transform Gumby into a foxy tennis star and failed totally. When she closed her eyes, all she saw was Gumby, with his sticking-up hair and his too-small mouth. *There's only one specimen of the male species under forty here,* she wrote to Serena, *a moronic sex fiend who constantly wants to jump my bones. . . .* She had to admit, she liked the way it sounded.

Day by day, Gumby's tactics grew more blatant. "You make me

crazy" became "I just wanna show you somethin" and then "I know you want it."

"You're so charming," she would say, mocking him, or, "Is that how people talk to girls up here in Vermont?"

"That's how *I* talk," he'd say, actually pointing to himself with both thumbs.

He loved to boast. He told her stories about truant officers, motorcycles, drowned cats, his POW cousin in Vietnam, fights with tough kids from New York. He was always the hero in some pathetic battle. Sharon felt sorry for the state of Vermont if this was what it was producing. "Had me an International Harvester last summer," he told her. "Borrowed it off my cousin. Got busted four-wheelin it up the ski slopes. Figured out who called me in and took care of their mailbox for em."

"I'll bet they were plenty scared," she said, mocking him.

"You're tellin me," he said.

Sometimes she let her defenses down, like an idiot, and he got to her. One afternoon he appeared out of the woods and asked her if she wanted to see something boys could do that girls couldn't. He looked at her with his little snail smile, then nodded downward, and she made the colossal mistake of looking. Down below the crotch, on the upper part of his right leg, his jeans were moving—pulsing, like a thumb pushing tight against the denim.

She practically choked. "You really *are* disgusting," she said. But she couldn't take her eyes off it. She felt herself floating into lostness.

"You make me this way," he said. He took a step closer. "Wanna touch it?"

She turned and ran.

Lying in bed that night, she kept seeing the image of the jeans. She wondered how he made his thing move like that. She remembered a group of dancers who had performed at her school, everyone laughing and freaking out because through the leotards of the male dancers you could see their things, pointing like little knobs.

She considered the possibility that she was obsessed with sex. She remembered seeing her brother's jock strap in the laundry basket—she must have been about six—and wondering what part of the body it could be worn on. In those days she was busy playing doctor with the Stopazzi brothers next door, but since she was always the patient and never the doctor, she never saw their things. Once in sixth grade she came home in the middle of the afternoon on a Saturday to see Lydia's car home from college; coming through the back door into the kitchen, she could hear loud noise from upstairs, and when she realized what was going on, she tore out of the house and walked around the block, trembling. When she sat across the table from her sister and her sister's boyfriend at dinner that night, she kept staring at them, trying to imagine it. It was as if they had a secret life as murderers.

Halfway through camp she saw someone she could imagine doing it with. He was an actor from a community theater in town. He appeared on the camp road in a purple sports car, top down. He had sunglasses and wavy hair and looked like someone famous. Sharon followed girls running from the boathouse over to the office. "Oh my God," someone said, "it's him." They saw him come out of Darnelle's office and staple a poster up on the bulletin board. Sharon watched tiny golden hairs where his legs disappeared into blue shorts. She looked at the sports car and imagined herself spread out in the back seat. Her palms tingled; she flexed her hands open and closed.

"He's king," a girl said. "He's God."

That night Sharon let Gumby sit next to her in the darkened barn where they sat watching a movie. He put his hand on her leg, and for a millisecond she closed her eyes, fantasizing that she was with the actor.

"I know who you're dreamin about," Gumby said to her afterward. She had gone out to the bathroom just before the film ended, to avoid being seen with him when the lights went on, but he had followed her outside and now stood leering in front of her. "And I got news for ya. He don't even do it with girls."

"What?"

"That's right, he's a faggot. Gay as a freakin blade."

"Tell me about it," she said.

"Once I was up the theater, I seen him going down on his faggot boyfriend. Right there under a bush."

She felt herself filling up with a completely new brand of hate. "You animal!" she yelled at him. "You moronic . . . ape!"

A counselor came over and began to hassle Gumby, telling him he wasn't supposed to be at the camp after 9:00 P.M., and he shuffled off, shaking his wristwatch and putting it up to his ear—a cheap digital like the ones that sold for five bucks on the street in New York. "Are you all right?" the counselor, whose name was Nancy, said to Sharon.

"Yeah," said Sharon, stepping back. "He's just an idiot."

Later on, back in her bunk, she thought about what to do. She saw now that a lot of bad boys had liked her over the years. She assembled them in her mind. They stood in T-shirts, always leaning against something, dark hairs on their upper lips, smoking cigarettes and squinting at her through the smoke. They spoke words like flat stones. They weren't good at anything, and they were proud of it. It made her feel ashamed when she walked in front of them in her Girl Scout uniform, with her book bag full of books. They saw right through her, while she could never be quite sure whether deep inside they liked or hated her. They kept rubbers in their wallets and showed them to her.

Parents couldn't handle bad boys. Sharon remembered Lydia's old boyfriend, Jeremy, who was kicked out of boarding school for smoking dope. He kept his hair in a long ponytail and wore tie-dyed T-shirts. "This house is off-limits to that kid," her father said to Lydia. "If he can't be trusted at boarding school, he can't be trusted with you."

"He doesn't *deserve* you," her mother added.

Gumby himself reminded Sharon of a kid named Roy that her family had taken in, a poor kid who had no father. When he slept over, he would stare at Sharon like some kind of zombie and try to break in on her in the bathroom. Finally he stopped coming over, and one day a few years later she saw him getting shoved into a police car downtown.

"Bad news," her parents would say about a kid like Gumby. "Going nowhere fast."

And it was true. Sharon thought about how Gumby boasted of having been to Montpelier and Burlington. He had no perspective. Back in Connecticut he would have his crowd, but up here it was different, just Gumby and three hundred girls with stickers of European cities on their suitcases.

Because she felt sorry for him, she listened to things she would never stand for at home. "You're a virgin, aint you," he said to her. "You never did it. Your mommy thinks it aint good for her little girl."

"You couldn't begin to imagine what my mother thinks," she said.

Gumby smiled. "Oh yes I can. She thinks she can keep you from being done to like she was done to by your father." He laughed, and punched his fist into his palm, three times. "But it aint possible."

"What are you talking about?"

"I'm talking about she's just jealous, your mother."

"You're crazy!" Sharon felt herself getting lost again.

"I know I am. You make me that way." He put his hands on his hips. "You aint just a little bit curious maybe?"

"Sorry," she said, backing off.

There was no place for a Gumby in the existence her parents had laid out for her, and she knew it. There were camps and ski trips with friends, and parties where you could make out with guys who would later come over for dinner, smiling and using their napkins constantly. Later there was college and romance, some unimaginable career in a strange city, and somewhere out there a person already moving slowly toward her from Chicago or Washington or California, the man whose neck she would in due time hang on to. Nowhere in any of it was there a Gumby.

And so she felt not guilt but only pity and a kind of justice when, in the fourth week of camp, she got him into the kind of trouble he had been pushing for. It was night, they were all in the cabin getting ready for bed, moths were shooting their shadows across the walls, and one of the girls screamed, "There's someone *out* there!" Mixed in the breeze off the lake, Sharon heard the familiar insane laugh; when a group of counselors came by, she went up to them and said, "It was Kevin." He was always lurking around, she added with extreme nonchalance, trying to get a peep at her.

The counselors went off. Back in the cabin, the girls stayed up late, analyzing Gumby's pervertedness and discussing how each one of them had been threatened by it. One loudmouthed girl named Rosa announced that Kevin had rubbed up against her in the lunch line. "And not just his leg," she said. Other girls sympathized. As the talk went on, Sharon found herself growing more and more resentful, until finally she put on her tape player with earplugs and blocked them all out. Harsh visions plagued her sleep.

Suddenly he was gone, banished from camp. There were rumors of horrendous punishment at home, of beatings and reform school. Gina was afraid. "What if he finds out you told?" she kept saying.

"It's not just me, you know," Sharon reminded her. "Half the camp knows what he does." Still, she was nervous when she saw him, four days after his disappearance, back in his old lurking place behind the office, waving her over. She held back for a second, then went up to him.

There were no bruises, but something was different. He wasn't trying to stare her down, for one thing.

"Hey Kevin," she said.

"You hear what happened?" he said. "Someone nailed me in the woods."

"Yeah," she said.

"My dad went nuts. Took my dirt bike and chucked it off the fuckin gorge."

She knew the place, there was a big waterfall and a platform where people could walk out and look down; she pictured a motorcycle tipping off the edge, revolving to the foam below.

"Three summers I worked my ass off for that bike," he said. He shook his head, and she watched him trying to change it into a shoulder shrug. "I guess them's the breaks though, huh?"

There was a silence. His hands clenched and unclenched in the pockets of his jeans. He dug one boot tip into the ground, working up a big clod of soil. "Hey, whadda you think a me anyway?" he said suddenly.

"Me? Of you?" She had no clue what to say. Her face flamed.

"I had you picked out from day one," he said to her. "You know that?"

She mumbled. "I kind of remember the van. . . ." She drifted off, then decided just to let her mouth go; anything other than silence. "Look, you're a nice guy, and I'm sorry about your bike, but I mean, I'm from Connecticut. I wasn't even going to come here. We were going to go to Florida, but my parents put off the trip till Christmas. . . ." She wished he would say something. "I mean, all of this, Vermont and everything . . ." She swept her hand over the view toward the lake. "It's nice, but it's just, you know. . . . Summer camp."

He nodded. "Yeah," he said, "it's a crock a shit, aint it?" His boot stopped digging the clod and now tamped it gently back into place. He looked at his watch and turned back toward the woods. Sharon could hear one of the huge trucks that carried logs on the road beyond.

"Hey," she called. "Was that you in the woods, anyway?"

He swatted his hand by his ear, as if at a fly, and kept on walking.

That night she wrote to Serena. *I had to tell this guy it was no go*, she said. *He took it pretty hard.*

With the Gumby episode behind her, Sharon decided to spend some time trying to enjoy camp things. She made a belated birthday present for her mother in Pottery, an ashtray in the shape of a heart. Only when a counselor kidded her did she remember that smoking caused heart disease. "I don't go around reading the Surgeon General's report," she said. But she worried about her mother's pack and a half a day, and didn't send the ashtray. Instead, she just sent a letter. *Dear Mom*, she wrote. *I'm sorry I sort of blew off your birthday. You are the most amazing mother anyone could imagine—I mean it. . . .*

She entered the camp tennis tournament and made it to the finals in her division, losing badly but with pride to a gigantic red-headed girl named Sally, who played a vicious serve and volley game. At the match there were line judges and ball girls, and at least fifty people watching, most of them rooting for Sharon as the underdog. It felt good to be cheered and congratulated; afterward, when they gave her the runner-up trophy and took her picture, she pulled her barrettes and shook her head, spilling ribbons of hair all over the trophy. She knew it was a silly moment, but she liked it nonetheless. Her brother and sister had played lots of tennis when they were her age, and they had never won a trophy.

She reached a kind of truce with Gina, and the two of them actually began to have fun. They talked at night until the other girls got mad, then sneaked outside and sat in their nightgowns on a huge rock by the lake. "Do you think he's around here somewhere?" Gina asked one night, looking out into the blackness.

"Who?" Sharon didn't want the subject raised. She had been avoiding thinking about him, and staying away from the path by the woods.

"You know, Shar, I was worried. I thought you really *liked* that worm."

"Be real," Sharon said.

Gina laughed. "And he's such a slime. You know who he reminds me of?"

They said it simultaneously: "Tommy Schotte." And they laughed until they cried.

Sharon saw she had been wrong about Gina; it was part of an overall negativeness she now set herself to correct. Gina still had a childish perspective on things, but it made life fun. Sharon let herself get silly, and the two of them played some of their old games, including Family: Sharon coming through the cabin door calling "I'm *home*, darling," dropping her knapsack on the floor, and Gina rushing up to kiss her and say "Oh, how was your day?!"

"Terrible! Horrible!" Sharon said, as the other girls in the cabin broke into hysterics.

When she didn't get a letter from home the whole third week and into the fourth, she wondered if her mother was hurt about the birthday screw-up. She regretted all the bad things she had ever thought about her, and hoped it was true that she could balance them with good. Instead of writing a letter that might not get there before she herself did, she decided to call. She went to the office after dinner, signed in on the Call Book, then waited for ten minutes at the Campers' Phone while a girl named Tara, who cried all the time, wetly begged her parents to let her come home early. Sliding into the phone booth minutes later, Sharon kicked aside the girl's bunched-up Kleenexes and felt sorry for parents. They had to take so much crap from their kids.

To her surprise, the phone at home was answered by Lydia. Sharon felt instant guilt for not having written to her in Boston, and said so. "Are you down for the beach or something?" she asked her sister.

"You know how the city is in the summer," Lydia said. "So how're you doing up there, Judge?"

Sharon told her about the reunion with Gina, the tennis tournament, and some details of the Gumby story. Something in the way her sister kept repeating "Great, hey, great," made her stop. "Liddie, is something going on?"

"No."

"Really? You sound weird."

There was a silence, filled only with the hiss of long distance.

"Liddie?"

"Listen, Judge. There are some things I can't tell you on the phone. . . ."

Sharon listened to her own voice. "Are Mom and Dad okay?"

"Fine, they're both fine."

"Let me talk to Mom."

"She's not here right now. . . ."

Everything seemed to come after a two-second pause. Sharon felt anger pushing at her from the inside. "Liddie—what is going on?"

There was a rumble on the line, and the smeared sound of someone's hand covering the mouthpiece. Then Sharon heard her father's voice. He told her not to worry; everyone was in one piece. "But you know, Shar," he said. "All people have problems at some point."

"Let me talk to Mom," she said tightly.

"Well, I can't do that. I wish I could. But your mother and I are having a little problem, and she went away for a couple of days to think things over. She'll be back by the time you get here—"

"You're going away, aren't you." She let it out quickly and then backed away from it, as if from a dangerous animal. She waited to see how her father would approach it.

"I'm not going anywhere, Judge," he said. "I'm standing right here."

"Do you promise you aren't going away?"

The smearing sound came and went again. "Judge," her father said. "I'm going to hand you back to your sister now. You'll come back home next week, and we'll all have a chance to talk about everything." She heard him breathing. "Things aren't always what they seem."

When Lydia came back on, Sharon listened not to the words but to the voice behind the voice. *I wish I didn't have to handle this* it was saying.

Soon she was outside and down the office steps, watching her own feet walk. The same paths led to the same paths. She thought about melting into them, like butter, like Little Black Sambo chasing tigers in the story her mother used to read to her. She thought about her father down in his office, with the Please Disturb—Paying Bills sign on the door; she pictured him listening for noise in the hall and reaching for the telephone, sticking his little finger in the dialing hole and clearing his voice while upstairs her mother stood by the back door with a packed suitcase.

"Hey."

The voice sliced through her thoughts. She looked up, focused, and found herself at the spot by the edge of the woods.

"I got somethin ta say to you."

She didn't walk the twenty steps but just stood there, feeling nothing. "You afraid a me now?" Gumby said, stepping out from behind his tree. He was carrying a bottle of beer. "You bitch," he said.

She watched him take a long guzzle, tilting his head back and then back further, as if shifting into high gear. He turned and threw the bottle at a tree; it exploded with a hollow pop.

"Think I give a fuck?" He jerked his head toward the office. "What the fuck else can they do that they aint done?" He looked at her. "What I wanna know is how come you don't party. Don't they party in Connecticut?" His mouth and lips wrapped themselves

133

around the word and squeezed it out, bit by bit. She knew he wanted her to be afraid, but she wasn't afraid. Behind him, the sun was flooding red through the trees, and she couldn't see his face too well. "Come on," he said, pulling another beer out of his back pocket. "Party time."

"We're supposed to go to the play," she said tonelessly.

"What, so you can see your faggot boyfriend?" He moved in closer. "You always got some nice fuckin excuse." He guzzled again, then whispered in a wet voice, "You act like you got no cunt."

The sun was now so red that she couldn't really see his face, only the silhouette of his head, like a bulb of stone. It helped, not being able to see him. She grabbed the beer out of his hand and took a swift, bitter gulp; she pictured the molecules of their saliva bouncing together in her mouth, and took a harder drink.

"You wanna do something about it?" she said.

He pulled back. The light changed, and she could see him now: brow squeezed together, his wounded-animal face pinched with its language of striking out and being struck. She poured some more beer down her throat and waited. She wanted him to make the first move. Her chest was burning.

There were questions in his eyes as he came in warily, suspecting a trick, and kissed her—lightly, like a good kisser. When he saw she meant it, the doubt slid off his face, his mouth glistened at the corners, and he kissed her harder. His tongue was in her mouth, his hands moving on her ribs. She was aware more than usual of his doglike quality; he wanted to finish her before someone came along and took her away.

"Hold on," she said. "Let's get out of the way."

In the woods, about ten trees back from the edge, they lay down. She felt pine needles. He kissed her and she kissed back. After a few minutes she was able to put her mouth on automatic pilot and con- centrate her eyes on a star revealed when his head, going to her ear or neck, moved out of her sight. Quickly he began making progress with her body. In the half-darkness she could see his hands scrabbling like white spiders on her chest; she could feel his hardness rubbing against her leg. He kept sliding up and up, trying to ease over on top of her, and she let him. His hands went up her shirt, and she was glad that she wore no bra for him to mangle. His hardness was between her legs now, and he was rocking.

She knew just how far she would let him go. She wouldn't let him get inside her, and he wouldn't care. She would make him shoot his scum somewhere else, on her stomach or leg, or better yet in his own pants. She could see the whole thing happening, right through to where he would pick himself off her and tramp away into the woods, back to wherever he came from. There would be no consequences; no one would believe him, and she'd be gone in a few days anyway. A hot shower would wash him off her.

The thought flashed through her mind that he might hate her for this detachment, as he had hated her all along. But she knew he had no idea. Her body was doing what it had to do: kissing where he kissed, pushing where he pushed. Her arms were around his back, her chin on his shoulder as he groaned hot noise into her neck. The only problem was the one she had wondered about for so long: what to say. But even this took care of itself. He rocked himself against her, she heard him grunt, and—very far away and small, as if from a deep well—she heard herself grunt back.

VIII

Arizona

There is only one porno theater in town, and he has often joked with her about going to it. "Shouldn't we see how people are doing it these days?" he'll say as they drive past on their way to the store or the post office. And he'll give her a smirking smile that says, *I'm only kidding, unless you say yes.*

Tonight she says yes. It is a limpid August evening, and she is doing the dishes after dinner, staring out through the picture window into the backyard. The phone rings, and he comes bounding noisily in to field it, taking it around the corner into the hall.

"Who was that?" she says when he comes back looking disappointed.

"Allan. He just canceled our game." She notices for the first time that he is wearing tennis clothes. He lifts his racquet from one of the kitchen chairs and takes a slow swing with it, his lips compressing the way they do whenever he thinks about something he won't be able to do as soon as he wants to. "Oh well," he says.

"So what will you do now?"

He looks at his watch. "Shall we throw morality to the winds and catch the early show at the Venus?"

She sees his knobby knees, the little tufts of hair just above each kneecap, and the socks pulled halfway up each calf. "Okay," she says, wiping the soap suds off her hands.

He goes upstairs to get changed, and not until he comes down and they are actually at the door does she have second thoughts. "Do we really want to do this?" she says.

He is already out and holding the door for her. "Who knows," he says. "Maybe this will help things."

For almost five months they haven't made love. It started on a Saturday afternoon. They often made love on Saturdays; with Lydia living in Boston, Toby off at college, and Sharon at dance lessons, the house was all theirs. But on that rainy Saturday in March when they took off their clothes and got into bed, nothing happened.

"Not this time, looks like," he said. She kissed him and put her head on his chest. Later that week and then again the next Saturday the same thing happened. "Is there anything wrong?" she asked him.

"Not that I know of," he said, smiling.

Since the previous fall she had been worried about him. He had been unusually moody, a moodiness she traced to September, when the two of them had driven Toby off to New Hampshire to start his first year of college. Through September and October he seemed tired and distant, too exhausted for washing his car or cleaning the garage, the kinds of things he usually liked to do on a Saturday. His appetite shriveled; on a Sunday afternoon she would bring him a sandwich as he watched football, and two hours later she would collect it, half-eaten, or see him feeding it to the dog.

"Are you all right?" she asked him.

"I'm fine," he would say, rubbing his eyes. "Just working too hard."

But she kept noticing things. "Do you know you never sing in the shower anymore?" she said to him one day in November as he stood in the bathroom, toweling himself off.

"Sure I do," he said.

"Well you weren't singing just now," she said.

"Wasn't I?" He frowned and looked off in the distance, then turned to her. "Well, then give me a song, and I'll sing it for you."

He missed their son, though he wouldn't admit it. He would read Toby's letters aloud to her, breathless letters full of professors and beer parties and girls. "What a life," he would say, smiling and shaking his head. Once she saw on his typewriter a letter to Toby, half-finished. Somewhat guiltily she began reading. *Well Champ,* she read, *while you revel in the freedoms of student life, your mother and I continue the slow and occasionally entertaining march toward senility. Half a century minus four, I find myself beset by bills, by patients with grievous head injuries, and by your little sister, whose dance steps up in her room sound like a veritable avalanche in the kitchen.*

As fall dragged into winter, his glumness deepened. It was as if someone had pulled a stopper in his life, and all the energy and joy had drained out. She did what she could. "We should do some new things together," she told him; they ended up going off one night a week to a Chinese cooking class, where along with three other couples they cooked meals under the direction of an elderly Asian man, meals they then proceeded to eat, fresh from the sizzling woks. He laughed, but she could see his heart wasn't in it. He looked like a sleepwalker. Knowing how much new cars could excite him, she suggested he trade in his Jeep for something small and snazzy. But he shrugged her off. "The Jeep gets me around okay," he said.

Just before Christmas she got him to have a complete physical. "You're so busy saving other people," she told him, "you never stop to think about yourself." When the doctor pronounced him fit as a horse, they celebrated at their favorite Italian restaurant, drinking Chianti and holding hands over the table. "I love you," she told him, and he smiled, but his eyes were pools of sadness. "Are you okay?" she asked him.

"Fit as a horse," he said.

Looking around at her friends and their marriages, she saw others in open crisis—separating, divorcing, changing careers, moving. Some women went to work in their husbands' offices; she tended to see this as thinly veiled spying. She remembered the times that had been toughest for the two of them, the bleak days of their early marriage, when he was a surgical resident and they lived in the slums of Hartford, or before that, when he was in the public health service and had taken her out to Arizona to live with the Navajos. There had been dismal days for them then, but faith in each other had gotten them through it. She felt the same way about whatever it was that was bothering him now: she believed that with her love he would emerge from it, as from some hibernation, and be himself again.

They park at the far end of the lot, closer to the supermarket than the theater.

"What if we see someone?" She tries to imagine any of her friends in a porno theater.

He smiles and holds up a finger. "I'm prepared for that." He leans over into the back of the car, and when he turns around he is wearing a Groucho Marx mask, with the nose and glasses and moustache.

"You silly," she says, kissing the phony moustache.

They pay their money to a little bald man who takes their ten dollars and shoves two tickets through the slot without looking up. The lobby beyond is like any other theater lobby. She is surprised to see racks of candy and a popcorn machine.

"Do we know when the movie starts?" she asks.

He laughs. "I don't think it makes much difference." His hand is on the door. "Now if there's anything you don't understand, just ask Daddy."

The theater is small, smaller than she has expected, and the screen immense. Muzak is playing, as in a dentist's office, and over it she can hear people moaning. But the gigantic images on the screen are confusing, and it takes her a full five seconds to figure it out: it is a huge close-up of testicles, of someone's balls, shaking and writhing like Jell-O.

She stops dead in the aisle and says, "Oh, my God."

Behind her, he bursts out in laughter.

It was in early spring that he began to come out of it, just as she had hoped he would. One freakishly warm February Sunday she awoke to the sound of him scraping dead leaves out of the window wells, and whistling as he did it.

"Well, hello!" she said to him, leaning out the window.

"You got a lot of sludge in these gutters, lady," he called back.

Gradually his interest in the world returned to him. He began playing tennis again, getting up twice a week at six to play for an hour with Allan Durfee, a new doctor in town. In the junk room he came across Lydia's old camera and developing equipment, unused for a dozen years; with the help of a library book, he set up a darkroom in the basement and began printing his own photos, mostly shots of dunes and driftwood on the beach. "What is Dad *doing* down there?" their thirteen-year-old, Sharon, asked her. "Does he think he's an artist or something?"

"Let him have his fun," she said. And it *was* fun, the way he came up the stairs with prints in each hand, comparing little details. Watching the images appear out of nothing, he told her, was like magic.

"I'm so glad you're happy," she said, hugging him.

Then came March. Just when he seemed himself again, their problems in bed began. She tried to ignore the first failures, but when a month passed, she was worried and wondered aloud whether they should get some help. Never in twenty-four years of marriage had they gone more than two weeks without making love. Let it wait a little, he said. They kept trying, and she did her best to love him; but in her hand, in her mouth, he was simply limp. Kissing his chest and moving downward, she felt him tensing. *You're not helping this*, she wanted to say.

She didn't know whom she could talk to. On the kitchen counter next to the fruit bowl, she had a stack of women's magazines, each one with an article about impotence. At first she had actually gone to the public library, had checked the card catalogue under "Impotence." There was nothing, and before she could look under "Mental Health" or "Sexual Problems," she lost her nerve and backed away. It seemed a betrayal of him to be there.

With each passing week she found herself unraveling a bit more. He, on the other hand, seemed livelier than ever—everywhere except in bed. He played tennis almost daily, rushed out after dinner to photograph sunsets, and even began to talk once again about building a playhouse in the yard for Sharon, a project he had planned and then dropped years earlier.

"You don't have to do everything, you know," she said to him. "Maybe you need to calm down a little. Save some of your energy."

In May, for his birthday, she took the occasion of a Friday when Sharon was sleeping at a friend's to prepare a surprise meal. She cooked a delicate veal piccata, chilled a bottle of champagne, set the table with candles in the dining room, and waited for him to come home from the hospital. Later, they took the champagne and candles upstairs—and again they failed. His penis seemed to have lost all life. Nothing she did mattered. For an hour they tried, and when she finally rolled over and gave up, she thought she heard him sigh, a tiny sigh of relief as he stood up and got out of bed.

"I have an unbirthday present for you," he said, walking naked to his closet. He brought out something wrapped with almost comic slovenliness in brown paper. "Did the wrapping myself," he said, smiling.

It took her half a minute, once it was unwrapped, to figure out that what he had gotten for her was a clock. It was obviously expensive, a glass-domed clock with a heavy mahogany base and brass fittings. But it was nothing that she, who never even wore a wristwatch, would ever think of owning. "I've never seen anything quite like it," she managed to stammer out. She looked up, hoping he wouldn't be too hurt; he was beaming at her and at the clock, as if he hadn't heard.

The next morning she sat for a long time in the kitchen after he left, drinking coffee and smoking, staring into the knots in the pine table. She thought about their early marriage, out in Arizona. In the dusty reservation town they had moved into a dingy house whose previous tenant, also a doctor, had died in a train wreck only a month earlier. They kept finding his stuff everywhere—rooting in a closet the third day there, she found a pair of dentures sitting in a glass of water. She jumped back out of the closet and stood in the kitchen, loathing the place. Outside, in the dirt street, two scrawny dogs were fighting over a severed goat's leg, hoof and all. Later that night she confided her dismal feelings in him. He held her and comforted her, then they had made love for a long time, as quietly as possible in order not to wake Lydia in the next room.

Upstairs, she stood looking at the pictures of her children, two of whom hadn't even been born on that day in Arizona. Now they were more or less grown. She didn't feel old enough to be their mother, not at all. Also on her bureau was the clock he had given her the night before. Looking at it again, she expected to see something new, something that would show her herself in the gift. But she couldn't find it. The little gears and weights were ugly. The guts of the clock were exposed, and the small face crowded with ornate Roman numerals. It was not made to be touched. She began to hate it.

They sit down near the back of the theater. As her eyes adjust, she can see the other people in the place, maybe twenty in all, couples and singles. Everyone is looking up at the screen as the testicles shake and the gigantic thing pumps in and out of a huge, glistening crotch. "I can't believe this," she whispers to him. "I can't believe what I'm looking at."

"Pretty wild, isn't it?" he says.

What shocks her most is the *size* of it all. People's parts are cut off by the camera and given a life of their own, hideously magnified, breathing and gleaming, moving of their own will.

"I feel like an ant," she says as a massive phallus jerks gobs of jism all over someone's heaving stomach.

After a while it is no longer shocking; it is just boring. It is like some National Geographic special gone berserk, one animal digging the same hole over and over again. She finds herself beginning to laugh. "Do you think people find this sexy?" she says to him. The screen now shows a man holding his own thing and diddling himself. He is big, but not very hard. She wonders how they are able to get it up, these actors, time after time, with strange women. She imagines the kinds of instructions a director might be calling out. *Diddle yourself! Diddle harder!*

She giggles. Daniel puts his hand on her knee. The actor keeps diddling his huge thing, which gradually and obediently gets huger.

"That can't possibly fit inside anyone," she whispers, and as he is leaning over to answer, the image on the screen flickers and catches, and the lights come on.

She blinks. Dan smiles a wide and sheepish smile, then drapes his windbreaker suddenly over her head. "I'll hide you!" he says.

The lights go out. "Hey," she says, freeing herself from his jacket. "I wanted to see if I knew anyone."

"But think how you'd feel if word got out that Mrs. Daniel

Slattery, noted community volunteer and good-deed-doer, was seen—"

The film again sputters, and the lights go on. "Projectus interruptus," he says, loud enough for people to hear.

One man laughs.

The third time the lights come on, half a dozen people walk out. She watches their faces. No one seems particularly upset. It really doesn't matter when you leave such a film, she realizes, or when you come in; it is all the same.

When she turns back, he is wearing the Groucho Marx mask.

"What are you doing, you silly?" she says to him.

"If you have to ask, then I guess I'm not doing it right," he says, doing the whole Groucho bit, with the fingers and the eyebrows and the cigar.

When the film resumes, he keeps the mask on. She watches the light reflect off the huge plastic nose. It annoys her, it is so dumb. Finally she reaches over and pulls the mask off his face. She watches him in the light of reflected depravity from the screen, and suddenly the horrible feeling comes over her that he is still wearing a mask—that hangdog, lopsided smile, the cleft in his round and meaty chin. Being funny is hard on him. His smile has become lopsided; one side of his face droops while the other climbs. She closes her eyes and tries to picture what his face looked like twenty years before. She sees him comforting her in their house in the Arizona desert. His whole smile was different then. His upper lip moved more; it showed teeth and even gums. Nowadays his smile doesn't gape like that. It protects itself more.

She opens her eyes and looks at him, trying with all her will to block out the actions of the white, writhing torsos on the screen beyond. The dismalness of the last four months fills her chest like flu. Somehow, she doesn't know when, she has stopped being part of him; she is outside him now, watching.

"I can't stand this anymore," she says.

He turns to her. "But we're just about to reach the stunning dénouement." Groping wildly in the dark, she reaches for her sweater.

Outside, she is shocked to find it is still light. She stands there blinking. Heat rolls upward from the ground, and through its shimmer she looks past the parking lot to the stores, the train station and war memorial, the river beyond. The normalness of town calms her. People walk, drive, eat pizza off wax paper, stroll from shop to shop. Their lives make sense.

He comes out the door, shaking his head and looking from side to side. "At least we made our escape before the lights came on," he says.

She is quiet. He puts his hand on her shoulder.

"I hated that," she says, nodding toward the theater.

"Didn't turn you on, eh?"

"It was about as big a turn-on as—" she struggles for the right image—"as melons."

They get into the car and drive through town. She is silent. *"Mona Lisa, Mona Lisa men have named you,"* he sings in his good voice. The sun is setting as they pull in the drive, and their house is pink in the light. Standing on the back porch, they can hear Sharon's black Lab, John Henry, yelping and throwing himself against the kitchen door.

"Dogs get so excited," she says.

He stands behind her, his fingers on her forearms. She feels him sway against her and is suddenly afraid, thinking about all the empty rooms in their house. She had wanted Sharon to go to camp, but now that she is there, the house seems too quiet without her. There has never been a whole month when all three kids were gone. "I miss them," she whispers. "I miss each one in a different way."

"Don't worry," he says. "They're all out there having a blast." He kisses her neck and sways against her again and says into her ear, "I think tonight might be our night."

He goes in to fix them a drink, and the dog comes shooting out, looking for fun, followed by their kitten, Poe. She sits down with the dog, pulling her head back to keep a distance from its large and slobbering tongue. She remembers how Lydia used to let their Dalmatian, Waldo, lick her face, even on the lips and eyelids, and how they all tried to get her to stop.

"Yes, John Henry," she murmurs to the dog, rubbing its ears. "You silly thing." Behind her she hears the clink of ice on glass, and her husband singing in the kitchen.

When he calls her, they take their Scotches into the TV room and sit down on the couch, under a wall full of photos of the kids. He sings along softly with Nat King Cole on the stereo. She closes her eyes and pictures him young again, in a white T-shirt, out in Arizona.

"Hey," she says. "When we were out west, what did we talk about?"

"Talk about?" He stops rubbing her arm. "I don't know. We talked about drunken Indians. We talked about the fact that the dirt out there was pink. Why?"

Eyes closed, she snuggles deeper into his shirt and the warm, thick smell of him. "It's just that I can't remember," she says.

"We talked about coming back east," he says. "You missed your mother."

"Oh, come on, Slattery. Don't make me sound like a child."

"We talked about our dream house. About a dishwasher and a real shower." He squeezes her arm. "About having a house big enough so we could perform the rites of marriage without having our children as spectators."

She sees a vision of the two of them making love on the rickety back porch of their house in Arizona, he still in his white T-shirt, hovering over her, extra gentle and slow because she is already pregnant. Just the two of them silently making love, under a million miles of blue sky.

"You were so cute then," she says.

"Some people think I'm not so bad now."

"Oh, you know what I mean."

She feels his hand leave her back, hears Scotch chug-a-lugging into his glass. "I know only one thing, *ma chérie*," he says in his Charles Boyer voice. "I know zat you are ze most beautiful woman in ze world, and zat I want to make love to you."

His lips are on the back of her neck, his leg sliding up over hers. She opens her eyes and stares at a button on his shirt. The grainy wetness of his tongue dips into her ear, and she shivers. Curly hairs on his chest look huge; it reminds her of the porno movie, and she closes her eyes. Instantly her vision fills with him in his T-shirt, smiling his boy's smile full of gums. She can see the blue sky, see him rising and falling gently in it, hear herself laughing, "I won't *break*, you silly." The vision is so big and so bright, it fills her up completely, and she feels suspended in a kind of dream. She hugs him.

"It's now or never," his voice whispers in her ear. "Let's go upstairs."

In June the whole family was home. He seemed happy, surrounded by his children, but she thought she could see shadows of desperation in his happiness. She watched him showing Lydia his darkroom, shooting baskets with Toby in the yard, showing Sharon where he wanted to build the playhouse. *Look at me*, he kept telling them. *Forty-seven years old, and not dead yet.*

She wanted some time alone with him. And so when he asked her what she wanted for Mother's Day, she said, "Let's get away for the weekend."

"What, and leave the whole gang here?"

"It doesn't have to be anything big," she said. "Just a couple of days."

They decided on Nantucket. He called a few places, and they discussed which of several promising inns they should go to. As it turned out, it didn't really matter, for the day before they left, he came down with a sudden cold, and though the place they had chosen was a beautiful inn overlooking the harbor, he coughed and hacked too much for either of them to enjoy it. On Sunday morning he stayed in bed while she went out, looking for an open drugstore where she could buy him cough medicine. She watched the people crowding the streets and docks, most of them college kids like her older children, young and careless kids whose sunburned faces shone as if lit from within by a luminous happiness. She bought some cough syrup, and as she came out onto the cobblestone street, holding the medicine in a small paper bag, it occurred to her that her husband had had similar colds twice before during the spring, sudden colds that had descended on him just before the two of them went away for a weekend somewhere. She thought of him sitting in their overpriced, romantic room, waiting for her. It made her tremble.

When they got back to Connecticut, he seemed to recover quickly; his cold evaporated and he was cheerful again. One afternoon he came into the kitchen beaming and grabbed her arm. "Guess what I did?" he said. "I finally took your advice." Outside in the driveway was a little white coupe, a Mercedes Benz. He had traded in the Jeep, he explained, and had bought the sports car secondhand from a car dealer who had once been a patient of his.

"What do you think?" he asked her.

"Snappy," was all she could say. "Very snappy."

After the Fourth of July the kids cleared out—Lydia to Boston, Toby to the Cape, Sharon to camp in Vermont. After dropping Sharon at the bus station, the two of them came home to a house so quiet it seemed soundproofed. She felt miserable, and yet something in his expression, some kind of dogged cheer, kept her from saying so. But that night when they went up to bed, their slow and shuffling progress up the stairs seemed to her yet another dreary trudge toward failure. And so it was. As they lay in bed afterward, silence pressing in on them from all sides, she felt how defeated they had become. He didn't even expect to be able to make love to her anymore.

"Listen Dan," she said to him afterward. "We've got to do something about this. I'm going to go crazy."

He nodded.

"I mean it," she said. "We've got to see somebody."

"Okay," he said quickly. "All right."

She woke the next morning to the sound of his new car pulling out the drive. Her vision focused on his side of the bed, empty and rumpled, and for a moment, still half-asleep, she felt a pulse of fear. *Tennis*, she said to herself, waking. *Of course.*

On an impulse she got out of bed, dressed, and went downstairs. In the garage she took one of the kids' old bikes and rode out the driveway, through the still, sleeping neighborhood. It was pleasant at that early hour; the air was cool but held a promise of heat. She waved to an old woman taking out garbage.

Approaching the tennis courts, she felt an unaccountable nervousness; it was the same feeling she sometimes had while driving, a certainty that something was about to go wrong, some awful, unknown breakdown. There was an ominous stillness in the air as she passed the grade school and Little League field; her lungs, weakened by too many cigarettes, seemed unable to take in enough air.

Then she heard it, drifting through the trees—the familiar, dopey sound of a tennis ball *pong*ing the strings of a racquet. She slowed and then stopped. Through the trees she could see them, hitting the ball back and forth on the tennis court. Allan Durfee, whom she had never seen before, was much younger than her husband, practically a boy. The two of them could have been father and son.

She watched as a long rally developed. She herself had always hated games with balls, never able to shake the feeling, as a ball whizzed toward her, that the opposing player was trying to hurt her. But what she saw now, as the two men stroked the ball from one side to the other, was something very different—a choreographed dance, the men hitting the ball to preassigned spots, gracefully running it down and then retreating almost on tiptoe; leaping suddenly to reach a high shot, swooping for a low one. She could feel pleasure emanating from the game, and hear it in the little grunts of surprise and admiration both men made as the point progressed. Finally, Allan Durfee hit a shot that went into the net, and both men collapsed to the ground on their respective sides, laughing and moaning.

"Jesus," said Allan Durfee. "That's just too good, Daniel."

She started to pedal forward, out of the trees. But something held her back. Out on the court, the men slowly stood, and began retreating to the end lines. "Remember the days when I used to win those points?" Allan Durfee said. "How is it that I keep getting older and you keep getting younger?"

She watched her husband breathe in deeply, his chest expanding, jaw jutting upward in a smile. "Good, clean living, that's all," he said to the younger man. She heard him laugh, a rolling, hearty laugh, and then she turned around and headed home to get breakfast ready.

This time it is happening as it used to happen. They sink to the bed, and she feels him pushing against her, harder than he has been for months. They roll over, and she is surprised to feel dizziness from the Scotch; she can't remember how many she has had. He drinks his Scotch off, puts the glass on the nightstand, and turns back to her, his fingers going to her belt buckle. Soon her shorts are off, and she is lying back in her panties and shirt, waiting. He takes his own pants off and kneels before her; they both look down to where he is sticking out through his boxer shorts. In his face she sees triumph rising like a flush. As he moves toward her, holding himself in his hand, she has a horrible flashback to the Venus theater.

"Dan . . ." she says. She wants to talk to him, but the moment is too fragile. His body is a match in the wind. Anything she says might extinguish him.

"*Chérie*," he hums. "*Comme tu es belle.*"

She watches his face as he slides her panties off and positions himself between her legs. She knows she isn't very wet, but it won't matter, as long as he goes slowly. He reaches for her breasts, and reflexively she raises her arms for him to take her shirt off. He doesn't, and she feels silly holding her hands up. Now he is lowering himself onto her; another small wave of dizziness washes through her, and she whispers, "I think I drank too much."

"Ummmm," he says in her ear.

"Dan, how many did I have?"

"Not very many," he whispers. The words lose themselves in the rush of his breath, the pushing and prodding of his body. He is almost in her now.

She pushes him off. "I have to go to the bathroom," she says.

"What are you doing?" There is a frantic note in his voice, and she glimpses bewilderment on his face as she crosses to the bathroom. Closing the door behind her, she sits down on the toilet. The bed mutters, she hears his feet on the floor. "I think I'm sick," she calls.

"But . . ." He is close to the door. "But this is what we've been waiting for."

"I know," she says. "I know. I'll be out in a minute." She sits there, breathing heavily, watching her own stomach go in and out. She needs time to figure herself out.

"Hey," his voice says. "Hello in there . . ."

"Wait," she says weakly, "wait just a minute." She can feel herself dissolving into tears, and now she does in fact feel sick, a hollow wave of nausea rolling through her. She gets up and begins to move toward the door. She imagines releasing herself into his arms. "I'm coming," she said.

"Well." His voice has turned cold. "I'm afraid it's a little late now."

She hears his feet move heavily back into the room. The bed creaks. She knows what his face looks like now, annoyance tugging his eyebrows up, disappointment etched into his smile. He is lying there waiting.

Terror seizes her. She gulps for breath, looking around at their towels, their toothbrushes and deodorants. It is all wrong. She isn't supposed to be here. She is supposed to be somewhere else, and someone else is supposed to be where she is. She wants to talk to Lydia, or Sharon, or her mother. But they are all gone. They have left her. She is all alone.

"Dan . . ." she sobs, and then is unsure whether she has said it or merely thought it. She doesn't want him to answer. There is nothing in his voice for her, and she is nowhere in it. It is all him, him, him. She gathers her voice, packs it together, and aims it through the door. *If you don't do this now*, she says to herself, *you will die*. "Dan," she says. "Dan, is there someone else?"

There is no answer. Again she is half convinced she hasn't actually said anything. Then the bed speaks in its springs, and she thinks she hears him sigh; her hand is slippery on the glass doorknob as she pictures him coming toward the door on the other side, young again as in Arizona, his face collapsing in love and concern, all of him focused on the doorknob, the door, and her. She turns the handle.

He is sitting on the edge of the bed, elbows on his knees, facing her bureau. The look he turns to her is pure in its blankness; for the first time in months, there is no smile wedged on his face.

"Aren't you going to say anything?" she says.

He turns away. She sees now that he has taken the clock he gave her off her bureau and is holding it. His fingers are tender, even gentle, on the glass dome. Motionless, he stares into the small world of the clock, and watches its gears turn and its tiny hand peck away at the seconds.

"Dan," she says, drifting toward him. "Dan, talk to me. Say something."

IX

Once More to the Cat Tree

My mother's love of cats is a fairly recent affliction. It began when I was a senior in high school, the year before my parents separated. My younger sister, Sharon, came home one night with a scrawny, big-headed kitten rescued from boys who were trying to drown it in the river. We had always been a dog family, but in the time before their separation, my parents acted unpredictably; we kept the cat. Given the task of naming the creature, my father called it Edgar Allan Poe because of a certain demented look in its eyes. My father never got the knack of holding the kitten; he would put it down on the floor and then pat it on the head, as if it were a small dog. By the time it was full grown, he was gone.

Soon after my parents separated, my mother took in another stray cat, and then another. Very quickly it was too late to turn back; by the time she and my father divorced a year and a half later, she was already a cat person. Owning a dog is simple, but cat owners become involved in a whole way of life. My mother has coffee cups and greeting cards with cats on them; she has cat calendars and cat plates and cat napkins. The air in her house is abundant with cat hairs, which float into your soup, your ears, your nostrils. "Those cats of yours drive me crazy," I tell my mother every time I am home.

"You hate them," she says. "And they know it."

On the one and only occasion when my mother called upon me to house-sit for her creatures, I did what I could to restore our black Lab, John Henry, to his former preeminence. Instead of feeding John Henry outside, I set him up in the kitchen, where the famished cats had to watch. When he was outside with his bone, I fed the five of them one bowl at a time, watching them bicker and hiss. Finally, when all the bowls were down and they were three-quarters done, I opened the back door to John Henry. He bounded in and went from dish to dish, wolfing the food down as the cats scattered in terror, their nails scrabbling on the linoleum. "You're the king, boy," I said to J.H. in the voice dogs love to hear.

When my mother came home, she took one look at the cats and turned to me. "All right," she said. "What did you do to them?"

Living with a daughter, a dog, and five cats in an oversized house has changed my mother's perspective. She has come to accept things that five years ago she would have rejected out of hand. Cats roam unmolested on kitchen counters. They pop up on the kitchen table during meals. My mother forgets that this is not normal, or else she doesn't care. I have seen her reading a magazine stained with cat piss. She makes a face, but she doesn't throw it out.

"It's getting to the point with these cats," says my sister, "where I don't even want to bring my friends over."

It's tough on my sister, who is seventeen. In the last three or four years, while she has been growing up, everything has been falling apart around her. Sharon has insomnia; she wakes up at night and is afraid of terrible things, rapists and murderers. Last month she got my mother to put a big lock on the basement door. "Anyone coming up through the basement would have to come through the kitchen,"

I reminded her, "and that would be enough to scare any murderer away." The kitchen is where the cats sleep. The thought of them sprawled in the darkness, their furry sides heaving in and out, scares me.

People are known by the animals they keep. Recently I called my mother's yardman, Mr. Wilcox, to ask him about a bill my mother had gotten. At first he was confused about just who I was, but then he straightened it out. "Sure," he said. "Your mother's the lady with all the cats."

With mistaken relish I told my mother about this conversation. It wounded her to see me identifying myself with people out there who explain away her love of cats as a kind of neurosis. When you get right down to it, love—even love of cats—is love, and bears no explanation.

Last month Poe, my mother's first and favorite cat, died. Poe was the only cat of my mother's that I had any use for. He was the only cat named after a writer; the others are named after actresses and Winnie the Pooh characters. I was home when the cat died, sitting at the kitchen table with Mom and Sharon, eating my mother's strange but delicious cabbage and peanut butter soup. Sharon was talking about her boyfriend Fred's high school graduation that night, when the doorbell rang.

My mother went out and came back carrying Poe, who had disappeared five weeks earlier. The cat was filthy, and his ribs were showing, but he was alive. My mother got a towel, put it on the table, and laid the cat on top of it.

"He was hit," my mother said. "The paper boy found him."

"And the person didn't even stop?" Sharon's voice rose. "That asshole! I hope his car blows up."

I try my best in these situations to sound brotherly and husbandly and fatherly all at once. "Hey, boy," I said to the cat. "Can you move these legs of yours?"

He couldn't. Poe looked at me calmly, his mouth set in what

155

looked like a smile. I noticed that the towel he was stretched out on was from a hospital where our father worked twenty years ago, when I was two.

"I'm calling Fred," Sharon said.

"Fred?" my mother said. "What good can Fred do?"

"Fred knows cats," my sister said. But she didn't call. In pressured situations she finds it hard to act. She analyzes decisions into the ground.

I called the vet, a woman I remembered from the time John Henry swallowed a bone. She told me to give the cat water, keep it warm, and bring it in for x-rays in the morning. When I hung up, Sharon and Mom were arguing about whether Sharon should still go to Fred's graduation.

"I want to stay with Poe," Sharon said.

"Fred's feelings will be hurt," my mother said. "Toby, tell her Fred's feelings will be hurt."

I shrugged and said nothing. My mother and sister have spent so much time together these last years that they have their own way of dealing with each other, and it is usually best for others not to butt in. So we just sat there in silence around the table, as tiny continents of fat coagulated and drifted on the cooling soups. I thought about calling my older sister, Lydia, in Boston. She has cats; she gives them names like Saskatchewan and Flying Buttress. I also thought, fleetingly, about calling my father. In the two years since he left, he has developed a habit of asking about events at Mom's house in a way that suggests he misses certain things. "How are the animals?" he'll say, or "How's your mother's menagerie?" A faint smile forms on his face, and he seems to grow nostalgic, but under that nostalgia I think he is glad he got out. I pictured him picking up the phone, or taking it from his wife, Ginny, and telling me he has no idea what to do with cats—a tremor in his voice saying, *Don't put your mother on.*

By 8:30 the sun was down, and we had cleared the table of everything except Poe. Mom fed the cat water from an eyedropper. The water dribbled out of his mouth onto the towel.

"I don't think he's getting any," Sharon said. "He could choke."

I looked at my sister's long hair, messily gathered up inside a baseball cap. She was wearing Fred's football jersey with his name across the shoulders. Sharon has been through a lot in the past three years; when Mom and Dad separated, Lydia and I were both off at college, but Sharon was here; when they divorced and Mom spent her evenings drinking wine and weeping, I was still in school, and Lydia was living in a house with lots of people in Boston, but Sharon was here. I remember partying my brains out for a whole semester at school, calling up drunk one night and getting Sharon and Mom in the middle of an argument. I couldn't deal with it, and hung up. Sharon is a good kid who gets into minor trouble every now and then, like failing gym or yelling at a guidance counselor. It's a way of trying to focus some attention on herself. When our parents first split up, Sharon went through a rebellious phase. She wore leather skirts and smoked a lot of dope and didn't eat enough. But in the past year she has changed a lot. She has settled down with one boyfriend; she likes to go to bed early and get up early to go running.

She and Fred are a placid couple. At night they watch Johnny Carson and old "Twilight Zone" reruns, and fall asleep on the TV room couch together. Fred works after school at a dry cleaner, saving money for a car. He is a great football player who quit the team and got a reputation for having a bad attitude, but you would never know it from the way he treats my sister, with love and a kind of deference.

"Hey Judge," I said, calling Sharon by a nickname I gave her years ago. "You can still make it to graduation. Why don't you go ahead."

"No." She shook her head, looking at Poe and Mom.

"Come on," I said. "You can even take my car."

I reached into my pocket for my keys. But at that moment the

cat on the table began choking and wheezing. The eyedropper broke
in his mouth, and Mom's finger was cut. She slapped the cat's back
as if it were a newborn child, and then my sister suddenly stood up
and started screaming; she stamped her feet in tiny steps and beat
her forehead with her fists. I grabbed her arm and took her toward
the door.

"Go on," Mom said. "I'm okay in here."

Outside there were stars and a whiff of garbage. John Henry
rustled out of the pachysandra, panting and wagging.

"I'm sorry," Sharon said. "I don't know what happened to me
in there. I got hysterical."

"It's okay, Judge," I said.

"It was just the sound. The sound was so awful."

We reached the corner, where dumb John Henry pissed and
then foraged in the Balthazars' ivy, and turned into the unlighted
alley that runs from Frog Hollow, our street, across to Clover Hill.
How pleasantly our streets are named! There is a light on Clover
Hill; when I used to walk our Dalmatian, Waldo, on his leash, I
would aim for that light on the far side of the alley and then run like
hell. Behind huge hedges on the left is Firelli's Ocean House—an
elephantine Victorian apartment house where Chip Butler and Nate
Holover and I would sneak in, ring the doorbells on the brass panel,
and run, a storm of outraged tenants exploding behind us. Now my
sister was crying again.

"Poe will be okay," I said. "He's a tough cat."

"It's not just that," she said. "It's Mom."

"Mom?"

"She gives and gives, and I just take and take."

"Hey—"

"It's true. She makes my lunch and washes my clothes and picks
up my room. And what do I do? Nothing. I see Fred. I do my absurd
homework. I have stupid phone calls with stupid jerks."

"Judge," I said, "calm down."

"Do you know Mom's bed is six feet across? I measured it. The cats sleep on Dad's old side. When I imagine being Mom, I just want to die."

Lights dim early in this neighborhood; sometimes I imagine that the children who have grown up and out of the place—my old gang—have somehow never been replaced by a new set. I have to force myself to realize that my sister still lives there, in her present, not in my past. We reached the corner of Clover Hill and stood in the halo of light. Sharon hugged herself, rocking from side to side and staring at the ground. I remembered a night in the first year of my parents' separation—Halloween, it had been—when our mother, in a fit of fury at Dad, had gone on a rampage in the basement, tearing up a whole box of home movies Dad took when we were kids. Sharon and I found her weeping in the basement. Upstairs was a man waiting to take her out on a date, and we had to tell him she was sick.

"Remember that Halloween when Mom went crazy?" I said to Sharon. "She's come a long way since then."

"That's true," my sister said.

We walked up Clover Hill, past the hedges that rim Firelli's Ocean House like a medieval rampart. I talked, rambling among memories of the neighborhood. I told my sister about Vera Waller, the ancient lady who lived in the Ocean House and doled out candies that smelled of moth balls; when we rang the doorbells, we always skipped hers. I told her about making out with Lucy Kreuzmann in the dark storage room under the apartment building. I described sneaking up to peer in the windows of the house across the street, where Mr. Haft lived—an architect who became a hermit when his wife left him and who was believed to hold seances in his attic. And finally I told her about the dead cat that Chip Butler and I found and carried under a blanket on his go-cart to the shade of a huge copper beech tree a quarter-mile down the road, where we buried it with full military honors. .

"So you haven't always hated cats?" she said, sniffling a laugh.

"Well, I respected that one. I felt it had been places. Like Poe."

"Is the grave still there?"

"No. About two months later, Billy Balthazar dug it up. We caught him." Billy Balthazar was the neighborhood bully, a truly frightening person.

"How disgusting," my sister said. "I'll never understand why guys do what they do."

Our large house loomed ahead. A car roared by on the avenue, hogging the middle. The shouts of kids passed through the neighborhood, bending and echoing.

"Toby." Sharon stopped, balancing on the curb. She looked at her watch. "Fred keeps talking about joining the Marines."

"Really?" I had never personally known anyone who joined the Marines. "How do you feel about it?"

"Sometimes I think he does these things to hurt himself. It's like he's saying to himself, 'What the hell, what am I worth anyway?' "

More cars blasted by on the street, their horns shrieking. I tried to remember the night of my high school graduation. There had been a bonfire on the beach with lots of beer. My parents gave me a watch with my initials on it. The other details were fuzzy.

In silence we moved through the backyard. On the porch my sister took a deep breath, which I could hear over my mother's wind chimes. "You know," Sharon said. "Sometimes I try to remember what it was like when Dad was here and you and Lydia were here. But I can't. I just can't *see* it—you know what I mean?"

"Exactly," I said. I thought of Chip Butler and myself heading back to the grave site of the dead cat, under the big tree, and finding Billy Balthazar at work with a shovel. "I got your cat!" he had yelled, dancing on the grave. And then I remembered something: we hadn't come just to pay our respects to Dead Tom. We, too, had come to the cat tree with shovels.

———

In the kitchen Mom sat Indian style on the floor, smoking a cigarette. Poe was a still form on her lap, the towel drawn up over his head. I remembered my mother saying that four cats was the number she really needed: one each to replace Lydia and me, and two for Dad.

"Don't bury him tonight, okay?" she said.

"Okay," I nodded.

"What will we do with him?" Sharon said.

"We can put him on the porch," I said. "The stones are cool out there."

"You know, it was your father who named this cat," Mom said. "He said he couldn't decide between Poe and Engelbert Humperdinck. I hate to say it, but I think he made the right decision."

I saw my sister looking at her watch. "Hey," I said to her. "Why don't you go out and find Fred now?"

She looked from me to Mom, who nodded, then turned toward the door, grabbing a handful of Kleenex from the counter as she went. At the back door I could see the other cats, circling warily, not really wanting to come in. " 'Bye, you guys," said Sharon, and the screen door banged.

"She really wanted to go," Mom said after a minute. "She just needs to be told sometimes."

I bent down and took the cat's body from my mother's lap. "Did you know all this about Fred? About the Marines?"

She nodded. "I don't know what to say to her, Toby. When I was her age, I never had to make any decisions. Everything was done for me. And I was so marvelously ignorant and self-centered! I mean, there I was in high school during World War II, but I have almost no recollection of the war. Here was this madman killing half of Europe, and the only thing I remember are the Navy League dances in Philadelphia. A bunch of us would go in and dance with the guys who were about to be shipped off. It was great fun. We'd take the train in to the city, or sometimes they'd even have cars that came out to get us. We felt very select."

The next morning I woke before dawn. The stairs creaked loudly as I went downstairs, stopping at the front windows to look at the eastern sky, which was crimson and purple and orange.

The cat's body had stiffened overnight, though not as much as I had imagined it would. I went out to a corner of the yard behind the mock-Tudor playhouse my father had built once for Sharon, and dug quickly through the wet grass, laying Poe at the bottom of a hole about two feet deep. I didn't like the way he looked, just lying there, and so I draped over him the ratty towel from the hospital where my father once worked, and filled in the hole. The shades were drawn in my mother's room. I imagined her dancing with young sailors forty years ago, flirtatiously smiling as she jitterbugged; she then heading back to her family's house to sleep it off, and they to fight in Europe.

A car stopped on Bay Avenue in front of the house, and my sister and Fred La Plante got out. They hugged each other, then kissed briefly, standing on the sidewalk. When they separated, their bodies peeled away from each other slowly, as if glued. My sister stood watching as Fred got in his car and drove off, then rubbed her eyes and headed across the front lawn, stumbling a little. I waited until she disappeared, then I tamped the dirt down flat and sat back to watch the sun come up.

X

Richard Butler
Dies at 60

Who were you?

You were always there in the background—alive, yes, but as utterly taken for granted by me as a lamp, a fire escape, a backstop behind home plate. You were a leather belt, stress-veined and narrow, below the newspaper, and half-lens glasses peering over the top. You were coffee grimly sipped in the next room. You were the referee's whistle.

Your son, my friend Chip Butler, hated the crusts of bread. They'd sit on his plate like jumbled Roman numerals. "You know I can't eat those," Chip said to me. He had a way of crossing his arms and leaning back from the situation, like a teacher. "I can't eat them cause I got wheat germ. It's a disease."

I was impressed, but Mrs. Butler at the sink laughed helplessly, said "Come on, Chip, not *this* again."

"I break out in hives."

"Chip."

"And have to go grunty."

This pleasing word, Chip's invention, was our signal for hysterical fun. We were seven, maybe eight. *Grunty grunty grunty let's all go grah—* Then that voice would come in from the next room: "Chipper? That's about enough of that." When Mr. Butler said something, it stuck. Those crusts went down.

Chip Butler and I were Best Friends. I was something of a mama's boy at heart, but Chip outdid me, happily for me. He was pale, husky, and heavy-assed; he had long, dark eyelashes and a hint of a lisp. In our football games Chip was always center, and I was always quarterback, calling plays in the huddle: Nathan, you square out right, Greg, go long left, Chip, you center. You hike. FIFTY-TWO, SIXTY-NINE RED OH ONE! I would bark meaningless numbers down the line, squatting over hiker Chip. At one point he took to wearing a towel tucked in the back of his pants, like a pro center. But in the pile-ups he would giggle and squirm, he and Bart Susskind. They would jump up laughing and chase each other with the football. "Homos!" the rest of us yelled. We were very serious about football. When Chip ran, his arms pumped furiously, his head bobbed from side to side, and yet his feet barely left the ground; the effect was of someone running on tiptoes through deep sand.

An old photograph I've taken out today shows Chip and me arm in arm, our backyard, circa 1961. Kindergarten. That elm tree no longer stands; the car is scrap somewhere; a different dog loiters and woofs over the grave of his predecessor. In the picture it is summer. Chip and I are smiling inanely. Both of us wear khaki shorts. Our bellies and heads are tremendous, our limbs puny. Chip's face features the pointy nose that won him the name Pinocchio, and his bellybutton thumbs his blue shirt like a person trying to reach out. From my pocket hangs a rope of red licorice. Our faces glow with chocolate.

Crew cuts for kids are out these days. But in our licorice years

Chip and I were fuzzy, cranially velvetized, and eminently touchable. Childless couples younger than our parents would rub our heads like crystal balls, smiling into their futures. Chip was, in fact, a bit too popular with grownups. In first grade he was chosen to recite some patriotic ditty he himself had written for Memorial Day at Wharf Hill School. The podium was a red, white, and blue mastless schooner—our town having been in its heyday a colonial port—and Chip stood high on deck in his maroon jacket and bow tie, gesturing like a mayor, his chin jauntily raised. Though I was his best friend, I wanted to punch that chin. "What My Country Means to Me," he began, as we sat squirming in folding chairs, all six hundred of us waving our miniature flags. I closed my eyes and ears.

Later that summer, Mr. Butler bought a fat black dog and named it Speaker. By September Chip and I were raking leaves in the Butlers' small backyard and lofting the puppy into the heaped piles, to see if maybe he could fly. From the living room came the voice: "That's enough of that, Chipper. How about if I throw *you* in the leaves?" The spoiler of fun.

Whirl of seasons! Politicians were assassinated, the newspapers I delivered told of a distant war, hurricanes and snowstorms pummeled our town and school was canceled, Chip and I waxing runners on our sleds; his Yankee Clipper against my Flexible Flyer. Summer again, and the Red Sox losing the World Series; Speaker died that very afternoon, hit by a newspaper truck—Chip calling to tell me just as George Scott was mightily striking out to end Game Seven. I lost fifty cents to Chris Raskin in that series, and when he came to collect, I called Chip for help, but he was busy; I paid. What Chip was busy with, it turned out, was another shameful slogan for another school contest. The theme was Obedience Week. My entry, "Stash the Trash!" didn't place, which was fine with me. Chip won with "Don't Be Bashful, Don't Be Bold, Always Do As You Are Told," which made him once again the darling of parents and teachers. For the rest of us, he became a target. I found a pretext—a trumped-up quarrel over Midget Weinstein's raincoat, which Chip had borrowed—and started the only fight I ever clearly won. We were coming home from school. Seeing me step out of the bushes onto the sidewalk in front of him, Chip put down his book bag and stood waiting. His resignation filled me with rage. "Why'd you steal Midget's coat?" I said bluntly. Moving forward, I punched awkwardly, once only, catching Chip high on the cheek. There was no resistance. Chip put his hand to his face and stared beyond me toward the mildly stinking cove at the bottom of our hill. "Nice punch, Toby," he said, his habitual lisp deepening into a sniffle. "Nice punch." Carefully he picked up his bag and shuffled off. Midget Weinstein came out of the bushes, laughing. "What a pussy," he said.

The next day my Little League team played Chip's, and Chip had a real honest-to-God shiner, his face yellow and blue and even green around the left eye. I was overjoyed at having produced these colors. As luck would have it, I was a first baseman, and Chip was the first base coach for the other team. We remade our friendship between pitches. Chip wore his eye like a badge; I was glad to have conferred it. "What did your dad say?" I asked. "He laughed," Chip said. "He told me I fight like grunty."

Mr. Butler was a junior high school principal, and belonged to just about every organization our town provided: Board of Education, Town Council, VFW, Knights of Columbus, Rotary. In addition, he was a licensed football referee. "Jeez, old Dick Butler can still haul it up and down the old gridiron, can't he," my own father said as we sat in the stands near the fifty-yard line, watching the high school team win. "Good for him." My father was only seven or eight years younger than Mr. Butler but spoke of him as if referring to an old man. We watched as guards pulled out on a sweep, and Mr. Butler followed on nimble legs made comical by the large, hard belly they supported. Behind us the high school booster club cheered steamily, breath sweet with memory and rum. *'Attababy, Admirals!* Those men, like Mr. Butler, had lived their whole lives in our town. My father, who belonged to no clubs, had come to the town as a grown man. In the late 1960s Mr. Butler was everything my slim father wasn't: his narrow ties and my father's bright, thick ones; his Oldsmobile and my father's Firebird; his crew cut and my father's shaggy sideburns; his love of town politics and my father's ironic disconcern; his grimness and my father's ease. My father was a good surgeon, and Mr. Butler a good educator; they could respect one another for this even if they never said nine words to each other, which I believe they never did. Beyond this, they were both old football players— my father a quarterback and Mr. Butler, surely, a lineman.

One season the Admirals were pressing for a state championship. They were winning by forty, fifty points a game. One wet Saturday in November, though, the team couldn't get untracked. Mud clogged the field. The ball squirted and slid out of players' hands like the maligned babies of bad jokes popular at that time among our crowd. Twice the would-be state champs crossed into the end zone; twice a drenched jubilation bubbled under the ponchos and umbrellas; but each time the unpiling of players revealed a sodden yellow flag. Mr. Butler, who was chief umpire that day, signaled the penalties. "Aw, go home, ya bum," a man behind us yelled, balling up a Styrofoam cup and hurling it toward the field. Sneezing, my father left at halftime, the Admirals down 6 to 3 and Butler a goat. "Too much excitement for your old man," my father said. "Tell me the details later."

In the second half a door opened in the citadels of cumulus above, and sunlight rafted through in beams. Rain ceased as if called back by parents, and the team answered with touchdowns. The drunks behind us furled their umbrellas, bellowing, "We're Number One!" Cheerleaders flashed soggy pompoms, the band milled against the fence, hoisting its tubas, and with a final touchdown making it 39 to 6, the announcer blurted over the PA system, "HEY, BUTLER, WHY DONTCHA THROW YER FLAG NOW, HUH?" Just then Mr. Butler slipped and fell in the muck. He got up quickly, but in the general delirium could be heard several dozen robust chuckles.

Poor Chip! To see his father dragged through such public mire! We hooted and howled. Chip had a portable cassette player, which he kept shoved to his ear, drowning us out with Blood Sweat and Tears and Stevie Wonder. This was 1967 or '68. Our country was fighting a war, and we were all but oblivious. I suppose eighteen-year-olds were busy signing up or chasing deferments, but we didn't know any eighteen-year-olds. Lenny Harmon, whose father would one day hang himself in the basement; Muss Hapsburg, the future driving instructor—they were our heroes, and they were still in high school. High school football players to us were men.

Though I had blackened Chip's eye and could have done it again, he was far from defenseless. He grew to be witty in a quick, sloganeering way, always a joke in the margin of every conversation. He outgrew the lisp, or modified it; laughing, he would suck on a small fund of liquid kept behind his front teeth, as if each joke were a fruity treat. And he came into possession of the Cave.

It was the era of home improvements, our neighborhood invaded by patios and tennis courts. The Butlers disposed of excess capital by extending their living room and adding a screened-in porch. Then they redid the basement and handed it over to Chip, who named it the Cave. The Cave was a subterranean fantasy chamber, with narrow windows high on the walls opening like gills to pale window-well light. A door leading to a small laundry room was the only concession made to the world of adults.

The place was boastfully indestructible. Chip crammed it, in his orderly way, with artifacts of the age. You entered through a spectral mane of plastic love beads hanging in the doorway, opposite posters of Jimi Hendrix and Carl Yastrzemski, of Abe Lincoln smoking a joint, of blue Earth seen from footprinted Moon. Leather peace signs dangled; incense smoldered. In the corners were two bean bag chairs sleeved in American flags, singed brown randomly where they'd sat too long against the electric radiator. One day as we were sitting around, Mr. Butler came down, took one look, and removed them without a word.

The Cave made Chip very popular among our crowd. We coveted darkness. Black lights replaced fluorescent and were in turn jettisoned for strobe, the small windows sheeted over with tin foil. In the epileptic light we danced wildly, windmilling our arms. Chip learned to juggle, syncopating the music with flying lemons. Gone were our road-racing loop and toy soldiers, replaced by a set of drums and then keyboards, Chip becoming a musician. Eventually a group was formed; I was not part of it. All I could do was sing a little. Laughing, Chip handed me a rattle to shake—a plastic egg in hemispheres of pink and white. It looked like something he had teethed on.

No longer were we Best Friends; no longer was he permanent hiker and blocker in our games. He did things to provoke me, like getting tickets to sold-out wrestling matches—thanks to Mr. Butler's infinite connections—and then selling them to me at double price, while giving them to Petie Mallon for nothing. Chip and Petie developed a whole private language I couldn't decipher. One afternoon a foul-smelling keg of beer surfaced in the coveside muck behind Petie's. We ran down toward this treasure, me leading the way. "Orffensneeber!" Petie laughed, and Chip answered, "Snorff!" They stopped ten feet behind me, Petie wiping his glasses with his shirt, as was his maddening habit. "All right, you guys," I said. "Cut the crap." I felt very stupid standing there, hands on hips, but found no alternative. And Chip answered, pointing, always pointing, "Alls we said's there seems to be a few large, wingy insects in the vicinity of the object. . . ."

But by then I was already stung. Chip and Petie ran for the house, and I chased them, pursued by the summer's last, sad bees. Locked inside the house, Chip and Petie pressed *Mad* magazine covers against all the windows as I stalked the grounds, furious, looking for entry. The impish grin of Alfred E. Newman taunted me at every turn. Bellowing, I bullied the garbage cans for a while, but they were the new plastic kind and resilient beyond my power to destroy, so I left. The Butlers' garbage cans were also on the street as I passed, good old aluminum and plenty bangable, but there was Mr. Butler in the front yard, pruning the cherry tree. He waved with his clippers. "Hello, Toby. Where's Chipper?"

Frying his ass in hell, sir.

Friendships, like fortunes and cloud banks, shift; Chip and I achieved a new balance struck more by diminished commitment than by anything else. The Butlers' phone number failed somehow to make one of our new lists. I became just one of a shifting clan, some of them girls now, who bunched like purblind reptiles in the dark Cave while Mr. and Mrs. Butler, a mere two feet above, must have sat there feeling their house vibrate and wondering just what they had created. We danced in the dark, someone banged a jumbled chord on the keyboards, doors opened and closed; then it was ninth grade, and Chip and I went to different high schools. Friends were shuffled like playing cards. The snapshots were tucked to sleep in Mom's cookbooks out in our kitchen.

Now I'm sitting in that same kitchen with those same cookbooks, a newspaper, my mother's mail. It has been almost five years since Dad has lived here. He has built himself a new house and a new life in a town fifteen miles up the coast, and he and Mom never see each other anymore. Still, letters addressed to him occasionally arrive here; Mom puts them in a big wicker basket and waits for one of us to bring them to him. Since we visit him infrequently, this pile can get pretty big.

I didn't see much of Mr. Butler after Chip and I drifted apart. Chip himself I would see on a summer afternoon, wheeling around the corner at Clover Hill and Bay in a car with flames and dragons very neatly decaled on the door. Typical Chip. He'd wave, leaning into the corner, looking over his mirror glasses. While in college we saw each other maybe twice a year; I remember him telling me about a summer and fall he spent working as a janitor at our old grade school, taking time off from the university, where he had become a music major. The kids at school would overturn his trash cans and unplug the ice cream machine, leaving him sockets of goo. Chip shook his head, telling me about it. I noticed his juicy chuckle had dried up. I tried to imagine him as a janitor and was surprised to find that I could.

I am taking out the snapshot again, two buddies, Richard Butler, Jr.; Toby Slattery, August 1961. Neither child has the look of one who is reading the future, that gauntness around the eyes that some kids have. The car in the background dates us; it is an old Checker my father bought from a cab company in 1959. My mother liked the jump seats. I swear I can't remember that lasso of red licorice dangling from my pocket; I've always hated the stuff. Chip Butler, Chipper, Chip off the old block—no one ever called him anything else. I place the snapshot back on today's newspaper, spread over the kitchen table, our small-town newspaper whose banner headline reads, "Richard Butler Dies at 60."

It's a quarter-mile from our house to the basketball courts at the new school. Six hundred dribbles of a Spalding basketball at walking pace gets you there. Today I do it at a trot.

He died at sea, which was fitting for a navy man. When I came home today for the first time in a year, the story was being told. My parents' old friend, Jack Cousins, who still visits my mother, was standing in the driveway talking with Mom when I pulled in. Jack had been with Mr. Butler, in a rented boat out in the Sound, a bunch of merchants, politicians, and sons of the city out bluefishing and enjoying themselves. The second morning Chip's father just wouldn't wake up. They found him stretched peacefully in bed, hands clasped over his stomach. "Now there was a solid one," Jack said to me.

171

"Since ninth grade I knew the guy, and you know, you'll never find a better one. Christ, the way Dickie Butler played football. Let me tell you, brother—" Jack always calls me brother, though he's older than my father—"there'll be some wet eyes around town tonight. . . ."

I take foul shots. The rim droops like a pouting lip; too many kids hanging from it. Slam-dunking, that's the rage these days.

A silver Camaro eases to the curb; it is, of course, Chip Butler. I haven't seen him in three years, since we were in college. He's grown a beard, as have I. I watch him get out of the car; it's something he's done ten thousand times, a reflex action that implies, somehow, that nothing ever changes. He sees me; we shake hands; I hold on. "You heard," he says.

"Chip. I'm so sorry."

Chip nods. He twirls his basketball on his middle finger, and I bounce mine, once, twice. "You know Stopazzi is married," he says.

"My God. Who took him?"

"Susskind, too. To a nurse. He's in med school."

"Yeah," I say. "Old Bart. Bart the fart."

Chip laughs, sort of. "You know, Toby, my mother retired last month when Dad retired. Thirty-one years. They were going to travel."

"Jesus Chip, I'm so sorry . . ."

Lay-ups, foul shots. A kid is banging a tennis ball against the tremendous brick face of the school. Chip shoots from the top of the key, and the ball hits high on the backboard; the whole thing jingles, loose. "Listen Chip," I say. "Wanna play some? Game of horse or something?"

"What? No. I don't think so. I'm still kinda dazed."

I feel clumsy around death. I don't know what to say. I'm remembering a snapshot Chip once showed me of his father as a young man. Mr. Butler was in his navy uniform; it was just before World War II, about 1940, which would have made him twenty. That frightening jaw, cleft chin promising muscular words and deeds, that un-

172

challengeable posture, and those eyes—God, those eyes. Those eyes were fixed on war clouds and on the golden spaces in between where one might slip through, to a second life.

I leap high and roll the basketball into the hoop, fingers brushing the rim. The ball sways in the rusty grasp of the net. I'm thinking of a stern man tamed, though never fully, by the life he built around himself: by the quiet of his neighborhood and the underpopulation of his family, by the statue of a stable boy rooted in the front yard, gloved hand advancing eagerly to greet him with a ring as he walked the thirty-odd flagstones neatly chickleted from drive to door; yes, tamed even by the additions to his house—the brick-red aluminum siding, the rubberized fence left over from the days of Speaker, the extended living room, the new porch that no one ever used. . . .

"I was sorry to hear about your parents, Tobe," Chip says now. "I always thought, I don't know, they'd be the last to go."

"Yeah, well. Thanks, Chip."

And finally you were tamed by your son. By his refusal to eat crusts and to fight, by his sense of humor indirect and slick, by his music, his demand for gadgets that you always granted, his fussiness over hair, his willingness eternally to hike and block, though poorly—his gentleness. You were that way, too. "We never hung out at my house much, did we, Chip?" I say.

"Nope. Always the Cave. The Cave was the place."

Sunset creeps up. Chip's basketball rolls in among the dark trees, and we leave it there. Back there in the shadows is the grave of a cat that Chip and I buried a dozen years ago, before the school was built—a cat we found in the dirt on the side of Clover Hill, Chip's street, and loaded on his go-cart under a blanket, humming dirges as we slowly proceeded. I wonder if Chip is thinking about this right now.

Above us the titanic spotlights begin to hum. Someone somewhere has pulled a switch. I fade into the corner and sink a long jumper, riddling the net. "Nice shot, Tobe," says Chip. *Nice shot.* I resist the urge to run into his arms. "I never was any good at this game," he says, "but neither were you. What happened?"

The ball is a scarred planet encircled by Chip's pale ex-janitor's hands. We peer at each other from behind our absurd beards, which hide nothing. He still looks like Pinocchio, and God knows what I still look like. If either of us says "grunty" right now, I'm sure we'll both dissolve laughing. But neither does. There is a dazed look on Chip's face—and yet still a hint of the old Chipper-Speaker smile, satisfied and prim: as when, at the end of one of our Battles of the Bulge, the Cave floor littered with the plastic corpses of armies green and brown, he would reach behind an ashtray or a stereo speaker, brandish the last unharmed soldier, and say, "Bang!"

XI

Punch Lines

"So, know any good cockamamie jokes?" Nate says over the handshake.

"Not offhand," I say. When we're both back in town, we tend to run into each other at bookstores and delis. But this time it's a tacky gift shop, where I'm looking for an ashtray my mother wants for her birthday, with cats on it.

"Well, how about this one? Whaddya call a man with no arms and legs you throw in the water?"

"Bob," I say. I don't remember jokes, only answers.

Nate's teeth as he laughs look more even than I remember. Maybe they've been filed down for his part as someone's daughter's boyfriend. His first role was Count Dracula; we were ten, and he did it without fake fangs. Nowadays he's doing a toothpaste commercial— all smiles and pectorals for three seconds on the beach. He's also had bit parts in soap operas. "Say," he says now, piping upward into an Irish tenor and turning to the salesgirl who has been waiting patiently behind the counter. "Didja ever heer the one aboat the fella havin' no arms and no legs who's lyin' oatside yer door? Now what might they be callin' 'im?"

The salesgirl gives us a panicked look. "Matt!" I say to help her out. Nate slaps my shoulder. He throws his head back, laughing in a way he's picked up in the city, mouth open wide.

"I'm sorry," the girl says. "I understand very little." She fumbles with a pink ribbon.

"You one a them damn furriners or somethin'?"

"I am a Russian," she says, "from Minsk."

"Oh." Nate has never quite known when to stop a joke, and when he realizes suddenly that he's been rude, he shuts up. All his life he's done voices: Jewish dentists, Texas oil kings, a Mexican bureaucrat with peptic ulcers. But now he plays himself—a semiemployed actor with a big grin and nervous fingers, home from New York on a visit. He looks down at his hands. The Russian girl pushes a package across the glass counter to him.

Today is Nathan's parents' anniversary. "You want a good joke," he tells me, "come on over for dinner tonight." He winks at me. Ten years ago I was Nate's straight man, and I feel swept up in the role once more as Nate's arm comes around me, pushing me toward the door, his voice graveling "Spasibo!" over our shoulders to the girl from Minsk.

Some people you remember for what they say, others for how they say it. Nate's mother, Eleanor, on the third hand, always had a way of *not* saying something. For instance: I'm fourteen or fifteen, Nate's not home, Mrs. Holover is telling me about relatives in New Jersey. "My niece Rebecca," she says. "Now, there's a girl simply too romantic for her era, Toby. Too romantic." Over the table she leans at me, close up, holding her cigarette out to the side so that I don't have to breathe it. She is walleyed, and cocks her head to look at the door, as if about to confide some great secret, while her other eye sweeps my face, side to side, like a searchlight.

She was trained as a lawyer, but by the time I knew her, she was always at home. I see her sitting in a chaos of cosmetics, head trembling in the glare of moonish vanity bulbs as she aims at her lips with a scarlet lipstick. Her aim is poor. "Albert?" she calls to her husband, saying it something like "halibut" without the *H*. "Alibut, can you hear me? I can't stand this mirror; it's like I'm being interrogated!" I hear her humming "Moonlight Serenade" very erratically down the amber hallways of the mansion, and shrieking out the windows at pigeons in the ivy, "A person cahn't concentrate in here with all that terrible googling! It's like some terrible, I don't know— some zoo!" What she had to concentrate on, I don't know.

Tonight Nate meets me outside in the circle drive. I walk over from my mother's house six streets away, and Nate is waiting for me on the fender of Eleanor's battered Caddie. The house spreads its wings over us—the biggest house in town. "Prepare to time warp," Nate says. "Yes, ladies and gentlemen, watch ten years disappear over the dinner table." He calls out like a circus barker. "Watch the Holovers turn their son back into a fifteen-year-old!"

Nate can be pretty cruel in dealing with his parents. He'll put on his Brooklyn-gas-station-attendant voice and say something like this: *My mother's experience with legal briefs was real brief. Found out pretty quick she'd rather try a case of gin than a case in court.* "And now Simmie's here, too," he says, rolling his eyes. Simmie is his older sister, who lives in Texas with her husband, Ted, a geologist for an oil company.

"I bet you can handle it," I say.

"You ever listen to my mother, Toby? It gets worse and worse. Listen to her trying to follow a conversation sometime. She gets from A to B all right, maybe even B to C. But that's it. Everyone else goes on and where's she? Back at A. It's like her head's inside a washing machine."

"I don't think it's that bad."

Nate just snorts. "And tonight's Friday. We'll be interrupting her holy drunk."

The kitchen is the same pale green. Mrs. Holover is at the counter, cutting little balls out of honeydew melons.

Nathan slams the door. "Good Shabbas!" he shouts.

"Go away. You're not welcome here. Hello, Toby. *You're* welcome, I'm sure." *Shoo-ah*, she says it.

"Hi, Mrs. Holover." I go over and kiss the wrinkled cheek she offers me. "Sorry we're late."

"You're not late. He's late." She won't look at Nate. "It was supposed to be a cookout. Now look at those steaks." I look at them. Nate picks one up and hefts it. "Nothing wrong with this," he says, imitating Lorne Greene. "Finest specimen American *bo*-vine." He tosses the steak up and catches it.

"Stop it, Tanny! Just stop!"

Up goes the steak, closer to the ceiling, brushing it.

"Tanny!" Mrs. Holover waves the melon knife at Nathan. "I'm sorry, Toby," she says to me. "But how I can ever get a meal together with him around, I have no idea."

"I'm sure it'll come out okay," I say.

Nate makes a noise. He has poured a glass of burgundy and is staring over it, now through it, at Eleanor. "Mother, I can tell this is going to be a truly Dionysian spectacle, this little meal of yours. Let's praise every grape ever to grapen in this most holy of holy drunks."

"Whaddya talking about?" Mrs. H looks suddenly frail. Nate takes my arm and leads me from the kitchen into the bewildering labyrinth of parlor and portraiture that leads to the front of the house.

"Elaborate speech just aint my mother's strong point," he says. His eyes are lit with a remorseless humor. "Let's go find her better half."

Upstairs, Nate's father watches a baseball game. Stretched out in bed, blankets back, he keeps gently waving the remote control at the TV. But the channel doesn't change. With his white hair long and combed back over his ears, with his half-lensed spectacles and deeply lined face, Mr. Holover looks oddly historical. He is George Washington in a silk bathrobe whereupon dragons breathe bright fire. When we were kids, we had great fun with his name—Halibut Haulover, Haul Over, Mister, and so on. Five years ago he represented my mother in my parents' divorce.

"Toby," he says. "So nice to see you!" He shakes my hand without getting up.

"Nice to see you too, Mr. Holover," I say.

"What happened to the cookout, Tanny? I thought we were having a cookout."

"I'm putting the coals on right now, Dad."

"But it's too late. It must be what, eight, nine o'clock?" Mr. H is a very big lawyer in town, but in the privacy of his own home, he indulges in a luxurious helplessness. He wheezes and whines.

Nate, for his part, brays like a donkey. "You couldn't've put the coals on yourself?"

"Simmie wouldn't let me."

"Whaddya mean she wouldn't let you? Who runs this place anyway?"

"Look, I don't want to argue." Mr. Holover looks at me apologetically. "Listen, Tanny, why don't you go down and keep an eye on your mother. She isn't capable." He looks at the TV for a moment, as an argument begins to develop between the manager and an umpire. "You see, Toby, she's upset today. It's a year ago today Edwin enlisted."

Edwin Sassler is a cousin, six years younger than Nate and I, who lived with the Holovers after his parents were killed in a terrible car accident. I don't think of him much because he wasn't living there yet when Nate and I were kids. As soon as he turned eighteen, he joined the navy; the Holovers wanted to send him to college. "So the whole evening's a disaster, Toby," Nate's father says forlornly.

"Look Dad." Nate is one of those people who can crook his index finger at the last knuckle. "I'm going to start the coals now. You just lie here, okay?"

"I'm not even hungry," Mr. H says. He waves the remote control at us. On TV the manager is now screaming at the ump, kicking dirt at him. Sometimes baseball is irrecoverably absurd. You keep waiting for the players to throw down their little gloves and bats and start bowing.

We stand there watching the manager kick dirt.

"Hey Dad," Nate says.

"What."

"Listen to this one. Whaddya call a man with no arms and no legs you nail to the wall."

"What's this now, a joke?"

"Yeah Dad. It's a joke."

Mr. H frowns. I say, "Art."

"How's that?" He looks up at Nate, at me, at Nate again. "I'm confused," he says.

"Forget it, Dad." Nate throws his hands out in front of him, then turns and walks out. "Just forget it," he calls back. "Come on," he says to me. "We got a cookout to do."

Outside the sky, chowdery all afternoon, flicks drops of rain. Nate soaks the coals in lighter fluid. As soon as the flame begins to die down, he pours on more lighter. "I ever tell you about the *real* Albert Holover?" Nate rubs his chin. "You'd never know it, but he's a shrewd sonofabitch, that man."

"Come on," I say. "I know your father."

"Oh, yeah? You ever hear him in court? Listen. It's a custody case, okay, and he's got some poor housewife and mother type on the stand." Nate imitates his father and a fatuous middle-aged woman. " 'So Mrs. Bellerman, your daughter is what, sixteen years old?'

'That's right.' 'And she's more or less attractive, Mrs. Bellerman?' 'Sure.' 'She has a normal social life?' 'Sure. I mean she goes out now and then.' 'I see. Is she engaged to be married, your daughter?' 'Who gets engaged at sixteen?' 'She have a steady boyfriend then?' 'Nothing special. No one in particular.' 'I see. In other words, she sleeps around.' "

"Objection!" I raise my hand.

" 'All right,' " Nate says, " 'I retract the question, Your Honor. Now just one more thing, Mrs. Bellerman. Your daughter, is she on the pill?' 'Of course not!' 'I see. In other words, it's all right with you, your daughter sleeps around unprotected.' "

"Jesus Christ." This blows me away.

"Yup," Nate says, becoming himself again. "The man's a real shark."

I try to imagine my father on the stand, being questioned by Mr. Holover. During the divorce proceedings five years ago, my mother would come home outraged by how *friendly* my father was trying to seem to everyone. To her, the fact that he had left her for another woman meant he had forfeited the right to present himself as a nice guy. Apparently Mr. Holover agreed. "Nathan's father," I remember her saying with satisfaction, "is not letting old Daniel get away with anything."

For his part, my father hinted to me once or twice that Mr. Holover had given him a hard time in court. I didn't want to hear about it then. But now I am imagining my father on the stand, frowning and squirming and experiencing mounting outrage as Mr. Holover pursues a line of questioning similar to the one Nate has just demonstrated.

I start to laugh. Nate laughs, too, and squirts more lighter fluid on the coals.

If anyone had been willing to bet me a hundred dollars, when Nate and I were thirteen and best friends, that in ten years it would be my parents and not the Holovers who'd be divorced, I'd have sold my ham radio and *Playboy* magazines instantly to raise some cash.

I'd never seen a family fight the way the Holovers did. What passed for an argument in my family was me forgetting to take out the garbage, then being quietly reproached by my father and going up to sulk in my room. In Nate's family, open warfare was a way of life. The best thing about having the biggest house in town, Nate used to say, was that you could always put at least four rooms between yourself and anyone else.

None of the Holovers seemed to care about my being there during their fights—in fact, sometimes they needed and used me as a kind of moral reference point ("Toby, do people in your family talk like that to each other?"). It was bewildering, the way things escalated among them. For instance: Nate and I are thirteen, Simmie sixteen, and I've come in the back door just as a fight between Simmie and Mrs. Holover is heating up over how late Simmie can stay out. "Mother," Simmie is yelling, "I can't be*lieve* you expect me back at eleven. You don't have *one ounce of trust* in you, do you?!"

And Mrs. H, her nasal but friendly voice rising, "It's not you; it's those people you go around with—they're just not appropriate!"

"Ap*pro*priate! Are they clothing? Are they napkins? Mother, you go straight to hell with your 'appropriate'!"

Enter Mr. Holover and Nate, bounding into the kitchen like firemen. "Simmie," Mr. Holover indignantly wheezes, "did I raise my daughter to speak to her mother that way? You're vulgar!" This sets off several explosions: Simmie proclaiming it's her mother who's vulgar ("Did you ever *look* at her lipstick? How can you kiss that, Daddy?"); Nate observing that Simmie's friends actually have great manners—they wipe off all their joints and needles before passing them along; Simmie jabbing her finger in Nate's chest and yelling, *"Stay the fuck out of my life, dipshit!"*; Mr. Holover turning red and saying how much it hurts him to hear Simmie sounding like a tramp;

Simmie cursing him as Mrs. Holover, belatedly reading in her husband's first words some great insult, turns her eye on him and says, "Whaddya mean *your* daughter, you raising *your* daughter?" Nate gives me the nod, and we escape out the back door.

Outside we head toward my house. Nate drags his feet through the gravel in the drive, as if to make a statement. He lights up a Marlboro and blows the smoke back over his shoulder. A door slams shut, and Simmie roars out of the garage in her mother's car, giving Nate the finger as she passes. Nate returns the favor and then takes most of the ten minutes between his house and mine to remind me how lucky I am to have cool parents.

Nate had a happy arrangement with my parents. Our house was a haven for refugees from screwed-up families, and of all our friends who ate dinner and slept over on a regular basis, Nate Holover was my parents' favorite. They loved him because he made them laugh, and he in turn loved them for laughing. His own parents thought his stories and voices were silly. But my parents took humor seriously. "That Nate Holover," my father would say from time to time. "Whatever his shortcomings, he sure has a gift for comedy." (The shortcomings were lousy grades, cigarettes, swearing, and daily incarceration in the principal's office.) With me Nate liked to play the tough guy. But in the stories he told my parents, he was always a helpless victim, overwhelmed by awkwardness and allergies, plagued by bullies, ignored by girls, tormented by rabbis and by sadistic counselors at any of the half-dozen camps his parents had sent him to over the years.

My parents' favorite Nathan Holover story—one they got him to tell over and over—was a tale of blighted romance. It had to do with a beautiful girl Nate had been hopelessly in love with in the fifth grade. He was invisible to her, he told my parents, and yet he felt compelled to talk to her. One day at lunch he was alone in the classroom, looking for a sandwich of his that Stevie Stopazzi had crushed into a little ball. The girl came in.

Already my parents are grinning. "Now it's up to me," Nate says, leaning into the story. "I start to open my mouth, but just then this huge sneeze comes up inside me—my allergies. My mouth goes wide open. She must be thinking I'm having some kinda heart attack. I put one finger to my nose while meanwhile my other hand is cruising around in my pocket for a Kleenex. I figure I'll take out the Kleenex, I'll sneeze into it, say excuse me, and begin again. Right?"

"Right," says my father, laughing.

"But no. I already used my hundred Kleenexes for the day. There's nothing in my pocket, and now the sneeze won't wait another second. So I just turn my head to the side, like my mother taught me, and let 'er rip. But now this humungous strand of mucus comes flying out of my nose. Without thinking I just sweep my hand across and catch it, the whole spaghetti. Now there it is, in my fist. I have to do something with it. What? I shove it inside my pocket and leave it there. Maybe she didn't notice. That's my only hope." Nate pauses, with perfect effect. "So I look up." He looks up at my parents, who lean toward him. "And there she is; she's just standing there staring at me and shaking her head. She's completely speechless."

My parents are beside themselves. My father is laughing so hard, he has to rub his eyes. "You've got a calling, Nate," he says. "No doubt about it."

Afterward, Nate and I go outside and cruise the neighborhood. We get some greaser to buy cheap wine for us at the liquor store, and head for a spot on Clements Avenue outside the house of Carol Ludtke, a girl we're both in love with. Nate is doing his tough guy act, hands in the pockets of his bell-bottomed jeans, feet shuffling, eyes slit to peer through the smoke of a cigarette wedged between his tight lips. I'm doing my best to follow suit. Clements Avenue is the unofficial boundary between our neighborhood and a tougher one closer to town; years later, in another comic monologue, Nate will claim that when we reached the end of Clements Avenue, we turned meek, throwing our cigarettes away and keeping our mouths closed.

We stop on the sidewalk under Carol Ludtke's window, which is dark. Nate knows it is her window because he has been inside the house once with his parents, who, like my parents, are friends of the Ludtkes. Our plan is to call Carol out and share a cigarette and the last half of our bottle of wine with her. She is a pretty girl, but not so beautiful that she will refuse us. We crouch behind the hedges. "Hey Stella!" Nate calls up in a strangled, nasal voice. "Stella!" When I ask him why he's calling Carol Ludtke Stella, he looks at me as if I'm crippled. So I call out "Hey Stella," too.

A light goes on on the porch. We duck behind the hedges. Through their tangledness we can just see the door opening and Mrs. Ludtke leaning out. Shit. "Nathan?" she calls. "Nathan Holover? Is that you?"

"Shhh," Nate whispers. "Be cool."

"Nathan?" Mrs. Ludtke calls out through a cupped hand. "Carol isn't here. She's at Eileen Lucker's bowling party!" Silence. "Would you like to come in for a Pop-Tart and wait for her?"

As Nate has often said since then, it's tough to be tough where we came from.

The tablecloth hasn't been set down quite right; there must be two cloths, one atop the other, and the lower one has folds in it. Mrs. H pulls at the top cloth, but the folds merely roll and re-form, coiling like snakes around the center fruit bowl. She waves her hand at them, giving up. All the silver is laid out in the right places; the plates are down; the steaks are cooked. There's a tray of candied tangerine crescents sitting there like a stock of gooey moons.

"One, two, three, four, five," says Mrs. H, pointing to our places. *"Dîner est servi."*

"This is lovely, dear," says Mr. H. "Just lovely."

"And who would've ever believed it, that I could raise this up all by myself. Would you have believed it, Alibut?"

"It's lovely."

"That's what I'm saying to myself—who would've believed it?"

"Not me, Mommy, that's for sure." Simmie sits down. She is short and nervous. In grade school she was supposed to be the genius and Nate the dummy. They had special puzzles for her to play with. "My God, Mother," she says now. "You'd think it was the feast in *Tom Jones* instead of five simple hunks of dead cow thrown on a fire."

"Simmie," says Mr. Holover, "don't be vulgar."

"All I'm saying," says Mrs. H, "is there were setbacks."

"All right already," says Nate. "Can we eat?"

Mrs. H sighs. "I only wish Edwin was here. He used to say the blessing. Toby, don't people say a blessing in your family?"

"Okay, Mom." Nate flourishes his knife. "Rub a dub dub, here comes the grub, yea God! Now can I start?" He slices his steak open and peers into it, cautiously. He's always been picky about food. When he used to come to our house for lunch, he brought his own jar of Miracle Whip for sandwiches because he didn't like our Hellman's. I tell this story now.

"He doesn't take things seriously, Toby," says Mrs. H. "That's always been Tanny's problem."

"For once I agree with you, Mother," says Simmie. "Have you heard about Tanny's latest film, Toby? It's called *Preppies on Parade*. The love scenes are being shot at Bonwit Teller."

"Funny, Simmie," Nate says.

"It's not enough he prostitutes his own talents, Toby. Now he's going to prostitute a bogus ethnicity." Simmie tips a ragged smile at me and stares out with huge eyes from behind her glasses. She likes to shock people. I remember the time she blurted out, in a family discussion of prenatal care, *You know, it's bizarre to realize that when Tanny and I were conceived, you two were just screwing the hell out of each other.* "Next he'll probably be playing a Latin gigolo," she says now.

"Well I'll be sure to hire you as a technical advisor," Nate says.

Mr. Holover jumps into the conversation, skillfully maneuvering past his children toward me. "So, Toby, I understand you've just come back from out west."

"That's right," I say. "I was in New Mexico."

"Yeah," Nate says. "Toby was a ski bum, and guess what. He worked in a hotel owned by a nice Jewish guy."

"Did you speak Spanish down there, Toby?" Mrs. Holover asks.

"He was in *New* Mexico, Mother," says Simmie. "Not Mexico. *New* Mexico. It's a part of the United States."

"But many people do speak Spanish there," I say to Mrs. H.

"Very interesting," says Mr. Holover. "Very interesting." There is a moment's slack in the conversation, and again he takes it up by turning to me. "Say Toby, did you by any chance know the Llwellyn boy?"

"Sure. Tommy Llwellyn?"

"That's right. Did you know he was killed last month in a fire in his apartment?"

"No!"

"That's right. He fell asleep smoking. His family is suing the landlord through my firm. The apartment building didn't pass fire inspection, you see."

I think about Tommy Llwellyn. In sixth grade he beat me up. He shoved bubble gum in my ear. He sat on my chest and farted. It's surprising how hard it is to feel pity for someone who sat on your chest and farted, even when he dies. "We weren't friends," I say.

"He farted in Toby's face," Nate says.

"Tanny, really," Simmie scowls. "Must you always be so disgusting?"

"Anyway," I say. "It was my chest."

"Whose chest? What chest?" Mrs. H seems very far away, down there at the end of the table. The centerpiece—some ferns, half a dozen oranges, a bunch of grapes—seems to block her from all angles. "Whaddya talking about down theyah?"

"Don't bother, Mother. It's morbid." Simmie waves a fork. "So Toby—can you see Tanny as a preppy jock?"

"Simmie," Nate says, "you have no idea about anything, okay?"

"And did you know he's going to change his name?"

"Simmie. Why don't you stick to something you know, whatever that might be."

"Alibut. Alibut are they fighting again?"

"You're in the same room I am, dear."

Nate turns to me. "If Simmie ever listened to me, she might learn something about the real world."

"Oh, tell me about it, Tanny."

Nate talks to me, but he is really talking to Simmie. "You go in for an audition. Maybe it's a soap, maybe a teen movie from some director you don't particularly admire. Big deal—it's work. So you go in to read."

"You'd read for anything, Tanny," Simmie says.

Nate keeps talking straight at me. "So there you are in the elevator. You've got your hair razor-parted, your assertive jaw as assertive as ever, your zits uncovered just enough to look honest. You're no rookie, you've got your whole education behind you: theory, technique, regional theater, good reviews, all that crap. You're ready. And then the door slides open, and right there in the lobby are these half a dozen guys who look just like you—same jaw, chiseled features, dimples, hair, smile, everything."

"Everything," I say.

"Down to the underwear. It's like some demented gene-splicer has created a race of people just like you."

"He'd have to be demented," Simmie says.

"Pass the potatoes," says Mrs. Holover.

"So in you go anyway," Nate says, ignoring both his sister and his mother. "Some little faggot with a tape measure comes up and starts measuring your chest. He turns you around twice, tells you thank you very much, and before you know what happened, you're back out on Seventh Avenue."

"Will someone pass the potatoes?" Mrs. Holover says again. Her voice is urgent, but the potatoes are way out there in the center of the table, where I can't reach them.

"Listen, Tanny," Simmie says. "I'm just waiting for you to get serious, that's all. What're you going to do, wait on tables and act junk roles all your life?"

"Well what're you gonna do? Make babies and be supported by Ted so you can sit around reading Kierkegaard all day?"

"All right," says Mr. Holover, "you're embarrassing yourselves in front of everyone now. Both of you." He looks weary and bedraggled, like a man who's been walking all day against a gale wind. Simmie plays with her knife and fork, laying one over the other in a T, reversing them, biting a fingernail, rereversing them.

"Forget the potatoes then," Mrs. H says. "Act like I don't exist. I mean, why change now?" She talks to her glass of burgundy the way some people talk to pets, not expecting them to answer but believing that they hear. "But don't you go calling yourself a waiter. Not in my house you don't."

Dessert. We all sit there eating little melon balls. More wine is poured. The melon balls float in raspberry brandy. In the midst of this fragrant sweetness, Nate tells the story of a drunk he had to bounce out of the restaurant he works at in the city. All the Holovers know this story and like it. When the man stood up, Nate says, he was at least six-five. Raving, he started to strangle Nate, who was forced to knee him in the groin and flee to the kitchen to hide behind the Haitian cooks; they cursed and waved their spatulas when the drunk came roaring in after him. "And get this, Toby. A week later the guy dies. Falls out of a building. No kidding. And the cooks take all the credit."

"Tanny always could tell a story, couldn't he, Toby?" Mr. Holover says when Nate has finished.

"He used to have my parents in tears," I say.

"Really?" Mr. Holover is genuinely impressed. Then he shakes his head. "You'd think that would be a golden ticket for an actor, wouldn't you?"

"Look at this table, will you," says Mrs. H, as if seeing it for the first time. "One, two, three, four, five."

Nate and Simmie get up and begin clearing the dishes. Mr. Holover asks me what my parents are doing these days, and I explain how my father and his wife, Ginny, take vacations all over the world, and how when they do, my mother keeps an eye on the paper and hopes for earthquakes and typhoons in the exotic places they travel to. Mr. H frowns vaguely at this, but Simmie, coming in from the kitchen with a gift-wrapped box, laughs loudly. "What a scream, Toby," she says.

Now Nate and Simmie place two small gifts in front of their parents. "Mom," Simmie says. "Wake up. Daddy. It's your anniversary."

"So it is, so it is," says Mr. H. He unwraps a pair of cuff links, gold 3s, thirty-three years they've been married. At times like this his eyes, deeply green, seem to fill with a vision not entirely his own. "Thank you," he says. "It's lovely."

"Mother, you have to press the little button." Simmie helps her mother with the lighter Nate bought today in the mall. "No, now you're holding it upside down. It's made to ruin your lungs, not burn down your house."

Mrs. H lights up. "I only wish Edwin were here," she says. The cigarette trembles in her hand. "But everyone leaves me."

"He didn't leave you, Eleanor," Mr. Holover says. "He just joined the service. He's serving his country."

"You mean threatening Beirut," Simmie says.

Edwin, I remember now, is on an aircraft carrier in the Mediterranean. I try to picture him with a crew cut. He has big ears, and they must stick out.

"Can't we just leave politics out of this and finish our dessert?" Mr. Holover says.

Simmie balls up her napkin and throws it down. "You think

your dessert isn't political? You think it isn't political when we stock-pile thousands of tons of grain to keep prices up while people are starving? You think it's not political when huge multinationals, some of which you probably represent, are taking over family farms and forcing people out on the street? I don't see how you can swallow a mouthful without biting yourself, Daddy!"

Mr. Holover looks helplessly at Nate and me. "I'm just an actor," Nate says, in his Ratso Rizzo voice. "I don't know about all that stuff."

"Listen," says Simmie. "Edwin's a nice kid, but I wish he'd find something better to do than play enforcer for American capitalism in the Third World."

"How can you talk like that, Simmie?" Mr. Holover is pained. "Edwin's out there risking his life. Every day."

"Hardly, Daddy. He's on a huge ship ten miles offshore, polishing doorknobs and waiting for some megalomaniac in Washington to tell him to push a button."

"Simmie. These people are trained. They're specialists." Simmie starts to interrupt, but Mr. Holover raises his hand, and she stops. "Now—let's change the subject." He turns away from Simmie. "How's Claudette, Tanny?"

Claudette is an actress Nate has been going with for the last two years in New York. His parents don't want him marrying an actress, and before Nate can answer, Mr. Holover turns to me and says, "You're not in any hurry to get married, are you, Toby?"

"No hurry at all," I say.

"Of course you're not. You're being sensible. You can always wait. Tanny knows how I feel. Women are fertile forever these days. They take hormones."

Simmie slams her coffee cup on the table. Coffee flies everywhere. "Oh great, Daddy. Load your system with estrogen. Get cancer. You think I'm losing my breast for some idiotic man to prolong his bachelorhood, think again."

I busy myself with my napkin. Our thoughts sway like building blocks stacked high on each other.

It's Mrs. Holover who breaks the silence, calling from her end of the table. "You know what? Edwin made a decision, that's what he did, and I'm going to tell you what it was. He decided he'd rather risk fighting in a war than staying with this family." She takes a long drag on her cigarette, and shrugs into the silence that these words create. Then she drains her glass, refills it, and speaks to it. "So. Tell me. Anybody know any good cockamamie jokes?"

We sit there. There we sit.

"Sure," I say.

Everyone looks at me.

"Okay. What do you call a man with no arms and no legs you throw in a pile of leaves?"

I wait. The problem is, I'm always the one who answers. "We give up," Simmie says.

"Russell," I say. There: a joke and its answer together. And once upon a time, somewhere, it was funny.

Nathan says, "Do you get it, Dad?"

Mr. Holover is flustered. "You people. You cut people's arms and legs off, you nail them to the wall, you throw them in the leaves. I have a client who broke his neck jumping into a pile of leaves."

"Oh *Gawd*, Daddy." Simmie pushes back in her chair. "Come off it," she says. And I'm about to say, *So no one likes the only joke I ever told*, when Mrs. Holover is suddenly laughing, a loose, sliding laugh like a flock of hiccups. "Russell! Russell!" She calls the name as if it's Russell himself who told the joke. She loses herself inside the laugh, looking out at us with the walleyed stare that Nate, in an inherited version, has used to advantage playing evangelists, schizos and con men; she has one eye on him and the other on Simmie, as if after all it were possible, though infinitely tiring, to keep your children in sight all their lives. She blinks, and then her head goes down on the table.

"Eleanor," says Mr. Holover. *"Eleanor."*

"Oh Gawd, Mother." Simmie's voice is like a wrecking ball battering an old house.

"Well, well, well," Nate says, raising his glass. "Here's to Dionysus."

I push my chair back from the table. Mr. Holover saves me from not knowing what to do next. "Come on with me, Toby," he says. "I'll show you something." As Nate and Simmie converge on their mother, Mr. Holover takes me by the arm and leads me away from the table. We head off through the house, saying nothing. Mr. Holover has a habit of taking a long strand of his white hair and crooking it back over his ear. It seems an anachronism, like something a guitarist might do in a studio between numbers. But Mr. Holover is seventy.

"What are you planning on doing with yourself now, Toby?"

I explain I might try to get a job with a newspaper. Or I might go back to school. Mr. H nods. We arrive in the television room.

"And how is your mother?" he asks me.

"Fine," I say. "She just got back from a vacation in Maine, actually. She's working now as a legal secretary." Even as I say this, I remember that Mr. Holover helped my mother get this job. But he smiles as if it's news to him, good news. He puts a cassette into the VCR. I think about my mother, who lives alone with her cats and dog in our old big house. She talks about moving to a smaller place, but so far she hasn't. When people ask me how she is, I never know whether to just say "Fine," or to get into explanations.

Mr. Holover puts a hand on my shoulder and leans close. "Eleanor has a problem; I think you know that," he says, not quite looking at me.

I nod.

"We're all trying to work things out, but it's never easy."

The tape finishes rewinding and flickers to life. It's a scene from a TV show, a soap, and the hero is in a bar surrounded by three thugs. He has already thrown the first thug through a window when I realize that the second thug is Nate.

"You see that tough guy, Toby?" Mr. Holover says as Nate,

wearing torn jeans and a leather vest, flexes his arms and growls at the hero. Mr. Holover waves the remote control and stops the picture, freezing Nate with a ferocious scowl. "I'd run from that guy in an alley, wouldn't you?"

We watch and listen as Nate sneers at the hero, in a voice full of hard edges, "You're finished now, friend." He takes a flying leap at the good guy. Again and again Mr. Holover stops the picture, freezing Nate five times in midair, then once more as he lands on the hero's back. Grimacing wildly, Nate is carried piggyback by the hero, then spun around and thrown over the bar, where he crashes against the rows of bottles and sinks out of sight.

"They had to pay him extra to do that," Mr. Holover says, laughing. I get him to go back and stop it with Nate in midleap, arms wide like a hawk's. It's very impressive.

"What woulda happened if we ever fought that way at Wharf Hill School, Toby?" I turn around to see Nate, the real Nate, grinning at me. He and Simmie and Mrs. Holover are standing in the doorway. Mrs. Holover is drinking a cup of coffee and leaning a little bit against her daughter. Nate is holding my jacket. "I kept telling the director, 'Hey, nobody jumps piggyback on someone like that.' He said, 'Just *do* it.' So I did." The Holovers laugh. Even Simmie looks conciliatory. I look at my watch.

After saying good-bye all around, I walk with Nate along the length of the house toward the front foyer. "Thanks for coming," he says.

"Not at all," I say. "You thug, you."

We squeeze hands, the door thunks shut, and the house heaves away behind me in its ceaseless scuffle with ivy. For some reason I am remembering the time when our fourth-grade teacher, Mrs. Tappan, dumped Nate's desk out on the floor. She lifted it high above her head, backed off to a place where no one was sitting, and tilted it so the top opened and everything came pouring out—books, rulers, erasers, baseball cards, Coke cans, pencil sawdust, and dozens of quizzes rolled up into little balls. "That's what happens when we refuse to keep our desks in order," she said, smiling to us and brushing off her hands.

I think of Nate now, being paid to act like a bad guy. It's perfect. A dozen years ago, when we were best friends, he was a "bad kid." I was a "good kid." As such, we struggled constantly. In the same ruthless way that we rated girls (Face, Body, Personality), we divided ourselves into categories and saw how we matched up. I had grades and sports, Nate had strength and (he claimed) sexual experience. But most of all, I had my family, happy and sound, while he lived with a bunch of screaming lunatics. And family, I kept reminding him, was destiny.

Memory is brutal. It reduces everything to a series of snapshots. I remember my father telling me he was leaving my mother, but I can't remember what he said or how I felt. I remember the look on Nate's face when the two of us, age fourteen, got caught drinking outside a liquor store after having sneaked away from camp. Nate was triumphant; he thought he had finally dragged me down. But the letter sent by the camp director to the Holovers said that Nate was a bad kid; the letter to my parents said I shouldn't associate with bad kids. Finally, I remember Nate's revenge, him luring me into an Ali-Frazier slap-fight outside his house and then pulverizing me. Like a gravely injured person, I lay in the driveway for ten minutes, hoping his parents would see me. *See what a bad kid Nate is*, I was saying. *Don't you wish you had me instead?*

Now I'm standing in that same driveway. The breeze ripples the ivy. Through the large windows I can see Nate making his way room by room toward his family, and I can see them, too, still clustered around the set, watching Nate the thug fly. If I look back for a second longer, I will see him rejoining them, so instead of looking back, I push on toward the street, toward our house where my mother lies asleep with her cats.

XII

My Father's Hot
Little Numbers

I drive a Ford Fiesta. It is brown, with good pickup despite its small engine. It has a sunroof, a radio, and no other extras. It looks like anyone else's Hornet or Chevette or Champ—about as distinctive as an eggcrate. To me, cars are just conveniences, like telephones and dishwashers.

The kid across the street thinks differently. Jimmy must be about nineteen, and he spends a large part of every weekend working on his Dodge Charger. Lately he's been parking the Charger, for reasons that elude me, on my side of the street. Backing out of the lot behind my apartment very early in the morning, heading for the school where I teach, I see Jimmy stooping to polish chrome on the front grill, or wipe the headlights, or wash clean the stripe of a whitewall. Late Sunday night I'm lugging the garbage out for early Monday collection, and there's Jimmy, huddled in the front seat, holding the door open with his leg to keep the overhead light on. It turns out he's installing an electronic alarm system that doubles as a horn. You can program different pitch sequences into it, so that the horn plays "Three Blind Mice" or "O Beautiful for Spacious Skies" in an electronic drone that sounds like cicadas keening.

"You never quit working on her, do you, Jimmy?" I say to him.

"You know how it goes," he says. "One stupid thing sorta leads to another."

And so it does. With the Charger Jimmy started by rebuilding the engine and getting a new transmission, then had the car painted twice. (Each time I thought it was a different car.) Then new tires all around, a new interior featuring sheepskin mats splayed like helpless victims over all the seats, dual exhaust, a rear suspension jacked up as on a dragster. Custom side-view mirrors on both sides gave the car ears. The most recent extra is a pair of rubber mudflaps for the rear wheels, featuring in bright colors the cartoon character Yosemite Sam.

Jimmy's sense of himself and his sense of his car are tied up in very complicated knots. As I back my Fiesta out of the drive, into the slant light of late afternoon, Jimmy will hurry to the front of the Charger, which faces me, and lean back against it, his butt on the hood. He'll jam his hands into his pockets and then pull them out to fold his arms. He'll lean back and cross his legs, and smile as if I'm about to take his picture. At the corner I'll look back in the rearview mirror and see him already leaping out of the pose, eager to turn back to the car again—circling, polishing, diving underneath to change the oil; coming up for air and then diving back again.

All of this makes me think of my father, who, like Jimmy and unlike me, loved his cars. New and restored cars were particularly exquisite to him. A picture of my parents on their wedding day shows the two of them standing arm in arm in front of the sparkling new MG they'd rented for the honeymoon. They were deeply in love then, and hopes were high, but looking at the picture, you get the distinct feeling that while my mother is staring up at my father as if nothing else in the world exists, my father is returning a look that, while equally loving, includes not only his bride but the car behind her—its headlights, its extravagant running boards and mud guards.

My mother, whose father had always had classy cars, took them for granted. But Dad, who was a caddy at the country club where my mother's father golfed, coveted cars. His family had been able to afford exactly one Dodge every twelve years, so when he became a doctor and got out on his own, he had a lot of catching up to do. The MG was only the beginning. He desired cars; he hungered for them; his mouth watered over them as if they were big steaks on wheels. "Now *there's* a hot little number," he'd say, watching a Triumph or Fiat round the corner, craning his neck as we drove in the opposite direction. And when he said this often enough, we knew it was the death knell for whatever car we were riding in. One evening, days or weeks later, we'd hear a strange engine in the driveway, and he'd come in, holding up new keys and saying "Guess what?" It was predictable. A new car would be sitting in the driveway, ticking irregularly as it cooled.

All told, my father went through at least a dozen cars between 1960, when I first became aware of cars, and 1976, when he left Mom and moved away. He held onto some of these cars for two or three years, but he let go of others almost immediately. The Pontiac Grand Prix, for instance. Three days after he bought it, he was miserable, but he couldn't admit it. So he drove it, forlornly, for another six weeks. We saw right through him. "You're miserable in that boat!" Mom said. "Go out and get yourself a new one! Be extravagant!" He winced as if he had heartburn, and shook his head no, but after three more weeks he gave in.

All this buying and selling must have delighted the car salesmen in our town. Twelve cars in sixteen years. It seems unreal. My sisters, Lydia and Sharon, are astonished that I remember, and can list in order, twelve cars. They can only come up with the obvious ones:

the Mercedes, the Jeep, the Corvette. "Come on, you can do better than that," I say to Lydia. "What were you doing all those years?"

She gives me a funny look and says, "I was about to ask you the same thing."

Sharon just says, "Boys will be boys."

Possibly. But there's another reason I know Dad's cars so well. The garage was almost directly under my bedroom. This meant that when my father had to go to the hospital at night, I always heard him leave.

He'd go at three, at four, at five in the morning. Sometimes it was the telephone that woke me, sometimes the back door closing; sometimes it was the sound of keys in his hand or the garage door heaving up in its ancient tracks. But usually it was the car starting that did it. The taillights glowed red on my window as my father turned in the driveway. In winter there was ice on the drive, and it crackled like radio static.

When we were small kids, Lydia and I sometimes went with Dad to the hospital in the morning. He would let Mom sleep late, and take us to the hospital cafeteria for breakfast. The fried eggs were runny, but Dad complimented the cooks and servers. He knew most of them by their first names. In the hallway just outside, he let Lydia or me flick the switch that lit up his name on the call board. Occasionally he was paged during breakfast: "Dr. Slattery, Dr. Daniel Slattery." He would go to get the phone, first putting a saucer over his coffee mug. "Guard that with your lives," he'd tell us. After breakfast we'd walk to our grade school nearby. One day we brought with us a human brain in a jar for show and tell, a compact ball of lobes bathed in formaldehyde, and at first no one believed what it was. Lydia became exasperated. "Look, my father's a *brain* surgeon," she said, as if that explained everything.

When I got older, I sometimes went in to watch my father work. At first these trips were brief and just for fun—for the excitement of watching him slap an x-ray up on the bright, humming screen, or of trailing him and his partner, Dr. Baylor, on their rounds. They swept through the corridors, smiling but businesslike, wheeling around corners with their jackets and ties flapping, like Secret Service men. The hospital then was like a big fun house for me. I was still too young to understand what my father did there. I knew certain words: malignant melanoma, subdural hematoma. They sounded terrifying, like someone beating a drum. But they were just words.

Later, I got to watch my father operate. I watched him scrub with an iodine soap for ten minutes, side by side with his partner, Dr. Baylor, their hands working up a reddish-orange lather that dripped into the deep stainless steel sinks. They talked about tennis and politics as they scrubbed. The hundreds of hours he must have spent washing his hands! Nurses wrapped the doctors in layer after layer of blue gown, until the men looked like desert raiders: all you could see were their eyes.

There was something in this dressing that unsettled me. My father held his hands out in front of him, as if sleepwalking, to have the rubber gloves thrust over his fingers by the nurse—up over his fingers and wrists, over his forearms. It was a reversal of everything I had always expected in men and women: here the men were delicate, vulnerable, and these women with the swaddling clothes protected them from germs. It was a conspiracy on behalf of the patient, but it had an intimacy all its own. Nurses were there to help, and that help had its special vocabulary. Clamp. Suction. Drain. Cauterize. If a doctor had an ache—*Christ, my neck is killing me*—a nurse rubbed it for him. Even, my father told me, if a doctor had to piss during a long operation, a nurse would be there with a beaker.

What would Mom think? I wondered.

"Let me tell you something, Champ, in case you're ever a doctor," my father said to me one day in the surgeons' locker room. "To nurses, there are two kinds of doctors: the single kind, and everyone else. They look for the wedding ring. If it's there, they don't care if you're Frank Sinatra. You're invisible." But still he smiled and joked with the nurses, especially the neuro nurses, whom he called "the Green Berets of the operating room." Hustling alongside my father down the green-gray halls of the hospital, I watched his smile as he greeted people with a quick wave and sometimes a joke. Some of the nurses had the same look in their eyes that people on the street had when they walked up and shook my father's hand. Their eyes seemed to reflect the amount of human life my father had saved over the years.

I must have seen my father operate half a dozen times over the years. My sisters never went with me, nor did Mom, whose aversion to hospitals was something of a joke in our family. She steadfastly avoided them. She would bake, shop, or babysit for a friend laid up in the hospital. But she wouldn't go in to visit. "Everyone's *sick* in there," she would say. "Who wants to go where everyone's sick?" She didn't approve of my going, either.

But still Dad took me in. Each operation I saw seemed a bit more serious than the last. The patients didn't always survive. There was an old man named Mr. Feracci, who had had dizzy spells and had fallen down some stairs. I saw him two days before surgery, when my father did an arteriogram on him that involved injecting a dye into arteries in the neck. Mr. Feracci lay there on the table as my father shouted at him. "Mr. Feracci! Can you hear me? You're going to feel a warm sensation in your neck and head! It may be a bit painful, Mr. Feracci, but it isn't going to harm you!" Then my father pinched and probed the skin on the old man's neck, stuck the needles in, and pushed the plungers, leaning over the old man as if great force was needed to propel the dye up into his brain.

"Mother a Christ!" The old man woke up staring. He tried to move, but his head and hands were strapped down with rubber thongs like inner tubes. I couldn't see his legs, but they must have been tied down too. "Holy mother a Christ, stop hurting me!" He moaned and strained at the thongs, and I turned away. Afterward, my father told me not to mention it to Mom. "Some things are just better kept between men, okay, Champ?" he said, his arm on my shoulder.

When I turned sixteen and was about to get my license and

begin driving his cars, Dad decided to take me in to see one of the accident victims on his ward. "They're kids, most of them," Dad kept telling me. "Just like you. They go out driving with their buddies, maybe they have a beer, smoke a little grass. Then *bam*, they're off the road, wrapped around a tree, and reduced to so much fruit salad." He shook his head as if all American teenagers were engaged in a plot to bereave their parents. "I'd like you to meet some of these kids," he said.

But it never happened. Mom refused. "Just because he's old enough to drive," she insisted, "doesn't mean he's old enough to see *that*."

"Well," said my father, "he's a sixteen-year-old male, and that means he's old enough to leave his brains strewn all over the highway. Look at the insurance rates."

My mother took a deep drag on her cigarette and let it out slowly. "Oh, insurance rates! Come off it, Daniel! The point isn't insurance rates. The point is that our son does not need to go in and see awful things."

My father left off talking.

At night, when my father went in to see awful things at the hospital, he would make as little noise as possible in order not to wake my mother. When the phone rang, he picked it up quickly. He could dress and be gone in five minutes, down the stairs and out the back door into the garage beneath my bedroom—his car waking me as he pulled out. In my half-sleep it was comforting to think of my father in his car, snugged down in the lush leather, his face lit by the dials, driving the avenues of town while the rest of the world slept. Dozens of times he must have seen the sun rising over the dashboards of those cars, or the moon falling, or the constellations infinitesimally swinging themselves across the sky while he ran his terrible errands.

Each of his cars had its particular idle, a special timbre of slamming door. In my room above the garage, I had to adjust to these changes. If the car was new, I'd wake outright, either when my father left or when he returned. But after a while I'd sleep through it, or half sleep, dimly aware of the car sliding away below me and later returning, as if a news flash crossed the bottom of my dream, announcing, without interrupting the show, that Dad was gone, that Dad was home.

My father left my mother after a year-long affair with a woman named Ginny Di Biasi. Ginny Di Biasi was, and still is, a nurse at the hospital where our father was (and still is) a surgeon. He was forty-seven, and Ginny was twenty-eight, a big-hipped and cheerful woman with three kids of her own and a husband who told her once that if he ever saw my father around their neighborhood again, he'd "damage him seriously and forever" with a baseball bat. He was a fireman in a town twenty miles from our own.

When the affair first came out in the open, my father was remorseful, and promised my mother he wouldn't see Ginny Di Biasi again. He would work with Mom to save the marriage. But after three months she accused him of breaking the promise. "So tell me," she said. "How is that woman?"

Dad was not adept at lying, at least not when put on the spot. He tried, but it was lame, and my mother stormed at him. "Don't try to hide anything, Daniel," she shouted. "I've seen the mileage! I've seen it!"

She had been checking the odometer in the Mercedes.

The Mercedes was a white 280 SL coupe. It was a beautiful convertible, a classic in the making, and the last car my father had that he really cared about. He'd gotten into photography somehow that final year, and walked around in the yard taking pictures, a bit aimlessly, of the dog, the dogwood tree, sunsets. I still have a picture of that Mercedes somewhere. The car is smack in the middle of the photo, and my younger sister Sharon's leg is dangling in at the side, amputated midthigh by the border, while the car sits there grinning, its top down, its blue leather puffy in the sunshine. I imagine my father driving this car toward Ginny Di Biasi's town, circling her block, parking three or four houses down from Ginny's, or even around the corner. But it is impossible to be inconspicuous in such a car.

Eventually, Ginny's husband changed his threat: he started promising to use his bat not only on my father, but on the car as well. My father responded to this not by staying away—neither promises nor grave threats nor, ultimately, a lawsuit could make him do that—but by trading in the Mercedes for a Renault Le Car. At the time my father did drastic and desperate things. I'm sure he had seen at least half a dozen movies in which irate wives deduced their husbands' treachery from the facts of the odometer, and yet off he drove in his new olive green Le Car, piling up the miles, day after day. Six weeks after the mileage confrontation he moved out, and a year after that—his Le Car still intact—he married Ginny.

Having had so many cars came back to haunt my father during the divorce. The lawyer representing my mother, Albert Holover, was the father of my old best friend, Nathan Holover—a particular favorite of my father's. Because of this, and because he was used to the deference accorded expert medical witnesses in court, I think my father expected a relatively gentle time from Mr. Holover on the stand. It didn't work out that way, however. I wasn't there, but recently I was told by Lydia, who was, that our father sat with a neighborly smile, which quickly dissolved as Mr. Holover, seeking a hefty settlement for our mother, launched into an exposé of our father's allegedly luxurious life-style.

"So, Doctor," he said. "I understand you drive a Mercedes Benz sports car."

"I *drove* one, Albert," my father said. "A used one. But I sold it."

"And what are you driving now, may I ask?"

"A Renault Le Car."

"I see. And is it safe to say that this Le Car is an imported European car?"

My father agreed that this was safe to say. According to my sister, Mr. Holover then proceeded to construct a list of vacations our father had taken since the separation, of theater trips to New York, a ski trip in Switzerland, a conference in San Francisco. He moved on to list things my father had purchased—stereo and ski equipment and the like—while my father tried to insist that this was misleading, that everything he had bought he had bought cut-rate.

"I'm just trying to get a picture of things, Doctor," Mr. Holover said. "And the picture I'm getting is of a person who likes the good life and who is more than able to spend whatever is necessary to afford it."

"That may be your picture," my father said. "But it's not mine."

"Well, then." Mr. Holover went to his desk and looked at his notes. "Why don't we take a look at the cars you've owned over the past ten years or so."

I can see my father rubbing his chin and wincing.

I don't particularly mind envisioning my father squirming on the witness stand. But recalling those dozen cars of his and reviewing them in my mind pulls me back to a time when things were different between us. I remember how much I liked his first cars, the little sports cars. There was an MG, black with red leather inside. There was also a Corvair, with the rear engine, and a green Triumph. I see myself riding in the passenger seats of these cars. We are pulling out of the parking lot at the high school, after a football game. The leather of the seats is soft; the instrument panel has dials round and luminous as moons. Smoke from my father's pipe swirls around the stick shift and the pyramid of rubber at its base. As we sit there waiting for cars to move, high school football players walk by, their pants covered with dirt and blood. My father, who was a quarterback in high school, talks to me of the great football players of his youth, like Sammy Baugh and Sid Luckman and Doak Walker.

If I was five then, my father was thirty-three, six years older than I am now. He spent Sunday afternoons washing, waxing, changing the oil in his little cars. To change the oil, he used Hills Bros coffee cans, the ones with the little genie, or Arab, on them; he wore a special T-shirt that Mom called "that odious shirt." Down on his back he'd go, rattling the cans and whistling Frank Sinatra songs. For a while there was a tiny car whose doors opened up like wings. It was a wreck, and my father never got it running. He bought cars cheaply then and sold them cheaply. One of those cars had a front trunk into which he put me, driving home from the gym where I watched him play basketball. All was warm and dark, and I tumbled around inside, laughing; I could hear my father singing in the front seat and shouting to me through the dashboard, "Guess when we're home!" He threw in some extra stops to trick me. When the hood finally opened, I squinted up into the light to see my mother, a look of hurt and dismay on her face. "He might have suffocated," she said. "He might have been killed."

The hot rod phase came next, in the mid-sixties. A GTO, a Firebird, a maroon Corvette—all these cars were American. My father was most like Jimmy in this phase. On Sunday he spent a quarter of an hour polishing the *backs* of the side-view mirrors. He boasted quietly about how fast his machine would go, and then never pushed it quite that far. On the highway he would gun it up a little, seventy, seventy-five. His hand was on the very top of the steering wheel, and he kept arching his wrist to look under it at the speedometer. What he saw made him smile.

After the Corvette came the ill-starred Grand Prix. His cars were getting bigger—an Oldsmobile, a brief fling with a Lincoln Continental—and then finally a Jeep. Like a lot of other people, my father went heavily into four-wheel-drive vehicles in the 1970s. We had a cabin up in snow country, at the top of a steep hill, and in my mind I still see him getting out of the Jeep to engage the front axles. It is snowing hard; bending to the hubcaps, my father disappears as if into a cauldron someone far overhead is furiously sugaring. Mom smiles; we can climb Everest in this.

He admitted now that those little cars he used to drive had been cute, but really they were just motorcycles with a couple of extra wheels tacked on. My mother agreed. With Jeeps we were safe. The Jeep Wagoneer was big—big enough to hold all my stuff when Mom and Dad drove me off to college.

It was the next summer, at the end of a strange, tense June, that my parents returned from a weekend in Nantucket, pulling into the driveway without beeping the horn. Our mother announced coldly, "Your father was ill," and went straight upstairs, without even bothering to help unload the suitcases, beach bags, and tennis gear they had brought with them for their vacation. Dad stood there, blowing his nose into his handkerchief. In July, as if the Jeep itself had become contagious, he suddenly unloaded it and picked up, second-hand, the little white Mercedes.

Back in the street outside my apartment, Jimmy waxes and waxes his Charger. I watch out the window. His car is now so water resistant, I'll tell him, that raindrops will spontaneously explode a good two inches above the hood. He'll laugh. I try to imagine the other cars parked in his future, but I can't. He is too devoted to this one.

Since his divorce and remarriage, my father has had one car and one only, a reliable Peugeot. Ginny has a matching Peugeot. They aren't really station wagons, these cars, nor are they off-roaders, nor are they luxury vehicles, nor by any stretch of the imagination are they sports cars. My father has changed. He has stayed with a single car for six long years.

In a way those twelve cars, those "hot little numbers," were twelve affairs my father never had. Each had its own pedigree, its nationality, its sound, feel, smell. *She really handles. Sweetness and light, oh baby, in the curves. I love her.* It was as if strict fidelity to his wife brought out promiscuity with automobiles. When he finally had a real affair, my father stopped giving cars such a hard time.

I've decided that Jimmy parks his Charger on my side of the

street so he can see it from his bedroom window. He doesn't even have to get out of bed; he just looks over the windowsill. He's more than responsible with the car; he's protective, he's tender. It's there in the way he soaps her up and sponges her down, slowly, humming under the music from the tape deck. It's there in his steadfast refusal to take her out during bad weather, and in the ornaments, gorgeous and absurd, with which he bejewels her. And it's there in the way he positions himself, though waving and smiling, between me and his car—arms spread, butt to the hood, as if to flaunt, shield, and secretly caress her, all in a single gesture.

XIII

Bread

These days she is always tired. In the morning when she slides out of bed and drags herself through the rubble of their living room, only the thought of coffee keeps her standing. At lunch, her eyelids are heavy as she eats her minuscule salad. At night, looking out over the assembled rockers and rollers at Hal's club, she feels as if she has grown a new, extra skin that she can't quite shrug off. "Why am I always so wasted?" she says to Hal.

He shrugs. "You sleep enough," he says, and turns back to the TV.

Lydia met Hal one night a year ago at Geronimo's, a club in Kenmore Square. Exhausted after a day cutting steak and peeling shrimp at the restaurant, she wanted a few hours of good rock and roll before she went back to her apartment. But the band of the night, a jazz trio, was so anemic, she felt herself falling asleep at the bar. "Jesus," she said out loud, "what kind of shit are they booking these days?" The guy on her left seemed sympathetic; she bought him a beer and complained to him about the sorry state of night life around town. He laughed; she liked the way the corners of his mouth turned up and his black eyes widened. By the fifth beer she was beginning to think that going home alone was not such a great idea after all.

His name was Hal. Half-drunk, she told him it sounded like a dog's name. "C'mere Hal, here boy!" She laughed at her own joke, and then apologized for it; the corners of his mouth curled up. The jazz trio mercifully disappeared, the place cleared out, and the two of them were the only people left. When the bartender went back into the kitchen, Hal, moving quickly, leaned over the bar and grabbed two shot glasses and a bottle of Jack Daniels.

She was startled. "What is this—you think you own this place or something?"

"Yes," he said, smiling and pouring out two large shots.

The bartender came back in and stared at them. "My friend Hal here," she apologized. "He thinks he owns the place."

"He does," said the bartender.

She looked from the bartender to Hal and back again. "Hey," she said. "I'm sorry about what I said about the music. I just don't like jazz. It's personal."

He laughed. "Are you kidding? They were terrible."

Standing out in the street, she sighed once and said to him, "Hal, I really like you a lot." A month later they were living together.

It was perfect at first. Hal knew everyone in Boston: artists, musicians, DJs, lawyers, writers. He was the most popular man she had ever met, and the most generous. Walking with him to Geronimo's in the evening, she watched him greet three old winos waiting in the shadows of an alley near the club; he shook hands with them and listened as they listed their aches and pains, then gave them five bucks and told them to stop by for a bowl of soup. "You're a helluva guy, Hal," they gargled, and she looked at his face and wondered, *Why me?* She wasn't used to feeling lucky.

In the beginning his passion for her seemed overwhelming. Sometimes he embarrassed her. "I'm really in love with Lydia," he would say, point blank, to her friends. But after the first few months, things began to change. He stopped telling her how much he loved her. He became silent, and when she tried to get inside that silence, angry. She saw how fanatical he was about the club, the long hours he put in, how weary it made him. But he would take no advice from her. They had been together for four months the first time he yelled at her. He was worried about money; he needed $2,000 to cover wages at the club, and when she suggested he borrow it from friends— "Christ, Hal, half of Boston owes you money"—he burst out at her with a murderous look in his eyes. She backed off, wounded, and his look softened. But she felt as if some third person, a mean and brooding stranger, had secretly entered the apartment and taken up residence.

She worked hard at understanding Hal. He had dozens of friends, but as far as Lydia could see, no one who really knew him from the inside. He was a secret, and she never knew when some item from his past would turn up to complicate the task of knowing him even further. One afternoon she came into the apartment to hear him berating someone on the phone in a harsh, bitten-off voice that was alien to her. She stood there listening, until with a final "Leave me the fuck alone!" he slammed the phone down and stomped around the corner, coming face to face with her. His face was red, and she could smell hot rage radiating from him.

"Who was that?" she said.

He went far away for half a second, then came back in a flat voice, "My ex-wife. I was married once."

"Oh, great," she said, beginning to shake. "Great."

Now, a year already invested in the relationship, she doesn't know what to make of him. Some nights he is the old Hal, the one she fell in love with, joking and smiling, sitting with his arm around her in a booth at the club. But the next day he is the stranger again, sullen and cold, and they argue about everything. Last month it was a phone answering machine she wanted; he called it a waste of money and screamed at her when she went ahead and bought it. Quickly he changed his mind; the machine gives him more possibilities for power. He sits there listening to his friends leaving their messages. "Answer it," she says to him; he holds up a hand and stares at the phone, smiling cruelly.

She has thought about leaving him. But the prospect of being alone, of coming home after a day of cooking steaks and lobsters to a dark apartment with only her things in it—this picture makes her stomach heave. Soon she will be thirty, and that is not a good age to be coming home alone.

The miles pass with undue slowness as Lydia drives south out of Boston. She rescues half a joint from the ashtray and smokes it, pulling the sharpness in deep and holding it there. Off the highway she sees woods and more woods. As a teenager she liked the woods, but now they inspire in her only a dismal sense of her own puniness.

She is headed to her hometown for the wedding of her high school boyfriend, Jeremy. She didn't plan to go until Hal, whose way of annoying her has in recent weeks reached a kind of perfection, drove her to it. Two days ago she got a flat tire in Kenmore Square, and when she called him, he let the answering machine take her call; she got home after paying a fifty-buck towing fee and let him have it, told him to fuck himself; she was going home to Connecticut for the weekend.

"Suit yourself," he said, shrugging and turning his back.

This morning when she woke, he was sitting slumped in front of the television, still wearing last night's clothes. "You need sleep, Hal," she said. "Human beings need sleep." He glared at her and poured a shot of bourbon into his soft, pale face.

"You're really pissing me off for no discernible reason," she told him.

Now she smiles, thinking of Jeremy Trumpy and his old crowd.

Fourteen years ago they were her corruptors, rebels in love with themselves and all of life. Most of them were boys a couple of years older than she; they liked her for her long, wild hair and her laughter. Jeremy and his friends talked about poetry, politics, music, Vietnam; she listened to them, and suddenly all the other boys she knew seemed mere children; they knew nothing about life. Jeremy's best friend, Carlton Bickers, knew every song Bob Dylan had ever written. In summer they stayed up all night, playing guitars and singing, drinking wine and smoking dope. "You're a beautiful person, Lydia," Jeremy told her. She fell in love with him; she thought about him day and night.

Her parents did their best to fight it. To them Jeremy was a hippie, a drug addict, and a seducer of innocent girls. Burying their own problems under an obsessive concern for her virginity, they monitored threatening developments in her outlook—interpreting her refusal to shave her armpits, for instance, as a sure sign of wanton sexual activity. With her younger brother Toby doing their spying for them, they compiled a dossier of evidence against Jeremy. "This kid is dangerous," her father finally said to her, "and I don't want to see his face around here anymore."

She exits at her old hometown, driving on roads that are always less familiar than she thinks they will be. New houses are everywhere, whole streets of them. People are building, building, building. She is early and parks across from the church, in the shade of a mammoth oak. The houses along this street, frame houses built with whaling and shipping money in the 1800s, shine blue-white in the sunlight. She looks at the pretentious Doric columns and curved pediments, at the plaques naming the original owners.

At ten she loved these neighborhoods, at twenty she hated them. She remembers the first time she hated them; it was the summer after her sophomore year in college, and she had made the mistake of deciding to spend it at home. She was beginning to see how impossible it was to live the life her parents wanted her to live. They didn't like her sleeping till noon; they didn't like her putting her mattress on the floor. ("That's what we have beds for," her father said. "It helps distinguish us from the lower life forms.") They didn't like it when she hooked up her bass guitar and amp in the garage and practiced. And they didn't like the friends who came down to visit her from Boston. Her friends were barely tolerated, while Toby and his preppy girlfriend, Sarah, were paraded in front of her again and again as Clean-Cut Young Americans.

Each night she wrote furiously in her journal, keeping track of how bad it was. What bothered her most was the iron sameness of her parents' life. Every day at exactly 5:15, her mother met her father at the back door, drink in hand, the same quick burst of kisses and smiles, her father sniffing the air and trying to guess what dinner was. Then a half-hour in the living room, dinner at six sharp, the same places around the table, the cup and a half of coffee, the agonies over dessert, the same worries about too much caffeine, too many calories, too little will power.

Mom and Dad, she wrote, *are slowly turning into robots.*

Her brother and sister couldn't see what she saw. She was all alone. One night she sat down at her father's place at the table, and everyone just sat there staring at her. Spontaneity was too much for them. *That's why they can't deal with me*, she decided. *I'm an alien here. But what they don't realize is that* they *are the strange life forms, and* I'm *the normal,* living *person.*

None of her old friends were around that summer—Jeremy Trumpy, just graduated from Cornell, was backpacking through Europe—and after two weeks she thought the boredom would suffocate her. Four nights a week she waited tables at a steak house, bringing drinks and massive slabs of meat to couples who gorged in silence. By twelve she was home and changed and ready to go out. But there was no place to go. Except for a couple of biker joints and sleazy pickup bars, the town folded up and died at midnight. She would walk around, looking for lights and listening for music and finding instead row after row of white, sepulchral houses, only the blue flicker of television through curtains signaling the lives entombed within. *I will never spend another summer here again*, she swore to herself.

Guests are arriving now at the church across the street. She wonders if her father will come. It is beyond belief that Jeremy Trumpy has become a doctor like her father, that the two of them work in the same hospital, have lunch together, know the same people, hear the same gossip. She has to laugh, remembering the day six years ago when her father took her aside and hemmed and hawed before asking her, Didn't she think Jeremy Trumpy would make a decent husband?

"You mean Jeremy the Communist, the hippie, the drug addict?" she said.

By that time Jeremy had already proposed to her, and her father knew it. She had already refused, and he knew that, too. She had no intention of marrying Jeremy, the outline of whose life was beginning to look suspiciously predictable. He was twenty-five and in med school, had cut off his beautiful hair and was in fact losing it on top. He was beginning to espouse the virtues of their hometown and to talk about going back there to live. She was twenty-three and living in Boston, going to cooking school and playing in a band. She had no money, but she thought of herself as having passion; when Jeremy proposed to her, it was as if he was speaking a foreign language. They were out on his sailboat, cruising around in the Sound, when he turned to her suddenly and said, "What would you think about getting married?"

"To whom?" She laughed.

"I mean," he said, "how would you like to be my wife?"

She turned away from him and looked out over the water. She wanted to laugh, but only if he would laugh with her, and she knew he wouldn't. "I don't think I'll ever get married," she said. "Not like that."

Jeremy was too late for her. By the time he proposed, she had already said good-bye to Connecticut and all it stood for and had set herself up in Boston. Her parents had split up two years earlier, their failure freeing her to be any kind of person she wanted to be; they couldn't tell her anything anymore. She threw herself into music, playing her guitar in two different bands, taking jobs only to scrape enough money together for meals and rent. She lived in a run-down but functional apartment with her friends, students and artists and music freaks, people whose energy she loved. When her father visited with his new wife, she could see them glancing around, ill at ease and scared of dirt. She got them to come see her band play, at a dingy, subterranean club where punks were slam-dancing on the floor. It was not one of her favorite places, a gruesome crowd by any standards, but it had the desired effect on her father. *I felt conspicuous the other night*, he wrote to her afterward, *by virtue of my age, my general cleanliness, and the large size of my wallet.*

It made her smile, to be living a life that her parents, with their trusty simplicities, simply couldn't comprehend. "Tell me who you are dating," her mother would say to her, cheerfully, on the phone. She had the same feeling with her parents that she did with Jeremy. The three of them spoke to her out of some ancient culture, their very language unequipped to handle the reality of her life.

But somehow things have changed. Looking back over the last ten years, she sees too many drugs; too many pointless, mindless jobs; too many bizarre and failed relationships. She went with one guy for three months, and they never told each other their last names; one morning she called him up and found out he had left, moved, zap. There are scenes from these ten years that her parents would recoil from in shock if they only knew. She wouldn't mind forgetting some of them herself.

She lights up the last morsel of roach and smokes it. The white houses she once despised no longer seem hateful, merely alien. They have smooth, painted boards; they have small lawns, closely clipped, and gardens. She would like to have a garden someday.

She is the last person inside. Over at the head of the left aisle, she sees Carlton Bickers, looking trapped but happy in an usher's outfit, his red hair shockingly short; he grins and waves as another usher, someone she doesn't know, takes her arm and drags her down the side aisle to where her sister and mother are.

"I didn't see you come in," she whispers to them as she sits down next to her sister, Sharon, who goes to a college not far away and often comes home to visit.

"How could you, silly?" her mother says, reaching across Sharon to squeeze her arm. "We were here before you."

Her sister shoots her a look of shock and amusement. "You *reek* of pot," she whispers, and shakes out a handful of Tic-Tacs. Lydia swallows them, remembering the mints her mother always had in church, square white mints she handed out continuously, trying to keep Lydia and Toby pacified.

"How long do you think it'll take for Mom to cry?" she whispers to her sister.

"I predict during the vows," says Sharon. They giggle. Their mother always cries at weddings, baptisms, funerals, and other ceremonies in which life passages are affirmed.

They wait. Time stretches and warps in a way that Lydia attributes as much to church as to the dope. She remembers the hours of her childhood spent here, suspended between boredom and elation: her mother praying; her father sitting with his hands clasped but not praying; she and her brother chomping mints and Neccos and getting their fingers stuck in the holes where the thimble-sized communion cups went. The only part of the service her father truly enjoyed was the hymn singing, when his excellent voice filled the area around them and caused people in neighboring pews to glance over in admiration. Her mother prayed intensely and privately, her head bent, her thumb and finger holding the bridge of her nose. She was silent during the hymns, which to her were beautiful but detracted from the solitariness she desired.

Lydia scans the church to see if her father is there. She looks back, close to the big doors, where he would sit to facilitate a quick escape afterward. But he isn't there. It occurs to her that she hasn't seen her parents in the same room since Toby's college graduation years ago.

"Can you still smell the dope?" she whispers to Sharon.

Her sister is beautiful. Men meet her on trains and planes and write to her for years. "I can't believe you came stoned to Jeremy's wedding," she says.

I bet Jeremy himself is stoned right now, Lydia is about to say, but suddenly everyone is standing; the procession has started, the organ cranking out the wedding march in a ponderous manner. Aside from Carlton she knows two of the ushers. One is Jeremy's younger brother, Sam; he was a little boy when she went out with Jeremy, and it is shocking to see how big and handsome he is, in the same outdoorsy way Jeremy once was. "What a fox," Sharon whispers. "I wouldn't mind jumping his bones."

The other usher she recognizes is Richard Rourke, the group's practical joker and the funniest person she has ever known. He catches her eye and winks lecherously as he passes. Up front she sees Jeremy himself. The fringe of hair around his bald head is neatly trimmed, and his body is bulky but in shape; he looks good, but he doesn't look like Jeremy.

As the group positions itself around the altar and the minister begins talking, Lydia inspects the person Jeremy has decided to make his wife. She is young and slender, and stands looking at Jeremy with an expression of beatitude. Her name is April. When Lydia was being forbidden by her parents to see the dangerous hippie Communist Jeremy Trumpy, April was in third grade.

The minister begins his charge to the congregation; he is a young minister who sounds like a swim instructor as he exhorts the audience in a thin and wheedling voice. "I ask you to throw open your minds and hearts to the witnessing of this bond," he says.

She closes her eyes. She sees herself and Jeremy, playing Frisbee in a green field. They are exhausted and silly, and when Lydia dives for the Frisbee, they collide; they wrestle together, and she gets lost in his long hair and round, sweet smell. Her own sexuality is a mystery to her, something that creates itself as she moves. She and Jeremy are in love. Wherever they are, they touch each other, twirling each other's hair, touching legs under the table at the pizza parlor as they laugh at Richard's jokes. She is fifteen years old, and for the first time in her life, she is speaking a language with her body.

She opens her eyes to see the young minister asking who will give the bride in marriage. Jeremy stands as if at military attention. Lydia's gaze floats up over the chancel, up to the high dome with its chandelier, to the gilded Latin scripture of the frieze. She remembers Mr. Duff, the ancient minister who, knowing the secret acoustics of the place, could make his deep voice echo and carom in that domed chancel until it became one, in her mind at least, with the voice of God. Now she is sixteen, that voice haunting her as she sneaks into church at midnight with Jeremy and tiptoes awed and barefoot down the nave. She is lying on the carpeted floor of the chancel with Jeremy on top of her, lost in their mingled hair, the oversized buckles of their leather belts clanking as they rub and rub their bodies together; *Oh God*, Jeremy says, *Oh God!* and they break out in blasphemous laughter—

"Psst." Her sister nudges her back to the present. Jeremy is intoning his vow in a wooden voice. "What did I tell you?" Sharon whispers, nodding to her left. Lydia looks. Tears are streaming down her mother's face.

Smiling, her mother cries silently through the exchange of rings and declaration of marriage. The organ strikes up a bright recessional; people rise and turn to the nave; cameras click and slide. The congregation rustles with happiness. Jeremy's face shines under a film of sweat as he passes. "That's Doctor Trumpy!" a little girl in the next row cries out, and people laugh.

"He's so *old* looking," Sharon whispers. "I didn't realize he was so old."

"It's just his head," Lydia says.

"I feel sorry for her," Sharon says. "She's *my* age."

Outside, the receiving line stretches from the church doors down a short flight of steps onto a stone landing. It moves with agonizing slowness. An old lady in a wheelchair is being lowered down the steps. Standing with Sharon in the mob of shuffling people, Lydia feels a tinge of claustrophobia. Her mother will not enter such crowds, and right now she is nowhere to be seen.

They look ahead to where Jeremy's bride is bending to kiss the old woman in the wheelchair. "Mrs. Jeremy Trumpy," Sharon says, chuckling. "Do you wish it was you?"

"No thanks," she says. And yet she is nervous, wondering what will go through Jeremy's mind when he sees her. It's insane the way her palms sweat and her smile quivers as the line moves her forward. Now Jeremy sees her, and his face—a square face made more for sternness, she sees now, than for laughter—smiles widely. "Hey!" he says in his deep voice. "Lydia!"

"Hey," she says softly, and hugs him tight, recalling in her fingers the amazing firmness of his back. For a moment she is lost in him, she is under him on the chancel floor. She pulls back and wants to say something to him. But he glances away, beyond her to the people up the line. She wonders how many women he has considered marrying in the last ten years.

"I'm so glad you came, Lydia," he says. "We didn't think you were going to make it." He turns to Sharon. "And is this Sharon? Good God, we're going to have to keep my brother's friends muzzled at the reception."

They all laugh, and she feels suddenly released, disengaged from the burden of their history together. She is happy for him and tells him so, then moves on to shake his young wife's hand and wish her the best.

From the stone landing she looks down the hill over the town, its rows of houses and yards tending neatly toward the river. Jeremy's voice floats in her ears, speaking in his polite, unerring way. The shape of his words is delicate; it is a shape that has no place in the bluntness and dishevelment of her life with Hal. She thinks of Hal, sitting in their apartment, luxuriating in alcohol and self-pity, and shudders.

Her mother is standing alone at the foot of the stairs. "How are you doing?" Lydia asks her.

"You know me," her mother says. "I'm a mess at weddings. How about you?"

"I'm tired," she says. "I'm so tired."

She sees love and concern in her mother's eyes. It is a look she has often turned away from.

"Why don't you come home after the reception?" her mother says. "Or are you in a hurry to get back to Boston?"

"No hurry," Lydia says.

They are in the kitchen, baking bread. When she was upset as a child, her mother did things with her designed to cheer her up—crocheting potholders, taking walks at midnight, making homemade play dough in bright colors.

"Which one of Mother's Magic Tricks would go well with today?" her mother said when she came through the door. "We can be as silly as we need to be."

"How about baking something?" Lydia said.

Now she has an apron over her good dress, and her mother is in shorts and a Club Med T-shirt. They sift the flour, crumble the yeast cake into water, and watch it foam and bubble. "It's alive," her mother says. "That's what I love about it. You have to get it to perform."

Side by side at the counter, they knead the dough. Lydia has never specialized in bread, and the sticky lump before her seems to sense this. Her mother talks nonstop about different kinds of bread. "When your father and I were out in Arizona, they had something they called fry bread. Very simple but very greasy. You made it with flour and water and baking powder, and fried it in a hunk of lard. When I was a kid, our cook Ilsa made a Hungarian sourdough. My father used to mop up gravy and grease with it. He'd even dip it into bacon grease. I'm sure it wasn't very good for him, but he loved it."

"How do you knead it so well?" Lydia asks.

"Use the heel of your hand, not the fingers. The tricky thing is that you've got to think of pulling it toward you and pushing it away at the same time." In silence they push and pull. "It's relaxing, isn't it?"

Lydia laughs. "Watching *you* do it is relaxing." Her own slender hands struggle over the surface of the dough, while her mother's power through it. The sound of her mother's voice and the motion of her hands in the dough are mesmerizing.

"Your father never liked home-baked bread. He thought it was peasant labor. He said, 'Why waste all that time and energy when down at the A&P they have one hundred and one different kinds to choose from?'"

"But it's such awful bread."

"Well, exactly."

"So what did you say to Dad?"

Her mother's hands stop for a second as she laughs. "On the outside all I said was, 'Yes, dear.' But inside I said, 'Okay, baby, if you can't appreciate it, I'm certainly not going to waste it on you!'"

With the dough in bowls under damp towels, they rinse their hands and sit down with a cup of coffee. "You know," says her mother, "one of the great things about being a woman is that so many of the things you love to do bring pleasure and sustenance to the people you love. I feel sorry for men, with their games and their teams. The things they love to do are so useless."

Lydia smiles but says nothing. For a moment she feels the emptiness of the rooms beyond the kitchen. She pictures her mother at the piano in the living room, drinking a glass of wine and sight-reading her way through songs from old musicals, missing a lot of the notes and scolding herself out loud for them. "When you were my age," she says, "you already had me, didn't you?"

"True enough, doodlebug," her mother says. "What makes you think of that?"

"I don't know."

Her mother sighs and purses her lips, looking into the past. "When I see myself then, I see a little girl lost in a woman's life." She smiles. "I think it's just fine you aren't the one getting married today."

When they uncover the dough, they find it puffed up double. "That's the magic part," her mother says. "Remember I used to tell you that the Bread Genie lived in there?"

She doesn't really remember. It is so easy to forget.

"But here comes the part I love." When her mother giggles, it is impossible to believe she is almost sixty. She raises her hand over the bowl, makes a fist, and punches it into the center of the dough, which collapses with a soft *oof*. "When your father left, I used to make a lot of bread. And this is why." She smiles.

"A surrogate target," Lydia says.

"Well, I was so furious at him. Every month something would go wrong with this house. The furnace. The water heater. Every month another repairman with hair sticking out between his shirt buttons, telling me I had to spend more money. I was so angry, I would go around the house trashing things Daniel had left behind. One day I couldn't find anything else, and that was the day I started making bread." Smiling, she nods toward the bowl in front of Lydia. "Go ahead. It can be whoever you need it to be."

Thinking of Hal's face, Lydia punches. The dough folds in around her knuckles. She hopes that somehow, up in Boston, he can feel it.

"You know," her mother says, "whenever I make bread, I think about all the billions of breads that have been made in the world and the billions of people who made them. I know my bread isn't particularly good, but that isn't really the point, is it?"

They knead the dough and let it rise a second time, then shape it into loaves, which rise again in the pans. Finally, they put the bread in the oven. "It's a lot of work," Lydia says.

"Exactly. That's what's so beautiful about it. You can't be in a hurry. You have to have a taste for the finer things. And you have to have faith in a process you can't see." She wipes a smudge of flour off Lydia's nose. "Anytime you want to stay here for a while, you don't even have to ask. You know that."

Lydia nods. She takes off the apron and looks down at her only good dress. It is four o'clock; she sees Hal drinking beer in front of the Red Sox game. "I'm going to find something to change into," she says.

Upstairs she finds corduroy shorts and a T-shirt that says Aspen. Hanging from the closet doorknob is a leather peace necklace Jeremy gave her. In the closet are old books and posters, boxes of letters and curled photographs, jewelry she wore in dress-up games as a child. The posters are of horses; she knows there was a time when she loved horses, but she can't feel it anymore.

On the hall phone she calls Boston. There is a click, and then she is hearing her own voice, saying "We're not here now . . ." in a tone that she meant to be funny but that, it seems to her now, is merely annoying.

"Listen Hal," she says after the beep. "I know you're out there." Nothing.

"I won't be home tonight. I'm at my mother's. We're baking bread." She waits for him to come on, and is surprised to feel no anger when he doesn't. "We have to talk," she says, and hangs up.

Downstairs the kitchen is empty. A whooshing sound from outside informs her that her mother is watering the garden. The smell of bread pushes itself into every corner of the room and into her nostrils; she goes to the oven, opens it, and looks at the loaves. She swears she can see them rising.

XIV

Primum Non Nocere

The day the paper boy got hit, Slattery and his wife and step-daughter were at home arguing. It was an April Saturday, gray and heavy with clouds. Slattery and Ginny were standing on the back porch when Tracey came out and dropped her bombshell on them.

"I'm not going back to school," she said.

Uh oh, Slattery said to himself. *Here we go.* He watched his wife's eyes narrow. "And may I ask why not?" she said in a rising voice.

Tracey threw her hands to her forehead and dragged them through her long blond hair, grimacing horribly. The gesture reminded Slattery of some of his patients, with their mysterious, agonizing headaches. "I'm just sick of it," she said. "It's so useless."

"This is about Eddie, isn't it," Ginny said. "It's all about Eddie."

The girl stomped back into the house.

Eddie Rindell was a pimply, nineteen-year-old ex-basketball player to whom Slattery's stepdaughter had attached herself early in her senior year in high school and from whom, a year and a half later, she now seemed inseparable. All fall and winter she had driven back from the state university every weekend to see the boy, who was unemployed and scrounging off his parents. Slattery had no strong feelings against the Rindell kid, who reminded him of any of half a dozen guys he had grown up with outside Philadelphia—guys who drank beer and loved practical jokes, who married quickly out of high school and went on to spend their lives grinding away in the paper mills and toothpaste factories their fathers worked in. The boy was harmless enough, and if Tracey wanted to hang around with him, it was no skin off Slattery's back. But his wife—who had married her first husband at eighteen—felt differently. She was afraid the girl would throw her life away on Eddie Rindell. Her older daughter, Trish, had married right out of high school and at twenty-one was now saddled with two kids of her own. Tommy, Ginny's middle child, had married at nineteen and divorced ten months later, running off to join the army. That left Tracey. "This kid is going to get through college," Ginny sometimes said, "if I have to drag her through by her toenails."

In the kitchen they could feel the music pounding in Tracey's room above them. "I'm sick of this," Ginny said. "I'm going out to shop and cool down."

Slattery looked into his wife's pale blue eyes. "Want me to talk to her?"

"Sure," she said, sweeping the cars keys off the table. "You can't do any worse than I have."

When his wife left, Slattery climbed to the top of the stairs and stood listening to his stepdaughter's music. Its willful mayhem reminded him how glad he was to have been young before the invention of the electric guitar. His own children had for the most part preferred folk singers and the Beatles, sane music that even he could listen to. He raised his hand to knock; the door opened, and he came face to face with his stepdaughter.

"Did *she* send you up here?"

"Who, your mother?" Slattery said, feigning surprise. "No. I was just drawn up by the dulcet strains of your music. May I come in?"

They sat down opposite each other on the twin beds, and for ten minutes he patiently explained why he and Ginny felt the Rindell kid was a dead end for her. "Let's face it," he summed up. "Some people in life go out and make it, and some sit back and watch."

"He happens to be a nice guy, you know," Tracey said.

"No doubt. But there's a surplus of nice guys. Take a look around sometime."

She said nothing, didn't look up, just sat there running her finger around and around in circles on her bedspread. He thought he had gotten through to her, but when he reached out to touch her forehead, she pulled back. "I see," he said. He felt himself getting angry. "Listen, if you want to waste your time on Eddie, fine. But your mother and I want you to know that as long as we're footing the bill—"

"Oh, *Christ!*" his stepdaughter shouted, clamping her hands over her ears and walking over to the window. "It isn't just Eddie."

"Then what is it?"

"I don't know. I'm depressed." There was a long silence, filled with the fluting voice of a bird outside. "Don't you ever get depressed?" she said.

He shook his head. "I don't have time to."

"But I mean, don't you ever wonder what's the point?"

"Look," Slattery said. "Tomorrow I operate on a forty-year-old woman with a tumor the size of a golf ball in her head. Now what good is it going to do her if she's prepped and ready on the OR table, and I'm at home sitting on my butt wondering what the point is?"

The phone rang. Turning from his stepdaughter, he picked it up and heard the voice of an emergency room nurse. A boy had been hit by a bus, multiple trauma, skull fracture.

"Okay," he said, "I'll be right in."

He rolled down his shirtsleeves and buttoned them, then looked up at the slim, wan girl facing him.

"What is it?" she asked in a small voice.

"A kid hit by a bus. I've gotta go in and put his head back together." He turned at the door. "Should I stop now to figure out what the point is?"

Downstairs he grabbed a sweater and walked out into a light rain. Four hours later, after attending to the open skull fracture of a boy who would never be whole again, he returned home wearily to find his wife waiting for him in the kitchen, her face lit with pleasure.

"I don't know what it was you said to her," she told him, "but it sure worked."

"What do you mean?"

"She went back! She packed and left!" His wife smiled. "You're a genius," she said, moving in to hug him.

For the rest of the weekend, he couldn't get his stepdaughter out of his mind. As he and Ginny worked around the yard together, the girl's pale, hurt look kept coming back to him.

On Sunday morning his son called from Massachusetts, Slattery recognizing instantly the understated and faintly ironic "Hello." He asked his son how things were going, and waited as they talked for him to get around to the point.

"I happened to talk to Tracey last night," his son finally said. "She sounds pretty depressed, Dad."

"Well, Tobe," Slattery said. It irked him how his children and stepchildren traded grievances. "She's got herself hooked into a pretty unproductive situation down here."

"Um-hmmm," his son answered in a slow, skeptical voice. The coming argument had the dreary inevitability of rain. "Don't you think it's best to let her fall down on her own?"

"Well, that certainly is a humane attitude," Slattery said, biting down on his words. Moments later, they tersely said their good-byes.

Of Slattery's three children, his son had been the most affected by Slattery's decision, ten years earlier, to leave his first wife, Mary Ellen, after twenty-five years. Since then his daughters had bounced back into closeness with him; but Toby remained aloof. In earlier years, Slattery and his son had done everything together, playing basketball and chess, going to Red Sox games, doing his son's paper route, sharing bawdy jokes. Nowadays none of this was ever spoken of. It was as if their former intimacy was an unmentionable secret. Such overtures as Slattery did on occasion tentatively make were met with a stonewalling cordiality. "Yes, I remember that," his son would say, unflinchingly neutral. Thus Slattery felt a whole body of experience fading unrenewed out of memory.

He blamed no one. He saw his life as a series of events in which the concept of blame had a very small place. His father, a pipefitter in a Philly shipyard, his mother, a secretary and part-time schoolteacher: they had made him. Living in a cramped brick house behind a police station where drunks raved in the cells on Saturday nights, they wanted more for him. "My boss walks in any day of the year and doesn't like my face, I'm a goner," his father endlessly said. "Don't let that happen to you."

He hadn't. Carefully steering himself from situation to situation, he had done well at school, entered college and a profession; had married and fathered children, provided for them, educated them. He had had vacations and new cars, and houses big enough to run around in.

But there had been costs. The love he had felt for his first wife, a girl whose father he had once caddied for, had been flawed with adoration. Adoring each other had been a kind of cloak under which their lives had begun secretly to diverge. She had stopped understanding what he did every day at the hospital, and he had allowed it—even, in some way he found hard to confront, had perhaps encouraged it. His wife had developed an aversion to hospitals, a squeamishness, and he had catered to it; steadily, the circle of her concerns shrank until, after twenty years, it no longer overlapped with the circle of his. Her breezy way of taking things for granted, which he had cherished at twenty-five, he found irksome at forty. She would write a check for four hundred dollars and come home indignant when it bounced, only to giggle when he pointed out to her that the three thousand she had thought she had in the account was actually three *hundred*. "Oh well," she would say, shrugging it off. "One little zero." Exactness eluded her completely. Numbers held no reality. He would read an article about the birthrate in America and, discussing it with her, would see she had no firm idea whether there were 25 million people in America or 250 million. "It makes a difference," he'd say, shaking his head in disbelief.

"Why? Will any of them stop existing if they find out they weren't counted? I wasn't counted, and I'm still here."

Sometimes he tried to make her see why such things mattered, but then she accused him of trying to make her seem stupid. To her, exactness was a kind of moral shortcoming, a failure of generosity. So he stopped trying to correct her, and opted for humor.

The break, when it came, came quickly. Within six weeks of his meeting Ginny, a quiet but comprehending nurse who was anything but the seductress some people would later try to make her into, he had known that sooner or later he would hurt his wife. It started in the winter after his son had gone off to college. Slattery had trekked to Providence to watch a basketball game, as he and Toby had often done. Sitting in the stands, he kept thinking he recognized the woman directly in front of him—a young, almost boyish woman watching the game with intense interest. "Excuse me," he finally said, leaning over, "but are you by any chance a nurse in Connecticut?"

Throughout the second half of the game they had talked, he moving down a row to sit next to her. He was surprised by how much she knew about basketball and about other things that interested him. She followed politics, read novels and biographies, liked to ski, and dreamed of traveling. He wondered why she was alone, and she told him, in a voice edged with irritation, that her husband was out drinking with his gang.

"And you?" she said.

Within two weeks they were meeting for lunch in the hospital cafeteria—casual lunches gobbled down in the company of other nurses and doctors. Eventually, when things between them became secret, they avoided each other in public. They agonized over their situation but kept moving onward into it. Slattery felt irresistibly drawn to Ginny Di Biasi, to her spunk, her tough persistence and good humor. She had not had it easy in life; her father had died when she was a child, and she had married at eighteen, missing out on college. Doggedly, and against the will of her boorish husband, she had taken night classes and read widely on her own, carving out an education for herself. She was a quiet person, but behind that quiet was a steady strength that Slattery found himself longing for with a desire whose power shocked him.

After several months, and before they were lovers in the technical sense, Ginny's husband found out; suddenly, Slattery found himself involved in scenes that he had never in his wildest nightmares envisioned. Her husband threatened him and on one occasion actually attacked him, barging in on the two of them in Ginny's kitchen and, bellowing, grabbing Slattery in a kind of headlock. As Slattery grappled with the younger man on the floor of his lover's kitchen, he knew he had gone too far to turn back. But it was months more before he told his wife.

Now, as then, he regretted having hurt his first wife. Even more, though, he regretted the walls he had placed between himself and his children. His new life was a good and solid one, full of friends, travel, and the satisfactions of work. But sometimes sentimentality about his children passed over him like a warm wave. His paper boy, a crew-cut, smeared kid of about eleven named Rusty, affected him particularly. Coming up the driveway, he would wave at the boy, who, walking lopsidedly under the weight of his newspaper bag, would wave back. "How ya doing, Champ?" Slattery liked to say. Sometimes the boy's crooked smile made him feel sad.

All Sunday, as Ginny polished and vacuumed, he found himself unwontedly thinking about his first marriage. He slept fitfully that night, and was glad the next morning to have a case to take his mind off himself. Standing with his scrub nurse in the sterile area by the patient's head, he gazed at the draped-out apparatus of the anesthesiologist. His mind flashed again to his ex-wife; he saw her sitting at the kitchen table in their old house, smoking a cigarette and staring at him.

He directed himself away from this vision to the task at hand. It was the woman he had told his stepdaughter about, a forty-year-old with a likely tumor near the tip of the left temporal lobe. He marked his line of incision with a scalpel, the scratch mark oozing a few drops of blood. Then he took a last look at the x-rays and CAT scans on the viewing screen, nodded to the scrub nurse, and went to work. The scalp incision completed, he turned the forehead down to the orbital rims, plotted and drilled his bur holes, and then sawed through to connect them, creating a trap door of bone, hinged at one end to the skull by the temporal muscle. This he swung open to reveal the brain, pulsing gently under the dura. Cutting through to expose portions of the front and temporal lobes, he moved slowly. In this hemisphere were the areas that governed speech, comprehension, and memory; whatever the nature of the lesion, he would do this woman no good if, in removing it, he threw her into a life without words, without memory. *Primum non nocere*—first do no harm—was the axiom of every surgeon who violated the cranial vault.

Afterward, Slattery undressed in the locker room. He remembered bringing his two older children into the hospital, two decades earlier. They would eat breakfast with him and then walk over to their grade school nearby. On occasion he would show them an area of the hospital, introducing them to nurses and technicians. His first wife had resented these visits, and when he wanted to bring Toby in to see him operate, she had opposed the idea. "He's too young," she had said. "It's too horrible." Now, as he walked through the bright, clean halls, he couldn't remember whether it had come off.

Turning into his driveway that afternoon, Slattery saw the paper boy crossing the lawn, and called out "Hiya, Champ!" before he realized it was a different boy.

"Where's Rusty today?" he said, stepping out of his car.

"He's hurt," said the boy, a chubby, dirty-faced kid. "He had a accident."

Slattery stopped. "Is it serious?"

The kid shrugged and rubbed his nose. "I dunno. They just called me to do the route. I'm only doing it today." He handed Slattery the paper. "See ya."

In the middle of the night, Slattery woke with a jolt. The blood-red figures on his clock said 2:27. He sat upright, blinking into the darkness. The face of Rusty the paper boy floated before him, and he reached for the phone.

"Hello, this is Dr. Slattery," he said when the night nurse came on. "Can you do me a favor and tell me the home address of the Kosniak kid, the multiple trauma I did on Saturday?"

"Sure, Doctor. Just a second." Slattery noted the curiosity in her voice. "Doctor? That's Richard Kosniak, 316 River Road in Hallington." There was a pause. "Hey, that's out near you, isn't it?"

"I'm afraid it is." He heard himself sigh. "Any change in this kid's condition?"

"Not really. Blood pressure down slightly. No reflexes . . ." Her voice trailed off.

"Okay," Slattery said. "Well. Thank you."

In the kitchen he poured himself a Scotch and stood in the dark by the window. Rain shot through the brightness of the streetlight, white like snow. He could see the place where the news truck dropped off the boy's stack of papers every afternoon. Slattery remembered helping his son with his paper route. He saw the two of them walking side by side up Frog Hollow Road, folding the newspapers and leaving them in mailboxes and porch doors. His son's crew cut was golden in the low light, and his own hand rested on it.

The Scotch was tasteless and warm. The Kosniak boy, he remembered, had been hit by a bus, had inexplicably ridden his bike right in front of it. He recalled the parents, a large couple huddled together in the ER, staring at him with glazed incomprehension.

"Richard has been very gravely hurt . . ." he had begun.

Ginny woke when he slid back into bed. She murmured and moved toward him. "What is it, Dan?" she said.

He told her the whole story. They lay there, touching each other in the darkness. "I'm surprised I didn't recognize him," Slattery finally said. "His face was fairly intact."

"Oh, God," Ginny said. "Those poor parents."

As his wife slipped back into sleep, Slattery stayed awake, thinking. Rusty's face glancing up from his stack of papers merged with the face of his son, cheerfully lugging his heavy bag, smiling the smile that always got him hugely tipped at Christmas. Getting out of bed, Slattery dressed quickly, dashed through violent rain to the garage, and drove off.

The doctors' parking lot was almost empty when he pulled in. Rain had ceased, and the whole world quietly gurgled as water ran off in the gutters. He said hello to a night janitor at the door and made his way up to E-1. Above the lusty snore of the patient in the first bed, Slattery could hear the whoosh and click of the respirator keeping the paper boy alive. The boy's mother sat asleep in a chair by the bed, one hand on her son's shoulder. KOSNIAK, RICHARD, read the printout on the bedpost, along with Slattery's name.

It was Rusty, all right. But he could see why he hadn't known it before. The boy's face was pale, bruised blue under the eyes, and swept clean of all expression. Slattery could see no resemblance to the mother, a darker woman whose dyed blond hair hung in chopped bangs over a long and narrow face. Rusty's mother was young, perhaps only a year or two older than Slattery's eldest daughter. In sleep she looked calm.

He laid his hand on the boy's ankle, imagining a reflex movement. The boy's chest rose and fell with the pump, his heartbeat on the oscilloscope showing regular but faint. There was nothing happening inside him except the bare minimum, the technical fact of life.

"Come on, Champ," Slattery said, his voice thickening. He gave the ankle a squeeze and then, before the woman could wake and see him standing there, he left.

Outside, rain had given way to a dense, still fog. Slattery remembered when Toby had had meningitis as a small child. Three nights in a row his wife had kept vigil in the hospital room, singing songs to their comatose son in her high and creaky voice. Her wide eyes trembled with tears as she changed the washcloth on Toby's forehead, or as she leaned against the wall in the hallway, smoking. "I have faith that this child is going to be okay, Daniel," she had said to him. And she had been right.

Returning to his senses, Slattery found himself in his car, driving. He was lost. For a moment he coasted, contactless, peering through the fog. Then a strange tree snapped into familiarity, dragging with it a row of houses, a store, a streetlight. He pulled to the side of the road and rubbed his forehead. The clock said 4:16. He was six blocks from his old home.

He woke at noon the next day, as late as he could remember waking in thirty years. Sunlight powered through the windows, and he rose to squint out at a world of green and yellow. He felt slowness in his bones; before the mirror, caught in a shaft of dust-specked light, he looked shockingly white, like a ghost. In two years he would be sixty. Most of his life he had looked young for his age, but at some point his hair had gone from gray-black to gray-white, and suddenly he had looked old for his age. His features were changing, his cheeks receding, his nose becoming more prominent. His mother, still healthy at ninety-two, was so pale and white-haired that in photographs she glowed, and looked superimposed onto the picture, or—as the kids always teased her—beamed down from another planet. Soon he would look like that, too.

On the kitchen table Ginny had left coffee and a note. *Call me*, her looping handwriting read. The coffee had gone bitter on the warmer, and he poured it down the drain. As a younger man, he had liked black coffee, but in recent years his taste for this, like his taste for very spicy foods and for the pipe he used to smoke, had disappeared.

Dialing the pediatrics ward where Ginny worked, he was glad to hear her serious, girlish voice answer. "I just wanted to tell you Tracey called this morning," she told him. "She says she's fine."

"You sound as if you don't believe her."

She laughed. "Just keeping my fingers crossed. I don't want to jinx it."

Slattery tried to reassure her but lost his train of thought in midsentence, and broke off. She asked him if he was okay. "You sound a little down," she said.

"Me? Nah," he said, brightening his voice. "I'm just tired."

"Well, enjoy your day off," she said. "Lucky you."

For a year or so, he had been taking one day a week off. Since his divorce he had pursued new interests: photography, cycling, sailing. He saw himself as a person who took great pleasure in activity, who needed projects to accomplish. His first wife had never understood that.

Today, however, nothing appealed. His darkroom reminded him obscurely of an operating room, and he backed away from it. He took a spy novel out to the back patio but could get nowhere; annoyed at himself, he laid the book down on his lap and frowned into his yard. The place was too well groomed. There was nothing left to do.

The basement was the only place where he could put himself to good use, fixing a broken shelf, dusting off patio furniture and hauling it upstairs. He lifted a bag of fertilizer, which split and spilled across the floor. He didn't mind sweeping it up, whistling as he pushed the broom slowly across the cement floor until every particle was gone.

Eventually he wandered over into the southwest corner, where a small stack of boxes held all the things he had saved from his first marriage. It wasn't much, only two carloads hustled out under his first wife's withering scrutiny. He lifted a lid, and a crayoned drawing of a stick-figure playing tennis stared up at him. *To Dad*, it said, *Happy 40!!!* Under this was a faded picture of his middle school football team, and next, folded in half, a program from a World Series game he and his son had gone to in Boston.

There was no system. The only order was the order in which he had grabbed things, hurriedly, his wife looking on bewildered and hurt, as if they had not agreed to separate. The second trip, when he cleaned out his office in the basement, she stood there, arms crossed, and battered him with a rocklike silence. All he wanted was to escape—and so he had never gotten to the huge junk room upstairs. He had left much behind. Occasionally he would remember, with longing, some trivial object he had possessed: a Mexican sombrero, an LBJ dart board, his old toy trains. But after a while these things ceased being a part of him and became in his mind attached to his ex-wife, hostages forming bonds with their captor. In the years since the divorce, he had seen his ex-wife only half a dozen times. She looked old.

Opening the second box, he found a lock of Sharon's red hair tied with a yellow ribbon. Reaching further, he pulled out a curled photo of his son, aged about six, posing with his best friend, a pudgy, amused boy named Chip Butler. Slattery looked at the crew-cut heads and found himself back in the kitchen at the old house, surrounded by a long-forgotten wallpaper of ferns and bamboo, ministering with electric haircutting clippers to the large head of his son. He had had those clippers when he and his wife lived among the Navajos in Arizona, and he gave haircuts; he remembered how the handle had vibrated warmly in his hand as he moved it gently over the surface of his son's head.

Slattery put the picture back in the box and slowly stood. He wondered if the clippers had by some miracle survived the years of his absence. He wanted them.

It took forty-five minutes to reach the old neighborhood. His route took him first to the beaches, then past his old buddy Jack Cousins's place, then finally, honestly, toward the big white house.

No one was at home. He slowed the car and watched the yard slide by, more unkempt than he remembered it. Andromeda ballooned high against the house; the two huge maples were dying; the place itself needed paint. He had heard rumors—not corroborated by his children, who told him nothing—that his ex-wife was thinking about moving; looking at the house, he imagined stacks of boxes, and furniture shrouded in sheets. After three orbits around the block, each slower than the last, he stopped. His ex-wife, he knew, was at the law office where she worked as a secretary. Looking to both sides and seeing no one, he got out of the car and walked into the driveway.

On the back porch he stood surveying the ragged yard and smiled, remembering the string of disastrous yardmen they had had. Only the garden by the back porch, a square of upturned earth six feet on an edge, showed real care. A stone near the side of the garden caught his eye. White and translucent, it was exactly the kind of stone his former wife had liked to use as a hiding place for the key.

Two minutes later, he was in the kitchen. His younger daughter's ancient black Lab, John Henry, heaved hoarse barks until Slattery called its name, then melted into tired and obsequious wagging. Slattery looked around, his eyes taking in unfamiliar furniture and wallpaper. He felt like a thief. In the front hall he closed his eyes and drew deeply into his nostrils an odor composed of burlap, sweet flowers and, more faintly, cat piss. He sensed neglect in the scent. A close look in the corners revealed dust balls, which fluttered when he moved past them.

Why he was there, he had no idea. He would think about it later; right now, what was important was to act. He took the stairs two at a time, navigated between a couple of bored cats circling on the landing, and entered Toby's room. The forlornness of his son's room, empty save for a few books and faded trophies, unnerved him. He moved quickly to the junk room door and shot back the bolt that he himself had affixed two decades earlier—to protect his son, as he recalled, from monsters.

Much had changed. The junk room had been insulated and plasterboarded. Boxes stood on boxes, many with labels; he stepped in and steered his way among them. Light shone through the single window where in his era there had resided a stained-glass mural, made by an old buddy of his from med school. He had failed to save it.

Sighing, he pushed his way into the room, past Mary Ellen's Zanzibari hope chest, past an exercise bicycle he had bought when he turned forty, past the ancient Victrola she had cherished in her childhood. Instinct took him to the darkest corner of the room and rewarded him there. Behind a small love seat was a yellow cardboard box with a big question mark inked on the side. Flipping off the lid, he saw a stack of pictures. The top one was from their wedding, taken right outside the church where they stood by the MG he had rented for the honeymoon. The next showed them in Arizona five years later, standing in the pink dust of the street outside their house. It shocked him to see how young they looked, and how foolish: his ex-wife with her bright lipstick and bunned hair, he fat and crew-cut in his T-shirt with the rolled-up sleeves, grinning like a trained seal. He couldn't remember ever having looked like that. Sifting quickly through the box, he found what he wanted, took them, and left. He took care to leave everything as he had found it, and hoped his ex-wife would not be able, through some sort of psychic radar, to detect his presence.

Driving away in the Peugeot, he turned right, as he had so many thousands of times, from Frog Hollow onto Bay Avenue. He watched the house shrinking in the rearview mirror and felt himself choking up. "So long," he said aloud, recognizing the gesture as sentimental and probably hypocritical, but enjoying it nevertheless. He headed toward the hospital, his left hand holding the wheel, his right hand tightly grasping the electric hair clippers, liberated from their decade of captivity.

The boy was fading. Slattery found his partner, Barry Baylor, up on the neuro ward, and Baylor told him that the boy's blood pressure had begun to fall early in the morning. "We speeded up the vasopressor," he said. "No response." Baylor looked at him quizzically in his jeans and sweater. "What are you doing here anyway?"

"Just happened to be in the neighborhood," Slattery said, shrugging.

"Opening a barber shop?"

"Huh?" Only when he followed his partner's gaze down to his own hand did he realize he was still carrying the clippers. "Oh. Just doing some attic cleaning," he said, shoving them into his back pocket.

Baylor nodded toward the room where Richard Kosniak lay. "You want to talk to his folks, or should I?"

"I will," he said.

He walked to the room; a nurse met him at the door. "Heartbeat is irregular," she said. "No pulse."

"Right," Slattery said, entering. His eye jumped to the parents: the woman still seated by the bed, her husband towering over her— a huge blond man, dry and summery as if made of straw. The couple turned to him a single face of exhaustion and pain. In an automatic

241

gesture, Slattery took their son's wrist and felt for a pulse. There was nothing.

"He's not going to make it, is he, Doctor," Rusty's father said. Though at least six-five, Kosniak spoke with the squeaky voice of a kid. He was huge and gentle, like a giraffe.

Slattery put his hand on the man's shoulder. "I'm afraid not," he said. "Your son is beginning to lose function in the part of his brain that controls cardiac activity." He nodded toward the oscilloscope. "You can see that his heartbeat is becoming less regular." As Slattery spoke, he watched a tear slide down the woman's face, slowly at first and then very fast. She tried to say something but could only gulp air; shaking, she whispered to her husband.

"We want to know what we can do—" Kosniak paused. "What we can do if we don't . . ."

Slattery nodded. *If you don't want him to go on.* "At some point," he said, "you may wish to ask us to turn off the ventilator and let your son follow his own course."

Kosniak nodded, blankly staring. His wife buried her face in his shoulder. Slattery felt his eyes sting. "I'm so sorry," he said. "Your son—" He struggled for composure. "Your son was a sweet kid."

On the way home he tried to imagine what the couple would do that night. Thirty years earlier, in Arizona, he had lost his first patient, a little girl with appendicitis, who had hemorrhaged, suddenly and massively. Slattery had gone home and wept in his wife's arms. For the next few years he had remembered all of the patients who had died under his care, remembered them by name and face and history; but eventually there were too many, and it all blurred together.

He pulled into his street of trim houses. Ginny's car was in the driveway. Inside, the note she had left him in the morning was still on the table. "Anybody home?" he called.

She was in the living room, folding clothes. He saw in the way she was batting out wrinkles in a T-shirt, with deft, angry chops, that something was wrong.

"You missed the fireworks," she said.

"Why, what happened?"

"Tracey called. She's coming home. She says she can't go on like this."

"Like what?"

"You got me." His wife threw a hand up. "It's this depression thing again."

"What did you say to her?"

"I told her if she's thinking about living here and seeing Eddie, she can just forget it." Looking up from the clothes, she frowned. "Where were you?"

"At the hospital." He rubbed his forehead; a headache had sprouted without his noticing it and was suddenly in full blossom behind his right eye. Hearing an engine in the street, he turned and saw the big black newspaper truck pull up to the curb; a bundle of newspapers came flying out, landing on the sidewalk.

"Dan," Ginny said behind him. "I just don't know what I'm going to do with Tracey. She says she's so depressed, even the thought of walking down the hall to brush her teeth is too much."

A breeze came up outside; he watched a corner of the top newspaper flutter and flap.

"What am I going to do with her when she gets back? Do you think you can work some of your magic again?"

The sun, as he came out on the front stoop, had just slid down into the woods, and the neighborhood was doused unevenly with a peach-gold light that meant summer. But his mood was bleak.

Despite what he had said to his stepdaughter, Slattery knew well what it meant to be depressed. A dozen years earlier, near the end of his first marriage, he had endured a depression that had transformed every minute of his life. His son's departure for college had been the small but crucial event that had frozen his psyche, almost overnight, into a block of despair. Slattery hadn't realized how much of his time had been spent with his son until he had to spend it

243

instead with his wife; conversations sputtered without the children there to ignite and fuel them. Dismally, he did alone what he and his son had done together—a pitiful figure making his solitary, sad excursions to basketball games and movies. But nothing really excited him. Mornings he would wake to the raw buzz of the alarm clock and push himself up out of bed, struggling with his socks and underwear, his shoelaces heavy as ropes; the day stretched bleakly before him, a landscape gray and featureless as the moon. In the shower, where he usually sang, he would try one verse and then fade off, standing dead still and listening to the water beating down on his head.

The blankness inside him had terrified him. He had told no one about it, especially not his wife. For six months he lived like a dead man. And then he had met Ginny, and escaped.

He pictured now his stepdaughter's arrival. There would be recriminations and turned shoulders, his wife's deep sigh, his stepdaughter's icy pout. And then there would be himself, the cheerful stepfather, carefully maintaining what he sometimes referred to as his "aesthetic distance" from the fray. With respect to his three stepchildren, Slattery realized he had settled over the years into a kind of permanent blandness, saying little, taking little offense or exception—a harmless godfather, perhaps, or a gift-giving uncle—at any rate not the eager father figure he had set out at first to be. He could see now how it had happened, the slow attenuation of patience, then of interest itself, as his stepchildren proceeded with mishaps and agonies that had no bearing on him, no matter how much he wanted them to. The lives of his wife's children were like novels he had begun reading avidly, then decided to skim. Somehow they had never become wholly real to him—never quite as real as the lives he had already, willfully, put behind him. The task of stocking a whole new store of memories with his stepchildren had proved overwhelming, and so he had given it up and concentrated solely on Ginny herself. He was too old, his stepchildren were too complicated, and after all they were not his own.

The newspapers flapped in the breeze. No one was coming to do the route. He imagined people calling the Kosniaks to complain, and shuddered. Kneeling by the stack, he slipped his hand under the plastic strap that bound the papers and pulled. His hand whitened under the pressure. The strap dug into the flesh of his palm, and just as he felt sure he was about to be cut, it snapped, and he went tumbling backward onto the lawn.

For a moment he didn't move but lay on his side, breathing in and out. Cheek to the grass, he stared at the stack of newspapers looming sideways in front of him. Get up now, he told himself. But he didn't move. The breeze kicked up again, and he watched the top newspaper quiver and then, freed of its restraining strap, blow apart, section by section. The pages caught the air and billowed like sails, soaring quickly out of his line of sight into the nothingness beyond.

XV

Atlantic and Pacific

For over twenty-five years, through thick and thin on both sides of the street, I've watched the Slatterys. And so it was a shock this morning when, slipping out in my pajamas to take out the garbage cans, I saw a big red moving van parked next to the Tudor house. The place looked quiet, all the blinds on the avenue side of the house drawn tight. One of Mary Ellen's many cats was delicately pawing its way through dew on the front lawn, hunting some phantom mouse. By the time Sonia and I came back from running, an hour later, the doors of the big red van gaped open, and moving men were already beginning to fill it with our neighbor's things. Sonia, who as usual had arrived far ahead of me, was across the street talking with a dark-haired woman whom I recognized as Lydia Slattery, the oldest of Mary Ellen's three kids. I waved to the women as I turned into our drive. I would have stopped to chat, but the boys were sleeping in the house, and I don't like to leave them alone for too long. My old man's legs were tired as I trudged up the driveway, and looking back at my wife and the Slattery girl I had to laugh, because I couldn't for the life of me figure out which of the two is older.

When I saw the van this morning, I did some quick arithmetic and dated the arrival of Dan and Mary Ellen Slattery at spring 1960. I remember it was a sunny day, and my first wife Lucy and I were in the kitchen arguing when she abruptly turned from me and looked out the window. Sure enough, a station wagon had stopped in front of the Lloyd house, and a young couple, two little kids, and a Dalmatian dog were taking their first careful steps onto the lawn. An hour or so later, Lucy and I ventured over—my first wife carrying a tray loaded so high with fresh fruit that I thought our new neighbors would have to open a canning factory to get rid of it. Immediately she and Mary Ellen Slattery began babbling rapturously, like long lost sisters. But I felt pale and old, fully forty-two, next to Dan Slattery, who, ten years younger, still had a crew cut and a cheeky, round face, full of boyish confidence. I watched as with a wobbly hand drill he made a small hole in a kitchen cabinet in which to sink a penny. When he and his wife discovered I was an architect, they wanted to know whether it was "kosher" to do this. I told them that while it was done in new houses and in newly renovated kitchens in old houses, it was, to the best of my knowledge, not usually done by new owners in old houses. Hearing this, Dan stopped turning the drill. "Well?" said his wife. "We're different!" She laughed, and Dan finished the hole. But when he went to sink the penny, he saw that he'd used too small a drill bit. He solved the problem by putting a dime in the hole. "I do it all the time in my work, too," he said to me. "Use whatever's on hand."

"What do you do?" I asked him.

"Brain surgery," he said immediately, then broke into a grin.

I liked them.

When our daughter Alison heard that a neurosurgeon had moved in across the street, she shuddered. She couldn't believe that anyone would *choose* to do that. (If she could have seen ahead eight years to her decision to drop out of college and move in with a shiftless bartender in Denver, she might have been less judgmental.) Alison assumed that neurosurgeons and their families were morbid; in fact, quite the reverse, in this case anyway, was true. Dan Slattery continually and cheerfully sang. He sang while out trimming bushes in the yard. He sang while waxing his car, while playing with his kids. If you were driving and he pulled up behind you in his car, you could see in your rearview mirror that he was singing—his eyebrows jauntily going up and down, his head syncopating the beat, his mouth comically hanging open on the long notes. Dan and Mary Ellen liked love songs from musicals—"If I Loved You," "The Girl That I Marry"—and they liked the smooth crooners. Sinatra, Perry Como, Johnny Mathis, Nat King Cole, Mel Torme—these were the singers who made the kind of sound my new neighbors wanted to hear. Sometimes, walking our old German shepard, Tarzan, slowly past Dan and Mary Ellen's place, I could hear the two of them banging out songs and harmonies on the piano. I wondered whether it would be safe to be operated on by a man who went around imitating Mel Torme.

People come to know each other in such strange and unpredictable ways! Three months after our neighbors moved in, Dan knocked on our door and told me that he wanted to build a playhouse for his kids but didn't quite know how to begin. I drew up some plans, in all of twelve minutes, to show how a simple playhouse might easily be built in his backyard. In return, Mary Ellen gave me a delicious chocolate pineapple upside-down cake, and Dan jokingly asked whether I needed any quick neurosurgery. In fact, my back had been bothering me ever since the afternoon I spent moving Lucy's piano from one side of the living room to the other (and back again). So I took Dan up on his joke and went into his office for some x-rays. When the pictures came through, he looked closely at them and then at me. How had I managed to go around for two years with a herniated disk in my back?

Having your neighbor operate on you is a risky business. As I went under the anesthesia, I envisioned Dan working away at his hedges with his huge, beak-bladed clippers, while singing "I Get a Kick Out of You." But the operation was a total success. I could bend again. Aside from being pleased by this, I was impressed, as an architect, by Dan's work. The human body is more changeable and vastly more unknowable than any building; Dan's work, as I imagined it, was more intuitive than mine, and therefore of a higher order. It is no wonder that architects, along with the rest of the populace, revere doctors. For what after all is a house but a facsimile of the human body, with a roof for a head, windows for eyes, beams for bones, a door for a mouth, and the hearth as heart or brain? Everyone expects (as they should) a building to stand up, but when a sick man is healthy again, the doctor is more than a hero. He is a kind of god.

My neighbor did what he could to dismiss these ideas of mine. "What I do is just glorified plumbing," he said once. And I had to laugh, for as I got to know Dan, I saw he didn't know the first thing about plumbing.

In my enthusiasm and gratitude, I made a piece of sculpture to give to Dan. It was a bronze cast of a section of spine. I worked hard and fast at it out in the garage, the first piece of sculpture I'd attempted since shortly after I was married. When the piece was done, Lucy sneered at it, as if it (and I) were some sort of tasteless joke. I certainly hadn't meant it that way; I was fascinated by the human spine, by its beauty and utility. But as I was crossing the street with the piece in a clumsily wrapped box under my arm, I suddenly felt that Lucy was right. I started to turn around, but it was too late; Dan was out mowing his lawn, waving cheerily to me over the old push cutter. He seemed genuinely to like the piece, and a few weeks later when we came to dinner, I saw it displayed, with suspicious prominence, in the living room. I overheard Lucy telling Mary Ellen that I'd intended it as a tie rack.

Dan put my back together, but no one could fix my marriage. Lucy was an alcoholic and a borderline manic-depressive. For a long time I didn't know the terminology; all I knew was that my wife drank a lot, and that the boisterous, moody charm that had attracted me to her had soured, grown capricious. She accused me of "turning her into a wife," much (she implied) as her father had done to her mother thirty years earlier—killing the woman through "slow spiritual asphyxiation." And just as it had been Lucy's father's fault that her mother had ended up with only the average, doled-out share of success and recognition and happiness, so was it my fault that my wife had never finished college, that she had no one who appreciated her, no job, no place in the world. She raged at me, and I pounded back with silences. Alison took to eating dinner at friends' houses, or even upstairs in her room. I can remember wanting to do likewise.

Across the street, meanwhile, was a tableau of happiness. Dan and Mary Ellen were prodigious hosts; at least twice they had so many house guests that they had to sleep some of them out on the lawn in tents. They established a tradition of annual costume parties, and for the first couple of years, they invited just about everyone in the neighborhood. The only time Lucy and I went, she caused a scene. I hadn't been excited about going in the first place—I think now I was never really sanguine enough about my own identity to take pleasure in imitating someone else's—but Lucy spent a whole week preparing herself for it. And a funny thing happened. Lucy went as a German beer frau, wearing something blousily daring, her dark hair bunned, red blush on her cheeks, and though my ex-wife must have been at least forty-one then, she looked beautiful and young, strikingly young. I'll never forget the look on Dan and Mary Ellen's faces when they opened the door and saw her. They both smiled hugely, right at Lucy, as if they had never seen her before. Of course, this both pleased and depressed my ex-wife, and made her spend the rest of the evening trying to prove that she was no older, physically or otherwise, than anyone else at the party. She drank too much, she threw her head back and laughed, she flirted outrageously. The sad thing is that if she'd only stopped at a certain point, it would have worked as she wanted it to; everyone would have gone home talking about that ravishing woman who danced on the staircase. But Lucy never knew how to stop. Her dancing dissolved into whirling, her singing into shrieking, and finally I had to more or less drag her home. Mary Ellen saw us to the door, and I can still see her face: not embarrassed, not annoyed, just concerned. My ex-wife, though dulled by drunkenness, was already drilling me with the "slow spiritual asphyxiation" look.

We fought about the costume party incident as we fought about almost everything—what college was right for Alison and why, whether our housekeeper should be fired for her alleged insolence, what exactly was the motive of Lucy's older brother in visiting for the first time in ten years just to tell her that their mother had been a "vicious alcoholic" who had drunk herself to death. "Some people don't have the guts to stand up for themselves," Lucy said to me after he left, "until other people are dead."

Loud argument gradually became our norm. Even today as I move through the rooms of my house, I hear thunderous echoes of the great running battles Lucy and I waged. I named different areas of the house after them: Appomattox, Gettysburg, Atlanta. Sonia and I joke about this; she'll ask me where I left the hammer, and I'll say, Manassas, meaning out in the hall. Once, just to gall me while I was trying to read, Lucy banged the piano keys crazily with both hands, as hard as she could. But after a minute she couldn't keep it up— the sense for beauty was stronger in her than the need for rage—and the keys under her fingers modulated into beautiful music, a difficult and wonderful piece, I believe, by Ravel. Lucy couldn't know it, and I didn't tell her, but in my study I put down my book and listened, and held my head in my hands.

The Slattery property is on a corner; Frog Hollow Road, the street that abuts it to the north, where the big red van parked this morning, empties out onto the main road—Bay Avenue—directly across from our driveway. On occasional mornings Dan Slattery and I would come head to head across the avenue in our cars. Dan would look from inside his gleaming new car (every tenth time we met this way, it seemed he had a new one) at my ancient, abused Oldsmobile convertible, whose blue skin, bleached green in spots, had never known a sponge. He'd shake his head and wave me on with a pitying look. Then I'd leave him in the dust. I've always been a fast, even a reckless driver. Dan was cautious behind the wheel, reverentially cautious, as if driving not a sporty car but a religious relic.

When my first marriage soured, it poisoned our relationships with our neighbors. Jealousy is straightforward in children, but as we get older, it begins to look like other things, friendship, interest, charm. If I was across the street with Dan, out in his backyard, Lucy would turn up in the kitchen with Mary Ellen, ostensibly baking or arranging flowers but really complaining about, and spying on, me. Childishly, I retreated to our house and, within this, to my study. I acquired a cot and a small hot plate. When Alison left for college, Lucy and I felt free to conform our domestic arrangements to the pitiful reality of our marriage, and we lived separately in the house for well over a year. Several large rooms separated my study from the parts of the house Lucy frequented. If I could have done it without having to call in outside people, I would have built a wall.

As things go bad in a family, it gets more and more desirable to pretend that the neighbors don't know. It also gets more and more difficult. When Alison was a senior in high school, in 1967, she was running around with a dope-smoking guitarist from a local college; this led to several full-blown screaming matches between my ex-wife and my daughter, which, despite my best efforts, kept spilling out of the house into the neighborhood. One morning Alison ran down the driveway, hands over her ears, Lucy following, shouting in her deep, cracked alto; I trailed numbly behind. If it had been ten years later, people might have mistaken us for joggers, but in 1967 there could be no doubt that this was a scene. As I ran out the drive, I saw Mary Ellen and Dan and their kids out in the front yard, but it wasn't until we were all the way across Bay Avenue, still parading in loud single file, that I realized the Slatterys were taking home movies. As if possessed of a photojournalist's instinct for live disaster, Dan Slattery swerved the camera from his happy, smiling kids to my wife and daughter, who obligingly stood still and began screaming at each other with renewed, bloodcurdling force. I turned around and skulked home.

That film stayed in my mind for a long time. I used to think of it tucked away in some dark closet or basement corner of the Slattery home, among reels of happy picnics and innocent afternoons at the beach. Morbid thoughts like this consoled me during the last year or two of my first marriage. Somewhere in my harangues with Lucy, I decided that marriage, like brain surgery, involved another kind of intuitive competence I would never have. So I gave up on it.

To her credit, Lucy was unable to do this. She needed to declare her grief. I can say without any rancor that Mary Ellen Slattery was a great help to my ex-wife during those years, and, I'm sure, one of her strongest local advocates. The two women would meet to chat at a spot right outside our drive; if I passed this spot, my ex-wife would turn her back, while on Mary Ellen's girlish face I would see politeness, commiseration with my wife, anger at men, and a lingering fondness for me, all battling for supremacy. She would float me a feeble wave.

I didn't find out until years later how thoroughly Lucy had vilified me. I cheated on her, I lied, I was abusive. I was a brute, a marauding ogre brilliantly disguised by this gentle and distracted mien. It all must have provided great grist for the mills of several overactive neighborhood imaginations. But since I had in effect ceded the neighbors to Lucy in return for a spurious peace, I was unable to broadcast across the street an opposing viewpoint. What Mary Ellen Slattery couldn't see were Lucy's screaming fits at night; the days of catatonia, when she didn't move out of the shadows of her room; the blatant paranoia that lumped not only me but various relatives, psychiatrists and neighbors together in a gang of thieves (I was, needless to say, the ringleader) who had stolen her looks, her career, and the sympathies of her daughter. Lucy ventured outside only when she felt able to control and manipulate these impulses. Mary Ellen Slattery, a cheerful thirty-five-year-old woman who had faced no crushing disappointments, was no match at all for my ex-wife. She was duped. But in the long run that didn't, or doesn't, matter. Mary Ellen gave my ex-wife a great deal of comfort. And, perhaps more than any other person, she helped Lucy do the thing she absolutely had to do to begin saving herself—leave me.

When Lucy left in 1968, I withdrew into the vast heartland of the house. My work was my refuge. Even today as I drive around town, I have to admire the structures I caused to be built or renovated during that time. Meanwhile, though, my own too-large home was falling apart around me, a House of Usher settling in a rubble of dead leaves, peeled-off paint, and ill luck. In my neglect I stopped taking care of the clay tennis court and the yard. Branches fell during storms and sat there. The place began to look like a tropical rain forest.

People don't quite know how to handle a neighbor who lets things go. Resentment coexists surprisingly inside us with pity, like oil that can burn atop an ocean of water. My neighbors felt sorry for me, deserted by my wife, but even sorrier for themselves, subjected daily to the spectacle of my yard. The mess was half hidden by a low wall along the avenue, but only half hidden, and the wall itself, crumbling and clotted with vines and moss, was a disgrace in its own right. People dropped hints. Everyone had a son, it seemed, who was always "looking for a little spending money." Casual conversations on the sidewalk turned regularly to the newest miracles of lawn management, sit-down mowers, magic weed-snuffers, mini-chain-saws. One afternoon I looked out the window and saw Dan Slattery's yardman mowing the Slatterys' lawn. As I watched, the man glanced across toward my place and then, with a look of determination, wheeled the mower out onto the sidewalk, heading my way. I was convinced he had been sent to mow my lawn, and I couldn't face it. I ran out of the house, got into my car, and tore out of the driveway, wheels spinning gravel, as if *I* were the surgeon, called to some vast emergency. I saw then that the yardman was not interested in my lawn, but merely in the little strip of grass between my neighbors' sidewalk and the road.

When, on a Saturday afternoon, I watched my neighbors sitting out on their wicker porch, talking to each other and to their orbiting children, I wondered whether I'd ever have it again, the repose and satisfaction and sweet necessariness of it all. My wife was gone, and my daughter had by now dropped out of college and wandered off to Colorado, from where she sent occasional postcards reviling the institution of marriage and requesting money. At night I'd watch the lights go out across the street, first in one of the kids' bedrooms, then later in the master bedroom, then finally, downstairs, in the den. One night I strolled by, walking into the yard a ways and then up to the den window; Dan was sitting with a big hardcover book on his lap. His back was to me, and I thought he was sleeping until he turned a page. When I shut my eyes, the lines of my own drawings, of ventilator shafts and spiral staircases, burned in my mind like so many cages.

A decade dissolved, leaving no taste in my mouth.

To neighborhood kids I was a great and irresistible mystery. In a child's mind only a tremendous evil, like a murder, can account for the willful ruin of a house and property. One Sunday Toby Slattery and the Holover boy appeared in my driveway, carrying tennis racquets and looking nervously about. Through the window I watched as the boys walked by the house, Toby kicking a pebble with admirable nonchalance. I had to cross quickly to another window to watch them come around the corner and stop still in shock, as I'd known they would, when they saw the utterly unplayable court with its huge cracks, its sprawling weeds, its anthills and rotted net. The boys turned suddenly and looked around them at the yard, then up at the house. I moved back from the window.

If Dan and Mary Ellen still had the cast of the spine I'd made, I'm sure their kids saw in it clear evidence of my ghoulishness. I didn't or couldn't do anything to correct this; I even aggravated it. One night around Halloween I heard a scraping in the ivy. Looking down from a second-floor window, I saw three boys, one of them possibly Dan's son, peering into my living room. Almost in spite of myself, full of wickedness and fun but also a kind of sad rage, I let out a low, quavering moan. The boys fled.

One unwritten rule in our society says that while divorce and remarriage are permissible, even healthy, no man in remarrying shall marry a woman younger than his daughter. To break this rule is to risk charges of lust, greed, and perversion. For many years I might have agreed—but then Sonia turned up, and my life unexpectedly came bobbing to the surface.

Sonia was twenty-four ten years ago when we met—a full three years younger than my daughter, Alison. She came in with a client of mine, returned to the office twice for no real reason, and then, in her brazen fashion, invited herself over to the house for a drink. I surprised myself by agreeing. Then I rushed home, and for three days I weeded, swept, painted, and raked, readying the place for our date. Carrying my rake, I walked out to the mouth of the driveway and stood there blinking into the sun. I was suddenly very hungry.

Sonia has been a Marshall Plan for my life. She handled my deepest problems metaphorically, insisting, for example, that we *do* something about the wreckage of the yard. So we clipped and dug and trimmed, and hauled things away. We stripped the hideous wall of its weeds, cut back the canopy of branches, and resurfaced it. Gardens grew. Windows opened. It became possible to see and breathe. After about eight months of this, Sonia and I stopped to get married, and then we resumed. And after we spent a year making the place livable, we decided it was a shame there weren't more people to live in it. Had someone twelve years ago told me I'd have three sons by the time I reached the age most people retire at, I would have laughed, faintly, and said that the requisite parts inside me—heart, mind, and groin—had long since ceased functioning.

At that time Sonia worked at the hospital (as she continued to do until our second son, Jason, was born five years ago), and it was she who first told me of the problems in the Slatterys' marriage. Dan, it seemed, was having an affair with a nurse. The woman and *her* husband had separated; it was a painful story all the way around. I remember going out into the yard after Sonia told me this and looking across the street at my neighbors' house. Dan was still living there, I think, but the house looked almost deserted. The older two Slattery kids were off at college. Sonia came out and joined me; she was pregnant with Andrew then, and as we looked across the street, I couldn't help thinking how things seemed to have reversed themselves. It had been some time—years, in fact—since the parties and music at my neighbors'. Things had gradually but completely quieted. No picnics, no volleyball, no music on the porch. Just a cat or two, and men who came to cut the lawn.

By the time our first son was born, Dan Slattery had moved out. There are two events I associate with his leaving. The first was the construction of the playhouse. I have seen couples do such things just before they split. New gardens, a picture window in the kitchen, even a tennis court. Building is inherently hopeful. It assumes a future. But there is more than a touch of desperation in building a playhouse for a last child who is already thirteen or fourteen, as Sharon Slattery must have been. I wondered what Dan was doing, hauling two-by-fours out into his yard. When the playhouse began recognizably to go up, I took a long look at the daughter Dan was building it for. I saw her get off the bus, and as I watched her slow, almost stately progress down the sidewalk, I knew she was just too big for the tiny house I'd drawn fifteen years before. I thought of calling Dan and Mary Ellen, but Sonia talked me out of it. Two months after the playhouse was finished, I heard that Dan had left.

The next fall I was out in the yard with Andrew one day, carving a pumpkin, when I saw Toby Slattery's car round the corner and turn into the drive. Simultaneously, as if cued by this arrival, a small object—a shoe, I think—came bursting out of an attic window on our side of the house. It landed on the lawn in a shower of glass. Through the thin hedges I could see the Slattery boy walk up the driveway, staring above him at the window; I picked up my own infant son, and the pumpkin and knife, and went into the house.

Just last month I saw Toby Slattery at a cocktail party. Toby is much bigger now than he was when I watched him walk up his driveway on that October afternoon eight years ago. He's bigger than his father in the shoulders and neck and cheeks—though even as I say this, I remember again the baby fat on my new neighbor's cheerful face. A quarter of a century is gone.

I talked with Toby for a half-hour at the party, and as I looked at the man the little boy had grown into, my face must have shown some of the patronizing tenderness that older people can't seem to suppress at such occasions. In return, Toby seemed surprised to find himself actually talking to me, hearing me return word for word. I introduced Sonia, and for a second I thought his eyes widened. He mentioned then that his father had remarried, which of course I already knew, and that Dan and his wife were at that very moment on a bicycle trip in Europe. I could easily picture Dan, pumping his way through Provence.

"Give my regards to your father," I told Toby as he moved away to talk to a friend. "And your mother, too."

He nodded and smiled, his mouth rising in a quizzical grin as he no doubt tried to figure out just how I had been transmogrified from a murderous ghost into this urbane and neighborly person.

"Hey, Mr. Haft," he said, turning. "Do you by any chance remember one night around Halloween, a long time ago . . . ?"

Sonia insists that I get out in the world. We take walks at sunrise, go swimming and picnicking, even take occasional ski trips on which I display my pathetic, giraffeish style for my young wife's entertainment. When I turned sixty-nine three months ago, I cut down to three days a week at the office. The boys love this, as does Sonia, as do I.

Today is one of those days off. I spend it playing with Jason and Kevin, raking leaves in the yard, helping Sonia paint the back porch. In between, I watch the house across the street empty itself into the moving truck. Big laundry bags sail out from an open window and land on the grass. Toby and Lydia Slattery, carrying books in plastic milk crates, stop to turn and look up at the house. The moving men take their time with the heavy furniture, spending their bodies as slowly as possible. *Atlantic and Pacific*, the big red van says on its side. Even though I had heard that Mary Ellen was trying to sell her house, the truck in all its redness and size is a shock.

At 2:30, Sonia and Jason and Kevin and I walk up to surprise Andrew on his way home from school. He's in third grade and thus not yet old enough to be embarrassed in front of his friends when his whole family leaps out at him from behind a bush, making ridiculous sounds. He even feigns fear to please us. And just as he's covering his face with his hands in mock terror, the big red moving van rumbles by in the street; the kids, even without realizing exactly whose life is being carried away, turn to stare a bit solemnly. When we near home, I can see that the house across the street is indeed empty. The Slatterys are gone.

Our boys run ahead, eager for the familiar romp of yard, table, fridge. I am quiet, as is my usually gregarious wife. When the Slatterys came, I was already past forty; Sonia was in third grade, where Andrew is now.

We gaze for a while at the empty house, then turn and walk arm in arm down our drive. She returns to painting the porch, and I take Andrew, Jason, and Kevin down for a walk to the beach. Whenever I walk with my sons, passersby smile at us, either indulgently, humoring Grandpa, or—if they know who I am—mischievously, with raised eyebrows. Some couples I've known for almost half a century, people somewhat older than I, say I'm crazy. They laugh and slap my shoulder; the men wink. But they love it, and so do I. My life is new again.

The sun is bright and warm on the sand. It's a summery late September, the kind of day when the two or three people who make it down to the beach come away with a sunburn, and smile as if they've cheated nature. A few seagulls placidly loiter. The Atlantic swills seaweed at the feet of my children, who find great joy in its patterns. Permission is granted for them to take off their shoes and socks. My sons seek out the treasures of the beach: smooth bits of wood, bottle caps, a feather. They squat to pry these objects loose from the sand, turn them over two or three times in their small hands, then rise and come running to me, faces wide with excitement. Sonia says the boys look like me, especially Jason, but I can't see it. It would be unfair to my sons, and to truth, to insist on a resemblance between faces so young and a face so old.

Running, my sons cleave divots out of the sand with their bare feet. If they challenged me to a race, I could win, but the time when, breathing hard, I will laughingly lose, isn't too far off. For now, I let my sons do all the running. A small pile of tribute accumulates at my feet as I stand, immobilized by happiness, looking out over the ocean. How did I find this life? Where did it come from? What did I do to deserve it? If I could tell my neighbors one thing, it would be this: if this can happen to me, it can happen to anyone.

XVI

The Last to Go

I

The clock by the bed galls her with its ticking. The sound flings itself across the room and lodges like grains of sand under her fingernails. Then it pushes up her forearms, under the skin. How many times has she said to him, can't we please get an electric clock?

I can't sleep without the sound, he says.

He has been in the kitchen since they got home, making ice, unloading the dishwasher, hiding out. She sits in the rocking chair, making tiny motions. Doesn't take off her raincoat, doesn't take off her shoes. "Want something to drink?" he calls in his hearty voice.

"No," she says. "Thank you."

The apartment is small, you can talk from room to room. He has a big voice, it floods into all the corners and hardens there like wax. "So old Nick is finally married," he says. "I can hardly believe it."

She says nothing.

"Yup," he says to himself. "Hard-ly be-*leeeve* it."

She thinks about him at the wedding party. Him sitting at the head table, rising to propose a toast, oh so witty, so funny. She looked around under the tent at all the people laughing nodding smiling. Wanted to tell them, *Hey, he's not really that great.*

When he finally comes out of the kitchen, he sees she is still in her dress and raincoat. If by some chance he didn't know she was angry on the ride home, he knows now. He plows straight across to the bathroom, the only other place aside from the kitchen she can't see from her rocking chair.

"What did you think of Gunderson?" he calls out. She can tell by his voice that he is combing his hair, pulling it up off his forehead, reminding himself he isn't going bald. "And how about van Bergh's wife—isn't she hilarious?"

"Pathetic," she says.

"And how about that old Nick?"

"Nick," she says, "is a truly nice person. In fact, I think he is a gentleman."

No comment. He comes out of the bathroom with his shirt off, swinging his upper body the way he does, and sits on the bed. "You going to get undressed?" he says, plucking at his shoelaces.

"No."

He shrugs. Starts winding his clock.

"Don't you want to know why I'm not getting undressed?" she says.

"Not really," he says. Winding the clock slowly as possible, click by click. At night he is the one who falls asleep instantly, his whole body radiating warmth and ease like a huge ember—while she lies awake turning and fretting.

"I'm furious with you," she says. She stares across the breakfast nook to the Matisse and Chagall prints on the wall. At the moment such colors offend her. "Did you hear me?"

He enters her line of vision, wearing only paisley boxer shorts and his wristwatch. "Look," he says. "I'm half-drunk, you're three-quarters, and in six hours—" checks his watch—"I have to get up and teach. So whatever you're cooking up over there, can we please save it for tomorrow?"

Her voice leaks out of her, a whisper, like smoke. "How can you treat me like you did today? Can you please explain that?"

"Treat you like what?"

"You know what I mean. Ignore me."

He sighs. Stands by the window with his back to her. The neighbors can see from there but he doesn't care. "Weddings are a problem for us, aren't they," he says.

What exactly is *that* supposed to mean? she asks him.

He shakes his head and goes back to the bed, picks up the clock, and tries to wind it, but it is already wound all the way. Gets into bed and turns his back to her, a mountain under the blankets.

"Hold on," she says. "I would like to know just what you meant by that."

"Tomorrow."

"No," she says. "Now. You come over here right now, and tell me just what you meant."

The mountain moves. A sigh, loud and wet like the blast of a whale.

I was only fifteen, but I knew I could marry her. Her name was Sarah, and she sat behind me in French class. What I liked was the way she snorted and whispered, "Oh, give me a *break!*" when Mademoiselle called her by her assigned French name, which was Françoise. She wore big flouncy sweaters, and the scent that floated after her was warm and sweet and dry, like something baking. She had deep red hair and a tiny mole on the side of her face, it drove me crazy.

My dreams about romance and my future were hardly original, but they were extensive. As I regularly confided to my best friend, Nathan Holover, I was convinced that at twenty-five I would marry a beautiful, blond virgin whose lack of previous sexual experience would not keep her from being transformed overnight, on our honeymoon and with my expert help, into a whirling, panting nymphomaniac. The two of us, financed by a lucrative career, would then retreat to a spacious white house on a corner, which we would stock with TVs and zippy cars and two or three loyal children, and lead lives whose smooth surfaces would be disturbed only by occasional ski trips to Colorado and by our continuing nightly ecstasies. This was essentially my parents' story repeated, with a few elements added in, like wild sex, in places where I felt my parents lacked good material.

But Sarah Clark was no fantasy. She was real, shifting audibly in her seat behind me in French class, taunting me with sarcastic whispers—"Très *bien*, Jean-Claude"; "Mon *Dieu*, Jean-Claude!"—whenever I volunteered an answer, until I deeply regretted having chosen my name after the famous Olympic skier. After a year of agonizing, I boldly asked her to a movie. Soon I was deliriously in love. To my shock and joy, she loved me back.

Sarah was proud, my friends considered her a bitch, and even after we were going out, she continued at school to treat me the way she treated any other boy, with amusement and faint sarcasm. But I loved her scorn—that hard shell of her defiance, which on a Saturday night past midnight on her parents' living room floor would finally crack under my ardor, revealing the soft, fleshy place inside where she, like anyone else, craved love and needed people and could be hurt. I felt this was my discovery, a place in her that no one else had gotten to, and as I watched her archly pretending not to notice me in school, I smiled, treasuring my secret and holding it carefully inside me.

My parents adored Sarah, and swept her into the family as if I had already married her. That first summer she ate dinner at our house at least once a week. She was an only child, and far preferred the noise at our table to her parents' monumental silences. My parents liked girls who gave boys a hard time. "That girl has spirit," my mother would say when Sarah left the room. "Doesn't let you [pointing at me] get away with anything." They thought we had a healthy relationship. I agreed. Sarah and I healthily lost our virginity together on the living room floor at her house one July night, a month after our graduation. We had been going together over a year and a half. College was looming in six weeks, we were already desperately missing each other. It was a warm night with a breath of breeze; we were on the floor rubbing and prodding and breathing, and then suddenly it was done—Sarah made a muffled, startled sound against my neck, then held me hard and groaned as I broke through to a rich warm softness that made me feel dizzy with desire; I wanted to shout, canned laughter from the TV was exploding in my ears, crickets screamed out in the yard. I looked down and saw blood on myself. Sarah was crying, and I didn't realize until she wiped a tear off my face that I was too. When I closed my eyes, the blond woman in the big white house had disappeared, and in her place was Sarah Clark.

It didn't happen that way. Life at college did not proceed according to plan. First, my parents suddenly split up and then quickly sank into their misery, like stones in a pond. The silence from home was overpowering. While this seemed to give me a real advantage over friends of mine whose parents called almost nightly to harass them, inside I was a mess. The stories my parents had always told me, stories about how the world worked and thus how my life in it should proceed, had fled from me like soldiers in a vast, hopeless retreat, leaving me standing alone on my own little island of ego. I dropped the vague idea I'd had of following my father into medicine, drifting away from the sciences and landing in the English department—the "Department of Unemployment," as my roommate, Dennis, called it. At about the same time, my value system was beginning to crumble under the discovery of beautiful women who seemed willing, if only I would invite them, to spend whole nights in my room, without worrying too much about the implications the next day. Of all my parents' abiding notions, the one taking the hardest beating was the myth of the One True Love, the spiritual Doppelgänger, that fated person whom you are supposed to recognize the moment you see her.

It took longer than it should have for things with Sarah to end. For the better part of a year, I existed in a state of complete contradiction. On Saturday night I would party wildly at my fraternity house, fantasizing about sleeping with whomever I was dancing with, and on a couple of occasions doing so. Sunday afternoon would find me writing Sarah a letter full of mournful longing and pledges of fidelity. I didn't feel like a liar. When I wrote those things, I meant them. It was as if someone kept turning a dial in me, one channel flicking to another and back again.

It all caved in during the second summer of college. I was housesitting a former teacher's apartment, glad to get away, if only a few miles, from the nasty sniping my parents had settled into during their separation. Each day I worked long hours as a house painter, and almost each night Sarah would come over. We would go out for drinks or a movie, then come back to the apartment to make love. To me it was an ideal setup, almost like living together; but as the weeks passed, Sarah seemed disappointed, even resentful. She was reverting to her old sarcastic manner. There was something sharp or bitter in our passion, some abrasiveness where before all had been smooth. One night we had just finished making love when she rolled away from me and said in a flat voice, "My parents wonder why they never see you anymore."

I couldn't tell whether she expected an answer or was just needling me. I said nothing.

"But," she said, "I guess you're a little too cool for that now."

"Hey," I said, staring at her back. "What's up with you anyway?"

266

She ignored me. "I mean, why go over there when we have this place, right?"

"Right," I said, uncertainly.

"I mean, it's practically like living together, right?"

The way she was twisting my ideas around irked me. "Why are you so pissed off these days?" I said.

"Oh," she said, sighing. "I'm not, I'm not." And she turned and smiled at me, forlornly.

Two nights later we were in our favorite bar, the Seafarer. Sarah was drinking vodka gimlets and I my usual half-dozen beers, which after ten hours of painting in the fierce sun were inducing in me a familiar, pleasant blend of horniness and fatigue. She wanted to head to another bar, where some of her girlfriends from high school were meeting. I wanted to go back to the apartment, and I was so busy impressing this idea upon her neck with my lips and tongue that I couldn't see how angry she was becoming at my insistence. Then suddenly I found myself pushed violently away.

I was shocked to see Sarah sneering at me. "If all you want is someone to fuck—" she landed hard on the word—"why don't you just go back to your fraternity and find some whore to do it for you!" She grabbed her pocketbook and strode across the bar. I followed, my mouth hanging open.

Outside I saw her walking away at furious speed in the gray-blue glow of the streetlights. Although my legs were twice as long as hers, I found I couldn't catch up without breaking into a run. When I finally reached her, she whirled around with such ferocity that I actually jumped. Her pocketbook belatedly bumped against me, and she jerked it back. "What?!" she said. "What do you want?!"

"I want . . ." When I saw the look on her face, I didn't know what to say. I knew what she wanted me to say and do in order to keep her, what she wanted me to be, and knew also I couldn't be it. All I could do was be angry at her for having shown me myself. I put my hands on my hips and leaned forward at her, shouting. "I want to know what the hell is wrong with you!"

She laughed, wildly. A couple passing on the sidewalk stared. "Oh yeah," she said. "Big working man, twenty years old, big guy. Works his ten hours, then comes home to his bachelor pad and fucks his girlfriend. Very big deal."

"You're crazy," I said.

She turned away and started walking, again with that impossible velocity, into the darkness. Her parents' house was at least five miles away. I ran to my car and cruised up to her, she looked horribly alone in the glare of my headlights, marching through dust and candy wrappers at the side of the road. I rolled down the window and called out to her to get in. "At least let me drive you home," I said.

She kept waving me off, but I persisted, and finally she got in, slamming the door.

We rode the five miles in silence. My anger dissipated like mist, leaving only the clear certainty that it was all over between us. At some point Sarah realized I wasn't going to say anything heroic to save us, and at that point I could feel her silence hardening around her. In the drive at her parents', I turned to her. "Look," I said, "we loved each other a lot. We both know that."

Hmph.

"It's just that we have different ideas about things. Different visions." I forget what I said next; whatever it was, she waited silently until I had finished, then got out of the car and closed the door carefully.

"I hope you find someone who shares your vision, Toby," she said. Then she turned and walked toward the house, where through the living room window I could see her parents watching television.

For some reason I found it hard to admit to anyone that Sarah and I had broken up—and especially to my parents. They were separated, and both of them saw in my relationship with Sarah a reminder of happier times. My father in particular kept asking me about her. I would visit him in the apartment he had moved into—the same rickety building his lover and her children had moved into—and always he would make a point of asking, "How is that girlfriend of yours?" One day late that summer he asked me if it was true that I had broken up with Sarah Clark.

"We decided to cool things for a while," I said. "Why?"

I think I expected some sort of rebuke. Instead my father merely nodded and observed that he had wondered how long it would last.

I was genuinely surprised. "What do you mean?"

He raised his eyebrows. "Well. Sarah always struck me as a nice girl. But not as someone you'd be settling down with."

"No?"

He shook his head and tilted a conspiratorial smile. "I remember the day your mother and I drove you to college. I took one look at some of those girls in your dormitory and said to myself, 'Man, oh man, were you ever born thirty years too early!' "

I didn't laugh. I hated the clammy sympathy he was offering me, bachelor to bachelor, so I picked up the conversation and re-routed it onto some political topic where we were sure to disagree, perhaps even vehemently. In those days I was always coming home from school armed with a critique of some dire current of American culture in which I felt my father and his whole point of view were deeply implicated. It was a rough time for him. All he wanted was to relax with his son, work up a pleasant, beery somnolence with the help of a few Michelobs, and talk about football and fraternity parties. I, on the other hand, kept chiseling away at the hard surface of his complacencies, hoping through a kind of intellectual catechism to get at the soft jelly of helplessness and confusion underneath. I wanted my father to admit that he had acted blindly and in desperation when he left my mother—that his philosophy had failed him, that the big white house on the corner was a fraud.

Still, no matter how much I harangued my father, I could not change what I had seen in Sarah's eyes on the sidewalk, or how I had felt a half-hour later as I drove away from her for the last time. The two times we had broken up in high school, I had gone off weeping, but this last time I drove away composed. Picturing Sarah walking into her house, brushing off her parents' questions, I reminded myself how sad I should be; but in spite of me, my mind kept flashing ahead to September and the return to school. All I could think of were all the women I had wanted to sleep with, and how free I now was to enjoy them.

II

"Okay," he says. "Here I am. All yours." He sits on the couch, tapping his fingers on the arm.

"Are you pissed at me now?" she says.

"Oh no. I love teaching Nathanael West to sixteen-year-olds on four hours of sleep."

"Well maybe you have a good quick explanation for why you ignored me all through Nick's wedding. Then we can go to bed."

"How exactly would you say I was ignoring you?"

"Oh, come on. You didn't sit with me, didn't talk to me. You danced with me, what—three times?" She pulls her voice back down into the calm range. "Then you sat around with your Bingham School people as if I didn't even exist."

"I'm not aware of any wedding at which the best man sits with his girlfriend, are you?" He pretends to wait for an answer, another rhetorical trick imported from the classroom. "As for dancing with you only three times, if we're counting, that's two times more than I danced with anyone else. And about the Bingham crowd, well, you were free to come over. You don't need an invitation from me." He looks at his watch and forces out a sigh that makes his whole body very quickly rise and fall. "So, now how was I ignoring you?"

"It was just an overall impression you created." She leans forward toward him now. "Look. Do you think anyone there tonight could have even suspected I was your girlfriend?"

The question annoys him, he is chewing his lip. "What was I supposed to do? Interrupt my toast to the newlyweds to say 'Excuse me, ladies and gentlemen, but at this point I would like to convey to you the impression that the woman in the green dress at the back table is my girlfriend'?"

She says nothing for a long time, then resumes in a voice two sizes smaller. "I don't know," she says. "I guess I just see Nick and Ginger drawing closer together, then I wonder to myself, how close are we?"

He stands up now and she hopes he is coming over to her. But he isn't. "Marcy," he says. "I have dinner with you five nights a week. We sleep together in the same bed. I edit your thesis and make your scrambled eggs, you put up with my bitching about students, and when your parents for some inscrutable reasons send us Harvey's Bristol Creme for Christmas, I write the thank you note. Isn't that closeness?"

Standing, he looks huge. She remembers what she liked about him from the start—how big he was. Sometimes she feels the apartment is only slightly bigger than he is, and he's wearing it like a loose jacket, and she's floating in a pouch of dark warmth between his body and the lining. She smiles. "Didn't you think it was beautiful when they said their vows? Wasn't that a beautiful moment?"

"Yes," he says. "For them." He turns away as he says it, walks to the window. You can never get him to stand still at the crucial moments. She remembers being with him at her sister's wedding. When it came time for the family photos, he escaped and hid in the bathroom.

"I just want to know you're committed to me, that's all," she says. "That I won't just wake up some morning and find you gone."

He stops. Tilts his head back and laughs. "So this is it," he says deep in his chest. "This is what it alllll comes down to." He seems to have a sudden, giant headache. Rubs his forehead and grimaces. No doubt she has caused this. "What do you want," he says, "some guarantee we'll always be together? What if I step off the curb to-morrow and get run down by a beer truck?"

"I don't care about beer trucks. I just want to know about you."

"Marcy." He jabs the air in her direction. "What I keep telling you is that I can't think the way you do about this. I can't deal with this frame you keep trying to put things in." He drops his hand to his side, it slaps on his thigh. "What do you want me to say?" he says. "That yes, I want to take the vows, just like Nick and Ginger?"

"That's how you see me, isn't it." Her face flares. Blood pounds in the hollow between her jaw and ear. "Some clinging female, some desperate person out to mug you into the nearest church."

"Oh, come on," he says.

"Well I've got news for you. You just may not be the piece of hot real estate you think you are. When I marry a man, I just might want someone who's capable of a little more hard thinking than you seem to be."

"I'm sure you will," he says.

"For instance. You say you can't plan the future. Well, let's get specific. Do you plan to be here one year from now? Can you tell me that?"

"As far as I know," he says. "I don't plan not to."

"But you can't commit yourself. Fine. How about six months from now? Or six weeks—will you be here in six weeks?"

"Yes. I'll be here in six weeks."

"Good. At least we have that established. You're capable of committing yourself firmly for six weeks."

He sits on the couch, head in his hands. She gets up from her rocking chair, her whole body is tingling. Goes to the kitchen and opens the fridge. For a long time she looks in, considering the pickles and cans of beer, the square block of tofu. Finally she opens the freezer, takes a piece of ice, draws it slowly across her forehead. The drops trickle down into her eye sockets, then down into her mouth.

Her anger is spent. Now she will go to him and dump herself in his immense lap. But when she goes back out, he is sitting there on the couch, making grotesque faces, pulling his cheeks and lips down with his fingers.

"Hello," she says. "You still here?"

"Right here," he says.

"Sometimes you make it seem so painful to be sitting here. Like it's torture."

"I don't know," he says. His face buried in his hands, he looks out between his fingers. "We've been over this so many times, Marcy. So many times. So many times."

She feels a speck of fear stuck somewhere inside her.

"Maybe we can't reconcile it," he says. "Maybe we're talking at cross-purposes."

"What are you saying?" The longer he keeps staring at nothing, the bigger the speck gets. "Toby?"

He puts his thumb and index finger across the bridge of his nose and squeezes and rubs.

Someone once asked me a tough question: how many women had I left in my life, and how many had left me?

I remember having no answer. I had never lined things up in my mind that way. But the truth is that after breaking up with Sarah Clark, I went back to college and slept around. Some women I thought I was in love with, some were friends; others were women I met once and then never saw again. Intimacy with strangers can be a wonderful thing.

After college I headed for New York City, where I moved into a loft on Thompson Street with my old roommate, Dennis. He was starting law school at NYU, and I was convinced I had to be a writer. Having been complimented on my style by a couple of professors, I considered my career already half launched. So I set up my Smith-

Corona and in short order produced a five-page piece on the first subject that came to mind—finding an apartment in New York. It was a lushly padded account of my own actual search, full of gritty urban details (dope dealers, careening Arab cabbies), and I didn't see how it could miss. I mailed it off to *The Times*. When five days went by, I began to worry; after ten days I got my courage up and called *The Times*, where I was shuffled from desk to desk until someone finally told me, unconvincingly, that my article "had been read" and returned.

I didn't want to believe him. "Are you *sure* you know the piece I'm talking about?" I said.

"Look," he said. "We couldn't use it. Feel free to try us again."

"Wait," I sputtered. "Will I get it back?"

"You sent postage, right?"

"Sure."

"Then you'll get it back." Click.

Of course, I had sent no postage, no return envelope, only the five sheets of my brilliance, which by now were stuffed in some huge trash compactor somewhere, or perhaps already burning in a dump in Jersey.

All told, I lasted eight months in the city—the time it took me to convince myself that it was the *place* that was all wrong, that no writers were writing in New York anymore. Everyone was out in Wyoming or Oregon or New Orleans, out in the real America, that limitless domain of laconic farmers, screaming evangelists, and soda jerks. Back home in Connecticut, I spent three weeks with my mother and my younger sister, Sharon, making big plans. On the kitchen table we spread out a map of the U.S. My mother seemed intoxicated by my freedom. "Who knows what's waiting for you out there?" she said, staring at the map, her fingers hovering with hypnotic slowness over huge patches of America. "Who knows?"

I traveled for three years. The money I needed I earned mostly as a painter, but also as waiter, tennis coach, baby-sitter, and substitute teacher. All the while I took notes, pouring America into little brown notebooks I kept in the back seat of my car. I was always just one stop away, I was sure, from some definitive revelation, some personal or artistic breakthrough. But somehow, none of those laconic farmers or screaming evangelists appeared to help bring this event into being—though one Baptist minister did stop to help me change a tire outside Biloxi, Mississippi.

And then it happened. A piece I had written about the Mardi Gras—I was in New Orleans by then—was accepted by *The Times*. What I had done was to get the stories of three people (all of whom I had met one night downtown in a bar near a building I was helping paint) for whom the previous year's Mardi Gras had been a disaster: one saxophone player from New Jersey who'd had his horn stolen and had had to buy it back at great cost from a fence; one ex-high school football star (local, Cajun) who had been falsely arrested and thus missed his own wedding; and one public works employee who spent three weeks cleaning up the whole mess, removing bushels of Mardi Gras beads from trees outside Tulane University dormitories. "The Lighter Side of Fat Tuesday," was the title I gave it and which, to my pleasure, *The Times* saw fit to use, running the piece on the op-ed page.

I bought out a whole newsstand's worth of *The Times*, collected my few friends (most of them from Peter's Painters, the outfit I was working for), and threw a party at which we all floated shouting on an ocean of beer and champagne. I was ecstatic. But eventually the smoke cleared, and I woke up alone in my still-trashed apartment, with only my dozen copies and a buzzing alarm clock, which told me that in thirty minutes I was expected to show up, brush in hand, at Peter's Painters. Nothing had happened. No publishers had called, no admiring agents. *The Times* had continued furiously churning out articles, hundreds of articles on subjects of immense importance, while my own small effort reeled steadily backward toward archival oblivion. My anonymity took my breath away. I had nothing new on my typewriter, and the couple of slim notions dancing on the horizon seemed suddenly pointless, even fraudulent. Nothing was real except the alarm clock, again raucously jazzing, and Peter's Painters.

Not surprisingly, I didn't make it to Peter's Painters that day, or ever again, and soon enough New Orleans was behind me. I headed west, with a few hundred dollars and twelve copies of my article—a fifteen-hundred-word joke saying, in effect, that Mardi Gras wasn't such a hot time after all. I felt like disappearing. San Francisco, where a friend of mine was working for a big law firm, was the ostensible goal. But I crept along, slower and slower, telling myself I was scouting local action, but really just running out of gas. In Amarillo, Texas, I almost landed in jail when the YMCA I was staying at was raided by the police in a drug bust. The night janitor and three friends were sitting stoned out of their minds in the TV room; I blundered in to request toilet paper, and three seconds later the police came rocketing up the stairs. We were all hauled downtown, where only a freakish streak of honesty in the janitor kept me from being booked. As I came back onto the street, I felt myself drifting into a lightheaded daze. I couldn't for the life of me remember where I was, and finally I had to turn around and read the name of the town on the police station. Ah, yes, Armadillo. I started walking, watching my own boots on the pavement, observing with wonder how solidly they seemed to be connected to my legs. It occurred to me I had no idea what I was doing, or why.

Then I met Joleen.

It was in Taos, New Mexico, a slow two-day's drive from Amarillo. There was a clean, sharp feeling in the air, and good skiing in the mountains. I found the cheapest motel, and as I registered I asked the owner, a fat, perspiring widower named Bob Rubin, if he needed someone to work for him. No, he said, looking me over carefully with a lopsided squint. But he smiled when he saw I was from the East—"From Newark myself," he said—and two days later, as I was heading out for dinner, he asked me if I wanted to be his night manager.

"When do I start?"

"Ten minutes ago," he said, tossing a huge ring of keys onto the counter.

I met Joleen in a bar the next Sunday—my night off. It was a skiers' hangout, packed with sunburned people drinking too much and calling heartily to each other across the room. There was a small dance floor, and among the swaying couples I noticed a woman dancing alone. She was thin, with pale skin and pale blond hair; she had a comfortable way of turning her body in slow, tight circles, her eyes closed. Best of all, she obviously wasn't a skier. I walked over.

"May I dance with you?" I shouted at her.

She looked me over quickly, then shrugged. "It's a free floor," she said, moving a little to make room for me.

After a couple of dances, I tried a conversation. "What's your name?" I shouted over the noise.

"Joleen!" She spelled it out.

"What kind of name is that?"

She closed her eyes.

Eventually I sat down. Joleen danced another half-dozen solo dances, then came over. "Hey," I said. "I didn't mean to be rude out there." I explained to her that I was new in town and didn't know anyone.

She took a cigarette out of a leather case and offered me one. "Good for you," she said sincerely when I refused. Each time she inhaled, her large, round eyes grew slightly rounder. "So. You want to know what kind of name Joleen is? The kind of name you get when your parents were Joe and Eileen and thought they were being cute."

"Oh no," I said.

"Yup," she said. "Doesn't that take the cake?" She laughed and shot out a plume of smoke. I don't like cigarettes, but I have always admired the way some smokers work them into their conversation, for emphasis.

"You're not a skier, are you?" I said.

277

She frowned at me. "Depends why you're asking."

"Just curious."

She said nothing and stubbed out her cigarette, which she had only just started. Then she went back out onto the dance floor. I liked the way she danced, all that smooth turning, and when she came back, I told her so.

"That's nice," she said. "But now I've gotta hit the road." She picked up her coat.

"Can I call you?"

She smiled slyly. "I've got a better idea. You give me your number, and I'll call you."

I gave her the number of Bob Rubin's motel.

Four nights later she called. I was sitting in the tiny office behind the front desk, watching TV, when the phone rang. "Bob Rubin's Motel," I said, answering as instructed.

"Oh, sorry . . ." It was Joleen's voice on the other end.

She called back seconds later. "That's you, isn't it," she said.

"I hope so."

"Why didn't you tell me?"

"Well," I said. "I don't like to give myself away too easily."

She liked that. She explained why she hadn't given me her phone number. "There are a lot of jerks and weirdos out there," she said. "I get sick of being hassled."

She asked me what I was doing at Bob Rubin's, and when I told her, she asked if I knew that Rubin's last night clerk had been shot, only two weeks earlier, on the job. "Right in that little room," she said. "Is that where you are?"

"You're kidding," I said.

"That's right. First shooting here in years." She sounded cheerful about it. "But don't worry. It was only his girlfriend."

The next Sunday we met for dinner at a tiny Mexican restaurant, then headed to the same bar. Again I watched Joleen dance, slow and easy like someone lazily swimming.

This time she invited me home. I followed her car, a dull-colored Chevy Nova, through town, past the stores with their adobe-style false fronts, up past the Kit Carson graveyard. She pulled in around a sudden curve at a small, square house.

"It's not much," she said when we got out. "But it keeps the rain out."

There was a light in the living room. A dark-haired girl, about twelve, sat reading on the couch. Joleen spoke to her in Spanish, and the girl smiled and left. "Make yourself comfortable," Joleen said to me. She disappeared into the back of the house. The place was crammed with jade trees and cactus. On the walls were paintings, in an Impressionist style, of Southwest scenes—sunsets, children on donkeys, sentimental things.

Joleen came back with a bottle of Spanish wine. A cigarette she lit was again snuffed after a few intense puffs. Then she sat back and asked me to tell her about myself. As I spoke, I watched her face, her strangely translucent skin through which I could see the tracks of delicate blue veins. She kept tucking a strand of blond hair behind her ear and laughing. I told her about the mess in Amarillo. "Ah," she said, "all of this reminds me of my own wild days."

There was a pause. In the corner I saw a pile of toys, and a small light flickered on in my mind. "Hey," I said. "Who was that girl when we came in?"

"Baby-sitter." Frowning at a fingernail, Joleen spoke tonelessly. "I have a four-year-old son. He's asleep in the back."

"Wow," I said.

"Scare you away?"

"No," I said. "I just didn't think . . ."

She let the sentence dangle. Then very matter-of-factly she told me how she had left her home in Pittsburgh at eighteen, how in St. Louis she had met an artist named Sammy who was heading for the Southwest, how they lived together for two years, first in Santa Fe and then in Taos, after which he announced he was gay, and ran off

279

to Mexico with a lover named Roberto. "Personally," she said, "I don't think he's really gay. He's too much of a bastard to be gay."

All he had left her was a stack of unpaid bills, some paintings, and a three-month-old son named Arroyo.

"Arroyo?" I said. "Arroyo?"

"Don't ask."

"But how could you," I said, "after Joe and Eileen?"

"You think if I'd had my head screwed on right to begin with," she said, "I would have stayed with his father in the first place?" Joleen shook her head, remembering. "No, Sammy was only good for two things, and one of them was painting." She waved her hand at the paintings on the walls. "I wanted him to make prints and start a mail-order business, but he wasn't together enough for success. Being a bastard was his main interest."

At about one o'clock Joleen looked at her watch. "Would you mind not spending the night here tonight?" she said. "I have to get up early to take Roy to the doctor's. He has a cold."

"Sure," I said.

"Thanks." She leaned over and kissed me; I felt the tip of her tongue on my lips. Then she pulled back. "Let me give you my number now," she said.

It was a number I ended up using a lot. After ski season ended, things quieted down at Bob Rubin's Motel, and far from worrying about being shot to death behind my desk, I feared boredom was slowly strangling me. Joleen loved to talk. We talked for hours. She told me about growing up in Pittsburgh with a brother and three sisters. Her father worked in the steel mills. They were good people, her parents; it was Pittsburgh she had left. Once she got back in touch, everything was okay. "As long as I had a roof over my head and wasn't selling my body to pay for it, they didn't mind. And as long as I wasn't doing drugs." Her older brother, she said, had been addicted to heroin. He was the wild one, always in trouble, and finally he committed suicide. She had flown back to Pittsburgh for the funeral with Arroyo, who was two and flew for free. When her father held Arroyo, he wept—the first time Joleen had seen her father cry.

For the last three years, she had been working as a hairdresser at Lorraine's Styles. It was Lorraine's business, but Joleen was the money-maker, and everyone knew it. The idea of cutting out on her own had occurred to her, she said, but she liked Lorraine; the woman had been kind to her. When Sammy the Bastard took off, Joleen had been desperate, had had a couple of stupid affairs with married men in town; Lorraine had given her the job and helped save her. "Besides," she told me. "This whole haircutting thing is just something I picked up along the way. They all think I have a diploma from some hot shit academy in New York." She laughed. "It's terrible when you're from the East. You can get away with anything out here."

She wanted to know about my life. There were things in it Joleen found fascinating, things I hadn't thought much about: that my sisters and I had had our own bedrooms, even as small children; that our father was a doctor and that I had seen him operate (she wanted this in full gory detail); that our parents never raised their voices, either to each other or to us; that our house had a laundry chute ("Was there a maid or something at the end of it?" "No, just my mother." "It always comes down to the same shit work, doesn't it, no matter how you wrap it up"); that I knew who my great-grandparents had been and where they were from ("*My* great-grandfather was probably just some dumb Polack who thought he could make a million bucks over here"); that at sixteen I had saved a hundred dollars to give my girlfriend a ring ("The first guy I went out with, all he ever wanted to give me was the same old thing, and it didn't cost him a penny"); and that we had lived near the beach and in summer could run five blocks and dive sweating into the ocean.

"It's like what I imagine the classic family to be," Joleen said to me one night on the phone. "You know, sort of Leave It to Beaver and Marcus Welbyish."

281

I reminded her that my father had divorced my mother and remarried, that nowadays my mother lived alone with her cats.

Joleen brushed this off. "Yeah, well, men are bastards," she said cheerfully. "You can't expect too much from them."

I felt this was too easy. What about commitment? I asked her. What about duty?

She laughed at me. "Keep dreaming, pal," she said.

Joleen and I saw each other on Sunday nights, on weekends, and on late afternoons between our jobs. Sometimes she came down to the motel at night, bringing a pizza and six pack (and Roy), and we sat in the office watching TV on Bob Rubin's huge twenty-six-inch Sony. The boy, Arroyo, was beautiful. He had soft, dark curls that surrounded his head like a halo, and Joleen's pale skin and huge blue eyes. His face was wide and guileless, and he had a ridiculous wide-eyed smile, his lips somehow covering his teeth in a way that made him look like a huge tadpole. After an hour Roy would be deep asleep, and when they left, I would carry his limp form out to Joleen's Nova and watch the two of them drive off—the boy invisible and Joleen sunk way down in the deep front seat, like an elderly person. On Saturdays the three of us would pack a lunch and drive up into the mountains or down to the Pecos River. To me the land looked pale and drained, but Joleen saw life in it. In buttes on the horizon or in clouds overhead, she pointed out shapes to me and to Arroyo—top hats, witches, trees. On the way back we would stop in some tiny pueblo and eat the fiery enchiladas Joleen loved. My insides were being slowly destroyed. At home Joleen might produce a softball or nerf football, and I was expected to teach Arroyo the things boys needed to know. In the middle of our catch, I would have to rush to the bathroom. Coming out one time, I found myself facing Joleen and Arroyo, both of them laughing at me.

"You're no tough guy, Toby," the boy said.

Eventually, Joleen and I got around to making love. Later, she would tell me she had wondered if I was gay, I showed so little interest. The truth was that I didn't want to add my name to the list of men who had slept with her and left. But one Sunday night after she put Arroyo to bed, she lit a candle and took me by the hand, through the boy's room to her room. "If you want to escape," she whispered as we stood by the door, "do it now."

She made love the way she danced, smoothly, eyes closed. Her skin in the candlelight was golden, and I had the hushed, reverential feeling of being in church. "I've never made love to a mother before," I told her.

"Yeah, well," she said. "We still have all the working parts."

We never discussed my moving in. There was a part of Joleen's life that was hers and hers alone; she had fought hard for it, and cherished it the way she cherished her son. I liked the thought that there were things going on in her life I didn't know about. Now and then someone would call when I was there, and Joleen would take the phone around the corner into the kitchen. "Who gave you my number?" I heard her say once. "If you think I'm in the business of distributing my personal number to any stranger who winks at me, you've got another think coming, pal." Then she hung up. Coming back in the kitchen, she was smiling at her own toughness. Sometimes when cars came too fast around the blind curve outside the house, she would stand on the front porch and throw eggs at them. She had put up a Children Playing sign and was outraged when people ignored it.

The months piled up. I thought little about the world beyond Bob Rubin's motel, Joleen's house, and the places in town where I ate and drank with a couple of acquaintances. Since New Orleans I had not opened my brown notebooks. The thought of doing so made me queasy. My old dream of being a writer seemed farcical to me now, and once when Joleen made me show her my *Times* article and was honestly impressed by it, I shook my head and crumpled the piece into a little ball. Joleen thought this was strange. There were some things about me she said she just couldn't understand. One day I mentioned that my parents had lived in Arizona in the fifties, when my father worked for the Public Health Service, that I in fact had been born there, in a Navajo town only a few hours from where we lived. "I can't believe you didn't tell me," Joleen said. She got the idea of visiting the place and wouldn't let go. It's your roots, she kept telling me. You should care.

The day we went was brilliantly clear. We drove Joleen's Nova. I took the wheel while she read aloud from a State of Arizona tourist brochure. Arroyo was in fine form in the back seat. "Where are we going?" he kept saying. "Tell me where."

"Arizona."

"Telephona!"

I remembered the stories my parents had told us about their Navajo town. In winter the sun shone all day, and then suddenly at night it would snow, flakes so light they barely fell out of the sky. Then there were the magic names: Window Rock, Canyon de Chelly, the Petrified Forest. On a table in our living room sat a chunk of stone from the Petrified Forest—an enchanted, fearsome place, as I imagined it, with towering trees carved out of rock.

The actual town Joleen and Roy and I pulled into was far from enchanted. It was incredibly dreary, even in bright sunlight. Nothing grew there but cactus gardens, scrub bushes, and a few dwarf trees. I thought of the millions of acres of lush lands behind us, which Indians had been tricked and chased out of for centuries. What we were looking at now was history's dumping ground. There was a gas station, a post office and bank, a few stores, a car dealership featuring used pickup trucks, some of them badly dented; there were three churches, a clinic where my father could have worked, and then bars—dozens of them, it seemed. "Toby was born here," Joleen said to Arroyo. But to me it didn't seem likely.

We took a walk around. The houses off the main street were low-slung and crudely hewn, some of them little better than shacks, behind split-rail fences. Telephone poles leaned crazily in all directions. We kept reaching the places where streets petered out into desert, and having to turn around.

Arroyo was getting bored. Each time we turned around, he sighed. Then he started kicking and dragging his toes in the reddish dirt. Finally he decided he wanted ice cream.

"Come off it, buddy," said Joleen. "Where do you think we are?"

"But I want it!"

"Good," I said. "Let's go find Roy some ice cream."

On the way home that evening I was silent. As soon as the sun went down, it got cold, and I turned the heater on. Roy fell asleep in the back, and Joleen asked me, as she sometimes did, to tell her about college. One school was the same as the next to her, she didn't care about any particular place. What she wanted to hear about was the life of a student, how you would go from class to class with your books under your arm, stay up late in the library, drinking coffee and writing papers. That was what she wanted for Arroyo, she said. Then she snuggled close under my arm and fell asleep.

Back at the house I was cold and stiff, and Joleen ran a bath for me. She had a great tub, an old cast-iron one, very deep, and I got in up to my armpits. No sooner was I in than Arroyo came in with a cold beer. He poured a little on my neck and then laughed uproariously when I shivered.

"Okay, Champ," I said, poking him in the ribs.

He poked me back, plunging his hand into the water. Then he got interested in my submerged body and, giggling, he poked me lightly between the legs. "Does it tickle there?" he said.

"All right, you pervert," I said, and I pinched his butt and tickled his armpits.

I looked up then. Joleen was at the door, staring down at us with distant, soulful eyes.

At the motel that night I felt restless. It was the end of November; ski season was coming on. I was thinking about life back east, about family and friends. I imagined one of my friends coming to ski in Taos and staying at Bob Rubin's Motel. What would I say? It seemed to me months since I had thought about my life. I had wanted to disappear and I had disappeared, tumbling over backward into my own life and letting it surround me, falling asleep in it. Now I felt I had to wake up again, into real life, before I forgot what real life was. It was a panicky feeling. It seemed to me that Joleen, the boy, and I were drifting willy-nilly into some relation that I was not at all prepared for. Far from resenting my intimacy with his mother, the boy seemed to want to join it. One night very late at the motel, he had awakened to find himself alone in front of the TV; barging into Rm #1, he found us in bed, and all he said was "Hey, where did you go, you guys?" As for Joleen herself, I thought I could sense her toughness melting away. The feeling that I didn't quite know where I stood with her had always been reassuring, and now it had begun to fade. Soon there would be no part of her hidden from me.

A week later we were sitting around at Joleen's on a Saturday afternoon. She was talking about Arroyo's kindergarten. Kids had been making fun of his name, and she was considering changing it legally to Roy. "Do you think that could cause some psychological problem for him?"

There was a heavy silence while I stared into space. She lit a cigarette.

"You can't take it, can you," she said.

"Joleen—"

"And now you'll leave."

"Look, Joleen," I said. "I'm sorry—"

"Don't be." Her voice bit the words off.

I muttered something, saying I knew she expected more from me, she had every right—

"That's where you're wrong, pal." She laughed. "I never expect anything. Company policy." She took a drag from her cigarette; I could see she was recovering already. "What were you going to do way out here, anyway?" she said. "Be Bob Rubin's gofer the rest of your life?"

I left town the next week, heading back east. Joleen threw a going-away dinner featuring a birthday-style cake with the blue frosted flowers Roy loved to eat whole. I was more than a little shocked to discover that her friendliness to me was not ironic. And this is why when I think about Joleen, it is hard for me to say who left whom. Physically I left her, to be sure. But because she knew much more about sadness than I did, she was in good shape, while I was heavy with guilt. Whatever hurt I had given her had already been stored away, deep inside, with other, larger hurts. And so I wasn't really leaving her as much as I was being released, even dismissed, by her. It was the secret to her enjoying my presence those last days: she had already written me off.

III

"I can't believe what's happening here. I can't believe where this is heading." The speck inside her is bigger now, a fist.

"You started it," he says. "I was half-asleep."

"Oh, great," she says. "Great." She waits, but he is wrapped in silence. "Are you really saying you want to break up with me?"

"I'm not saying anything."

She tears off her raincoat and flings it away from her. "What do you think this is, a press conference?" Her voice rises, and when it cracks, she knows she is yelling at him. "Talk to me, damn you! Sure, you're great when everything's smooth, witty guy, funny guy. But a little rough going and you run and hide."

As she talks, she sees him tensing. He keeps a moat of good humor around him, but if you manage to get across it, watch out. Now muscles in his jaw are going, now tendons in his neck. She can either stop it now or push him over. "How dare you ignore me all night and then say I started it?"

"Goddammit!" When he jumps up from the couch his foot catches the leg of the coffee table and he kicks it free. The table jumps, flips, vase and ashtray and flowers flying. He roars like some tortured beast, and though she is prepared for this, it still startles her. By the window he turns and yells at her, and with each word his head jolts, and he beats the air with his meaty fist. I. Cannot. Stand. Your. Jealousy Marcy. "You read my private letters," he says. "You can't stand it when I go somewhere for the weekend. You can't stand it when you hear about some former girlfriend of mine. I see your nostrils flaring. All I have to do is mention I ran into So and So, and your nostrils start flaring."

Always it happens: as soon as he fills up with anger, she finds herself drained empty, as if the two of them shared a limited supply. "One letter," she says to him softly. "I read one letter." She looks at the coffee table lying legs up like a dead bug. Shards of the vase. Somehow the ashtray has proved indestructible. If her nostrils flared every time she had to hear about one of his old girlfriends, she'd have a nose the size of Nebraska by now. But this isn't the time for a joke. "I'm sorry about that letter," she tells him. "I was wrong. But maybe I wouldn't act that way if I were more sure of you."

He doesn't listen. Inside his head he is developing an idea. "You're even jealous of my students," he says.

"Oh, give me a break." Suddenly she can't bear to see him. Goes back to the kitchen. Opens the fridge for another ice cube, but she has left the tray out, and they are all melted. She looks at the things in the kitchen. Only the clock and a frying pan are his. Some spices maybe. Quick inventory of the whole apartment. How flimsy and few his possessions are. All the heavy stuff is hers: bed, couch, bureau. But he, he can pack and be gone in an afternoon. What he can't pack he'll chuck, or leave for her to deal with.

She charges back out at him. "You think I'm jealous of your

precious students? Well, maybe I am. But the more interesting question is why they're so precious to you in the first place. And I think I know the answer: they *leave*. That's what you really like about them, isn't it? That they leave! You have them for a year, maybe two, and they adore you, and then they disappear—still adoring you, of course. It's your perfect situation." She pauses. "Well let me tell you something. I won't go off adoring you. I'll go off hating you."

She crosses to the bedroom, takes off her clothes, and puts on a robe. Inspects her face in the bathroom. Two pimples have sprouted during this stress. She thinks about the people in the other apartments in the building, dozens of them, and then the dozens of buildings in the neighborhood, and so on. Impossible to imagine these scenes endlessly replicated. The city would sink under the weight of it.

He will leave her. Maybe not right away, but eventually. She knew it earlier tonight, at the wedding party, but talked herself out of it. Now she feels she should write it down somewhere. Otherwise tomorrow she will be weak and will forget. But she has no idea where her journal is, it has been months and months since she has written in it.

When she comes back out, he has righted the coffee table. Is on his knees, picking up the vase piece by piece and gently piling it on the table.

"I'm sorry about the vase," he says. "I'll try to find another."

"Ming Dynasty," she says. "Irreplaceable."

He doesn't hear her joke. "Why do you provoke me like that?" he asks.

"Sometimes," she says, "I think it's the only way I can get through to you."

"But that's not me," he tells her. "I don't believe that's me."

She sits on the edge of their bed, which is really her bed, and hugs her robe around her. "I know you don't," she says. She is beyond all anger now, and she likes the way her voice sounds. "I know how you see yourself. Deep inside you see yourself as a basically carefree guy, a ready-for-anything person. One eye always on the road. Keep all options open."

He says nothing. Inspects the crooked edge of a chunk of broken vase. "It catches up to you, Toby," she says to him. "Don't think it doesn't. Do you think people become happy that way? Do you think that's how solid lives are made? It takes care to make a solid life."

"Please," he says.

She wants him to remember this the right way. "Isn't that what you want, a solid life? You're twenty-nine years old. How long do you expect to keep living this way?"

"You make it sound as if I'm halfway out the door," he says. "I didn't say anything about my going. You did."

She takes this in. She has the feeling tonight that anything he says comes into her rough and dirty, and comes back out a polished pearl of truth. "Toby," she says. "How many women have you left in your life, and how many have left you? Honestly."

Long, frowning silence. "I didn't think this was a baseball game," he says. He has finished stacking the shards of crockery on the table, and now one by one he lays the flowers across them.

For three years I taught English in Massachusetts, at a small private day school (for Boys and Girls) situated among towering maples in a quiet town deceptively close to Boston. While the Bingham School wasn't one of the obscenely rich, inordinately famous old academies, it was no pauper's den. Many of the students inhabited frankly opulent palaces in the shady suburbs. They had state-of-the-art car stereos (not to mention cars), and designer clothes and sunglasses. After every winter vacation they wore their golden suntans proudly, like war medals, sidling up to each other in the halls to compare arms while we faculty members, pale green and dizzy with head colds, trudged like decrepit polar bears among them.

Many of my colleagues on the faculty were outright apologists for the school. Others were sunk in terminal envy and irony. But there was a small group of rebels, those who in one way or another did not openly embrace the state of affairs posed by a Bingham School. The group was headed by a history teacher named Nick Pieroni. Nick was Bingham's in-house radical, a bearish former college linebacker three years older than I with a huge forehead, demonic laugh, Rasputin-like eyes, and a pedagogy based on his refusal, as he put it, "to fine-tune the neuroses of the future ruling class." Nick could be brutally funny. I remember having to flee the Bingham Room, stifling laughter with a violent, faked cough, after listening to his whispered commentary on one of the stunningly myopic slide shows Bingham kids typically gave after a trip to Europe ("This is the Champs Elysées. There are a lot of really cool cars there. . . . This is a French café. You can see the people—they look really. . . French. . . .").

Nick and I saw ourselves as missionaries to the unenlightened bourgeoisie. But it wasn't easy to trouble those Bingham kids, to disturb their sense of well-being. The dream of the big white house raged full force. *Success* was the magic word, and the school did produce "successful" graduates—frighteningly confident kids, armored with their parents' certainties; sleek, handsome kids who snappily raised their diplomas like trophies at graduation while video cameras rolled and parents looked on with a wild, vicarious glee. "There goes another cog in the machine," Nick would joke as the latest valedictorian strutted beaming down the aisle.

Still, we pecked away. Some students we singled out for special attention—the ones with "possibilities," the ones in whom we thought we spied a glimmer of subversive potential. Our favorite project was Luke, a big, good-looking boy whose Bingham transcript was packed not only with good grades but with the assorted sports and activities that made him another example of what our headmaster gloatingly liked to call "the total Bingham kid." Luke was far and away the best writer in my junior composition class. His essays had none of the weedy clichés that choked the prose and minds of so many

Bingham students. But when I tried to praise him, Luke brushed me off with a smile (perfect teeth) and a wave of his hand. Writing was fun, he said, but only as a kind of hobby. What really mattered were physics and calculus; those were the subjects you needed to become a doctor. A *doctor*? I said. That's right, said Luke. His father was a doctor, and he planned to go into practice with him someday.

I rushed to find Nick. "What do you make of this Luke character?" I asked him.

He shrugged. "Another cog, right?" I showed him the essay, and he read it, frowning. "That kid wrote this?"

I nodded.

"Tragic possibilities," Nick said. "He needs us, fast."

Our simple goal, we told Luke, was to get him to renounce his career plans and throw himself open to worlds to which his mind, if he would trust it, had the keys. We kidded him constantly. We called him Luke the Apostle, for his unswerving loyalty to the Gospel of Bingham. He resisted us all the way. One day, when we praised a paper he had written and told him he could make it as a writer, he shook his head and said, "But writers don't *do* anything. At least doctors save people." Nick and I howled at him. Didn't Plato do anything? Didn't Whitman? James Joyce, for God's sake?

"And besides," Luke said, ignoring us, "I want to make money. I'm not ashamed to admit it."

We hooted as he smiled and walked away. "So that's what it all comes down to, isn't it, Lukey boy?" Nick called after him.

Once I was invited to Luke's house for dinner. At the table we all bowed our heads while Dr. Jeffries—Ed—intoned a blessing. Then followed an explosion of family clatter as Luke and his younger brother and two sisters launched themselves into the meal.

"Luke says you run a sharp class," Ed Jeffries said to me over the noise of his family.

"Well, he's a sharp kid," I said. "In fact, he's the best."

"Luke has always had a flair for writing," Ed said.

"Just like his father," said Mrs. Jeffries—Carol.

"Well." Dr. Jeffries flashed a bashful smile. "Let's not go overboard." He turned to me. "I did minor in English. Even thought about journalism."

"Come on, dear, don't shortchange yourself." Carol Jeffries turned to me. "Ed was editor of his college newspaper," she said. "Then he got to med school, and they told him the only books he could read were anatomy textbooks."

"Almost quit right then and there," Ed said.

"Mr. Slattery had an article in *The New York Times*," said Luke.

The Jeffrieses were impressed. Too many doctors, Ed Jeffries said, had no concern whatsoever for language. As a result, he could barely bring himself to read what was written in the medical journals. "In fact," he said, "I told Luke if he wants to major in English in college, he should go right ahead. He can pick up enough science credits on the side to get into med school. We *need* more literate doctors."

After dinner we went into the living room—Luke along with the adults. It came out at some point that my father was a doctor, that he had trained at Hartford Hospital some ten years before Ed Jeffries. "Please," said Carol Jeffries. "Don't remind me about his residency!" As she went on to tell me about it, I kept hearing echoes of stories my mother had told us about her early years with our father, when he was in surgical training and the two of them lived in gallant poverty in a series of inner-city tenements. Eighty-hour work weeks. Spaghetti concocted out of tomato soup. Cockroaches the size, it seemed, of small turtles. Did you have cockroaches where you were? I asked the Jeffrieses.

"Did we have roaches?" They smiled at each other. "They were like house pets," Carol said. "We used to give them names."

We all pleasantly laughed. The Jeffrieses couldn't know it, but behind my laugh I was a saboteur, an assassin, a note of chaos they themselves had invited into their orderly universe. It was all so painfully familiar to me—the way Ed and Carol finished each other's sentences, the way each child at the table was invited, in ascending order of age, to tell his or her day; the comments elicited, advice given, problems solved; the judicious doling-out of after-dinner chores, the buoyant good nature and steady teasing. There was a sickening sweetness in it. It made you wish for something bad to happen. I wondered if there was some way to make such a family explode.

Luke was the key. In class and out, I tried to punch small holes in the smug assumptions Bingham dished out, holes he could peep through. The misery of slums, the defiling of the land, the lunacy of Mutual Assured Destruction—there were dark shadows stretching far behind the shining certainties that Bingham parents were pushing. I wanted Luke to see them. Nick and I tried to explain to him the idea of a counterculture. We took him on a camping trip for a weekend in Vermont, where some people Nick had known in college ten years earlier had built cabins in the woods and were living in a kind of grand commune, working as carpenters and seamstresses and smoking a lot of dope. We wanted him to know that he had choices, that just because he went to Bingham didn't mean he had to buy wholesale into the philosophy.

It was futile. We couldn't budge Luke Jeffries, and ultimately our mission dwindled into a friendly game, a ritual. He was, after all, a good kid, and we liked him. Somewhat ruefully we congratulated him on his acceptance at Brown University (his father's alma mater), where he planned to enroll as a pre-med student. At his graduation, Nick and I gave him a small treasure chest of essential books, from Marx and Freud to Jack Kerouac, with a card that read, *What every Total Bingham Kid needs.*

"I'll come back next year," he promised, hefting the books, "and give you two radicals the low-down on these."

But the next year I was gone. Very few people knew it on that graduation day, but in fact my departure had been looming for months, since the revelation to certain members of "the Bingham community" of my misconduct with the (married) mother of one of our students. The actual affair was limited to three hectic nights spent together during Christmas vacation, while her loutish husband was off at another of his frequent conventions and the daughter was vacationing with friends in the Bahamas. Somehow word got out, and by February I was embroiled in a limited but nasty scandal. The headmaster (a pleasant, docile fellow named Gunderson, whom Nick and I privately referred to as "the Flaming Moderate" and "The Tower of Jello") never actually fired me, but in his gentlemanly, private school way, bit by bit he made me feel unloved enough that eventually I had to resign.

The affair with Mrs. X perplexed friends of mine who knew about it. Why are you messing around like that? they said. You'll bury yourself. Even Nick Pieroni seemed annoyed, as if in sleeping with a student's mother I had broken some unstated boundary, shrewd observance of which had kept him at Bingham, despite controversies, for eight solid years. Nor did my actions endear me to Marcy, the woman I was involved with at the time. We had other problems. For months she had been wanting to formalize our relationship in a way that made me shiver. I remember the sinking feeling I had when at her sister's wedding her family insisted on dragging me into the family photograph, and assorted great aunts and grandmothers swept me head to toe with approving glances. For a while Marcy and I seemed to teeter on the edge of matrimony. The fiasco with Mrs. X put an end to that.

I was not sorry to leave Bingham. I felt that if I stayed one more year, I might have stayed twenty-one more. And the figure of the dedicated fifty-year-old teacher, the father-figure, Mr. Chips—that was not for me. What my friends couldn't see was that far from burying myself, I was digging myself out. I didn't have any particular plan, only the exhilarating sensation of leaving. As I drove off the school campus for the last time, my books and papers in the back

of my car, I looked up at those huge maples swaying in a dull June
breeze and almost hyperventilated with happiness.

IV

If only he would look. Once would be enough. She hates herself
for feeling this way. But there it is.

It is crowded under the tent. Raining outside, and the tables
have been pushed in from the edge, jamming the center. Her table
is near the back. When she turns she can see him at the head table,
next to Nick and Ginger. The waiters hover. Bottle after bottle of
champagne at the head table, but at the back they run dry, and no
one comes.

The woman next to her is an old friend of Ginger's mother. Are
you here for the bride or the groom? this woman asks.

The best man is my boyfriend, she says.

Oh, is he? Well, he's certainly a nice-looking young man. Is he
a teacher, too?

Yes, she says, turning to look again. He is leaning back laughing.
Slapping Nick on the shoulder.

One of my sons is a teacher, the woman says. In Ohio.

Mmm-hmm. Nods. Is remembering the first time she saw him,
in the museum. She leading a group of old ladies through a Dutch
and Flemish exhibit. He lurking in the background. Every time she
looked up, she saw him, their eyes locked. It was blatant the way he
lurked. She thought he was rude but found herself wanting to know
more.

Now she finds herself saying mmm-hmm to the woman next to
her without any idea what she is agreeing to. This makes her mad,
at him. Mad she has to crank her neck around to see him, mad he
is always a course ahead of her in the meal, mad he can shovel chicken

Kiev into his mouth with such robust and obvious pleasure while she is there losing her appetite and he pretending not to notice her.

Of course, I was only twenty when I married Roger, the woman says.

She can't pinpoint when he started pulling away. Eight months they have been living together, and the last two three four? of them she has felt him straining and pulling. He pulls away, and she knows it only makes things worse, but she can't help it, she holds him tighter. They went down to his mother's house in Connecticut, the place he grew up in, a beautiful place near the ocean, a house with a yard, neighbors, and was there anything wrong with her imagining them living in a place like that someday? But you could see him getting surly, minute by minute, she clearly was not allowed to find anything beautiful in the house yard neighborhood or anything.

Look at me, damn you. Just once.

It is Nick who catches her eye and smiles. Hard to trust someone with eyes like that. But at least he has the decency to notice her. Unlike him. He by the way was quite upset when Nick and Ginger broke their news, quite upset indeed. Tried to hide it. Couldn't.

The man wants a normal life, she said to him, anything wrong with that?

No, no, no, of course not.

Now at the head table they have finished dessert. Toasts to the bride and groom. At her own table there are people who push their plates away and people who start eating faster. How about you? the woman is saying. When is it your turn? She pretends not to hear.

Toast follows toast. Fathers, brothers. Only men are allowed to speak. Now it is his turn. Stands up, right hand in pocket, he is jingling his keys, she knows. Raises his glass and smiles. The best man has the worst job, he says—he has the groom before the ceremony but doesn't know how to calm him, has the ring in his pocket but doesn't get to keep it, and has the vows memorized but doesn't get to say them.

Everyone laughs. The woman next to her grabs her forearm and knowingly nods.

She feels physically ill. His toast goes on, she looks around, everyone with mouths half-open ready to laugh. He's not really so great, she wants to tell them. Now he raises his glass higher. Creates a pause, and in the pause swings his gaze across the audience.

When she was a child she would tell herself, If even one star is out, it is good luck, if even one snowflake falls, it is winter. Now she says, If he looks at me even once, everything will be okay. And it's coming; his gaze is rolling toward her. She moves a fraction of an inch to get in it, but suddenly it is too late, he has somehow missed her, quite efficiently it seems, his gaze making a little hop right over her and then turning back to Ginger and old Nick. She falls back into her seat and sees the people with their open mouths. "Here's looking at you, kids," she hears him say.

This is the year all the old holdouts get married. Dennis Petersley, my roommate in college and briefly on Thompson Street in New York, is a district attorney in Pennsylvania, and six months ago wrote to say he had married a woman who as a public defender kept winning cases against him. Then Nate Holover, my old best friend, who now plays a ruthless doctor on a soap opera, married a French actress he met on a movie shoot.

Then my sisters married, bang bang, in rapid succession. My older sister, Lydia, moved back from Boston to Connecticut last year and quickly met and married an Amtrak conductor named Tony. The two of them are renovating an airy, dilapidated Victorian house, and my sister works as a chef in a popular vegetarian restaurant, the Impudent Carrot, located in what used to be a barber shop about a half a mile away from where we grew up. Meanwhile, my younger sister, Sharon, had gotten engaged to her college boyfriend, Hector. Hector is a software genius with one of the Route 128 companies, and the two of them are searching for a house in the crazy Boston market.

Both of my sisters had small and elegant weddings. Sharon's was up in Maine, where our mother, who left Connecticut almost two years ago, manages and partially owns an inn called Waldo's—named after an old dog of ours. Lydia and Tony were married in the living room of their new/old house. At both of these ceremonies our father, now almost sixty and talking about retiring, was present with his wife, Ginny, to whom our mother, after a decade of pointed silence, was heard to utter her first historic words. "So," she said, a tense smile on her face. "Does he still hide his dirty handkerchief under the pillow?"

Also present at both weddings was our grandmother, my father's mother. She is ninety-four years old, a very sharp ninety-four, and likes to ask me hard questions. "Now what about you?" she said to me after Sharon's wedding. "Doesn't it bother you that your little sister is twenty-six and married, and you're thirty-one and all alone?"

"It's not a race, Grams," I said.

She ignored me. "Have you *completely* given up on the idea of settling down?"

"Grams. I'm still a young man. Still exploring the world."

"Oh, go on with you," she said, and walked away.

At Lydia's wedding she sought me out again. I saw her heading my way, her mouth set in a quivering frown. "Grams!" I said, before she could get set up. "Isn't it great that two-thirds of the children in our family are married, bringing us in line with the national average?"

Her eyes squinted reproach. "Let me tell you something," she said, actually pointing at me. "You were not raised to be some kind of vagabond."

Apparently, neither my stint as an English teacher nor my current job as general assignment reporter for a small Rhode Island daily paper (circulation 30,000) can convince my grandmother that my situation is not either fundamentally shifty or desperate. Sometimes I feel the same way. In my current apartment I get a lot of junk mail addressed to Kurzler (sometimes Kurtzler), J., the guy who lived here before me. Sometimes my only mail for the day is a sweepstakes offering to him, or a note from the Evangelical Library Association of America to Melissa De Gange, the woman who lived here before him. The other day I was in the foyer when the mailman came, with letters for both of these people.

"They don't live here anymore," I told him. "They moved."

He took the letters back with a broad sigh. *You'll move, too,* his eyes said, *and then I'll have some other drifter getting your junk mail.*

Generally, though, being a kind of nomadic renter pleases me. There is a thrill to walking in and out of situations. I got my current job by walking in off the street and talking (and writing) my way into it—not neglecting to mention, I'm ashamed to admit, my prior work published in *The New York Times*. I like the job, and it is satisfying to be, finally, a writer of sorts, but almost every day I'm aware that, given the right combination of events, I might be doing something else ten months from now. I'm not restless, just open to suggestions. And as for women, I have friends I go out with, one or two I occasionally spend the night with. There is a sportswriter at the paper I go skiing with; she and I drive up on weekends to a beautiful inn in Vermont, and when we come back, we don't broadcast it around the newsroom.

So I am hardly all alone. But nowhere on the horizon is that spiritual Doppelgänger. And, in truth, I don't expect her to show up, because I don't believe in her, or in the big white house. Of course, I could have told my grandmother this, but I see no need to treat someone her age that way. She thinks this is just a phase, and will surely die thinking that. My parents are less sure. For years they worried that their own failures had somehow ruined the idea of marriage for us. But the idea of marriage has a magical resilience. Marriages collapse and collapse and collapse, but almost no one concludes that the *design* is faulty. They just keep blaming the builders and materials. If any architect tried this, he'd be thrown in jail, but people are far less reasonable about relationships than, say, bridges. My parents held their respective breaths as Lydia and I cruised straight through our twenties without marrying. Now they are relieved; with two out of three gone, they can relax a little, knowing they didn't destroy their children after all. They don't need me to marry to prove this. Nor do they complain about my rootlessness. They were renters once themselves, they remind me.

Yesterday Luke Jeffries, my old student, showed up unexpectedly at the paper. Over the clatter of the newsroom, I heard the receptionist saying my name and, looking up, saw a bearded, somber figure in ragged jeans and T-shirt moving toward me.

"Hey, Mr. Slattery." He stuck his hand out, and only then, when he smiled, did I recognize him.

"Luke," I said. "Pull up a chair."

We talked for half an hour. He was on his way home from Brown in Providence, and he had found me; he wanted to tell me that it had taken him almost two years to do it, but he had finally finished all the books Nick and I had given him. "And you know what?" he said. "You were right."

"Oh really?" I smiled. "Right about what?"

He stroked his beard, through which I kept trying to see his face as I knew it. Flashes of it would come to me, then disappear. "Right about everything," he said.

"Well, that's nice to hear," I said. "But can you be any more specific?"

I sat back, then, and listened. Luke told me about his disenchantment with college. Most students weren't real *students*, he said; they were pre-professionals, cynically preparing to milk the system. And while there were a few "amazing" professors, ones with real vision, most of them had given up, too, either hiding behind Standard Academic Bullshit or (the scientists) selling out to the military, doing government-funded research to feed the war monster. "The whole thing looks great from the outside," Luke said, "but when you get to the core, it's all money, money, money—just like you said."

"Did I say that?"

"Yeah, and guess what—I think I'm dropping out of school."

I didn't know what to say. The clack of keyboards and babble of telephone conversations at my colleagues' desks poured into my ears and drove out all thought. "What do your parents think?" I asked him.

Luke frowned for a second, then resumed stroking and pulling at his beard. "Well, naturally they don't think too much of it. But their lives are so screwed up, I really can't see where they get off telling me how to run mine." Briefly, Luke described how empty his parents' marriage was, how they had given up years ago trying to *say* anything to each other. As far as he was concerned, they might as well be divorced.

I asked him how old he was.

"Twenty next month," he said. "My father keeps saying if I do this now, I'll get off the track. That's how he sees life. A track. I'm not into tracks. I try to explain that to him, but it's hopeless." He smiled, somewhat wanly. "Actually, I'm thinking of taking off, going cross-country. You did that, didn't you?"

I nodded. "Yes," I said. "Yes, I did that."

When we stood up, he again shook my hand, and smiled at me through the beard. "Anyway, Mr. Slattery," he said. "I wanted to thank you. You were really important to me, you know. And if you see Mr. Pieroni, tell him the same goes for him, okay?"

I said I would. As Luke walked away, a well-thumbed copy of Kerouac's *On the Road* sticking out of his back pocket, I almost called out to him across the newsroom, *Wait!* But then he was gone, waving to me as the elevator doors closed over him. I went to the window and watched him come out of the building three floors below and get into a smashed-up Pontiac, which he drove off amidst billowing exhaust.

"Good luck, Luke," I said.

That was yesterday. After work I came back here to my apartment, picked up my mail (*You, J. KURZLER*, May Have ALREADY WON One MILLION Dollars!), and sat down in the kitchen, thinking about all the places I have lived in the last decade. Sometimes I can't remember them very well; whole parts of different houses blur into each other, or simply drop off altogether, leaving big blank spaces. What happened, for instance, when you turned right at the top of the stairs in the house I briefly lived in with four other people in New Hampshire? You would come around the turn in the stairs, reach the second floor, pass one bedroom, and then—what? Blankness.

Last month I visited Lydia and Tony in Connecticut, and after dinner my sister and I bicycled across town past our old house. We stopped out front. There were new birch trees in the yard and a bright flower garden where the pachysandra had been. The horrible bulging andromeda, which I had always loathed, was gone. As we watched, a man and two tiny children tumbled out the front door and began playing kickball. My sister and I joked about rushing up to him and telling him to uproot those birch trees, replant the andromeda, and leave the place the hell alone. Then, standing there with our bikes, we began to tour the house, room by room, recalling to each other the smallest details, from the print on the wallpaper in Sharon's diaper-changing room, to the secret liquor cabinet behind the bookshelves in the living room. There was not one inch of that place we didn't know.

After opening J. Kurzler's sweepstakes letter (he hadn't actually won the million dollars), I cooked myself a meal of hamburger and creamed corn. I watched the news, drank a couple of beers, failed to reach Nick Pieroni on the phone, and then, tired, went to bed early. I tried to read, but I was drowsy; I had the feeling that dreams were reaching out to me, fully formed, from the world of sleep; that their soft, rubbery hands were already on my ankles, on the back of my neck. I reached over and turned off the light.

I am running across the front lawn. It is summer and dusk. Cut grass stings my legs. My mother is ringing a bell. It seems I am racing the sun toward the horizon, and winning; the soles of my feet are leathery with calluses and black dirt, and carry me skimming across the lawn. "Toby, Toby!"—my mother's voice echoes through the yard, everywhere, sliding down off the maple branches, bouncing back from the hedges and thumping upward from the ground, wrapping itself around me. I glide faster. My father's car rounds the corner, honking. The big white house looms overhead, a whole city; I know its secrets, every alley and passageway, every corner, every dark nook. "Tooooo-byyyyy!" Everything is in place, where it belongs. It will always be there. It will never go away.